Hench

Hench

A Novel

Natalie Zina Walschots

HARPER LARGE PRINT

An Imprint of HarperCollinsPublishers

Text message bubbles © Adobe Stock

Excerpt on pages 98 and 99 from Ilan Noy © VoxEU

HarperCollins books may be purchased for educational, business, or sales promotional use. For information, please e-mail the Special Markets Department at SPsales@harpercollins.com.

FIRST HARPER LARGE PRINT EDITION

ISBN: 978-0-06-304057-1

Library of Congress Cataloging-in-Publication Data is available upon request.

20 21 22 23 24 LSC 10 9 8 7 6 5 4 3 2 1

For Jairus,
whose hands I'll recognize in heaven

Hench

1

When the Temp Agency called, I was struggling to make the math work. In one window, I was logged in to my checking account; in the other, I was whittling down my grocery delivery shopping cart into something that would fit into the sliver of overdraft I had available. I kept dragging different configurations of noodles and vegetables in and out of the cart, grimly trying to ward off scurvy until one of several outstanding invoices was paid.

I had my phone right next to me with the ringer on as loud as it would go, so when the call came in it scared the crap out of me. I fumbled to answer, leaving greasy fingerprints on the cracked glass of my phone's screen.

"Anna Tromedlov," I croaked.

"Am I speaking with . . . the Palindrome?"

"Fucking hell," I hissed before I could stop myself.

"Um."

I coughed. "Sorry, yes. This is she."

"Do you prefer your civilian name?" There was palpable distaste in the voice on the other end of the call. Some of the recruiters took their work too seriously.

"If you don't mind." I tried to sound breezy, but my voice was still hoarse and anxious.

"I'll make a note of that," the Temp Agency recruiter lied.

I closed my eyes for a long moment, regretting once again filling in the "aliases" section of my hench profile. Two years later, the rookie mistake haunted me in the form of every recruiter addressing me by a nerd's idea of what a villain's name might be. At least the punishment for hubris was on brand.

"Miz Trauma'ed-love, this is a courtesy call to inform you that there is a screening session at the Luthor Street branch of the Temp Agency that includes opportunities that match your skill set. Are you able to attend?"

"When is the screening?" I hunted on my desk for my phone for a moment, to check my schedule, before realizing it was in my hand. I opened a new tab with my calendar.

"Eleven A.M., Miz Trauma'ed-love."

"Today?" That call time was less than an hour away.

"Is that going to be a problem?"

"Not at all, that sounds great." It didn't. "I'll definitely be there."

I wouldn't have time to shower. I decided showing up covered in dry shampoo and desperation was better than missing a chance to pick up a contract. It had been a few weeks since I last worked; the villain I was semi-regularly henching for had their largest aquatic base raided, and almost all of the henches working off-site had our contracts canceled to cover the cost of the rebuild. It was nothing unusual, but I had gone just long enough between jobs that I was getting a little uncomfortable. You can only eat so much instant ramen.

"We look forward to seeing you in person, Miz Trauma'ed-love," the recruiter lied again, before hanging up.

In the tiny tile rectangle of my bathroom, I discovered last night's winged eyeliner was in decent shape and could be repaired. With a lot of mouthwash, fresh lipstick, and a severe-but-vampy bun, I looked almost presentable. I squeezed myself into my tightest suit (tweed) and called my cab.

Oscar was a new driver. There weren't a ton of cabbies who would work with us, so it was hard for any villain who couldn't hire a personal driver to get a ride in the city. It turns out when some asshole in tights picks up the rideshare you're in and flips it over like a confused tortoise, that's a one-star review. A few cabbies, though, decided that being able to double their rates was worth the threat of getting their car ripped in half by some costumed dirtbag. I'd had to break up with my last driver when he got a little fond of me and told me I was "too nice for this life." When they start getting attached, it's time to move on. Next thing you know they're developing a savior complex and turning you in "for your own good." I was already grocery shopping in the middle of the night after the same cashier saw me buying a single bag of Doritos one time too many and started giving me life advice. I'd been emotionally preparing myself to give up my favorite pizza joint if the delivery guy kept being friendly.

Oscar, though, I liked a lot so far. He'd barely spoken a handful of words since I started calling on him. I could count on his curt nod and a quiet ride wherever I was going; I also got to admire the shocking thickness of his eyebrows in the rearview mirror.

Halfway to the Temp Agency, my phone started to vibrate aggressively. It was June.

> Feeling lucky?

> I hope so because I feel like shit

> You on your way?

> Could you hurry I'm fucking freezing

> Are you getting coffee

I didn't write back, but instructed Oscar to take a detour through a drive-thru and ordered a pair of too-expensive lattes.

I spotted June a block away from the Temp Agency, tucked around a corner to keep out of the line of sight from anyone in the building; I asked Oscar to drop me off there. Her body was curled against the intense February chill, her face turned toward the brick wall in front of her. Her smart navy blue trench coat was too light for the weather, and the tips of her fingers were shaking from the cold as she held a cigarillo.

June had been henching longer than I had; she'd dipped a toe in the dastardly end of the freelance world for the first time almost three years ago, and had been invaluable when I followed suit. She was the first person to admit to me that she worked as a hench, and surprised me by generously helping me through my Temp Agency application. I was a shaking mess before my first intake interview, expecting a roomful of hardened and battle-scarred evildoers. There was a remarkable lack of black lycra and metal masks when I finally walked through the doors, though, just desperate temps, who looked as likely to have decent typing speeds as demolitions experience. She made fun of me relentlessly for being so scared, and we quickly became inseparable.

She'd hit a rough patch recently, much longer and deeper than my raid-related few weeks out of work. June had powers, and her skill set was extremely specific; that meant she was both expensive and niche, feast-or-famine. There had been too much of the latter, too little of the former. Her shoulders, even hunched against the cold, showed a lot of tension.

I unfolded myself from the cab and strode toward her, clearing my throat so I wouldn't startle her. She flicked her cigarillo into a small pile of filthy snow and

I heard it sizzle. She reached for the coffee with grabby hands.

Her eyes were a little bloodshot. "You look like crap," she said. She took a sip of the latte, leaving lipstick marks on the plastic top of the to-go mug.

"Probably," I agreed, too cheerfully.

"They give you any idea what to expect?"

"No, just that something fit my profile. They tell you anything?"

She shook her head. "Same as you." She took another swallow and flinched. "Drinking this is like eating a vanilla pod's ass."

"I told them to go light on the syrup, sorry."

"It's fine." June's voice seemed especially weary. She had an advanced sense of smell and taste, which sometimes made her valuable as a hench, but usually just made her life miserable, especially in the city. There was a shine right under her nose; she'd spread mint chapstick there, a trick doctors and coroners used beneath surgical masks, to block out some of the odors around her.

"No one tells you how much supersenses hurt," she explained once. "It's fucking agony. You know some lucky assholes can't feel pain? Like, not as an ability. Their pain receptors don't work, so you get these toddlers breaking toes and chewing off their own tongues before they learn to stop fucking with themselves. Turns out, if you can't feel pain, you can't smell anything either. Think about a bad smell, how you recoil from it, like it hurts. It's like that, all the time." We'd both been drunk as balls and I babbled about how sorry I was until she threw what was left of her drink at me. She was even worse at feelings than I was. She'd been wearing nose plugs to the bar that night, like a swimmer.

She never said so, but I suspected the reason June moved to henching in the first place was that the work she tended to get evildoing was generally less unpleasant. She worked for the border patrol, once, to sniff out explosives in the airport (mostly she found coke and contraband cured meats). She was miserable there, surrounded by the smells of body and breath, of everyone coming off long flights, of dirty clothes, of airport food. There was also the aroma of panic and exhaustion. Mostly, though, she hated dealing with cops. Now she helped villains design packaging her sense of smell couldn't penetrate, or sniffed their drinks at parties to make sure the liquid hadn't been dosed. In between jobs, she smoked like a chimney, dampening her sense of smell and taste in tiny, merciful increments.

"Let's get inside," I said, drinking my coffee and watching her shake.

She shrugged. "Let's get it over with."

I pushed the heavy doors open and we walked through them together, the heels of our boots clicking in time on the wet tile floor. The Temp Agency's reception desk was in a long, bleak room. Smaller, windowless interview rooms branched off of it, reminding me of holding cells. One of the sickly fluorescent lights flickered. My eye twitched.

There weren't many of us there that morning, barely a dozen, in moody coats and unnecessary sunglasses and sharp-shouldered suits, chipped manicures and threaded eyebrows, all doing what we could to cast the illusion we were intimidating. No one was sitting. Two temp wranglers sat behind the desk: a man in an ill-fitting blue suit who was trying to make himself look less baby-faced by growing a thin blond beard, and a frighteningly neat woman with glossy black hair, pecking irritably at a tablet.

June and I elbowed our way closer to the front of the pack, making a point of taking up space while trying not to look too keen. I smiled at a man in what appeared to be low-key hard-boiled detective cosplay when he glared at me.

"How bad do you think it's going to be," I asked June quietly.

"Abysmal."

"Half of us leaving without work?"

She tossed her head, gesturing to the hench-hopefuls behind us. "At least. I say two-thirds walk out of here with nothing."

The man in the blue suit stood, and the muttering around me quieted. I stood a little straighter.

"Where are our drivers?" he asked.

Three people stepped forward: a broad-shouldered blond woman with a buzz cut and two young men who scowled at each other, both wearing leather jackets and white T-shirts. Their matching, perfect pompadours trembled as they eyed each other aggressively, like the wattles on a pair of roosters.

"Wore the same dress to the prom, I see," June said in my ear, and I nearly choked on the coffee in my mouth.

The woman looked up from her tablet; her eyes were shark black. "We need a chauffeur with first-class getaway. Who has a stunt background?"

The blond woman raised her hand. "I'm certified." She dropped her arm back to her side. Her dress shirt was rolled up her forearms, and her biceps strained the material. It made my stomach flutter. "I have a lot of on-set work, mostly commercials."

"You got references?"

"Of course."

"Let's head out to the track." The blue-suited man started to walk out of the room, gesturing for her to follow. He paused to glance back at the two men, who looked even more deflated than they had moments before. "Sorry, guys. Next time."

The two disappointed drivers turned to leave at the same time, and had to endure the awkwardness of stomping out together, both refusing to pause and let the other go first.

"It'll be a summer wedding," I predicted. June choked on her coffee.

The woman with short hair followed the blue suit out the back of the Temp Agency; I watched her carefully close the heavy doors so they wouldn't make too much noise behind her. I imagined her being led to the supercar she'd be driving for the rest of the day. If she was any good at all, I expected the job would be permanent. Good drivers got snapped up, and were relatively rare. I found myself hoping I wouldn't see her back, that she'd get a good assignment and have a long life span (though I realized with a small pang that would mean I wouldn't get to look at her well-muscled arms again). I always found it sad when someone kept turning up at the Agency every few weeks, looking for more work. Like me.

The remaining temp wrangler was spitting out assignments, rapid-fire. Most of them were skill specific: a call for a safecracker, another for a network security specialist. That last one made me scan the crowd for a face I knew.

"Where the hell is Greg?" I said, a little louder than I'd meant to. "That's a perfect job for him."

June opened her mouth to answer, but then the woman with the tablet said she needed someone with "exceptional sensory perception" and June's attention swung away from me and toward the promise of work.

They discussed details I couldn't make out, and after a few minutes June signed the surface of the tablet with the tip of one finger. She walked back looking positively jolly.

"Six weeks on-site, possibility of extension," she told me, sweeping her box braids back over her shoulder and rubbing the back of her neck to get rid of some of the tension she'd been carrying.

"On-site, though."

"Yeah, see, I'm not a coward like you."

"I'm sorry, I am still rather attached to my mortal well-being."

"Still, eh?"

"Anna Trauma'ed-love?" I glared at June instead of responding and walked to the desk to get my assignment. It was too late to correct the way the temp wrangler had said my name, but it still annoyed the crap out of me. I forced a rictus smile. "We have a remote data entry assignment, if you're interested." The tone of her voice indicated she didn't think I would be, but she was wrong. I was willing to stoop to all manner of soul-destroying work that didn't require me to put on clothes.

"Just what I'm looking for."

Mercifully, she didn't bother making eye contact.

"Sign here. You'll be emailed login credentials. Sixty hours to start, with the possibility of indefinite extension." There was something about the way she said it that indicated she felt she'd given out a sentence.

"I like the sound of that!"

She rolled her eyes.

I cringed.

I walked back to June, who grabbed my arm when I showed her my assignment; I could feel her nails through the fabric of my jacket. She would be working on-site for the same villain who'd hired me for remote work. "Let's get breakfast," she hissed. "I'm picking the place, though. I'm sick of your bougie white girl bronsch."

As we walked toward the doors, the temp wrangler announced that there were three other positions available the rest of them would compete for; I didn't envy the poor assholes the gauntlet of micro-interviews.

As soon as I touched the heavy metal door handle, it was wrenched out of my hand. I wobbled in my heels and Greg, the out-of-work network administrator in front of me, had to draw up short to keep from slamming into us in his hurry to get in the building.

"If you're here about the security gig," June said cheerfully, "some rando a quarter talented as you nabbed it." She took visible pleasure in the crushing disappointment that blossomed on his face.

He backed up and I let the door slam behind us.

"Shit!" He raked his hand through dark, messy hair. "Shit."

"It was one of the first they called," she said. I couldn't tell if that was meant to comfort or turn the screws a little tighter. Probably the latter. June started walking down the sidewalk brightly and I followed; Greg skittered after us.

He was quiet for a long, sour moment, sulking. Then, "I was on the phone with The Scarlet Hood," he said. "He's worse than my fucking mother."

"Oh?" I called over my shoulder. Greg jogged a couple of paces to catch up.

"He called me yesterday because he forgot how to eject a CD from a drive. This morning? I shit you not, he'd forgotten to charge his laptop and couldn't get it to turn on."

June laughed. Her finding work after a drought combined with Greg's misery had put her in a great mood.

I elbowed him and he yelped. "Come with us, we're getting breakfast."

"Ugh. Sure." He shoved his hands deep into the pockets of his down coat and hunched his shoulders. "Like, I appreciate he keeps me on retainer. But it's costing me better work now."

I nodded. "He should just hire you. Make you a hench."

Greg's head jerked up. "Fuck that. He already calls me at three A.M. If I was his hench my life would officially be hell."

Greg's phone rang the moment we reached the doors of the diner. He mouthed a curse and fumbled in his pocket, while June and I escaped the cold and let the yawning server lead us to a booth. The comforting vinyl seats were tacky and creaked as I sat down. I ordered Greg a tea and greedily accepted the coffee that was placed in front of me.

"Tech support for supervillains." June watched him, eyes narrowed, through the window as he paced outside in the cold. "Can you fucking imagine?"

"It's not like data entry is any more glamorous." Through the glass, I heard Greg ask, "Have you tried turning it off and turning it back on again?" He winced and pulled the phone away from his ear at the response.

"Data entry's less risky," June said, scanning the laminated menu.

"Maybe I wouldn't mind a bit of risk."

She flicked her eyes up at me. I was as surprised as she was. "That's new. Growing a spine?"

"No, just getting bored."

She made a noncommittal sound. I looked back outside at Greg's impatient, pleading face. He caught my eye and mimed shooting himself in the head, his first two fingers pointed to his temple.

"You like being bored, though," June said. "I think it would stress you the fuck out."

"Probably." But I felt a little deflated.

She raised a pointed finger. "But, if you want some on-site work, I'll refer you."

"Oh."

"Think about it."

"Okay."

"Want to make fun of dudes on Tinder until Greg comes back?"

I grinned. "Yeah."

I sidled closer to June and she unlocked her phone.

"He looks like he was just arrested for shitting himself at a Denny's."

"He looks like a bear in a kids' show who is also a cop."

"He looks like a Muppet who is here to teach me about sharing."

We were cackling by the time The Hood mercifully let Greg off the phone and he bumbled in, stomping his feet in the doorway to warm up.

"His ferret chewed through the fucking cable, I swear to Christ," Greg snarled, swinging himself into the booth. I inhaled some of my coffee and June had to pound me on the back to keep me from choking.

Hours later, wearing stained track pants and nested into an afghan, I logged in to the Electrophorous Industries website and started working.

I fell into the easy rhythm of updating the spreadsheets in front of me, sorting and tidying the data. There could be something satisfying, almost trancelike, about ordering the columns and rows. I wasn't able to hit that meditative place, though; I tried to focus, but my mind kept wandering back to my surprising assertion I was bored, and June's offer to help me make the move to on-site work. I tried to pick apart if I had meant what I said, and it was like a dull, annoying buzz in my brain over the hum of the data.

I got up and stretched, carrying my laptop and afghan over to my desk, hoping the change of view would help me focus.

I rarely knew what I was working on when I got the assignments, but sometimes I could infer or piece together something from the data. What was in front of me was easier to parse than most: a huge cache of news stories, clips, photos, social media posts, and video and audio files, all selected because they contained some specific detail about a hero's description. They included mentions of injuries, pictures of scars, grainy surveillance videos with glimpses of birthmarks, interviews that mentioned tattoos peeking out from under a costume. I sorted them by superhero and added the information to a spreadsheet tracking the details, building the basis of what was obviously an identification database.

As soon as the data became a puzzle to solve, I couldn't tear myself away. In a few days, I had rebuilt the spreadsheets to be more efficient and comprehensive, and taken a few stabs at guessing the odd civilian identity. I burned through my hours and asked for more; the Temp Agency relayed that my request was approved. It was a good sign.

It was foolish to think I had found a holding pattern I could work with. A satisfying steady state. It lasted three weeks. When I got the news that the villain who held my contract wanted to interview me for a long-term position, I called June, stress eczema already breaking out on my hands.

"Tell me about your gig right now." I tried to sound casual. Sitting on my kitchen counter, waiting for the toaster oven to preheat, I couldn't stop my leg from bouncing.

On the other end of the phone, June took a bite out of something crunchy. "Electrophorous? It's okay."

"But what is it *like*."

"Normal. Boring. An office. The lighting is terrible."

"But is it. You know."

"What."

"Weird." I hesitated. "Or evil."

She laughed around a mouthful of . . . popcorn? "No. The vibe is much more shitty start-up than lair."

"Oh."

"Did you think there was a fucking lava moat?"

"Shut up."

"You did."

"Shut *up*."

When June stopped laughing, she said, "Why do you ask."

I shifted the phone to my other ear. "Electrophorous wants to pick up my contract for an extension, but it would have to be on-site."

"Oh shit! That's great."

"Thanks!"

"Here comes that sweet referral bonus."

"I'm so happy for you."

"It's win-win."

"So I should take the job?"

"Okay. Listen. There are some things you need to know."

I felt my chest squeeze. "Yeah?" I hopped off the counter and stood awkwardly in my tiny galley kitchen, between the fridge and sink.

"It's mostly about the boss. Electric Eel."

"Is he scary?"

"No! Not at all."

I flinched, feeling very stupid. The toaster oven dinged. Three hundred fifty degrees—perfect for whatever bargain nugget or other sadness dinner I found in my freezer.

June was struggling to find the words. "He's—man. He's not . . . Huh."

I put my hand on the freezer door. "Is he a pervert. Is he going to touch me."

"No! Calm down—shit. He's a supervillain, not a fast-food assistant manager."

"I have never done this, okay."

"Oh, I know. Look, the office isn't on a fucking airship. There is a piranha tank, but it's decorative and not for feeding lazy interns to. The computers are out-of-date and this one personal assistant microwaves fish every fucking day. It annoys the shit out of me. You'll love it."

"Okay. Sorry. But tell me about the Eel."

"Oh right. So, the boss. He likes you to call him E. And he wants to know how you're feeling."

"What."

"Yeah. He wants a 'real answer' when he asks how you are. It's fucking creepy. And he'll probably tell you what kind of 'energy' he 'gets from you.'"

I felt myself relax a bit and started digging in the freezer. I came across an ancient box of puff-pastry hors d'oeuvres. The box said *Perfect for Entertaining!* There were dumplings, some kind of quiche, sausage rolls. I dumped the variously shaped beige chunks onto the toaster oven tray and banged the door shut.

"Is he going to talk to me about my chakras."

"Definitely. While making *so* much eye contact."

"All right. I can handle that."

"When do they want you to start?"

"I'm coming in for a meet-and-greet stealth interview on Friday, and if I don't tank it, next week."

"Good luck. I probably won't see you if you stick to the main floor."

"I'll live."

"Probably."

"What?"

"It's just . . . don't let the retinal scan freak you out. It needs servicing so it might tell you it's going to incinerate you but it for sure won't."

"So I impress them with how cool I am in the face of stress."

"Exactly. Don't fuck it up."

She hung up before I could respond, a retort caught in my throat. I put my phone down on the counter. While the toaster oven continued to hum, I hunted through the crumb-filled utensil drawers, looking for some leftover plum sauce packets from the last time I ordered takeout. Instead, I struck gold:

Taco Bell hot sauce.

A hand curled around the edge of my monitor, startling me. The nails were buffed and a huge turquoise ring adorned the middle finger. I took a breath and tried to make my face as serene and welcoming as I could, despite having been shaken out of deep hack mode.

"Hey, Anna," the Electric Eel said, too slowly.

"Hi, E." I raised my eyes and he smiled down at me, sculpted brows arched high over his sunglasses. I hoped that acknowledgment was enough and let my eyes wander back to my monitor. I was not in the mood for a lecture about "our culture's fear of intimacy," but I also didn't want to encourage him. "How are you?"

He let go of my monitor and flexed that hand. "I've been really missing the coast lately. I think I'm going to have to head out west soon, get a little beach time in. My partner and I have been talking about opening our relationship, and it's going really well." He sat down on the end of my desk and I met his eyes again, resigning myself to the fact I wasn't going to get rid of him quickly. His mouth, surrounded by a perfect black goatee, became more serious. "But, Anna, how are you?"

"Oh, I'm well. I get quite buried in my work."

"Mmm." He steepled his fingers and pressed his hands to his mouth. "Is anything bothering you lately?"

That seemed loaded. I could suddenly smell the sharp cucumber and citrus of my deodorant as I started to sweat. "Nothing immediately comes to mind!" I knew I sounded too chipper but couldn't stop myself.

He sighed. "Anna, has anyone been bothering you."

I was taken aback. "Look, I am sorry that my ex called looking for me. I promise that won't happen again."

"I don't think we're communicating," he said mournfully. I imagined lighting him on fire with my mind. "This is about someone in the office."

Oh. "Is this about the Knifefish's personal assistant?"

"Yes. Jessica."

"I feel like we resolved the matter."

"She filed a grievance yesterday, Anna."

"I can understand why she would do that."

"And you don't feel like that should be addressed?"

I considered my words, tilting my chin up. "If she felt the need to file a report, I respect that decision. I do feel like I got my message across to her."

"You hid her phone in a spooky pumpkin."

I glanced over to Jessica, sitting a few desks away, hunt-and-peck typing on her phone's screen. She'd had a habit of leaving that phone unattended on her desk, sometimes for hours, with the ringer on. After listening to it blare a few bars of some awful pop song over and over for weeks, I'd taken matters into my own hands. There was a plastic pumpkin looming on top of a filing cabinet in one corner of the office, a forgotten Halloween decoration. One afternoon I'd picked up her still-ringing phone and hidden it inside. The pumpkin had distorted the sound just enough that it had taken her until the following afternoon to find her phone. I sent June updates via chat for the next day and a half while Jessica searched the office with a coworker's borrowed phone, head cocked to one side, listening for the ringtone like a bird-watcher straining to hear the call of a rare specimen.

I couldn't help but smile. "I did indeed, yes."

The Electric Eel seemed confused. "Do you see an issue with anything that happened?"

"Well, she hasn't left her ringtone on again."

"I see." He took off his sunglasses to give me a long, grave look. "I understand that you were frustrated. So how about you—and Jessica, of course—take a conflict resolution workshop, just to clear the air? Then we can drop the grievance."

I looked back over at Jessica. She was glaring at me now. I smiled and waved, and she dropped her eyes back to her phone, her lips pinched. "No, thank you. I think the problem has been solved."

"Then you'll have to be written up." E seemed at a loss.

"That's fine, I'll have two more incidents before I will have to talk to HR about it formally, and I don't expect I'll need that."

"Well. Mmmm. Okay, Anna, if those are the consequences you are comfortable with." He stood up and brushed off his trousers, sighing.

I gave him a genuine smile. "It only seems fair." I thought it was safe to let my attention wander back to the work in front of me, but the Electric Eel lingered, contemplating the drop ceiling.

"Hey, Anna."

I exerted a mighty effort not to sigh. Interacting with him was like talking to a robot that had just discovered emotions. "Yes, E?"

"How would you like to get out of the office."

My stomach dropped. "Am I in more trouble than I thought?"

"Oh, no!" He put a warm hand on my shoulder to reassure me; I fought not to cringe away. "Not at all. I was just thinking about how you're cooped up in this office all the time and that must be frustrating. I thought some fieldwork might be a welcome change of pace."

My silence became awkward. I wasn't sure how to answer that question. I felt safe behind a screen and keyboard; there was functionally little difference between my work and that of anyone else who worked as an administrator in an office. If I was feeling so inclined, I could pretend there was nothing illicit at all about my work while I filled out spreadsheets trying to match up scars with the known injuries of super-heroes.

"Let's do it," I said finally. The sureness in my voice startled us both. "That sounds fun." To my surprise, I believed what I said. The entire point of making the move to on-site work was owning that I was, in fact, a hench. In for a penny.

E smiled. He held up his hands, palms out. "Nothing dangerous, I promise! We're having a press conference and could use a second pair of hands."

"I'm in."

He slapped his thigh. "Spectacular. We'll meet in the lobby at nine-fifteen on Friday morning. Thanks, Anna!"

He wandered off, whistling. I could have sworn it was "Sandstorm."

"Namaste," I muttered as soon as he was out of earshot.

I took a couple deep breaths and was about to dive back into the spreadsheet in front of me, when a window of my chat client popped open.

Fieldwork!

It was June.

> Have you bugged my desk

Nah I just saw your name on the brief

> That's rather presumptuous of E

I'm sure he sensed you'd say yes

What's the press conference about?

> Not sure, some tech unveiling thing. We're supposed to be a startup, after all. I'll probably have to sign a billion NDAs

Well that sounds mercifully boring

Also it means E likes you

Well I did just get written up for the pumpkin incident so let's not get ahead of ourselves

Ha! Nah he probably thinks you're showing initiative

What?

You know, real villain material

Sure

Karaoke to celebrate?

I can't tonight

Why the fuck not.

I have a thing

Bullshit

It's a date

WHAT

Don't make fun of me

Is it someone from the office?

Jesus no

You're not seeing you-know-
who are you

I made a face even though she couldn't see me.

God no

Is it Julie? She was okay

Uh, no

Matt?

NO. It's someone from
Tinder, okay

I mean, probably that means they are less likely to murder you than your exes

We're having sushi

Are they a hench?

No, just a guy

Does he know?

No, and I would like to keep it that way until I get laid at least once this year thank you

Check in when you get home

Yes, mom

Pardon me for wanting to make sure some rando hasn't made your skin into a lampshade

Bracken smiled. There was a black sesame seed caught in his teeth. "I had a really nice time."

My smile was too wide; my cheeks were beginning to hurt. I reflexively covered my mouth with one of my hands, which I hoped looked demure instead of painfully awkward. "Me too."

I couldn't tell if I was actually attracted to the objectively handsome young man sitting next to me in the back of the cab, or if I was just so relieved to be on a date that actually seemed to be going well. But the conversation had been easy, he'd even asked me a question or two about myself, and I'd caught myself laughing for real rather than politeness more than once.

Bracken turned toward me, and his knee brushed against my leg. I didn't pull back immediately, and decided I didn't mind this bit of contact. It was a novel feeling. "I'd like to see you again," he said, perhaps even a little nervously. His dimple was showing.

"I'd like that." I tucked a wisp of hair behind my ear. My french braid was coming undone.

We were a few minutes away from both of our apartments. We'd discovered we lived only a few blocks apart and decided to split a cab home. It occurred to me, quite suddenly, that in just a few minutes my night was about to be over. That Bracken, this investment banker who played a lot of first-person shooters and still got together on the weekends with his college buddies for Ultimate Frisbee—this nice, ordinary man—was about to see me to the front door of my building, maybe give me a peck on the cheek, and then continue on his way.

To my shock, I found the idea disappointing. Sure, his name was stupid and he'd been a bit rude when the server had forgotten his deep-fried yam roll, but the delicious normalcy of him drew me in.

I glanced at my phone. "You know, it's kind of early," I said lightly. "Would you like to come in for a while? We could watch a movie."

Bracken's dimple deepened in pleasant surprise, which was a relief. He raised his eyebrows, visibly pleased with himself. "I'd like that, Anna."

I giggled when he said my name. I suddenly felt too hot, blushing from my chest to the roots of my hair. In the six-month dry spell since the end of my last bad relationship, it seemed I had forgotten all the basics of human interaction. I hoped my fumbling was at least as endearing as it was clumsy.

I glanced nervously up into the rearview mirror, trying to catch a glimpse of my face to see how flushed I was, and accidentally made eye contact with Oscar. I'd called him to pick us up from the sushi restaurant on instinct, even though I probably could have used a civilian cab. He waggled his thick eyebrows at me and I bit my lip hard.

"You're going to have to excuse my place. It's about the size of a shoebox."

Bracken stretched a little, the picture of casual serenity. "No problem. We can go to my condo next time."

I smiled harder, thrilled that there might be a next time. "So." I gathered whatever scraps of courage I had and rested my hand on his knee. "What would you like to watch?"

He smiled expansively. "Anything you'd like."

"I have so many horror movies. What kind of horror do you like? Ghost stories, classic slashers, that kind of thing?"

His smile visibly faltered. "Yeah. I don't really do horror."

"Oh, that's fine!"

"The problem is, I actually get scared." He put his hand on top of mine. "I'll be up all night thinking there's a murderer in the kitchen."

"I'm sure I have something you'd like." I tried to remember if one of my exes had left behind any shitty comedy DVDs, or anything to help convince Bracken I was a human person with normal interests. Not that I expected—hoped—we'd be *watching* anything, given my hyperawareness of the warmth and weight of his hand on top of mine.

"I am sure you do." It was a terrible line, but I let it work on me all the same. I looked up and he smirked at me. I tried not to stare at The Seed.

A loud, awful squawk went off inside the cab, startling us both badly; our hands leapt apart like we'd been caught. Oscar swore and fumbled at the dashboard, trying to shut the shrill alarm off.

"What the hell, man?" Bracken glared at Oscar, then gave me a little "can you believe this fucking guy" hand gesture.

"Sorry, sorry." Oscar stabbed at the tablet mounted to his dashboard agitatedly. "Priority call."

I was hit with the sick wave of certainty that calling on him rather than a regular cab had been a terrible mistake.

"Is there any way you can drop us off first?" I asked weakly.

"It's E. Your boss."

"Oh god." I felt ill.

"Your boss?" Bracken's brow furrowed in confusion.

"Company car," Oscar explained, coming to my rescue. "She's very important." I mentally doubled his tip.

Oscar tapped the screen one more time and put the call on speaker, to my utter horror.

"Hi, Anna! How are you this evening."

I am so sorry, I mouthed at Bracken, stricken.

He waved his hand, a little "don't be" gesture, but he was clearly still agitated.

"I'm fine, E."

"Listen, I know this isn't in your job description, but I'm in a pickle. I need some Meat transported and your driver is the closest one who works with us. I was wondering if you wouldn't mind sharing the cab and supervising the process."

"I mean, I can . . ."

"Great! That's just great. Should be quick. Have a lovely night!"

The call cut off.

"So what's that about?" Bracken asked.

"We just might have to make a quick stop," I said as vaguely as I could. I looked up, trying to meet Oscar's eyes in the rearview again. "Do you know how out of the way we need to go?" I was not looking forward to having to share the cab for any length of time with a brooding, sweaty kneebreaker.

Before Oscar could answer, the right-hand rear door of the cab was wrenched open, before we were even completely stopped.

"Oh fuck," I said, as a huge man heaved himself inside and across the back seat. His head hit the window next to me and his shoulder bashed into the center of my chest. One of his elbows dug painfully into my thigh, and his hips and legs slammed into Bracken, who had flung his own arms up in disgust.

"Drive!" The Meat's voice was a bark.

"Get off me!" Bracken was trying to shove the man, whose combat boots were trickling slush all over Bracken's expensive raw denim, off his lap and out of the cab.

"Shut the door!" I yelled. Bracken looked at me in disbelief. I elbowed him. "Do it!"

"Shit." Bracken pulled the door shut, furious.

The cab lurched forward and Oscar picked up speed. The man in my lap was younger than I expected, with an immaculate fade. His eyes were glassy and panicked, and his complexion was going gray.

Bracken let out a disgusted yelp. "He fucking pissed on me!" He shoved the Meat and tried to recoil farther into his seat. Then he froze; his palms had come up bloody.

Right then, something shifted in my brain; instead of panicking, everything inside me got very calm and clear.

"Where is it?" I asked. The Meat pointed to his

thigh and a rip in his black tactical pants. It was difficult to see the tear because of all the dark blood pooling underneath. "Goddamn it."

"This is gonna be extra," Oscar was grumbling. "Extra for bleeding in the car."

"Bill E." I started to hunt for something I could use as a tourniquet.

"You pay me and expense it," he countered.

"You'll have to take a card." I pulled my scarf off and tied it around the Meat's leg above the gash as tight as I could, then stuffed the rest of the fabric against the wound. The Meat mewled pitifully.

Oscar huffed. "Fine."

"You need to keep the pressure on." I took one of the Meat's hands and pressed it against the bloody wad of fabric along his leg. He gasped but nodded.

A thin voice warbled, "Oh shit." I glanced up at Bracken, whose face was suddenly wet and greenish. "Oh shit."

"You are both going to be okay." I hoped I didn't sound too annoyed. The Meat's eyelashes fluttered and I poked him. "You stay awake. What happened. Tell me."

"Fucking . . . one of those throwing star things."

My lip curled. "Bearded Dragon?" One of the brooding vigilante types, he had a proclivity for using bladed weapons that resembled the frills of a lizard. They cut deep.

"Yeah. It was him."

"Did you pull it out?"

"Huh?"

He must have been new. "Never pull them out. You do more damage."

"I didn't know."

"It's fine. They'll patch you up." I looked at Oscar. "We almost there?"

"I'm sorry." The Meat sounded lost.

I awkwardly patted him. "It's your leg, not mine, you don't have to be sorry."

"I'm going to puke," Bracken announced. He started to roll down the window but didn't quite make it, and sprayed the glass inside and out with half-digested sushi.

Oscar was having a fit. "This is going to be a god-damn nightmare to clean!"

I was about to say something snarky, but he pulled over so quickly that the side of my head bounced off the window. We stopped in front of the mixed martial arts academy that served as a front for the Meat Market, where villains went when they needed some muscle, just like they went to the Temp Agency when they needed someone to answer the phone or be cuffed to a briefcase or reset the routers. The only difference between the two staffing agencies was violence. When you needed human cannon fodder to throw at a hero or someone to break a few bones on your behalf, you went to the Meat Market. The average life span for Meat was not particularly long, but the Market did maintain an infirmary, staffed mostly with cutmen, med school dropouts, and disillusioned "doctors" of questionable licensing status.

One of them, an enormous Samoan man wearing black scrubs and latex gloves, was waiting at the curb with a wheelchair. As the cab stopped, Bracken fumbled weakly to open the door, and as soon as the latch caught, the Meat kicked it open.

The man at the curb poked his head in, the freshly shaved, bald skin gleaming under the cab's interior light. "Can you stand?"

"Dunno." He swung his head back and forth in agony.

"Try." The medic reached in and, gently as he could, started to wrestle the injured young man out of the cab. The Meat whined and hissed, sucking air between his teeth, as the medic eased him down on the seat of the wheelchair.

"Thanks, Oscar," the medic said, patting the roof of the car and then shutting the door behind him. Oscar made a disgusted noise and pulled quickly away. I caught a last glimpse of the Samoan wheeling the injured young man toward the building, where two more staff were holding the doors open, ready to stitch the kid up and pump him full of painkillers.

There was an awful beat of silence in the demolished, reeking cab. "Where to," Oscar said eventually.

I looked over at Bracken, whose striped dress shirt was visibly smeared with blood and vomit, and who was holding a filthy napkin up to his mouth. "Um. Can we drive you home?"

"Stop the car," he said, very quietly.

"Eh?" Oscar craned his neck to hear better.

"Stop now," he bawled. Oscar brought the cab quickly to the next curb, as Bracken fought to free himself from his seat belt. "I'll walk. Just let me out."

"This isn't the best neighbor—"

He slammed his way out of the cab and swayed on his feet for a moment. I reached for him in alarm and then quickly withdrew my hand; his disgust was palpable. He braced himself against the car for a moment, and as soon as he got his head together, he fled. I watched him quick-march away. I'd have run from me too.

The car slid back into the flow of traffic, moving almost sulkily.

"You, uh, want to go home?" Oscar asked, not un-kindly.

I nodded. In my bag, my phone started to chirp; it was June, checking in to make sure I had survived the evening.

> I don't want to talk about it.

I hit *send*, and tucked my phone back in my bag, ignoring the buzz of her repeated messages. I pressed my hot face against the window, watching the liquid city lights, defeated.

"Then my credit card was declined twice."

June was gasping for air, laughing so hard she'd stopped making any recognizable sounds and was just wheezing. She had a pair of swimmer's nose plugs on to shield her from the scents of sweat and body spray and spilled crantinis at the karaoke bar.

"Oscar finally took pity on me and said he'd in-voice E."

"Shit, dude." She gasped, fanning her face. "It's so terrible. So terrible." She tried to take a swallow of Chardonnay, but almost choked. I pressed my lips to-gether and looked toward the stage, where Greg was belting out show tunes.

"Your empathy moves me."

"I'm dying."

"So is my sex life."

"Are you going to call him again?"

"Oscar? Yeah, he's a good driver, it wasn't his fault."

"No, you idiot, Bramble."

"Bracken."

"Whatever his terrible name is."

"Obviously not." I looked down into my gin and tonic, stirring it fretfully with the little straw.

"It could be a funny story one day. Your dramatic first date."

"He was covered in blood and puke."

"The start of a whirlwind romance. Your child will be named Decorative Hedge."

"You know I'm naming my firstborn Worf." I drained the rest of my drink and rattled the ice in the bottom of the glass while she cackled. "I need another." I stood, wobbling in my heels.

I passed Greg on my way to the bar; he'd handed off the mic and was trying to attract the bartender's attention to get another Long Island iced tea. He spotted me and lifted his hand for a high five; I walked right by, leaving him hanging.

He scowled and dropped his arm. "Cold, Anna."

I leaned on the bar and ordered for both of us, as

it was clear the bartender was going to continue completely ignoring Greg as punishment for singing "Mr. Mistoffelees." Going out the night before the press conference, my first bit of fieldwork, was a mistake, but one I needed. I'd feel like shit in the morning, but the hangover and being made fun of by my friends might wash a little bit of the reek of failure that had been clinging to me ever since that decent-looking man had probably the worst date of his life in my company.

I slid Greg's drink over to him. He picked it up and nodded in thanks; his phone had rung and he was struggling to give tech support over the tinny synth and off-key singing.

"Have you tried pressing *ctrl-alt-delete*? Yes, the buttons. Yes, at the same time." He put his drink down and stuck his finger in his ear to try and hear better. I took a sip of my drink.

He hung up a moment later and we walked back to the table together. June had somehow acquired a martini and was fishing out a pearl onion with her pincerlike fingernails. She flicked it at me. She was still grinning.

"At least work seems to be going well," she said, too cheerfully.

"You're enjoying this."

"I'm cheering you up."

"So magnanimous."

"Shut up. Also, I mean it. E likes you, likes your work."

"Yeah."

"He was talking you up to Electrocutioner," she admitted. There was a tiny bit of sourness in her voice, an edge of jealousy. It made me believe her.

I sat up a little. "That's something."

Greg had been nodding along. "It is something," he agreed. "Going out in public with a villain is for-real henching. You're part of the entourage."

I smiled despite myself. "Let's hope my energy is aligned tomorrow."

June lifted a talon-tipped finger. "Also, stop dating civilians."

My smile twisted. "Yeah."

"You're just going to get blood all over them. Start looking in the talent pool."

"Another hench?"

She shrugged. "Or a villain."

"Yeah, I already have one ex who stalks me, I'm good."

"I've found the professionally evil are much more reasonable," June said, theatrically drinking. She wound up spilling a bunch of martini down her shirt.

"Is that why you keep dating that one piece of Meat?"

She paused to glare at me. "We are *not* dating. He's a semi-regular booty call at best. Also, don't knock it till you've tried it."

"I could just warn the poor civvy next time."

June swiped at the front of her shirt angrily. "Pointless. They either write you off immediately or get a hard-on imagining you robbing banks in a thong and goth boots."

"So I shouldn't wear that to work tomorrow."

"I mean, follow your heart."

"Anna! How *are* **you?"**

I flinched and turned to find E striding toward me across the Electrophorous Industries lobby. He was positively beaming, walking with a long, confident gait and wearing a dark blue pinstripe suit. His teeth were so white they seemed to glow, and his tan seemed especially deep. In one hand, he was holding a device that looked a lot like a gold dinner plate attached to a pair of brass knuckles. Two people from R&D skittered behind him nervously, their eyes fixed on the device, hands twitching, certain he was going to drop it.

I swallowed and smiled, hoping my face was not too drawn. His excitement was aggravating my headache.

"I can't wait to see what the day has in store." I took a sip from the gigantic coffee I was holding.

"Good! Good." He fiddled with one of the knobs on the apparatus in his hand, and one of the researchers next to him grimaced.

"Is that the new model?" I didn't have to fake my curiosity. The gadget looked like a more advanced version of a prototype he'd had in development for ages, something called the Mood Ring. It was supposed to be able to scan emotional states, or "read auras," if you were feeling particularly pretentious. June was adamant it didn't work and E just made all the readings up.

"Yes! Well, sort of." He turned another knob and the Mood Ring started to emit a low hum, like a tuning fork. "No spoilers before the press conference, but it has a few new features."

"Oh yeah." I tried to sound game. E swept the Mood Ring up and down in front of me, then around my body like a handheld metal detector sweeping for weapons. He brought it a little too close to my face and almost knocked my glasses off. I smiled through my annoyance and nausea.

The Mood Ring pinged and the humming faded to a low buzz. "Ah!" E eagerly brought the thing close to his face to get a better look at the tiny digital screen that displayed the Mood Ring's readings. It reminded me of the screen on a calculator watch. "Hmm. It says you're stressed." He looked up, his dark eyes liquid and concerned. "Are you stressed, Anna?"

I tried to stop my heart with my mind. "Good stress will still read as stress," I finally offered. "I am keyed up for the presentation."

E nodded sagely. "True. True. I should adjust the calibration for that." He fiddled with the device for another moment, then shrugged and tossed it to one of the hovering R&D guys. The developer caught it with a kind of fumbling panic, like E had thrown a baby at him.

More henches had gathered in the lobby while we talked. Several administrators buzzed around carrying tablets and paperwork, and a half-dozen Meat, all wearing suits and earpieces, loitered about, exhibiting a look I liked to think of as *semiformal murderer*. One of them, with a tattoo on his neck of a jaguar, had been working with E for some time. I accidentally caught his eye and he winked at me. I turned away too quickly and a little bit of coffee leapt out of the lid of the travel mug, splashing my shirt. My head throbbed.

E's phone chirped, and he became even more animated. "Our chariots await!" He strode out the front doors, flanked by his bodyguards, and the rest of us followed.

Just outside the doors a long, midnight-blue super-car waited, purring like a contented tiger. E climbed in along with the stony-faced R&D guy holding the Mood Ring and Jaguar Neck. The rest of us piled into the pair of SUVs parked just behind. I chose the car with the most admins, hoping it would be quieter, but as soon as the vehicle started to move the interior cabin lit up, painfully bright. A pair of screens, one for each row of seats, sprung to life, displaying E's grinning, ridiculously pleased face. The video bounced; he was clearly recording with his cell phone. It made me seasick.

"Hey, team, it's the big day!" The sound in the car was tinny and too loud. I moaned audibly. One of the researchers sitting next to me—a woman with red hair in a tight bun—giggled quietly. "Thanks to all of you for being a part of this. Now, everything's going to be pretty straightforward once we get there; it's a teleconference being broadcast live, so there won't actually be anyone in the space but us and the camera crew." The image shook violently; he was doing excited jazz hands. "It's going to be big!"

Then the screens went dark and I sighed in relief. I spent the rest of the trip chugging my coffee and dabbing in vain at the small stain on my shirt.

The press conference was scheduled to take place in one of the boardrooms of a nearby hotel. When we arrived, the camera crew was already there, going through the last of their preparations. E hollered with delight as soon as he strode through the door, startling all three of them badly.

The boardroom was considerably more well appointed and well lit than anything in the gray-and-beige Electrophorous offices. There was a long window along one side of the room, which had E very excited, chattering on about how good his skin looked under natural light, while one of the crew, a young Indian woman with a braid that went down to her hips, fitted him with a wireless mic. The set, such as it was, included a long, dark wooden desk for E to sit behind and an oversize forest-green armchair. The arms were carved into elaborate curls and made the seat seem a little like a throne. E sat down and squealed in delight.

In addition to the woman with the mic, there was a stocky camera operator who was already strapped into a stabilizing rig and a third man—an aging Irish punk with a side shave—handling a pair of laptops and a seemingly ridiculous number of cables, who I vaguely inferred was in charge of the broadcasting part of whatever was about to happen. I thought I might have recognized the punk from the Temp Agency, but not well enough to say hello.

Once E was wired for sound, the pair of techs from R&D busied about setting up the Mood Ring on the desk in front of him, placing it on an elaborate stand.

"Move it a little to the right, guys?" the camera operator instructed, face contorted in a squint as he looked into the camera.

The researchers looked miffed as they carefully shifted everything over, a piece at a time.

"We want to see your boss, after all," he added, and one of the lab techs scowled.

E smiled expansively. "Can't have anything obscuring this *visage*, eh?" He gestured toward his high-cheekboned face. I thought he might have been wearing a little bit of eyeliner for the occasion. I had to admit it suited him.

While the R&D folks continued to bustle in front of E and the Meat arranged themselves around the room—a pair at the door and the other four behind the boss—I felt vaguely useless. I wandered over to the woman with the braid.

"So, uh, where do you want me?" I asked, hoping she had some sense of what the hell was about to happen.

She looked up at me and then down at a call sheet. "Anna, right?"

"That's me."

"Great. E wants you to stand with his bodyguards as part of the entourage. He felt it was imbalanced to have 'only men standing behind him' when he 'considers himself a progressive employer.'" She did a performative this-guy-is-an-idiot voice when delivering direct quotes.

I felt foolish for thinking I'd earned this. "I'm one of the booth babes." The sour truth bloomed in my stomach.

She looked at me sympathetically. "That's how it goes." She gestured for me to join E and the Meat behind the desk; the pair from R&D had finished their work and taken their own place to E's left, directly behind the Mood Ring. She told me to stand on E's immediate right.

I took my place, shifting back and forth according to the camera operator's instructions until I was in exactly the right place. I tried to look engaged and attentive, but the wind had been knocked out of my sails.

"Isn't this great, Anna?" E stage-whispered to me. He sounded like he was vibrating with glee.

I smothered the urge to stage-whisper, No. "Yeah, really impressive. This is a great space."

He nodded. "I made a good choice." His head suddenly swiveled and he fixed me with a look for a moment. "Anna, thank you for getting Andre patched up the other night."

"Oh, it was no trouble." My voice was equal parts syrup and poison.

E only heard the sweetness. He smiled and settled back into his chair, facing the camera. I wondered what it must be like to be so mediocre and so confident at the same time.

"You handled it well. Really kept your composure." He nodded to himself.

"Thanks, E. It means a lot to hear that from you." I tried to tamp down my bristling annoyance and sound as pure and genuine as I could. Between his compliment and the press conference, I was beginning to nurse a feeble hope that maybe, just maybe, that gratitude he was feeling might blossom into a full-time position. Maybe one day I would be able to visit a dentist again.

"Dare to dream," I accidentally said out loud.

Luckily, at the same time the punk with the laptops suddenly stood up. "Everyone, quiet for a moment. We're going live in just a couple minutes. Mr. Eel, I have us tapped into the municipal feeds covering today's transit debate; we're ready to cut in at any time."

"Splendid. We're ready when you are. And please, call me E. Mr. Eel is my father." The Meat behind him rumbled a collective, obedient laugh, which set me giggling.

I struggled to get my face under control. The bodyguards behind me were all wearing practiced scowls and even the R&D nerds had managed expressions of somber menace. *Mean nerds.* What would a villainous lady do with her face? I tried a smirk, to see if I could hold it.

"Okay, everyone," the woman with the call sheet said, clapping her hands for a moment of attention. "Remember your job is to make your boss more impressive. Loom, but don't mean-mug too hard. Try to project some intensity, but take your cues from E and don't go overboard. You're like . . . evil bridesmaids. You're here to make him look even better."

The Meat behind me grumbled at the comparison and I fought against another smile. I tried to project a sense of menace. I indulged in some revenge fantasies and hoped they carried to my face.

"We're live in ten!" the camera operator called, and then continued to count down on his fingers. E sat a little straighter on his makeshift throne. He dramatically steepled his fingers and allowed one corner of his mouth to quirk up the slightest bit. I found myself suddenly gripped by nervousness. With a final thumbs-up, we were live.

"Mr. Mayor. Councillors. Chief Danczuk. Pardon me for interrupting this municipal session on, what was it, public transit?" E paused a moment, mentally counting out a few seconds to allow for the sounds of shock and outrage he imagined had erupted on the other side of the closed-circuit channel he'd invaded. "Please, I promise not to take up too much of your time.

"At the bottom of this screen there is a crypto-wallet address. This is a very simple ransom demand: the equivalent of five million dollars, delivered within the next five minutes. Nothing outrageous, nothing that would bankrupt the civic purse, just a little nest egg to get my next project off the ground."

E glanced meaningfully across the room, where two of his bodyguards had been standing by the door. One of them nodded and touched his earpiece, barking a quick command. The other held the doors open. A third man walked in, bigger than any of the other Meat, half dragging and half carrying a long-limbed teen boy with him. The kid had grass stains on his knees and was wearing a jersey emblazoned with the logo of a dough-nut shop; he must have been grabbed from soccer prac-tice. As the thick-necked man holding him dragged the boy closer to the desk, I could smell the salt of his fresh sweat and a high note of panic. One of the kid's feet was bare and it looked like his own sock was stuffed into his mouth.

One of the Meat behind me kicked me in the back of the leg, and I realized my mouth was hanging open. I struggled to compose my face.

"Of course, I understand that you need some incentive for such a business proposition, so let me provide it, along with a demonstration of the new project I am working on," E said jovially, gesturing the Meat closer. He dragged the boy into the frame of the camera. E paused again for a reaction he couldn't see on the other end of the video feed, then plucked the sock out of the boy's mouth. The kid shook his head and spat.

"We'd like to thank Jeremy for volunteering for this demonstration." E stood. He picked up the Mood Ring and set it humming, much louder this time; I could feel it in my teeth. "Jeremy, your dad is watching, so try to put on a good show for him. I'm very excited that you were able to help us out."

"Where is my dad?" Jeremy's voice was a lot higher than I expected.

E pointed to the camera. "Your father can see you, Jeremy, but I'm afraid that you can't see him. Now, answer me this: How do you feel, Jeremy? What would you say your emotional state is like currently?"

Jeremy attempted to kick the Meat holding him with the foot still wearing a cleat. "Let me go! Let go!"

E nodded. "Upset. Would you say that's fair?"

Jeremy's lip was trembling. He was even younger than I thought he was at first glance; what I had originally taken for a skinny fourteen was probably more like a tall twelve. He was close enough to me now that I could see the scabs on his knees and the dirt under his fingernails. I was struck at once by how vulnerable this poor kid was, and the fact that I was standing almost directly behind him while we were live-broadcasting his kidnapping. The room swam and I suddenly felt like I was going to barf.

"Okay, Jeremy," E was saying, his voice even and soothing, almost hypnotic. "We're going to try something together." He adjusted the settings on the Mood Ring slightly, and the vibration seemed to rattle around in my sinus cavities. E brought the Mood Ring close to Jeremy's head, and the kid yelled and struggled against the huge hands around his upper arms. "Now. Tell me how you feel."

The reverberating hum became a deep pulse. My jaw ached, but something in me relaxed. Where I had been panicking a moment before, I now felt a strange, artificial serenity.

Jeremy stopped struggling completely. His eyes had been feverish with panic but now they glazed over. He rested in the hands of the man holding him, where he had frantically resisted seconds before. A little drool pooled in one corner of his mouth and he absently wiped it away with the back of his hand.

E patted the shoulder of the Meat restraining Jeremy, and the big man slowly let go. The kid made no attempt to move or get away, just shifted his weight, looking around the room with vague curiosity.

"Feeling better?" E's voice was encouraging, almost gentle.

"Yeah. I am." Jeremy's voice was slow and wondering. His face was relaxed now; he looked almost sleepy.

"I'm glad to hear that, Jeremy." E gestured for the boy to join him behind the desk. Jeremy ambled over and stood next to E obediently.

E squeezed the kid's shoulder gently. "What do you feel like doing right now, young man?"

Jeremy's brow furrowed as he thought. "Well. That depends on what you want me to be doing, mister."

E's face split into a grin, showing white wolfish teeth. "Very good answer, Jeremy. You're a very bright boy. And please, call me E."

"Okay, E."

"That's perfect. Now, there's a small favor I want you to do for me, Jeremy. Would you like to help me out?"

At the prospect of being given something to do Jeremy's face lit up. The boy nodded, a deep swoop of his head. "Sure!"

"Wonderful." E made a demanding gesture toward one of his bodyguards, who reached into the tactical messenger bag he held and produced a long, rectangular box. It was heavy and closed with a latch, not unlike a jewel case for a necklace, but larger. E took it eagerly and laid the box on the desk between him and Jeremy, who was watching the exchange, calm and intent.

E turned to me then. "Hold this," he said, so casually, and handed the Mood Ring to me. I held up my hands to fend it off, but he calmly took my wrists and curled my fingers around the handle of the device. I could feel the weird pulse that it was emitting become dampened, like a current was passing through my body, but I was safely grounded now, letting it pass through.

"Keep it close to his head," E said conversationally. "Works better that way." My arms shook but I held it, gritting my teeth against the weird keening and wondering if this meant I was going to jail.

E rested one of his free hands gently on Jeremy's back, between his shoulder blades. He lifted his head and directly addressed the camera. "As you can all see, young Jeremy here is terribly obedient and open to suggestion." Jeremy looked at him adoringly and E smiled. "By the time we're done with this demonstration, I bet you're all going to want one yourselves." He laughed at his own joke.

He raised his other hand, as though being sworn in. "I would like to assure everyone watching that Jeremy won't be suffering any ill effects from the Mood Ring, at least not at this setting." He tilted his head to one side. "I can't say the same is true for what he might do under its influence, however."

E turned his attention back to Jeremy. "Now, are you right- or left-handed?"

"Left, E."

"A lefty! Me too. Okay, in that case, lay your right hand on the desk, nice and flat."

"Like this?"

"Move over a tiny bit, so the camera can get a better angle. Yes, perfect, great job."

Jeremy's hand looked very small and dirty on the polished surface of the desk.

E opened the long box in front of them, and I sucked in a breath sharply between my lips and teeth. "Now, take this. Be careful, it's heavier than you'd expect." He placed a cleaver in Jeremy's left hand.

The boy bobbed the blade in his hand for a moment, testing the weight. "It *is* heavy!" His voice was so calm and curious.

"Do you have a good grip on it?"

"Got it."

"Great. Now, I would like you to cut off the tip of the little finger on your right hand—just the tip, now—to complete the demonstration. That would be very helpful."

"Sure thing, E." Jeremy shifted his weight and planted his feet a bit more firmly, getting a slightly more secure grip on the cleaver. He spread his fingers farther apart. He raised the cleaver a little higher and wiggled back and forth, concentrating, like a cat preparing to pounce. Numbly, I kept the Mood Ring pointed at his head.

Then he paused, lowered the cleaver a fraction, and looked up at E again. I felt a wave of incredible relief. It wasn't going to work.

"I'm worried," Jeremy said. "I might not be able to do it right."

"What do you mean, kiddo?" E reached back and took my wrist, pulling the Mood Ring a little closer. His voice was still chipper but there was a hint of worry in his grip.

"I'm worried I might miss."

E grinned, relaxing. "Don't worry, Jeremy! You can always try a few times. I won't mind."

Relieved, Jeremy nodded and turned his attention back to his hand. He raised the cleaver again.

E stared directly into the camera. His eyes shone. I watched a bead of sweat trickle down his temple. "If the money arrives promptly, we'll restrict this demonstration to a single digit. Does that sound fair to you, Mr. Mayor?" He took out his phone and looked at it. "No transfer yet." He shook his head.

I closed my eyes.

Several things happened very slowly, and all at once. The huge window, through which all that beautiful natural light was streaming, exploded into the room. I felt shards of glass hit my arms and face. I reached up wonderingly and touched my cheek, my hand coming away bloody. I had time to feel lucky that none got in my eyes.

E lurched toward me and tore the Mood Ring out of my other hand. I held on a moment too long and his sudden movement wrenched me forward and threw me off balance. I grabbed hold of the desk to steady myself, my hands landing just a few inches from Jeremy's.

While everyone else in the room was yelling and diving for cover, Jeremy stayed completely calm and intent on his work, even though he was covered in glass. I could see the tip of his tongue sticking out at the corner of his mouth in childish concentration. My throat went dry. I reached toward him, but I knew I was already too late.

He swung the cleaver down.

The blade never completed its arc. There was a blur, and a smell like ozone, and a gloved hand caught Jeremy's a moment before the cleaver made contact. Accelerator, the fastest man on the planet, held his hand cupped around Jeremy's. The sidekick gently pried the knife out of the boy's hand and tossed it away. I took a step back, and found myself in an immense shadow.

Supercollider stood there between Jeremy and the Electric Eel. Accelerator tucked the boy behind him, creating a distance between the kid and the Mood Ring, trying to break its thrall. One of E's bodyguards ill-advisedly lurched toward the two of them, and Supercollider kicked the Meat across the room. There was a wet crunch where he landed. Now behind the hero's broad, impenetrable back, Jeremy started, blinked, and shook his head, like he was waking up.

E took a step back and hissed.

"I have you," the hero snarled, his perfect quarterback's jaw clenched tight. As Jeremy became more alert, he started to shiver uncontrollably and clung to Accelerator's arm.

I'd run into the odd hero now and again in the course of my work, usually C-list at best—Sapphire Mask sat next to me in a bar once and tried to talk to me about my life choices, while the Nucleus had come to the Electrophorous office once on a diplomatic mission—but I'd only ever seen Supercollider on the news. I stared at him stupidly, at the perfect wave of his blond hair and the impossible breadth of his shoulders. On his chest, two gold, concentric rings seemed to burn in the sunlight against the dark blue background. I tried to creep away from him, backing away slowly, easing my feet through all the glass.

"Slow news day?" The Electric Eel's eyes were wild. I wondered if he'd ever been in the same room as Supercollider. Usually the champion would be averting a natural disaster or stopping a nuclear warhead from detonating, not swooping in to save our mayor's kid's pinkie.

"I was in town, as luck would have it. News of your depravity reached me in time." Supercollider sounded profoundly disgusted. I kept backing up slowly, letting the two of them talk it out, hoping to slink to safer ground.

"Surrender," Supercollider demanded.

I looked behind me to make sure my way was clear. The two Meat who had been guarding the door were utterly stunned, frozen in place. This was well above their pay grade. Accelerator was keeping an eye on them, darting back and forth like a barracuda in front of Jeremy, unable to remain still.

There was a hum over by the shattered window and, almost lazily, Quantum Entanglement stepped through. She hovered just a couple of inches off the ground for a moment then let her boots sink into the high-pile carpet, crunching delicately on the glass. She strode into the room like a windstorm, her bleached-white hair swirling around her. Like Supercollider, I'd never seen her in person and, in shock, I seemed to have time to stare. The tattoos on her lips and chin were beautiful, complex and interlocking shapes that defined her already striking face.

I expected the Electric Eel to freeze and panic, like the rest of us. Some part of me was waiting for him to hand over the Mood Ring and put his hands on his head, to kneel. E looked down at the device in his hands for a moment, then his lip curled sharply. The air around me seemed to crackle and I could feel the hair on my head writhe, my skirt clinging to my legs with static; he had activated his shock gauntlets.

He actually intended to fight.

A blue arc of electricity shot out of E's hands. It wasn't especially powerful, but it was bright and loud, and that startled the hero. For all his strength and durability, Supercollider's reaction time and mental capacity were still entirely human. He blinked and took a step back, instinctively tucking Jeremy a little more fully behind him to protect the boy. That gave E the room he needed . . . and the villain bolted.

He ran past me, and I saw him grinning with a kind of unbridled, ecstatic fury. It dawned on me he was enjoying this, that drawing the attention of a hero—of a real hero—was his greatest accomplishment as a villain so far.

"Cover!" As soon as the Electric Eel shrieked, the Meat seemed to come to life. The two by the door pulled out guns. Deeper in the room, one of the three survivors, the one holding the bag the cleaver had been in, pulled out something strange and circular, like a thick saw blade. The weapon spat out a gout of red, wet light in a messy arc, like a spray of lava. The three heroes darted and rolled to get out of the way as the light cut a swath through the room, eating aggressively into the floor. One of the pair from R&D, the giggly woman with red hair from the car, didn't get out of the way in time when it splashed near her. I saw a chunk of her fall away from the rest, an arm and a flash of white rib, accompanied by the smell of burning flesh, and she collapsed.

Supercollider used his invulnerable body to shield Jeremy from the spray, keeping the boy carefully behind him. With the hero occupied for a few precious seconds, the Electric Eel managed to make it to the door. He cackled as he left, sprinting down the hallway toward his supercar and escape. Accelerator tried to intercept him, but the spray from the lava gun was too unpredictable and he had to dive behind Supercollider to avoid being cauterized. While he was incredibly fast, the sidekick was almost as fragile as an ordinary person.

With E gone, all of the henches were left alone with the heroes. Quantum Entanglement made her way over to Supercollider and the pair exchanged a couple of hushed words. She threw up a force field around her and Jeremy, scooping the kid away from her partner. She lifted Jeremy easily, and the traumatized kid wrapped his arms and legs around her as if he were a much smaller child. He stuck his thumb in his mouth.

Supercollider nodded to her and she levitated herself and the kid out through the broken window and toward safety. I could hear sirens below; in a moment he'd be safely in the hands of some EMTs. The rest of us, however, were trapped with Supercollider and some maniac with a lava gun. The hero's face was a blank, stern mask. I sank to the floor, trying to become invisible.

Supercollider began to slog through the spray of liquid heat still being poured onto him. It couldn't damage him, but it made him grimace as he fought forward. It was slow going and seemed to sting. The carpet and the soles of Supercollider's boots were melting together, each step a stretch of blackened rubber. The weapon began firing more erratically as he approached, running out of power or beginning to malfunction. The red light sprayed out in a thinning spatter pattern, like water from a broken nozzle. A bit splashed dangerously close to me and I scrambled up, trying to put more distance between my body and the furiously hot, rapidly disintegrating floor.

The Meat shifted his aim, sending the staccato spray toward Accelerator, thinking perhaps he'd have better luck doing harm to the sidekick, who had been using his speed to dart ever closer. Supercollider took the opportunity to rush the Meat, and unluckily, trying to keep myself from being burned to a crisp, I had stumbled into the hero's way.

He absently moved me aside, out of his path, as though I were a piece of furniture. He might not have been trying to injure me, but it was like a glancing blow from a transport truck. His flesh seemed impossibly hard, the way jumping from a great height into water is the same as hitting a concrete wall once you reach a certain velocity. I felt my body buckle and give.

I was briefly airborne and landed badly. I sat, stupidly, in the middle of the floor where I'd fallen, legs splayed out, in shock.

The heat weapon sputtered out entirely. The Meat holding it threw the useless thing at Supercollider, who grimaced as it bounced off the side of his face. The Meat threw a punch and Supercollider caught his hand; he screamed as his fist was crushed. No longer worried about getting sprayed with liquid magma, Accelerator began darting around the room, disarming the other Meat. Supercollider followed behind—still holding the Meat by his jelly hand, dragging him along—parting them from their consciousness. Each of them fell bonelessly, in terrible limp heaps. Often the arrangement of their necks and limbs seemed impossible. He absently punched the Meat he held one last time, then dropped him in the pile. From my angle, I couldn't tell if his face was swollen or caved in.

The camera crew was huddled in one corner. The man who had been working with the laptops was sobbing in long, keening gasps; the woman was silent. The camera operator tried to climb out of the broken window, but stopped when he realized how high up we were. He fell back to the floor, his hands bleeding from the glass shards clinging to the frame.

I tried to stand by myself, but my left leg collapsed under me, refusing to take my weight. It didn't feel like it belonged to me somehow, ground beef and shattered porcelain wrapped in someone else's skin. I stared at the offending limb, confused. There was something wrong with the angle, the familiar lines of my body warped and alien. Then, pain finally found purchase in my gut and wrenched down hard. I turned my head and puked, coffee and stomach acid.

Suddenly the room was filled with lights and noise; I started to lose track of things. The room seemed weirdly still for a moment, then I blinked and it was full of cops, pointing guns at everyone and demanding they put their hands on their heads, or get on the floor. I lifted my arms uselessly, palms open. One officer grabbed me, about to haul me to my feet, and I screamed. He took a closer look at me, and the meat of my leg gone wrong, and flinched away, releasing his grip. A second cop bent down on one knee and asked my name. Instinctively, I asked if I was being detained. She said something in reply, but I was more concerned with the vomit in my hair. I noticed the first cop wiping his hand on his leg in disgust. I asked for a tissue.

Someone started to cover the bodies with tarps.

Once it was clear that there was no one dangerous left alive or present, the EMTs were allowed in. I screamed as they maneuvered me onto the stretcher, every little jolt of movement hammering into me like a railroad spike. One medic, a young woman with green hair, threatened to tie me down if I kept fighting them; I hadn't realized I was resisting. I tried to keep it together. The other EMT, who had a deep tan and incredibly kind eyes, apologized. He found me a vomit bag and a couple of moist wipes for my face.

The ride in the ambulance was a wailing blur, both muffled and too bright. The friendly medic kept talking to me, trying to keep me awake, but I kept losing little bits of time. The louder the sirens became, and the more forcefully the medic spoke, the easier it became to slip away inside myself. Sliding into shock was almost comfortable, like falling asleep, only cold instead of warm.

I didn't lose consciousness, but I did lose track of things for a long while. I knew the shock was wearing off when I got annoyed. No matter how often or how slowly the nurses or doctors explained things to me, it was incredibly difficult to retain and process any of the information. I was so tired of being confused and miserable that my brain kicked into gear again.

I was asked over and over for my name, if I knew where I was, if I could remember what happened. The nurse had to try three times to get my IV in, but once I was finally hooked up, the steady drip of painkillers went a long way toward helping me communicate. At first I was only able to blurt out the odd word here and there, but as the pain became more manageable I worked my way up to ugly little sentences.

"Thrown."

"He threw me."

"The hero threw me."

"Supercollider. He threw me across the room."

I repeated it over and over, the simple fact of the cause of my injury, and it made almost everyone who heard my answer grimace and blanch, and change the topic. Only one doctor pursed her lips together and nodded, as though unsurprised. She didn't look much older than I was, with luminous black skin and long, deft hands. She seemed exhausted but projected an air of utter competence that was incredibly comforting.

"I should have been a doctor," I drawled. She smiled.

"Maybe. What you do seems dangerous. Might have a longer life expectancy than working with heroes."

"Wrong side, I'm afraid."

She shook her head. "Don't say that too loud or too often."

"Fair."

"Explains why you're in such bad shape, anyway. Before I saw your chart, I assumed you were in a car accident."

"I feel like I got hit by a semi."

"Your femur looks like you did." She was gravely considering some X-rays.

"My leg?"

"Yes. Bones don't distinguish between trucks and someone who can throw trucks."

I was fitted with a brace, a grotesquely painful process that made me squeal, even with the drugs. The imaging confirmed what was already apparent from how badly my leg was twisted: that the break was bad and complex. At first, I wasn't able to process much more than my body's steady, dreadful bleating *there is something wrong with my leg*, like an internal siren.

Later, I would become intimately, obsessively acquainted with everything that was happening under my rapidly swelling skin. But at that moment, I couldn't understand why they didn't just slap a plaster cast on me and call it a day.

I had broken my wrist once, in middle school. A quick trip to the emergency room and a neon-green cast later, and I was home watching TV and eating a popsicle. I missed a couple of days of school, almost ceremonially; it didn't even hurt very much, just a deep, weird ache and later the terrible itch of healing. Lying there now, I thought at first they just needed a bigger cast, and soon I'd be home with some Percocet, bingeing on Korean horror films.

"I want a black cast," I announced to no one in particular, imagining I could pick the color again, like I had as a child.

"It's a bit more complicated than that," my doctor said, and I looked up in mild surprise that someone had bothered to answer.

"What?"

"You're going to have surgery in the morning."

"On what?"

"Your leg." I could hear the struggle for patience in her voice.

I stared at her, blank and confused. She tried to smile but managed only a weird tightening of her lips.

Later, a nurse helped clean some of the vomit residue off my neck and chest, and I made a feeble attempt to wipe more of it out of my hair. He also brought a cup of ice chips; I had to keep my stomach empty before going under anesthesia, and I sucked on them fretfully. At least it helped make my sour, acidic mouth feel cleaner even if it couldn't dispel the unsettled emptiness that had taken the place of hunger.

That night, my blood pressure began to dip. Things began to become vague again, but without the chilly, numbing edge of shock this time. A couple of doctors conferred at the foot of my bed for a moment. I couldn't make out what they were saying, but the hushed urgency of their voices was an almost soothing, slightly distant susurrus.

My eyelids startled open when one of them tapped my good foot to get my attention. My doctor, who somehow seemed both more exhausted and more in command every time I saw her, told me then I needed a transfusion to stay stable enough for surgery. My femoral artery was intact, so I wasn't going to bleed out, but the leg had shattered down to the marrow, and blood was pooling in the soft tissues of my leg.

I tried to distract myself from how deeply distressing the idea of internal bleeding was by focusing on weird details. I wondered whose blood I was getting. It seemed so intimate and alien—and strange that I would never know whose red and white blood cells were shoring me up, keeping my brain wet enough to function.

What no one tells you about a transfusion is that the blood goes in nearly ice cold. The bag of gore they hook up to you comes straight out of the refrigerator. I expected something hot, arterial, life-affirming, but what hit my body was cold and sluggish. It takes hours to transfuse and I ended up needing two units to keep pace with what I was losing into the sinkhole of my injury. I shook with cold harder than I ever had before in my life, the arm my IV was attached to frozen and livid. I couldn't get warm, no matter how many thin, terrible blankets the nurses brought me, and I shivered all night.

The next morning, when the anesthesiologist covered my nose and mouth with a mask and told me to count backward from one hundred, I was simply relieved at the prospect of getting some rest and finally feeling warm.

While I was unconscious, surgeons inserted a metal rod into the marrow canal of my femur. The bone— harder than concrete, the thickest and sturdiest in the human body—was in pieces. It was not a clean break; later I would learn the phrase "comminuted fracture" to describe the way shards of bone were left floating in the meat of my leg. The doctors scooped the broken pieces back together and packed them in place, hoping they'd mend as well as possible. They made a second incision in my knee, matching the one at my hip, and attached the rod to my bones at both ends with titanium nails.

Waking from anesthetic isn't like shaking off sleep. The weight of your unconsciousness has to wear off. It's a slow swim back to the surface of your mind, a fight against the drag of grogginess. I found myself clinging to uncomfortable little sensations to anchor myself, like the ache from the IV and the terrible cold—which hadn't, as I'd hoped, gone away—the huge new throb of my leg all the painkillers couldn't quite wipe out. My skin was clammy and seemed to itch everywhere. In the recovery room, finally being able to fill my mouth with a little cold water was bliss. I made a joke about setting off metal detectors at the airport for the rest of my life. No one laughed.

By that evening I was sitting up, hands curled around a cup of tea (which, if not hot, was at least blessedly warm). My doctor reappeared, bearing the air of someone who'd just showered and changed their clothes in lieu of sleeping.

She showed me new X-rays, the rod and nails showing up crisp and vivid against the ghosts of my bones. "It went well," she said, satisfied. "It was an ugly break, but surgery went as smooth as it could have. You may be able to put some weight on that leg in a few days."

That sounded promising. I tried to think of what I knew about breaking a bone. "So, what, in eight weeks I'll be back to normal, then?"

"Six months."

"What?"

"I've known a break like this to heal in a little less time, and you are young, but considering the type of spiral fracture this was, I wouldn't be surprised if it takes longer. You'll be on crutches for most of that, maybe a cane in the last weeks. You'll get a referral for physio."

She might have said more but I lost it. I stared at her earrings, fiercely bright diamond studs, focusing on them to keep from panicking.

She pressed on through my unresponsiveness and blank, horrified expression. "Do you understand, Anna?"

"What?"

"We're keeping you for a day or two longer, to make sure no complications arise. Then you can go home."

I managed to nod, and she left to deliver terrible news to someone else. A wave of loneliness hit me, and for the first time it occurred to me I should try and tell someone where I was.

This was harder than I expected it to be. My purse had, almost miraculously, made the trip to the emergency room with me, and was stowed in a small locker beside my bed. The bag had been stepped on repeatedly, either by cops or capes, and my phone's battery was dead and the screen even more badly cracked. I realized that I didn't even know June's number off the top of my head, so I couldn't call her from the terrible, strangely sticky landline in the room.

My best nurse, whose name was Nathan and whose muscular arms were covered in full-sleeve tattoos of tentacles and warships, found me a charging cable and managed to plug in my wrecked phone. It took me three tries to input my password and I sliced my thumb open on the shattered glass of the screen, but the device still worked. Dozens of texts and chat messages from June arrived in a squawking swarm of notifications.

Her messages started out affectionately mocking (good luck today, dick), but quickly became concerned (what's happening over there? holy shit you're on tv!!). After the footage cut out, there was a string of panicked messages detailing how everyone on-site was told to clean out their desks and leave, that the building might be raided; someone ripped the hard drive out of June's computer while she was still in her office, putting on her coat. Eventually her messages devolved into her alternating between calling me a bitch, sending poop and explosion emojis, and begging me to call her.

I managed to peck out the message hey, I'm alive and was working on a follow-up before my phone lit up from her calling me. I let her scream at me for scaring her until her voice gave and she was hoarse and panting, and then I slowly explained the horrors of my last forty-eight hours. She felt bad enough for me, or forgave my radio silence enough, to promise to swing by my house and come by with supplies in the morning.

I spent another fretful, shivering night, unable to get either comfortable or warm, and managed to sleep just as a thin gray dawn was starting to filter into my room. I was startled awake a pitifully short amount of time later by my morning nurse, who sang hello to me and plopped a huge fruit basket down on the table next to my bed.

"This came for you! Isn't that exciting?" She stared at me expectantly.

I flailed and cursed. Every time I got any sleep at all, even just nodding off for a moment, I woke up stickier, smellier, more physically abject than I was before. My leg was stained with iodine from where they had painted my skin in prep for surgery, and my skin had broken out everywhere the adhesive from the surgical tape had touched me. I felt like one-third of my body was a rash. The backs of my hands were the worst, aching from the IVs and seeping lymph. There was no fruit basket yet created on this hell earth that would have been capable of making me excited.

Batting away the cellophane, careful not to disturb any of the tubes attached to me, I fished between the

apples and fig jam and a tiny box of artisanal crack-
ers until I found a card tucked between the leaves of
a pineapple. It was emblazoned with the familiar eel-
and-trident logo of Electrophorous, and I felt a sudden
surge of warmth toward E. He might have placed me
right in harm's way, but at least he cared. Maybe when
I returned to work, I thought, I could negotiate dental
coverage. I opened the envelope.

It was not the "Get well soon!" card I expected, but
an HR document, typed neatly on official company
letterhead. I was thanked for my "good" work, told I
had been a "valuable resource under difficult circumstances." However, since my injury meant I would
be recovering "indefinitely," and my employer found
themselves in a "state of flux," they were "regretfully"
severing my contract.

> In acknowledgment of your service and efforts
> while under our employ, a standard reference letter
> will be added to your agency file. Once you are able
> to seek employment again, please feel free to sub-
> mit a new application to Electrophorous Industries.

I held the letter nervelessly, staring into the middle
distance, and could barely muster a reaction when
June entered the room with a small duffel bag over one

shoulder. She drew up short when she saw my face, and I held the letter out to her, unable to come up with something to say.

It wasn't often I got to see June speechless—her quick-witted viciousness was one of her best qualities. But in that moment, staring at the huge fruit basket on the side table near my hospital bed, her powers left her.

I sipped some lukewarm ginger ale through a bendy straw and basked in her outraged shock. She opened her mouth to say something, then closed it again.

I managed an uneven grin. "I know."

"I can't." She shook her head with brain-rattling force.

"Drink it in." I gestured grandly.

"An actual fruit basket."

"It's next level."

She turned her back, walked away from it, and suddenly turned around, as though if she looked away for a moment, the basket might disappear.

"Those fucks! I'll fight a bitch," she spat. Her outrage was more comforting than a hug. I managed my first real smile in some time and gathered the motivation to reach for the bag she had brought me.

June was wearing nose plugs, but it was still obvious how gravely uncomfortable she was in the hospital. The odor of disinfectant, new and old wounds, sickness and shit, would be awful for her (and to be perfectly clear I didn't smell delightful either). But she'd brought me warm socks and my favorite hoodie, basic hygiene supplies, and even my lipstick and eyeliner. It went an incredibly long way toward making me feel human again.

Her generosity had limits, of course.

"I'm not helping you in there," she said flatly, though she did agree to find a nurse to help me hobble to the bathroom to make a first pitiful attempt to clean myself. After brushing my teeth, applying a few cucumber-scented body wipes, and using an elastic to tie back my gritty, greasy hair, I was downright cheerful. While I slowly navigated my way back into bed, June read the letter from HR over and over, brow knit together in fury.

"It's the cliché of the fruit basket I find particularly offensive," she said finally. "Of all the shitty ways to deliver this news, they chose the worst bad joke."

I reached into the basket and fished around. "Would you like a plum?" Opiates and emotional devastation were making me giddy.

"No."

I shrugged and bit into the stone fruit. Juice pooled in my palm and ran down my arm.

"Greg's here."

I sucked on one of my fingers. "That's nice of him. He taking a call?"

"Yeah, out front. He should be up in a minute." She looked me over critically, taking in my swollen and splinted leg, limited mobility, gray face. "When are they going to let you out?"

"Tomorrow, maybe the next day. As soon as it's clear I don't have staph or a clot."

"Shit, I thought you'd be here a month."

"Nah. If you're not in immediate danger of shuffling off this mortal coil, they get rid of you pretty quick to free up the bed. I'll have to come back eventually to get the stitches removed and for some checkups. But soon I'm on my own."

"What do you mean, 'on your own'? You can't even piss by yourself. You gonna waddle down the stairs in that shitty Terminator leg brace to get your delivery tacos three times a day?"

"No."

"So what are you going to do?"

My throat suddenly felt like it was closing. I took a bite of the plum to try and buy some time before responding, but I couldn't swallow and had to spit it out. I wiped my face and stared into my lap. "I don't know."

Her face softened. "Your folks might help."

"Absolutely not."

"Yeah, fair. Do they know?"

"I hope not, but probably."

"Want me to call them?"

"No. I will, eventually. Just to let them know they don't have to throw a funeral."

She was quiet for a long moment. I thought she was letting me get my composure back, sparing me the embarrassment of crying, but it turned out June was thinking.

"You should come stay with me," she said all at once. "The couch folds down and I have a tub; you just have that tiny shower. You wouldn't have to move around very much."

"Are you sure?" I wanted her to have an out, though I'd be completely screwed if she took it.

She sat on the bed. I could still smell myself under the cucumber; I was amazed she could stand to be that close to me. "We can give each other makeovers and everything."

Greg mercifully bumbled into the room, sparing me having to deal with my emotions. He was even more flustered than usual and his long limbs were everywhere at once.

"I'm sorry, I'm sorry, I shouldn't have taken the call and come right up, but you know what he's—" He stopped talking suddenly, looking me up and down. "Shit, Anna."

"Thanks for coming, Greg. It's been boring as hell."

"You're a disaster." He groped for a chair near my bed and sat heavily in it. Whatever he had been expecting, I looked worse.

"They did a number on me, that's for sure." I tapped my hip with my bruised, intubated hand. "I got a metal rod and everything."

"We saw you on the news, with that thing in your hands. You looked like you were going to shit your pants."

"Trust me when I say I did not go into that room expecting to hold a mind control device tethered to the mayor's fucking kid."

"Obviously." He looked over at June, then said hesitantly, "What was it like? You know. Meeting *him*."

"'Meeting' is an interesting way to say it." He stared at me helplessly. I sighed. "You think you know what it's like to be hit. You've taken a punch. But that was something completely different. He barely had to touch me at all, and I'm totaled."

Greg was leaning forward, his brown eyes very bright, gripping his knees tightly with his hands. His phone rang in his pocket; he reached down and declined the call. I was touched.

"Anna," he said. "Do you know what this means?"

"That I may never walk normally again?"

"You fought Supercollider! You're, like, a real supervillain!"

"Greg." June's voice held a note of warning.

I tried to wave her off. "If by 'fought' you mean 'bled internally,' then, yes, the battle was long and valiant," I said.

"This is big!" He stood and started to gesture wildly. "There are, like, serious villains who've never even been in the same room with him, let alone fought him! This is major league stuff, Anna!"

"Shut the fuck up, Greg!" June hissed, and he shrunk in his chair, chagrined.

"It's a big deal," he said defensively.

I managed a thin smile. I couldn't muster any enthusiasm, but I also didn't have the heart to swat him down for excitement. June, however, had no such problems.

"I'm pretty sure Anna doesn't care how cool you think her devastating injury is, clown." She crossed her arms.

Greg looked at the floor. It occurred to me that he might actually be a little jealous.

They stayed for an hour or so. Greg installed some games on my broken phone, and June promised to check in so she knew when I'd be released and could pick me up. Eventually, Greg couldn't ignore the constant muted buzzing in his pocket that meant someone's weapon of mass destruction wasn't booting up the way it was supposed to, and he fled the room to take the call.

June stood at the foot of my bed and squeezed my dirty toes, poking out the bottom of my brace.

"You should see the other guy, eh?"

Later that night, after she left, I realized that at some point while we were talking she'd written "Supercollider was here" on my brace in silver marker.

I dozed again, for a while. Sleeping deeply was challenging, but I nodded off frequently, usually to be awakened by someone prodding my leg, taking a blood sample, or running some minor cognitive tests to make sure I didn't have a concussion.

I was finally feeling hungry, but that didn't survive dinner service very long. The chicken was oddly soft and seemed breaded with sawdust, and the soggy corn had revoltingly combined with my mashed potatoes, but at least the pudding cup was edible. I was scooping the last bit of butterscotch out of the container with my finger when I became aware of a hushed bit of commotion taking place outside my door.

I recognized the voice of my doctor, who sounded extremely annoyed, but none of the several men she was speaking to.

"Shouldn't be more than a few minutes," someone said. "Standard procedure; she's the last interview we have to do."

"Visiting hours are technically over, so please keep it brief. She needs rest."

"We'll be gentle," someone else promised.

"When is she being released?" The third voice sounded strange, like someone was deliberately speaking a full octave above their natural register.

There was a pause. "We're not sure yet. Hopefully tomorrow."

"Thank you, ma'am."

The door swung fully ajar and three cops stepped into the room. Or, rather, two cops and Supercollider. The hero was wearing reflective aviator sunglasses (at night), a hastily applied fake mustache, and an obviously borrowed uniform that was markedly too tight. It would have been hilarious if the sight of him didn't make my mind go bloody.

He hung back by the door while the two actual officers approached my bed, a combination of solicitous expressions and threatening body language.

"How are you feeling, Miss Truelove?" The first

cop who spoke was the shorter of the two, built like a fire hydrant and sporting a few days' worth of stubble. His partner was taller and wiry, with salt-and-pepper hair and a slash of a mouth.

"Fine." My heart was hammering against my rib cage. Part of me was terrified, certain I was about to be placed in electrified handcuffs and dragged off to some supermax villains' prison where I'd be freeze-dried for all eternity. Below that fear, though, was the deep calm of a surprising fury. I found my gaze locking on to Supercollider. I hoped it was the pure venom I directed toward him that made him look uncomfortable under his disguise, instead of the uniform pants that were probably cutting off his circulation.

"Good to hear, miss," the first officer said. His partner took out a notebook from his back pocket and flipped to a clean page, then fished a silver pen out of a breast pocket.

"And it's *Troh-MED-lov.*"

"Certainly, miss." The first officer spoke in the tone of someone who had no intention of changing a thing they were doing. "We don't want to trouble you, we just have a few questions about what happened at the Giller Hotel."

I didn't say anything. I just kept staring at that stupid fake mustache.

The second officer sighed heavily. "Look, we're only charging the Meat and the suits. If you want a lawyer, you can call one and we'll come back tomorrow, but this will take five minutes." He spoke in the resigned voice of someone who expected his already terrible day to get even more annoying.

"Okay."

He looked visibly relieved. "Can you tell us what you were doing there, Miss Truelove?"

"Working. I was at work."

"I see. Now, we can't find any record of you being an employee of the hotel or a known associate of the Electric Eel. Who were you working for?"

"A temp agency."

"Ah, I see. So, what, you were getting the coffee or sandwiches or something?"

"Sure," I said, still staring at Supercollider. He had crossed his arms across his chest, causing the fabric of his borrowed shirt to creak and the buttons to strain.

"Why were you standing next to the Electric Eel?"

"They told me to."

"Did you have any idea what was supposed to happen at the press conference?"

"Happen?"

"Did you know about the weapon, or the kidnapping, or the Eel's plans?"

"Oh no—of course not." That seemed like a question to have asked before they decided not to charge me, but I wasn't about to do their jobs for them. The cop taking notes looked up from his pad and stared critically at my face for a moment. Then, satisfied, his gaze turned back down.

"Just a couple more questions, ma'am. How did the villain injure you?"

"Well, he sent me this fucking fruit basket, for one."

"I'm sorry?"

"Sorry, I was confused. He didn't. It wasn't the Eel. It was Supercollider."

The taller cop immediately stopped taking notes and again looked at me—hard. His partner raised his hands.

"Now, are you sure about that, ma'am?"

"Positive." I pulled the blanket back, and right at the top of the brace on my leg there was a massive bruise in the unmistakable shape of a handprint. There was no way the Eel had put that mark on me. Only someone with superstrength could have done it when he swept me aside. Supercollider shifted slightly.

The taller cop put his notebook away. "I can understand how you would be confused, ma'am."

"Confused."

"About exactly what happened. All that commotion."

I didn't reply, but let my jaw tighten.

"Thank you for your time, miss," the first officer added, suddenly jovial and dismissive. "I hope you feel better. And get a better job."

They nodded at me and walked out of the room too loudly. Supercollider let them pass in front of him and then turned to follow.

"Nice mustache," I said quietly. He faltered a moment, then brusquely left the room.

I buzzed the nurse and waited, fuming quietly, until someone finally came to help me to the bathroom again.

2

For the next few weeks, everything smelled like lavender.

It was one of the very few smells that June could tolerate consistently, even find pleasant, and so everything in her apartment was tinged with the soothing fragrance. Some of her pillows and blankets had sachets of the dried flowers sewn into them, and there were bunches of it hanging from the ceiling.

"I appreciate the aromatherapy."

"You're making fun of me." June pursed her lips. She did not like being challenged.

"Not at all, it's like a spa in here."

"It's relaxing, bitch."

"It's not a diss!"

Convalescing was awful. I was impatient with my

new physical limits, and was constantly making things worse, reinjuring myself in a thousand tiny ways. The only thing that could make me better was the passage of time, in maliciously slow increments, and I seemed determined to sabotage that already excruciating process whenever possible. I'd move too quickly and rip out stitches, push myself too hard one day and be too exhausted and in pain to do anything the next. For long weeks I was a rancid ball of frustration, with constant tension headaches from clenching my jaw too tight.

I was hurt just badly enough that follow-up medical care was its own nightmare, as I tried to navigate my injured body to and from the hospital or to specialist visits. I canceled as many appointments as I could, going so far as to take my own stitches out with a pair of nail clippers and some tweezers, hoping that rubbing alcohol would keep me from dying of a staph infection. In my darkest moments I felt like my life couldn't get any worse, but the bleak pragmatist in me knew it absolutely could.

I was constantly choosing between suffering through the brain fog of being on an awful lot of painkillers and suffering through the pain itself. I hated feeling vague and clogged, all my perceptions and responses cottony and dampened, but not taking anything was terrible. I ended up weaning myself off the Oxycontin as soon as

I could and chose being miserable, which was at least as uncomfortable for June as it was for me, because being in that much pain turned me into a cranky asshole.

Crankier asshole.

To her credit, June was as patient and nurturing as her personality allowed. She built me a kind of permanent nest on the pullout couch in her living room, a blanket fortress of pillows and snacks. She and Greg brought over more of my things from my apartment; she even enlisted the help of her barrel-chested not-boyfriend to be an extra pair of arms. She tried her best to make my presence in her house seem like an ongoing slumber party instead of a gross imposition. A few days after I moved in, she painted my toenails purple. It was her favorite color and looked a lot better on her than it did on me, flattering the deep, warm brown of her skin while accentuating the livid bruises around the pins in my ankle. We laughed at how swollen my toes were, like cocktail sausages poking out of the bottom of my brace. She wrapped up her hair and we put sheet masks on, as though skin care could cure anything.

It couldn't lift my mood for long, though. June was quickly reemployed, this time helping a "research firm" develop sniff-proof packaging for "secure shipping" (smuggling). While her day job meant that she could continue to feed and shelter me, it also meant that I was alone for too many hours with nothing to do but think.

I couldn't stop running the math in my head, over and over. Every day, the cost added up. Every day I couldn't work, or move; every day that passed in a haze of pain and obsessive misery-making added to the total. As soon as I was alone with my asshole brain, the counter at the edge of my mind was whirring away, telling me exactly how much Supercollider cost me that day, that hour, that minute. Every time I felt my guts twist from the bone-deep anguish of moving wrong, or dropped the remote and couldn't reach it for hours, that number jumped.

It could be worse, I told myself one day, endlessly circling through Netflix for something I hadn't half watched that had at least one murder in it. I could be that redhead from R&D who was sliced clean in half. I thought about the glimpse of her rib cage I caught as she fell.

Of course, rationalizing ended up making it worse anyway. I was suffering; her suffering was ended, forever. Whatever her future might have been, whatever she might have discovered, whatever great love or disaster of her life—all of that possibility was gone. She might have lived sixty more years, making wonderful or terrible things, and it was gone . . .

My brain shuddered to a halt at that thought. It was so startling that I sat up straight, hurting myself. Digging out my laptop, I started looking for a way to calculate exactly how much he cost all of us. There had to be a way.

It didn't take as long as I thought. After putting many variations of "disaster math" and "how to measure collateral damage" into a search engine, I eventually came across an academic paper called "A DALY Measure of the Direct Impact of Natural Disasters" by Ilan Noy. I'd been thinking about Supercollider the wrong way, I learned. I had been thinking about him as a person—an immensely destructive person, but a human being nonetheless. But he had more in common with a hurricane than a person, and once I adjusted my thinking, I realized there was a whole system devised to describe such forces, and what they cost. The currency was years of human life.

Lifeyears lost due to mortality are calculated as the difference between the age at death and life expectancy. The cost in lifeyears associated with the people who were injured (or otherwise affected by the disaster) is assumed to be defined as a function of the degree of disability associated with being affected, multiplied by the duration of this disability (until an affected person returns to normality), times the number of people affected. This disability coefficient is the "welfare-reduction weight" that is associated with being exposed to a disaster.

The last component of the index attempts to account for the number of human years lost as a result of the damage to capital assets and infrastructure—including residential and commercial buildings, public buildings, and other types of infrastructure, such as roads and water systems. We use the monetary amount of financial damages, and divide it by the monetary amount obtained in a full year of human effort. To proxy for this last quantity, we use income per capita as an indicator of the cost of human effort in each country-year, but discount this measure by 75%, as much of human activity is not spent in gainful employment.*

---

* Noy, Ilan. "A DALY Measure of the Direct Impact of Natural Disasters." VOX, CEPR Policy Portal. VOX, March 13, 2015. https://voxeu.org/article/daly-measure-direct-impact-natural-disasters.

I flailed around the couch, clawing for anything that I could reach and write on. I came up with a few napkins and receipts, and a ballpoint pen lodged between the couch cushions. Hazy with painkillers, I tried to run the math.

I started with the Meat whom Supercollider had kicked across the room thoughtlessly, who landed with a sodden thump I still heard sometimes while I was trying to fall asleep. If he'd been twenty-five years old, and been the average civilian, that meant he'd have had fifty-two years of life expectancy left. I tried to account for the fact he was in what we'd call a "high-risk position," so I cut that in half. It was still twenty-five years gone.

The woman from R&D was a different story. She was around thirty, I guessed, and had a safe desk job, which meant she was looking at another fifty-three years. Even if I decided to knock off another 25 percent because of her employer, that was still *forty* more years ahead of her, inventing new guns or new microsurgery techniques.

That was sixty-five years lost, just between the two of them, just that one day. That wasn't even taking into account yet my own injuries, or the two more dead Meat, or the others who were hurt (probably at least one spinal injury, two with severe concussions, a host of broken ribs and fingers), or the property damage. Looking at it all written down, watching the numbers add up, it seemed like a high price to pay for a pinkie finger and some cryptocurrency.

I was doing calculations on how henching compared to Alaskan crab fishing when it came to high-risk professions and life expectancy, when June came home. I explained what I had been working on, but she seemed less enthusiastic than I had been about the importance of my calculations.

"So today was the day you finally went full conspiracy theorist." She curled her lip. "Honestly, you took longer than I thought."

I was too feverishly amped to succumb to her sick burn. "I'm onto something." It was hard to keep my eyes off of what was emerging on the screen: a picture of the actual human toll of just a few minutes of Supercollider's presence. It was appalling.

June was saying something. "What?" I asked, trying to pay attention this time.

"I said you've gone stir-crazy."

"These numbers mean something."

She dropped her bag and coat onto a chair, and took off her nose plugs with an audible sigh of relief. "If I come home and there's a bunch of string and post-its about how Supercollider's an inside job, I'm kicking your ass out."

"Would only post-its be okay, though?"

She disappeared into the kitchen.

Late into that night, and over the next week, I worked to describe and quantify the disaster of Supercollider. There was a lot to account for, and a lot of numbers I had to guess or invent. I nearly tore my hair out trying to work out figures for hospitalization times and lost income for people I barely knew. I pored over endless crowdfunding pages, slowly becoming numb to the ordinary horror of house fires and tornadoes, to properly calibrate how much disasters were costing people. Within a few days of slow, foggy calculations, I had a number that seemed solid.

Those few minutes in a hotel conference cost all of us 152 years of our lives combined. Supercollider had decided that a kid's little finger and the Eel's ransom demand held more value than 152 years in hench lives. Maybe a lot of those years wouldn't have been terribly good, and would have involved a lot of busting heads and driving recklessly and working for villains. But they were *our* shitty years, and they'd been taken from us by an asshole in a cape playing judge and executioner.

For all her teasing, at first June seemed relieved I had something to do. I think she hoped that once I landed on a number that made sense, I'd lose interest and become a reasonable person again. To her dismay, I immediately began to examine Supercollider's greater toll on the world. If that one morning cost us so much, how much damage was he doing every day?

The next project took much more complex thinking and more time; I was slow, and sometimes had to stop and close my eyes for hours until a headache passed. I was forever waiting until the drugs were fading just enough that I could think a bit, but not so much that the pain made working impossible. The fact that I could focus at all in the state I was in convinced me I was doing something important. And in those little windows of time, I started to build something.

To start, I only went back six weeks, and found four incidents (including the press conference) that I could run some numbers on. Only a few days before my leg was shattered, Supercollider was chasing Nerve Gas and backhanded one of the getaway vehicles into a parked car. One of the henches was thrown free from the wreck, through the windshield, and was shredded on the pavement. Supercollider dragged the other two henches out of the car and restrained them by tying them up with the car bumper and front axle. While it was not mentioned directly in the news reports, there was no way they weren't injured in this process, because human flesh is squishy and he tied them up with *huge chunks of steel.* I counted one dead, two injured, and two totaled cars.

A couple of weeks earlier, Alkaline managed to mind control the psionic hero Dendrite, and things went haywire in a penthouse downtown. Supercollider had a run-in with the gas stove, and in the resulting explosion, the condo was seriously damaged and both Alkaline and her hench were badly injured (Dendrite was fine). More than two hundred residents were evacuated from the building that night. The villain was sent to the hospital in serious condition with burns to her face and 40 percent of her body; the hench was luckier, and got away with burns to 20 percent of her body. Alkaline never stabilized, and ten days later she died of complications. I counted one dead, one injured, and two hundred displaced, with $400,000 in damage.

A month and a half back, Supercollider and Accelerator had busted up The Gash's warehouse operation, and the building caught fire. Three Meat died on-scene, and three firefighters were nearly killed when a wall fell on them. According to a follow-up news story last week, they were "still dealing with the effects of their injuries." That fiasco racked up three dead, three injured, $1.2 million in damages.

Then there was the press conference. The body count was on the high side at four, with a lot of injuries, but a mere $70,000 in property damage.

I ran the numbers. In six weeks alone, Supercollider was responsible for 468 lifeyears lost. Those years bought a pinkie finger, Dendrite getting her faculties back, Nerve Gas and a handful of Meat being arrested after a botched robbery, and The Gash losing an awful lot of coke. That was what 468 years of our lives were worth to him. That was how little I mattered. A black pit opened in my stomach, and I wasn't sure if fury or despair waited at the bottom.

June tried, to her credit. She treated what I was doing as though I had a weird new hobby, like I'd suddenly become obsessed with knitting or model trains. She'd even listen to me give a quick summary of the day, about the complex spinal or traumatic brain injuries I'd tracked, about the buildings demolished and cars totaled. I learned how long to talk before her eyes glazed over or she got annoyed, and let her lead me away from the spreadsheets and toward a new horror movie or stories of her nightmarish coworkers. But all the while, in my head, I was adding up the cost.

Once I had worked through those first six weeks, I sat on the thing I had made for a little bit. I needed to take a break from the work, but it was never far from my mind. I spent a few days eating and sleeping more and doodling terrible equations a lot less, but I couldn't stay away for long—Supercollider had been active since he was a teenager, and I had so much catching up to do. I intended to work backward, going through this back catalog of horrors, but before I did that, I looked forward.

If the six weeks I examined turned out to be an accurate core sample of the average cost of Supercollider being a superhero in the world, that meant some terrible things. For every day he was alive, he cost over ten lifeyears; he ate up an average of seventy-eight years of life a week. If he continued at this rate for the next forty years, that was a staggering 162,240 years of human life he'd cost the world.

The only events that I could compare him to were catastrophic. Years ago, a 6.2-magnitude earthquake hit New Zealand; 182 people died, thousands were injured, and there were billions of dollars in damage. The entire downtown core of Christchurch was leveled. There was no question in anyone's mind that it was a disaster. It cost, according to the researchers who wrote the paper, 180,821 lifeyears.

Supercollider was as bad for the world as an earthquake.

I was overwhelmed with the feeling I had to do *something* with all of the terrible numbers that I'd been torturing myself with for weeks. I needed someone to know, or at least someone to have a chance to know, aside from me and June (and sometimes Greg, though he didn't have the attention span to listen to me for very long). I decided to go the traditional crackpot-with-a-theory route and started a blog.

I called it the Injury Report.

I assumed I would scream into that echo chamber for the rest of my days, or until I got bored and defeated by it. I updated the lonely site regularly with Supercollider's activity, present or past, and sometimes did profiles when other heroes happened to cause an egregious degree of harm. I created a few anonymous social media accounts and dutifully sent out the links every time I finished a new one, little digital messages in a bottle that I never expected anyone to read. Just sending them out there made me feel less lonely, less isolated. But one day one of those bottles bobbed up on the shore of a journalist who was trolling superhero hashtags for a story, and dug deep enough to find me.

The piece he wrote was not flattering. He positioned me as some kind of obsessive maniac, scribbling away in a basement, when actually I was obsessively scribbling in a third-floor walk-up, thank you very much. "Superhero sour grapes" was the best quip he came up with, dismissively assuming (correctly) I was a castaway hench bent on revenge. His audience mostly agreed with him.

But someone decided to check my math, possibly to make fun of me more effectively. And when they did, they discovered that it worked. They looked at the research I linked to online and it was legitimate, and a counterpoint emerged that I might be onto something here.

And just like that, the Injury Report took shape. While my primary focus was always Supercollider, I started to run the numbers for other heroes, and nearly every one of them came out in the red. I started to get requests, and I'd oblige, looking into a particular incident and coming back with a damning number. They all told the same story: superheroes, for all their good PR, were terrible for the world. They were islands of plastic choking the oceans, a global disaster in slow motion. They weren't worth the cost of their capes; whatever good they did was wiped out many times over by the harm.

Soon, my messages weren't lonely at all. Every piece I put up was boosted and recirculated and syndicated.

I got tips every day about devastation and death and loss, accounts of family businesses now crippled by debt, and previously cheerful young people suddenly changed into shells of themselves by head injuries or PTSD. A morgue worker complained that my numbers were low, far too low; for every hench casualty the media reported, there were three more Meat on a slab.

I thanked every single person and added their numbers, and their credit (if they wished it), to the report. The stories about it were still sometimes insulting and dismissive, but more and more readers cautiously allowed that I had a point. At any rate, people were reading it and fascinated by the horror show of it. I could count on tips and rubberneckers at the very least, and every day the total rose.

June's support evaporated the moment I had an audience. Working on my theories alone seemed harmless, but once people started to pay attention, she panicked.

"Why the fuck do you do this," she snarled one evening, while I was trying to respond to a backlog of DMs.

"I—what?"

"Why the fuck do you make this awful thing every day? It's your whole life now."

I slammed my laptop shut, startling her. "Because it *is* my whole life now." I gestured toward my body, trying to encompass the abjection of it.

"But why wallow in it? You could be doing anything. Write live recaps of shows you're watching, fucking learn to knit, I don't know. You could do anything else."

I shook my head. "I can't do anything else." And I lifted my laptop lid and tried to slide back to work, to the grim disaster math consuming my brain.

A hand waved in front of my face. I looked up, surprised, and June was standing directly in front of me.

"I don't like it," she said.

"Okay? You don't have to, and I can stop talking about it."

"No, I don't like that it's happening *here*. In this apartment. It's not safe."

I made a you're-being-ridiculous face. "No one knows I'm here. I worked with Greg and have a VPN set up. It's fine."

"No, Anna—it's *not* fine. You're calling them out while in my fucking house."

"Nothing is going to happen!"

"She says, as she tallies the human life and property these people destroy every day."

"Are you going to kick me out?"

"Wh-what?"

I'd surprised her. "Is this an ultimatum?"

She threw up her hands. "Fucking—no! I just don't like it and wish you would stop."

I nodded. "I'm sorry," I said, and meant it.

And then I went back to work.

After that, I saw her less and less. Her contract ended and she picked up more work from the Temp Agency, something that required longer hours; she didn't tell me what. As much as she tried to be hospitable—and when she was home we both tried to enjoy each other's company—it was clear she found what I was doing with the Injury Report deeply uncomfortable. She stayed out later and later more often, and sometimes now didn't come home at all. I missed her badly, and also felt terrible guilt, like I'd kicked her out of her own place. More than once, I seriously considered heeding her request and shutting the whole thing down. But every time I came close, some hench would wind up in traction or a deli would be liquefied, and not carrying on because I was sad and she was unhappy was an equation I couldn't balance.

It was hard to be lonely, however, when I started to attract a different kind of attention. Henches and minor villains I had never heard of before dropped me lines, sending texts from unfamiliar numbers and sliding into my DMs. Being the latest of Supercollider's casualties gave me a weird kind of notoriety: I'd met the hero and lived. There were lots of professionally bad people who wanted to share in a piece of that, and reached out.

The pleasure I took in the sudden spike of my villainous social capital was sullied by what a great time the Electric Eel was having. In the wake of the press conference, he'd gone to ground, but even in hiding he was enjoying a huge bump in charisma and notoriety; his public profile had never been higher. I would torture myself sometimes by searching for news stories and social media posts with his name. Every time I found something new, a knot in my stomach tightened.

Meanwhile, I was running out of money. My cards were long maxed out and I was burning through my savings. The little bits of money that trickled in irregularly from donations and slightly more reliably from Patreon didn't cover my groceries, the upgraded internet connection, and my not insignificant medical supplies and prescriptions. As flattering as they were, none of the villains were moved enough to hire me. I might be interesting, but I sure had baggage. I tried to apply for municipal Superheroic Insurance—the public purse set up to help anyone whose body or property was destroyed because of "heroic activity"—and was summarily turned down. The paperwork required a copy of the police report from the press conference incident, which I discovered contained no mention I had been injured at all. All of the injuries and fatalities were ascribed to "nefarious activities," blamed on the bad guys. I was probably "confused by all the noise and violence," my rejection letter assured me.

I thought about Supercollider having the gall to appear in my hospital room wearing a stupid fake mustache and reflective highway patrol aviators. I added the rejection onto the pile of wrongs done to me, burned that indignity as fuel. Soon it would be just one more number to run.

One day, June and her Meatfriend went to my apartment to bring over the rest of my clothes; they came back with the eviction notice that had been tacked to my door. June didn't interrupt me while I ugly cried, and then stage-whispered advice and gesticulated wildly at me during the painful and incredibly terse conversation I had with my soon-to-be-former landlord. In the end he threatened to sell all my stuff if it wasn't cleared out immediately, and I choked on a laugh and told him he'd be doing me a favor. She high-fived me when I was done and graciously refrained from mentioning that I now couldn't even go back to my shitty apartment and vacate her couch if she wanted me to.

The next day, a bouquet arrived.

It was a cheap and thoughtless arrangement, something you might grab at the grocery store, mostly baby's breath and carnations and a single, anemic rose. But it was delivered by an expensive courier, and the card that accompanied it was of thick, weighty stock.

June snatched up the card before I could open it, preying on my still-slowed reaction time.

"I don't like this." She pried the thick, velvety envelope open with a talon-like fingernail.

"It's probably nothing." I rubbed one of the rose petals between my fingers until it disintegrated, enjoying the tiny waft of fragrance it released.

An idea occurred to her that made her visibly relax. "Maybe it's from that guy. Bustle? Brindle."

"Bracken. Oh god." I had almost managed to suppress the memory of him entirely. I winced in embarrassment, picturing the vomit on his chin and the outraged way he slammed out of Oscar's car. "Perhaps the last date I will ever have in this life."

June opened the envelope and froze. Her hair had fallen in front of her face so I couldn't see her expression, but her fingers curled around the paper hard and I saw a little tremor in her hands.

"Dude. What is it?"

For a moment, she didn't reply.

"June." I said it louder than I meant to, a panicky croak.

She turned and threw the envelope at me, furious. "How the fuck did he get my address?"

The card she had begun to pull out of the envelope, now creased from her grip, was embossed with the twin circles of Supercollider's logo. I swore.

"He knows you're here!" Her face was panicked, her lips grayish blue, like she'd just stepped out of a cold pool. "I fucking told you!"

"Of course he knows I'm here—he's fucking Supercollider. He probably knows how many pizza rolls I have eaten in the last month."

"It means he knows where *I live*, it means—"

"It means exactly jack."

"What about this? What do these mean?" She snatched the bouquet out of my hands and grabbed the stems hard with both hands, like she was trying to wring its neck.

"I don't know."

"What does the fucking card say?"

"Nothing."

"*What?*"

"It's blank." I opened it and turned it toward her; there was nothing written inside the fold.

"Why would he send you fucking flowers?" The accusation overflowed from her voice.

"This is not my fault."

"How is it not?" She stared at me a moment. "Nothing else better come."

"The next time we have tea, I'll ask him not to send any more tokens of affection to the apartment."

She dropped the strangled bouquet into my lap, stormed out of the room, and slammed into her bedroom.

After she left, I sat stunned for a few moments, staring at the smashed flowers and trying to steady my breathing and my hands. When I looked up, I noticed something on the carpet where she had been standing, a small slip of paper. I painfully dragged myself up, using a crutch and the coffee table, and retrieved a business card that had fallen out of Supercollider's envelope.

The business card was for Sherman Moving & Storage, a local place with an address in the suburbs. Written in tight, angular letters on the back of the card were the words "Your belongings are in Unit #311" and a jagged initial "S."

I felt the strangest twist in my chest. On one hand, this meant Supercollider felt guilty for the swath his casual backhand had cut through my life. On the other, fuck him.

I lay awake very late that night, wondering how much longer my welcome at June's would stretch, going through the very short list of other people I could call on if I needed to suddenly leave. And when another unexpected delivery arrived the next day, I was absolutely certain I was going to be homeless. The courier didn't know what to do with the simmering rage radiating off June while she signed for the package, but when the sender wasn't another goddamn hero she settled a little.

A *little*. "Explain to me," she said, clearly making a mighty effort to keep her voice calm, "why the Villains' Union also has my address."

The Union was a joke. The loose association of second-tier baddies and ambitious henches thought having meetings, taking minutes, and participating in panel discussions on popular topics of villainy were the best ways to advance their careers; they were generally considered horrifically uncool.

I held the heavily padded, rectangular package addressed to me from the Union carefully, wondering the same thing she was. A light went on in my head. "What are the odds," I said slowly, "that this is Greg's fault."

June pressed her lips together, and a little more of her anger toward me evaporated. "High. Fucking high."

I tore open the package and found my suspicions were confirmed: inside was a framed certificate, decorated with the garish official Villains' Union coat of arms and scrawled over with overdone calligraphy. It read, "Congratulations, you have been Supercollided!" and included the time, date, and circumstances of my encounter with the hero. It was an honor bestowed on every villain or hench upon the occasion of their first verifiable encounter with the world's greatest hero. Sure enough, Greg was listed on the certificate as my union sponsor.

June called Greg to scream at him for handing out her address while I texted him my heartfelt thanks. The frame came with a little stand, and I proudly set it up on the coffee table by the couch. June took the certificate down and used it as a TV tray for her dinners or a place to rest a coffee mug at every opportunity, and each time I would defiantly replace it. The stupid Villains' Union logo, with a snake and a bat and a skull, made my lip curl in a smile every time I saw it.

Things between us continued to be tense. It was clear she felt endangered by my presence in her house; I was acutely aware that I didn't have an alternative place to go back to even if I wanted to. I felt precarious, and that anxiety wound itself around my brain and into every one of our interactions. I no longer felt like I had the luxury of a reasonable recovery time. I started to cut back on my painkillers even more drastically to alleviate some of the opiate brain fog, and started to look for new work again in earnest. It was hard to pry my time away from the Injury Report, but I reasoned that I couldn't continue the work if I didn't have anywhere to work from.

Almost exactly two months after the collision, I came across some data entry and content creation work for a fairly run-of-the-mill shadow corporation, which seemed to be a supervillain's off-site property rather than their everyday operating base. It looked boring and safe, which seemed like the best possible outcome. Instead of running math, I spent a day redoing my résumé and quickly secured an in-person interview. It would mean traveling much farther from June's than I had since my injury, which made me intensely nervous, but it seemed like my best shot at somehow righting the tipping ship of my life.

That night, I dreamed about being measured.

I was little, and standing with my back to a doorframe, as though a parent were about to tell me how much I had grown. But around me, there were towering figures in lab coats, with clipboards and calipers and measuring tape.

I could hear the squeak of latex gloves close to my ear as one of them wrapped the tape around my head. Another pinched my scalp with the calipers, and goose bumps rose on one side of my body.

"There should be something here," one of them said, annoyed, "but I can't get a reading."

"She's got some of the markers."

"Do you think it's worth further testing?"

Then my alarm went off, the violence of waking suddenly fixing the dream, like nebulous gel stiffening into an image in a Polaroid. It wasn't exactly a nightmare, but I was sweaty and limp with relief to find the dream hadn't been real.

I gave myself hours to get ready in the morning, beginning the long and laborious process of becoming presentable while June slept. I was almost used to navigating the tub by now, carefully propping my leg up and keeping it out of the water. I stayed in the water until after it cooled, trying to keep myself calm; I was profoundly aware of my physical vulnerability, and traveling across the city on crutches was intensely daunting. Eventually, I heard June starting to bang around in her bedroom, and left the tub and my wallowing behind.

Dressing for an interview was also suddenly stressful, as I simply could not fit into most of my sharply tailored clothes while still confined to a bulky hip-to-ankle leg brace. Even if I could get them on, maneuvering in those clothes while on crutches would have been doubly impossible. I ended up settling on a much softer outfit than I would have preferred: a long, charcoal-gray sweater dress with a cowl neck, with a single stocking on my good leg and a dainty little sock on the other. It felt like I was walking into a battle without my armor on, and I tried to compensate by channeling all the imposing energy that I could into my eyeliner.

I balanced in front of a full-length mirror, looking myself over critically, while June bustled behind me, leaving for work.

"You'll do fine," she said, popping in a pair of earrings and then patting herself down for her keys. "They might even have heard of you by now. It'll help."

My throat closed. I unexpectedly found myself fighting tears; that was the nicest thing she'd said to me in weeks. I couldn't answer for fear of my voice breaking. I nodded, and she left. I shook my head to clear the unfortunate emotion. After a final, critical look at myself—I took a last deep breath and summoned Oscar. Wondering if he'd give me shit for not ringing him for months, I began the slow and painful process of navigating myself down to street level from June's third-floor walk-up.

I stepped out onto the cold sidewalk, enjoying the sharp, freezer-burn smell of threatening frost the way only someone who has spent weeks and weeks inside can appreciate. It took a moment too long to register that it wasn't Oscar's serviceable car with the rust rings in the rear wheel wells that was waiting for me. Instead, there was a thrumming supercar, the looping, muscular shape of it recalling a predator, muscles coiled tight and ready to strike. The exterior was a strange matte black that appeared to slither like scales, with oddly liquid-looking windows. A woman stood by the back door wearing something that looked like a cross between tactical gear and a tuxedo. She was more muscled and confident than she'd been all those months ago, but I recognized her short blond hair, face, and bearing as those of the driver I'd seen hired through the Temp Agency.

She was looking at me expectantly, obliterating any confusion I might have had that she was there for someone else.

I nodded to her. "How can I help you."

"Your ride, ma'am," she said, opening the door for me.

"I have a ride coming." The *I have a boyfriend* of getting into strange cars.

"Oscar has been informed."

That both disturbed and impressed me. She approached, offering me an arm to help me enter the vehicle, which even at rest felt menacing. The escaping warmth of the interior hit me like an exhalation.

I took her proffered arm. She smiled at me from behind her dark glasses, which were not sunglasses, I saw, but smoked lenses that obscured the details of an internal display. The potential danger of the situation didn't detract from (and maybe added to?) the flutter in my stomach. She took my crutch from me and together we slowly moved toward the car. "I was going to an interview," I told her. I wasn't sure if I was protesting or not.

"You still are. Just a different one than you expected." She lowered me into the back seat. As soon as I was settled, legs tucked in and crutches resting at my feet, she shut the door with an authoritative snap.

I felt a brief surge of panic rise and fall in my chest. I let it come up, held it a moment, and then let it dissipate. In its wake, a strange calmness and resolve came over me. It was entirely possible something awful was about to happen to me, but at least it wasn't the bleak future I'd been staring down a few moments before. Something was going to happen, which frightened me less and excited me more than I expected. It had to be better than the shambles of my current life. I settled back into the leather seat, which held me almost fondly.

I touched the wall comm, opening the panel that separated the front seats from the back, as soon as the driver took her position behind the wheel. "I recognize you," I said. "From the Temp Agency."

She chuckled. "Those were dark times."

"You been back?"

"No, thank fuck. I got my contract picked up."

"The placement worked out?"

"Incredibly well." She steered the car with a sensual, buttery smoothness.

"I'm Anna." She probably knew that, but it seemed polite.

She made eye contact with me in the rearview, and I hoped very hard I wasn't blushing. "Melinda." I could see green lights flickering in the periphery of her lenses, some kind of digital readout.

"Can I ask you a stupid question."

"Fire away."

"Am I about to die?"

"Ha! Not stupid. But no, definitely not. You do have an interview; that part is true."

I leaned back. Even if she was lying, I decided to enjoy myself and luxuriate in what might be my last ride in a supercar. There was a mobile espresso machine in the back seat, and with a few button presses I was enjoying an entirely passable flat white.

It was a long drive, clear past the other side of the city, through industrial parks and the edges of several suburbs, and then long minutes of emptiness, just highways and frost-burned fields. Finally, we came to the edge of a huge, walled compound and stopped at a pair of gates. A light passed over the exterior of the car, scanning it, and Melinda tapped something on the center console. The gates rose like a portcullis.

We coasted slowly down a few of the interior roads, not unlike driving through a university campus, before coming to a stop in front of a huge, glossy steel-and-glass low-rise building. It was a brilliantly sunny day, and the roundabout where the car came to a stop was flooded with chilly white light. Along the walkways between the buildings of the compound, as well as the sidewalks and in the small green spaces all around us, people hurried to get back indoors; it was unusually cold, and their breath was visible as they walked and chatted.

"Here we are." Melinda hopped out of the car and came around to my door to help me out, carefully getting me steady on my feet and handing me my crutch. "I'll take you all of the way in."

There was a welcome desk inside the bright, stately foyer, where we began the process of signing me in. I needed a "guest pass," which was actually a small lozenge I had to swallow, as well as a single-use contact in my right eye for the retinal scan. Blinking back tears (I was never good at getting contacts in), I managed to survive the light blasting into my eye that permitted the elevator doors to open, and a full-body scan that allowed the lift to move.

There was no panel of buttons, nothing to push; the elevator operated on voice recognition only. Melinda put a hand to her mouth to indicate I should stay quiet as the doors slid smoothly closed behind us. Then, she said a single word: "Leviathan."

I laughed in the hollow of the elevator then, and she grinned at me. "I couldn't believe it at first either when I was brought on board," she admitted.

I'd been going over in my head which of the villains might have decided to grant me this audience. Firewall had seemed like an obvious choice, valuing information as they did, and I could imagine being quietly put to work in the data mines; it seemed peaceful. If I'd had to choose, I'd been hoping for Cassowary, who was known to be brutal to heroes, but had a strong reputation as a fair employer to her henches, offering more support, benefits, and structure than most. It had even occurred to me that it might be Megalodon, who was rumored to be working on a superweapon called the Jaw and was actively hiring, but I didn't want to flatter myself too much thinking someone that famous would have taken an interest in me.

But Leviathan? Leviathan was the monster lurking beneath the surface of the world. Most heroes hoped to never be in the same room with him. Now, we were about to be breathing the same air. When the elevator stopped, Melinda walked me down a long hallway to a room with a set of massive double doors made of copper and dark wood. Despite the weight they opened like silk when she touched an oxidized handle.

The room beyond had the odd electric crackle of many quiet machines operating in unison, the inaudible but palpable buzz of a server room. It was large but not cavernous, with a few deep leather chairs in one corner for intimate meetings and a long, sleek table that was clearly a work surface. One entire wall was a massive screen, currently split and displaying four different newscasts, all with the sound off.

Behind the desk, watching the screen wall intently, stood Leviathan. His stance had a courtly formality to it that was also wrong somehow, eerie and reptilian. He wore his armor, which he was never seen without. I'd heard it described as a mecha suit, but it appeared more like snakeskin than metal at this distance: dense and sleek and oddly organic. Bits of it shone, like the shell of a beetle. Rumor had it the tech in it was so advanced it was functionally indistinguishable from magic.

It was also rumored that Leviathan was hideously ugly or inhuman under that suit, though no one had ever come forward with evidence of what he might actually look like. Of all the villains and heroes, his identity was the most obscure. All that he was now completely obliterated whomever or whatever he might have been.

Melinda nudged me and I started; I hadn't realized I was both frozen in place and openly staring at him. I gave my head a tiny shake and moved into the room, walking with Melinda's help.

Leviathan didn't move as we crossed his office to his desk. Once there, Melinda carefully helped me sit in one of the two chairs across from his (a hyperergonomic monstrosity that looked a lot like an alien spinal column, but had excellent lumbar support). Once I was seated, he turned slightly, inclining his plated head toward Melinda in a weird gesture of acknowledgment and thanks.

"Wait outside a moment," he said to her. His voice was warm and oiled, but also slightly metallic, as though distorted by digital interference. "This won't be long, and Miss Tromedlov may need your assistance again."

Melinda nodded. "Yes, Sir," she said, and gave my arm a barely perceptible squeeze in solidarity before leaving the room.

Leviathan didn't sit down at his desk, but remained standing behind it. When the doors slid shut with a muffled weight, he finally turned his full attention toward me. He didn't rush to speak and break the tension in the room, but took a long time assessing me, studying my face, my leg and its brace. I straightened my shoulders with what I hoped was a bit of shabby dignity and waited.

"It has come to my attention you may be in need of new employment, Miss Tromedlov."

The world shimmered around me for a moment, but I held it together. "I am."

"Apparently your last contract was terminated somewhat prematurely."

"Yes. It's certainly limited my options."

"While I do take a particular interest in anyone who has been victimized as you were, you have other qualities that drew my attention."

"That's flattering." I couldn't quite believe this was happening, and felt like someone else was speaking using my mouth.

He made a small humming sound. "Your agency file is a fascinating mix of exemplary work and boredom."

I couldn't contain a real laugh; the sound seemed to startle him, but not unpleasantly. "I don't think I have ever heard my career summed up so perfectly."

He watched me again for a moment. His eyes were dark, and the sockets in his armor came right up to their very edges.

"It was your research into the cost of heroism, which you dubbed the 'Injury Report,' that I find most interesting."

From the way he said the word "interesting," I could not immediately tell if this was a very good or a very bad thing. I decided "thank you" was the safest response.

He gave a small nod. "You've done much with nothing, seeming to spin straw into gold from the most meager bundles. I would see what you can do with my vast storehouses."

I let out a weird, uncontrolled laugh. Did this monster just make a fairy-tale reference? "Are you threatening to chop off my head or take my firstborn if I can't repeat the success?"

He made the oddest sound. "I've no use for your head detached from the rest of you."

I realized I might have made a mistake. "I mean, of course you don't. I didn't think you were going to decapitate me. I mean, you could, but you won't! Um." I managed to make myself stop talking and wondered if spontaneous human combustion could be voluntary.

His face didn't change, but I sensed his raised eyebrow. He decided, after a moment, to have mercy on me and continue. "I am curious what you are capable of with resources far less finite, yes. Would you continue and expand the Injury Report under such circumstances?"

"Absolutely, if such an opportunity was even possible."

"It is." There was no doubt in his voice.

"What exactly are you offering me, Sir?"

"That depends. I have one more question."

"Okay."

"Do you hate them now?"

I was shocked by the intensity of my reaction. I felt my chest tighten and a weird acidic burn crawl up my throat. "Them" was such a vague word, but the hate I felt was extraordinarily specific, and right at the front of my mind. There was the petty disloyalty of two-bit villains like the Eel. The ineffectual brutality and brown-nosing of the police. The blithely ignorant wrecking machines that were all of the heroes, unaware of the human and material costs of their every stupid, impetuous move.

And then there was Supercollider, the disaster that had derailed my small, pitiful life and shown me exactly how precarious and nearly loveless it was.

"Yes." The response seemed to come from somewhere else, some deep recess of my body.

Leviathan nodded. "Good." He touched a comm pad on his desk, and raised his voice a little. "Melinda, you can join us again." He looked back down at me. "The specifics of the position are negotiable, and I am confident we can offer you a package that you will be content with."

I heard the doors slide open and Melinda reenter the room. "This feels too easy," I admitted.

He made that odd rumble again and I realized it might be a quiet laugh. "It seems to me like it's been quite difficult for you indeed." I blanched. He looked over at Melinda. "Please take Miss Tromedlov to her new apartment, and once she's settled see to it her orientation takes place on schedule."

"Of course, Sir." She bent down to help me stand, and I found that I was unexpectedly wobbly. Leviathan and I had been alone only a few minutes, but I felt incredibly drained. She let me take a moment to get my bearings.

"Thank you," I said to both of them. Leviathan nodded, his attention already turning back to the screens in front of him. Melinda gave my arm, which she was supporting, another quick squeeze, and then carefully helped me navigate my way out of the room.

She was cool and businesslike until the moment the doors shut behind us, when she leaned in, grinning. "I think you're really going to like it here."

"Wait. Did I just agree to take this job? And did he just say 'new apartment'?"

The rest of the day was a blur. The first place Melinda took me was the snug little suite in one of the residence buildings, a spartan studio that was neat as a pin and had a lot of east-facing sunlight. I was overwhelmed by the sudden prospect of a job, but a place to live that wasn't also June's couch was too much to process. Melinda seemed to clue in to the fact that my brain was misfiring and left me alone rather than marching me down to HR. I was so stressed out I almost immediately fell asleep on the velvet love seat that was now apparently mine, for the time being.

I was awakened by knocking. The light had shifted— hours had gone by, and I shot up in panic. I shuffled, shattered and bleary, to the door to find a pair of red-faced and overly cheerful movers, bearing my few earthly possessions. I had a string of text notifications from June, presumably about my unceremonious departure. I chose to ignore them while the friendly, too-loud men deposited laundry hampers and garbage bags of my clothes everywhere they could find floor space.

Once they left, I wandered around my three small rooms, hanging up some clothes in the closet, setting up my laptop, placing books on the shelf. My view overlooked a little green space, and though the lawn was brown and patchy, the star of still-visible desire lines through the grass seemed to promise it would soon be full of people enjoying nicer weather.

It occurred to me that I wouldn't even need to get my few pieces of bashed-up furniture out of the storage unit Supercollider had rented for me, out of guilt or pity. I wondered how long I could leave it there, how many months he'd keep picking up the tab before it went to auction. The thought of him forgetting and paying to store my scratched-up bed frame for years amused me.

Early that evening, a bustling, extremely polite HR representative paid me a visit to fill out paperwork and go over the particulars of my injury, treatment, and rehab. I was worried that my medical file might change their minds about hiring me, but HR assured me that their vision was "long-term" and that for the next few weeks, my job very well might just be healing, if their on-site doctors determined that was for the best. Afterward, they even pointed me in the direction of a lovely little café right across the green space from my suite. Once I was alone again, I braved the cold and had a celebratory meal of spaghetti carbonara and a bottle of wine.

Sitting at that small bistro table, I pulled out my still-smashed phone for the first time in over twelve hours—and was hit by the realization that June had no idea whatsoever what had happened to me. The number of panicked messages on my phone, in order of rapidly descending coherence, confirmed this.

What had happened from her perspective, I quickly pieced together, was that when she left in the morning she knew I was headed to an interview. Not only did I never come home, but when she came back that evening, every one of my belongings had been spirited out of the house as though it had never been there. Her door was as locked as it was when she left, and nothing had been disturbed, as if my existence had been neatly deleted.

So of course she assumed I had been disappeared. She reasonably guessed that the Draft, or some nameless hero, or Supercollider himself, had finally taken enough umbrage at my pointing out how much worse they made the world for everyone that they decided to simply remove me from the picture rather than endure my continued, annoying presence on this earth.

I stared at all of her messages and tried to think of how I could possibly apologize for scaring her so badly. And, in the process, apologize again for how unsafe I'd made her feel, and how unwilling I had ultimately been to change anything about what I was doing for her comfort.

I did the worst possible thing, of course. She picked up immediately when I called.

"Hey," I said, "I got the job."

3

It took about a month for me to get medical approval before I could get to work. I learned that, at first, my duties were going to consist entirely of medical appointments, evaluations, and a very proactive treatment plan. My medication was adjusted slowly, sometimes in daily increments, and I was assigned a sweet but diabolical physiotherapist. I hated every part of it, but I had to grudgingly admit it worked.

One thing that did not recover was my relationship with June. She tore into me for letting her think I was dead or worse for a whole business day, and hung up on me before I could muster even a feeble apology. I sent her chat messages and emails; I even called her twice, letting it ring three times before hanging up like a coward. Over time, my deluge of contrition slowed to a trickle. I was deeply lonely, but eventually accepted that she needed time and space.

Only after my physiotherapist, a doctor, a psychiatrist (every incoming staff member had an extensive evaluation), and an orthopedic surgeon agreed it was reasonable did I have my first work-like experience. I met with a being made of data with goggle-thick glasses named Molly. Their hands had been completely replaced with robotic equivalents that ended in sixteen superfine fingers, each tapering to a small textured nub for added grip. Molly's glasses weren't just to correct nearsightedness either, but served as small, secondary data displays. Molly was the head of several small departments, one of which was called Information & Identities, which was where, they suspected, I would be most at home.

I expected to be handed tasks, to be told what my job was going to entail. Instead, Molly and I worked through my file together, essentially *building* what my position would be. I showed them the Injury Report and all of the research that went into it, and what my methods had been (limited as they were).

"Good, this is good." Molly nodded enthusiastically, lines of text ticking by on one of their lenses. "I like the way you move information around. I'm going to introduce you to the Information & Identities team—I think you might be a good fit here."

I was given a desk in I&I, and after a round of introductions I was left to my own devices. To start, I was to continue working on the Injury Report and look for opportunities to expand it, as Leviathan's resources allowed.

What I had to do, I slowly realized, was come up with something to do with it all.

For two weeks, I drank a lot of coffee and got around awkwardly on my crutches, fretting semi-regularly that I was going to be fired at any moment for not doing anything particularly groundbreaking. No one gave me any flak, however—just provided space and watched me from a distance. I spent a great deal of time circling between fussing at the data and clicking aimlessly around my social media accounts, until I had what I was sure was a very bad idea. It was, however, my first and only idea, so I asked for a meeting with Molly and spent a couple of days assembling a proposal.

Of course, when we were actually in the room together, I didn't even bother to fire up my first slide before I leaned forward and said, with more excitement than I expected to hear in my own voice, "What if we fuck with them."

Molly had been tinkering with a technical readout when I arrived; rarely anyone got their full attention, but I managed to startle them into making eye contact with me. Their eyebrows and forehead seemed to be at war with each other as they tried to raise and furrow their brow at the same time.

I saw my opportunity and pounced. "So, exposing secret identities is passé, right?"

"Right."

"And most of the heroes are out and the rest we can make a pretty good guess at. Even if we're right, we don't gain much outing them. But we have *all* of that data."

Molly nodded. "Fifteen-odd years of tracking careers, powers, activity and inactivity, battles, defeats, injuries, associations."

"Besides what we've gathered ourselves, we've got access to so much more." I was not prepared, when I took the job, for exactly how impossibly vast the data pools were. After finding some surprisingly detailed numbers once, I'd asked the data scientist who provided them exactly what databases we had access to. Social media, retailers, advertising networks—it didn't matter. They'd casually stated, "If it's on a corporate hard drive, we can get it. If it's on a government hard drive, I give it even odds."

I'd been nearly giddy when I heard that.

"What if," I continued now, "instead of focusing on who they are, and what they've done, we put that data to use trying to anticipate what they're going to do."

Molly's frown deepened, but not angrily. "You're talking about predictive data modeling."

I nodded eagerly. "Exactly! We take that fifteen years of hero behavior we've tracked, and we connect it to the literally billions of points of consumer data we have access to. We integrate those databases. Then we hire an army of data scientists and start running simulations. We know what they've done in the past and we know how much damage they've done; we can start modeling what we think they're going to do. Once we have a model that works, we run more direct experiments."

"Experiments?"

"We start exposing the heroes to stressors."

"What kinds of stresses do you have in mind?"

"Like I said, we fuck with them. Fighting them head-on, we lose more often than not. But if we go at them sideways . . ."

"Go on."

"We make their private and public lives as miserable as we can. Make them late; make things go wrong around them; ruin their dry cleaning and dinners and marriages. Fuck with their social media profiles and public perception."

Molly scanned my face. "I see." They kept their voice even, but they were deeply interested.

"It's not entirely out of pure spite," I clarified, picking the chipped polish off my nails.

"I mean, I appreciate spite."

"Oh, I do too. But I think we can make it actively strategic. People whose lives are falling apart have a harder time being heroic. So we find the cracks and we widen them. We find the stressors that make them as ineffective as possible. And this further gives us opportunities to expose them behaving terribly in ways that are less socially acceptable than pulverizing the Meat. We give them every opportunity to be small and petty and mean."

"And when they do fuck up and punch an old lady or kick a kitten?"

"We do everything in our considerable power to make sure as many people know about it as possible."

"That's terribly unpleasant." They smiled.

I felt myself grinning. "Well, we are villains, after all."

Molly helped me assemble an actual proposal. If I'm honest I didn't expect it to go anywhere, but inside of a week Leviathan had reviewed and signed off on it, and suddenly things were moving very quickly. I was told to put a team together, and in a bit of a panic, I reached out to just about everyone I'd met so far who'd been helpful or competent in my presence. I hired Javier Khan, who had been introduced to me as "the Excel Pervert," to build me beautiful spreadsheets to handle and direct the flow of data. Nour had been doing some front-facing administrative work, but her extraordinary charm and poise made me bring her on for social engineering. Darla started out in Technology, but after they repeatedly helped me hack into systems we couldn't cheat or charm our way into, I poached them to join I&I full-time. Within reason, we could access Leviathan's network of undercover agents and plants for inside jobs.

Within a few weeks, I'd carved out an extremely demanding and deeply satisfying position utterly ruining as many heroic days as humanly possible. It was immediately the best job I'd ever had.

I continued to use an encrypted service to message June every day. At first, there was only silence in response, which I suppose I deserved. I endured it stoically, knowing if she really didn't want me to message her at all, she'd tell me directly to fuck off. Instead, she kept me on read for weeks. I started to look at the little check that told me she saw my messages as its own kind of reply; I knew when she was reading along and present by how quickly the read receipts came through.

Eventually, she couldn't help herself. I sent her all the juiciest tidbits from the archives and that was the bait that got her.

> Of the original Four Corners—Doc Proton, Neutrino, Siege Engine, and Cold Snap—which one was closeted?

I expected to wait a moment for dramatic effect and then tell her, but after the read receipt, the three small dots that meant she was composing made my heart all but leap into my throat, and reminded me again just how much I missed her.

Doc

I almost dropped my phone; my hands were suddenly shaking and clumsy.

> No everyone knows he'd fuck anything

Neutrino then

Siege Engine

Fuck you no way

I swear. It was his big secret. He and some cop had this long term thing even

A COP? You better not be full of shit

After that, we cautiously, tentatively started making fun of each other at regular intervals again. I'd send her selfies of my eye bags or photos of the livid scars on my leg where the pins had gone in. She'd tell me how bad I looked and that I'd have to leave one hip-high sock on if I ever wanted to get laid again. She'd tell me all about the terrible Meat she was still not dating and I'd criticize her choices until she threatened to stop talking to me. Then I'd back off, not wanting to risk she might be serious. But within an hour or a day, she'd be sending me screenshots of her terrible work Slack conversations and things seemed secure again.

Our relationship wasn't the only thing that continued to heal. Soon, I was getting around with only a cane, as my first doctor had promised. Even if I became tired quicker and the movement itself was more painful at first, the freedom it afforded me gave me a massive morale boost. I started to own my significant limp; I started to feel at home in my body again.

A thing I quickly learned about carrying a cane, regardless of how necessary it was, was that it immediately tripled my theatricality. Every gesture gained additional layers of affectation. Every morning, walking into my team's office felt like the beginning of a performance.

"What have we got today?" I beamed at the rest of my team, balancing on my cane.

Nour put her headset on *mute*, wished me a quick good morning, and went back to the animated conversation she was in the midst of having; it sounded like she was posing as a customer service rep for a charter flight company.

Jav, surrounded by external monitors, raised his hand in greeting. It was all of him I could see, but I could hear him fine. "Right now, we're in the process of making Pneumatic and Typhoid's charter flights to Austin as uncomfortable as possible."

Nour's ability to transform into any imaginable corporation's customer service representative was extraordinary. Hostile or helpful, dull as a spoon or scalpel sharp, she could tell someone exactly what they wanted to hear or serve as a human roadblock. There was also a quality about her that people trusted, something in her voice that assured you everything was going to be okay. She was an invaluable weapon. I heard an apologetic note creep into her voice as she relayed over the phone the bad news that there were going to be delays. So many delays.

A little warmth bloomed in my shriveled apple core of a heart. "Great. What else?"

"Eclipse Computing has a product announcement next week, so we're DDOSing a bunch of their clients." The COO of Total Eclipse Computing was the alter ego of Absolute Zero, a hero with heat-sucking powers.

I navigated my way over to Jav, coming to stand behind his shoulder so I could see what he was looking at. "Sounds lovely. On my way over, I heard that there was a media tour today of the new megaprison, Dovecote. It's just north of the city."

"That's right, the replacement for Kensington supermax." Jav pulled up another spreadsheet, opened some news sites, and Googled a press release on three separate screens. "Yep, that's starting in a couple of hours: 'Press is invited to an in-depth, hands-on tour of the facility, including some special containment procedures.'"

"Excellent."

Nour hung up after ensuring that the suspected heroes' luggage would be misplaced by the airline they'd chartered and that they'd be stranded for several hours between flights. Her lovely face beaming, she scooted her rolling chair over to us. "I'm pretty sure I heard about this; one of the containment rooms they're going to demo is a flash-freezer that supposedly doesn't damage flesh." She was visibly excited.

I raised an eyebrow at her. "Does it work?"

"Seems to."

"But . . ."

"There are some reports that thawing out can be slow, painful, and cause temporary incontinence. But it's not like they're going to be thawing prisoners very often."

"Perfect. Who do we know is going to be there?"

Jav started digging; I let him work. Nour had a steaming cup of something wonderfully fragrant in her hands.

"What is that? It smells lovely."

"Oh, the break room has chai now."

"I am so getting one of those in a minute."

Jav made a trilling noise of excitement; he'd hit on something. "This journalist here, who's tweeting about attending?" He pulled up a woman's profile. "She's almost certainly Tardigrade."

I frowned. "That's a new one."

"She used to be Glassblower's kick: Blast Furnace."

A light went on. "Oh right—I know her. They broke up, it went thermonuclear."

"Sure did. She just struck out on her own maybe six months ago, but the name is newer than that. It has to do with her ability to withstand extreme circumstances and endure inhuman levels of punishment, or something like that. She's pretty much unkillable."

I nodded, my earrings bobbing. They were shaped like tiny axes, dripping with enamel blood. "This is the one."

"What's happening, terrible people?" Darla was standing in the doorway, carrying a tablet and a stack of papers, fresh from their meeting.

"I think we're going to flash-freeze Glassblower's former sidekick." I allowed myself to sound exactly as pleased as I felt.

Jav shook his head. "This is some *Demolition Man* shit." It wasn't a criticism.

"That's why you're in charge, Anna," Darla said

I smiled at the compliment. "Darla, see if you can get Tardigrade registered as an inmate. I think we have a tissue sample and fingerprints on file. It's older information from her Glassblower days, but should work fine. Jav, pull up everything we have on her."

"You got it," Jav said. Darla put two fingers to their temple in salute, added the papers in their hands to the hellscape of their desk, and started working.

"It's important to love what you do," Nour said sweetly.

After a quick trip to the break room to grab my own cup of chai—which was even spicier and more delicious than I expected—I settled back at my desk, got my own suite of external monitors lit up, and started opening as many live feeds, social media platforms, and news sites that were engaging with the Dovecote opening as I could find. Nour helped me monitor social, and we fired links back and forth.

A few hours later, the team was clustered behind me, watching gleefully as the Dovecote media tour got underway. What began with a cool, sober air of penal efficiency was about to quickly descend into utter chaos. We were all a bit breathless when the media were invited to walk through the flash-freezer to demonstrate how it was completely safe to anyone who wasn't a registered inmate of the facility; when the freezer suddenly sprang to life and locked down around Tardigrade, we cheered like it was a touchdown.

The livestream kept rolling as security was trying to hustle all the media out of the room and get the obvious cameras shut off. A cluster of people in lab coats scurried around the flash-freezer in a state of utter panic, furiously flipping through notes and fiddling with controls. One of the researchers even kicked it.

Just before whatever cell phone that was running the livestream was finally knocked off the tripod, I caught a glimpse of the woman trapped in the containment field. I managed to grab a screenshot.

"That's going in the next progress report, isn't it." I could hear the grin in Darla's voice.

I nodded. "Spectacular work, everyone."

"Hey, isn't Tardigrade-née–Blast Furnace supposed to be doing a meet-and-greet at a children's hospital tomorrow?" Nour asked cheerfully.

"It will be a chilly reception," Jav said.

"I wonder if she'll be thawed by then," Darla mused aloud.

"I wonder how temporary the incontinence is," Nour said pleasantly, and Jav gave a weird, hiccuping laugh.

I felt an extraordinary surge of pride for my team; they'd kicked ass this morning. All three of them were looking back at me, expectant and eager. "All right, who else can we freeze or make shit their pants before lunch?"

The problem with ruining a hero's day is that often we did it *too* well. Because we were in the business of public humiliation, our activities tended to rival the more typically aggro, smash-and-grab enforcement missions for media coverage. Sidekicks and henches duking it out was still news, of course, but Tardigrade being turned into a popsicle went viral. We'd given her a shockingly unpleasant experience and embarrassed the entire security team for a supermax prison, which would have been a success of its own, but there was something about her particular experience that people really latched on to. It got passed around with the kind of despicable glee that we couldn't have predicted or bought, and the media saturation was beyond anything we could have hoped for.

As spectacular as it was to watch one of our enemies become a meme, we never could have anticipated Glassblower's reaction to it all. We didn't think he'd be thrilled that his former partner and recent ex had broken the internet by being turned into an ice cube (though, hell, she thawed in record time and had only a relatively mild case of uncontrollable diarrhea as a result). So we thought he might release a public statement condemning whatever negligence or malice caused the events (Jav joked at one point we should change the name of our department to Negligence or Malice, considering how often our activities were thus attributed in the media).

We couldn't have imagined that he'd release a rambling, almost incoherent video swearing vengeance on whoever had wronged his beloved. Jav happened to be working late, saw the video moments after it was posted, and, thinking quickly, saved a copy. When it was taken down in the morning by Glassblower or one of his teammates or handlers, we had a copy we could keep in circulation, reposting and releasing it whenever another was taken down, making sure the video was always hosted somewhere.

We could never have dreamed that our luck would hold, but it did. Over the next few days he would keep a vigil outside Tardigrade's hospital room, despite her adamant refusal to see him. We paid more than one orderly to capture regular cell phone footage of him lurking about. He spoke to the media often and at length, despite his team's obvious disapproval (and occasional horror), demanding that anyone with knowledge of what had happened to Tardigrade tell him all they knew or "face his wrath."

It was clear he was on the brink of something. If his team, or their civilian handlers, truly intervened, it might be staved off. They might talk him down, he might come to his senses, and his mildly weird behavior would recede as the news cycle moved on.

But we weren't about to let that happen.

"That is a man," I said to the team, "who is about to have a meltdown. What we need to do is make sure that it happens, and that the incident is as spectacular and public as possible." We were all watching the video for the eight hundredth time; I was eating the last third of a container of strawberry ice cream to cleanse my palate after too many cheeseballs.

"What's the first step?" Nour asked.

I licked the spoon, considering. "We need to know what happened between them, because it's clearly more than the usual strain between a hero and a kick."

"We know they fucked," Jav said.

"Yeah, but we need terrible details. We need timelines. We need *receipts*. Then the path to ruin will become clear."

We dug in.

The heroes had done a pretty piss-poor job of covering their tracks, to be honest. It would have been adequate for anyone who was willfully turning a blind eye to the situation, like their teammates, or law enforcement, or any of their more obtuse associates and handlers. But anyone who decided to go looking, like we did, would have been able to string together the dinner reservations under badly chosen assumed names and hotel bookings in the city where they both maintained apartments, to figure things out.

They had gotten together while Glassblower was still trying to work things out with his now ex-wife (good for her; Debra seemed like a nice lady who had no time for all of this bullshit), a couple of years earlier when Tardigrade was still Blast Furnace and very much his sidekick. They got into the habit of subterfuge and never really shook it. Even after Glassblower's marriage definitively ended, they kept sneaking around out of habit. (Or maybe they got off on it? I'm not here to kink-shame.)

Eventually, it was the former Blast Furnace who called it quits. She made a bid to become a full member of their middle-tier superhero team and Glassblower actually blocked her, pulling the standard "you aren't ready" reticent-mentor bullshit. What it was really about was that things had hit the rocks; he wanted to get more serious, and public, about their relationship and she had turned him down. He tried to put her in her place, and she not only left the team to strike out on her own but changed her name, distancing herself from him even further.

What began to emerge as we followed the pattern of their relationship, gleaned from hastily assembled press releases about her departure and some screenshots from Glassblower's more erratic social media posts, was that he took the break very, very badly. His teammates were struggling, and increasingly failing, to cover up his behavior.

It didn't take a lot of digging before the team was once again clustered around a monitor, this time Nour's, while we watched the surveillance footage she'd found of an incident at Prime Tower. The terribly named high-rise held the offices of more than one superhero team, including the Alliance of Justice, of which Glassblower was still a member and Tardigrade had left.

Apparently, about a month earlier, she'd teamed up with her old associates to help foil the perfectly nice armored car robbery Escape Velocity was trying to pull off, and the team had called a meeting to see if they should try and invite her back to work under the Alliance banner again. Glassblower decided to take the high road, by which I mean show up to the meeting stinking drunk and cause such a scene that his teammates escorted him from the building. A security camera captured footage of the disgraced hero sobbing in the lobby while his former teammate—and, by all reports, best friend—Lambda Lad stood by helplessly.

"This is better than HBO," I said, passing around some leftover Valentine's Day candy I had stored in my desk.

"Oh, this isn't even the best part," Nour said. She queued up a second security video, this time from outside the fetish club Oil & Leather.

"No."

"Yes."

"Jav—I don't think you're old enough to see this."

"How dare you."

"Here we see him follow her in . . ."

"Unbelievable."

"Do you think he followed her all the way from her place?"

"Probably, creepy fuck."

"Ex-boyfriends, man. They're worse than us."

"Shut up, you're going to miss it."

"Sorry."

"Ah, and here's where the bouncers turf him."

"This is beautiful."

"Is that dude wearing a gimp mask?"

"Play it again, play it again!"

"He gets serious air when they throw him and everything."

That ugly little incident wasn't public knowledge yet, as the Alliance was just barely able to cajole and threaten the club into keeping quiet about the whole thing. Besides, when you're a club with a St. Andrew's Cross in the back room, you're not really in the habit of narcing on your clientele. Still, we learned two crucial things from the encounter:

- Tardigrade was a top who frequented a BDSM club (okay, so I guess part of my job *was* to kink-shame).

- Glassblower was ready to tip over into a complete breakdown, and Tardigrade's accident seemed to have made things even worse.

"He holds it together here. He doesn't melt anyone to the floor, he just takes it. He's not quite at rock bottom yet. All he needs," I explained to the team, "is a little nudge. We are going to be that nudge."

"I'm shocked he bounced back from this," Darla said, gesturing toward the monitor, where Nour and Jav were still giggling at a loop of Glassblower getting his ass handed to him by two men wearing chest harnesses and assless chaps.

I shook my head. "I'm not. It's bad. It's embarrassing, but that's all it is. There is no way anyone at Oil & Leather is shocked by one whiny sub having a bad night."

"So you think he's got room to get worse."

"I do. And when it happens, I want him to be surrounded by people holding their phones, smoking rubble everywhere, and great lighting."

The proposal we submitted was unquestionably our most ambitious to date. Glassblower was weakened, vulnerable, and poised on the brink of a breakdown. He was already acting out, sending flowers to Tardigrade that she refused to allow first into her hospital room and later into her high-security apartment. His teammates were trying to play it off like this was just a manifestation of his extreme concern as a former teammate and colleague, but he was every inch the jilted lover about to snap. The time to strike, we noted, was now.

Which meant we needed to deploy a tactical team. I wasn't entirely sure I was even allowed to do that, but I requested one anyway. I proposed that we get some run-of-the-mill villains to take the fall for Tardigrade's unfortunate accident, have them release a video gloating over their success, and then appear very conspicuously in public. When Glassblower struck, we'd provide cover for them to get away as safely as possible; they'd have the notoriety (which often led to more-high-profile villainy) and we'd have, we hoped, Glassblower forgoing every standard of professional heroic conduct and straight up trying to murder whoever he thought were the culprits. We'd make sure it happened somewhere public, highly populated, and very surveilled.

I was so certain that I was going to be immediately shot down that when Molly called me into their office a matter of hours later, my first impulse was to be worried I was going to be fired.

"How bad is it?" I said, sitting down. The desk, a disaster of paper and components and neglected memos, stretched between us.

"What?" They sat down slowly, looking for space to fold up their long legs in the mess.

"How much trouble am I in?"

"Oh, none, really. It's all good news."

"They're going to let me do it?" An entirely different kind of panic came to replace what had been there before. If it was good news, I might actually have to execute this ridiculous plan.

"There's good news you are going to love, and good news you are going to hate."

"Give it to me."

"Starting with the pure good, you made Leviathan cackle when he saw and approved your proposal, which is a sound I have not heard in too long."

I found myself suddenly unable to control my face and grinned awkwardly. "You're lying."

"Absolutely not. You impressed him."

"So what's the part I am going to hate? Because right now I feel like nothing could ruin my mood."

"The field mission is approved on the condition that you are present."

The smile drained out of me like a plug had been pulled somewhere just below my diaphragm. "I'm sorry, what."

"They want you there. *He* wants you there."

"I don't do fieldwork, Molly."

"I know."

"I am a fucking delicate flower."

"Blame Keller."

"Fucking shit balls." Bob Keller was the head of Enforcement & Tactical—our in-house Meat department—and I was generally under the impression that he hated me. He seemed to have decided that, since he wasn't sure what my job was (to be fair, I was still figuring that out), I was a useless waste of space. This was, I was certain, some kind of a test of his. My body couldn't decide if it was furious or in a state of panic.

Molly looked as sympathetic as their lean, robotic face allowed. "Keller said that you had to be there, since it was your mission, for 'accountability.' He wants to make sure your 'strategic vision' is properly implemented."

"Bullshit. He thinks I won't do it, and then the mission will get shit-canned."

"Will you?"

I felt my mouth tighten. "Leviathan signed off on it?"

"He did, and agreed to Keller's terms."

I sat for a long moment, thinking. "Can you, like, put a panic button in my cane?"

They held out their hand for it. "How about a taser? I'll hide it; that way you look clean if you all get detained."

I sniffed. "That sounds nice."

A horrifyingly short few days later, I found myself on the verge of a panic attack in the back of a car.

"It's going to be fine," Melinda said soothingly. Her voice and face were calm, but she was eyeing me with deep concern in the rearview mirror. I was too upset to be awkward around her.

I looked for a way to recline the seat in the back of the tactical vehicle in an attempt to loosen my shoulders, but quickly gave up. I rubbed my forehead.

"I know. It's not a big deal." *It was a huge fucking deal.*

"You're not even getting out of the car, there isn't a police cruiser built that can keep up with us, and we'd be a catch-and-release anyway."

"We've been over this," I said a little too sharply, then, "I'm sorry; I know. I'm just anxious."

"Take your time. They've all been briefed, they might not even need to hear from you. The comm's still muted."

I nodded and looked away, out the narrow window in the side of the slip car. This was a very different kind of vehicle from the one she'd picked me up in for my interview. While the shape of that automobile had evoked the muscle and grace of a puma, the slip car was shaped more like a toad: squat and sturdy. What it lacked in aesthetic appeal it more than made up for in armor thickness and evasive capabilities, with precise friction controls and shocking acceleration. If we needed to get out of a situation that went sideways fast, this was the thing to be in.

I tried to use that thought—of how safe I was in that car at that moment—to still and anchor me. A fragile little sprout of confidence and composure had started to grow in me over the past few months, and I tried to draw on that for every possible ounce of strength available.

I clung to that tiny island of serenity, while all around me roiled a vast, crawling ocean of anxiety. It wasn't just my body that Supercollider had injured; the prospect of enduring another risky encounter with a hero filled me with so much dread it felt like a physical weight was crushing my chest.

I told myself that this time would be different. I was safe in the car, and actually valued by my employer. The tactical team deployed to engage Glassblower had specific instructions to guarantee my safety. I had my own exit strategy and getaway driver. My role was almost ceremonial. Still, the certainty that something terrible was about to befall me made me chilled and nauseated.

"They're moving into position," Melinda informed me.

My heart started to hammer harder against my chest, and my focus narrowed. I activated the display screen in the rear console with a swipe. Two blocks away, the tactical team was taking up positions in nearby buildings, while Defense Mechanism and Denial, the two supervillains Leviathan was "collaborating with" (a term used to mollify their superegos—he had hired them for a not insignificant amount of money), made an extremely dramatic show of taking a seat in the window of a small café together. Their disguises were terrible: trench coats and false beards. Thin as tissue paper; exactly what we needed.

Our own tactical team members, Leviathan's grade-A Meat (they tended to refer to themselves as Filet Mignon), were cool and professional, but the three heavies Denial had insisted on bringing were amped-up and jumpy, cluttering my comm feed with chatter.

"S'gonna be sick."

"Gonna break some heads, brah."

"Time for some action."

"Shut up and clear the line," said one, who was mocked by the other two for actually having displayed good sense and discipline.

As annoying as the first two were, I found I sympathized with them, all coiled energy and cramped nervousness, nothing to do but let the tension build until the hero actually showed. *If* he showed. As much as I was afraid of what might happen, waiting for it was exponentially worse. I closed my eyes and pressed my fingers into my temples.

"I bet this goes nowhere." That was Keller's baritone growl. He was openly furious that I'd taken his bait and become, however temporarily, part of this tactical mission.

Something about his snark centered me. I toggled the mute on my comm off. "Your mic's live, Keller." I sounded a lot more cheerful than I felt.

There was a fumbling, coughing noise as one of the Meat frantically muted their voice before laughing.

"I know it's live, Tromedlov. This is a waste of time. How do you know Glasshole's going to show."

"Glasshole! That's great." I was genuinely impressed.

He grumbled audibly. I caught myself smiling. I felt a glimmer of hope that this wasn't going to be as awful as I expected.

"He'll show," I said.

"How do you know?"

"Bread crumbs."

"What?"

"Trust me."

What I meant was we had left a strong trail of bread crumbs for Glassblower to follow. We'd laid a deliberate trail, using everything we knew about him. Defense Mechanism and Denial had gleefully taken the fall (the video mashup of Tardigrade being frozen to

Foreigner's "Cold as Ice" was a nice touch), and had been "spotted" meeting at nearby locations a few days in a row. All of our research showed that Glassblower was decaying in his mental state and was spoiling for a fight and a grand, romantic gesture. I'd felt awfully confident when I called for the tactical mission; I tried to unearth that sense of surety again, if only to use it as a shield.

Keller was getting impatient. "Tromedlov, I trust you as far as I can—"

Melinda suddenly slammed her comm live. "Here he comes," she said.

I looked back at the screen and, sure enough, there was Glassblower, walking just a little unsteadily, but with extreme aggression and purpose. He stomped toward the café where Denial and Defense Mechanism were very visibly sitting, doing their best impressions of ne'er-do-wells planning dastardly deeds.

I felt an incredible adrenaline surge. It was one thing to bank on him being reckless and foolish enough to try to win his former partner back with ill-advised violence, but to have bet correctly was exhilarating.

I tapped my comm again. "Let Glassblower fully engage with D&D before you move in. I want to see property damage before you confront him."

"Tactical is aware of the mission parameters,

Tromedlov," Keller snarled. I bit back a laugh; his annoyance was delicious.

"Here we go," I said to myself as patrons started to hurriedly flee the restaurant. Glassblower was standing next to the villains' table, gesticulating wildly and swaying just a little on his feet.

"Steady," Keller said. Glassblower had grabbed Defense Mechanism by his lapels, hauling the skinny man to his feet while Denial shoved himself back, reaching for his concussive knuckles.

I couldn't see exactly who threw whom, but suddenly the front patio window exploded outward and all three tumbled onto the sidewalk, nearly squashing a young woman walking a schnauzer.

"Go, go, go!" Keller bellowed.

Our four-person tactical squad and the trio of Denial's Meat leapt into action. Two of our team were supes with low-level, thermal-based abilities and, using their breath and psychic powers, respectively, began working to drop the ambient temperature around the battle as much as possible. Keeping things cool was critical, and not just for comfort on a surprisingly muggy spring day. Glassblower's powers involved creating tiny, superheated pockets in any substance he touched. He often kept sand on him, which could be manipulated into liquid-glass weapons in an instant, but anything would do in a pinch. So as he picked himself up, he began scooping chunks of asphalt out of the road around him and throwing the suddenly molten projectiles at the incoming Meat, like balls of bubbling pitch.

One of Denial's goons took a molten hunk of sidewalk right in the face. His screams were awful. Glassblower's normal level of typical hero restraint had been eroded by his alcoholic bingeing, rage, and misguided quest for vengeance. It didn't make it any less terrible to watch.

Seeing one of their fellows down, another of Denial's Meat screeched, "Motherfucker!" and threw a punch at Glassblower. The hero, enraged and distracted as he was, dodged the blow.

I slammed my comm on. "No overt attacks!" I yelled. "Let him look like a fucking monster. Defensive moves only."

That was easier to say from the back of the car, but it was crucial for the plan to work. Whether or not we won the fight was entirely secondary.

The two unpowered members of our tactical team were providing covering fire for Denial and Defense Mechanism, trying to let the villains withdraw to a safe distance. Glassblower noticed the focal points of his rage were trying to escape and began grabbing chunks of shattered glass up from the sidewalk. He threw the suddenly liquefied, superheated glass all over the feet of the nearest Meat, who howled and toppled, while our two cold guys did their best to deflect the worst of his assaults from themselves. This was the break Glassblower needed and he surged after the pair of retreating supervillains. The situation was starting to get out of our control.

"Tase him!" Keller ordered.

"I can't get a clean shot!"

"Fucking hell," I spit out, then muted my mic.

"I'm going to pull us back," Melinda said, activating the slip car. "They're getting too close to us."

"No, stay." Our eyes met in the mirror. "We might be the last thing that keeps this idiot from beating us."

Melinda didn't say anything, but the deep thrum of the engine wound down.

Glassblower was herding the pair of increasingly panicked villains and two of our tactical unit closer and closer to the alley where my car was parked, trying his damnedest to reduce them to piles of steaming offal. Our unpowered team members were both wielding long-range weapons—glue and net guns designed to slow, rather than kill—but Glassblower was craftier and angrier than they were. They were forced to dodge more than they could attack, and the raging hero was coming perilously close to getting his hands on one of D&D. In the state he was in, he very well might shove a bubble of superheated concrete down Denial's throat. Another gruesome injury caught on video would have been an asset, but it was a level of violence I didn't have the stomach for yet.

I got out of the car.

"Anna! . . ." Melinda began, but I gestured violently for her to be silent. I could hear the sounds of conflict on the other side of the building. Denial and Defense Mechanism were no longer playing decoy, but genuinely fighting for their lives while our team tried, precariously, to hold Glassblower back.

I pressed my back against the damp brick wall of the alley, right at the lip of the street. The fight would pass by me in moments. I slid open a small panel that had recently been installed in my cane. There were several buttons inside, and I placed a thumb over the largest.

Suddenly, he was a couple of feet away. Glassblower's back was to the mouth of the alley, one foot stepping into it as he shifted his weight. He was grabbing bricks straight from the wall now and lobbing them, smoking and incandescent, after his quarry. I could smell the sweat and staleness of him, the unwashed, rank despair. His costume was stained at the armpits and his hair stuck in sweaty clumps to the back of his neck.

I raised my cane so that the handle was level with his shoulder blades and pressed the button. The two electrodes, trailing wires, shot out and sunk deep into the flesh of his back. He wrenched backward, contorting at the surge of electricity, and dropped hard to his knees with a croaking yelp. Our two cold-weapon units, who had been unable to get as close as they needed to him, saw their chance and leapt in, one jamming a gas pellet into his open mouth, the other covering his face with a fume hood to keep the gas from escaping. Glassblower went limp and they let him crash to the ground unceremoniously.

Once they were sure he was incapacitated, one of the tactical squad immediately turned his attention to me.

"Ma'am, are you hurt or distressed in any way?" he asked.

"No," I choked out. "I'm okay."

"Okay, ma'am. I think you can deactivate the weapon," he said gently.

"What? Oh." I realized that Glassblower's body was still jerking from the effects of electricity, and that I was still pressing the button so hard my thumb ached. I forced my hand off the button, and the taser powered down. The prongs detached and their trailing wires immediately retracted into my cane with a surprisingly kinetic swoop.

"Thank you, ma'am." He started to return to the violence in front of him, but before he could I reached for his arm and he turned his attention back.

"Yes?"

"Could you do me a favor and just help me sit a moment?" I asked.

"Oh, of course." He led me over to the curb and lowered me into a sitting position, surprisingly gently.

I was too agitated to say thank you.

While two of the tactical squad quickly assessed Glassblower, and a third radioed in evac for Denial's injured Meat, he went in search of a bottle of water for me. A few feet away, I could see still-smoking scorch marks in the asphalt from where the hero had ripped up chunks of the street. I put my head between my knees.

By the time I could lift my head without feeling like I was going to puke or pass out, everyone around me was clearing out in earnest. Two of Denial's Meat were in bad shape. The man whose feet had been pinned to the sidewalk by melted glass had been freed; one of our cold squad had managed to cool it relatively quickly and then carefully broken him out. He was still badly burned, even through his protective boots, and couldn't walk unassisted. But it was the man who had taken a chunk of burning asphalt to the face who was far worse off. I had a hard time even looking at him wheezing and gurgling.

The one uninjured heavy who had come with Denial shook her head as she watched her fallen colleagues get taken away. After handing me the bottle of water, our tactical-squad member walked over to her and punched her on the shoulder gently.

"Hey," he said, "you're too good for them." He gestured vaguely. Denial and Defense Mechanism had fled as soon as there was an opening, leaving the Meat they'd brought with them to their fate, in typical villain fashion.

The Meat frowned a bit, taking her abandonment in stride but clearly annoyed. "Nice of you to say."

"I mean it. Hey, I recognize you. You train at Pig Iron, right?"

"Yeah!"

"Thought so. Power lifting?"

"Yeah, that's me."

"Here." The tactical-squad guy handed the Meat one of our business cards. "We're hiring."

"Thanks."

"See you."

It was like the meet-cute scene in a rom-com directed by Gareth Evans. Downright heartwarming. I swallowed some lukewarm water and screwed the cap back on with difficulty.

Melinda came out of the alley then, looking back and forth anxiously as she made her way over to the curb where I was sitting. "We have to go, Anna. The police scanner says we have less than three minutes before law enforcement arrives."

I nodded. She helped me stand; my head swam, but I steadied myself quickly, getting my legs and my cane under me.

Nearby, two of our tactical squad were guarding Glassblower, who was just starting to moan on the pavement. One noticed me standing and turned to face me.

"What do we do with him?"

"Leave him and get out of here. Let everyone find him in the middle of this mess." I gestured to the smoking ruins around us—the glass and torn-up streets. A stop sign had been ripped out of the ground, partially melted, and then thrown, javelin-like; it had speared a mailbox.

I turned toward the two injured Meat, who were being ineffectively helped by their colleagues. "Them too."

"What?" Keller was suddenly behind my shoulder. "We have medical evac on the way."

I shook my head. "Have them intercept the ambulances, or collect them from the hospital."

"Fuck, why?"

"I want there to be a chance someone gets a glimpse of what he's done to them. Press might get here before things are cleaned up, and there are going to be rubberneckers here any second."

He looked like he was about to object, but couldn't quite get his thoughts together. Then, far off in the distance, I heard the unmistakable keening of sirens.

"Move it, everyone," Keller snarled, and he and his Meat hustled to their vehicle. The last survivor of Denial's squad hesitated a moment, then jogged after them and boldly hopped into their transport van. I liked her, I decided.

Then, Melinda was hustling me away too, helping me into the slip car and then all but running around to the driver's side. As we took off, weaving and bobbing through the narrow backstreets, making less noise than a bicycle, I couldn't stop smiling. I turned my cane over in my hands, feeling the weight of it.

"Did that go the way you wanted?" Melinda asked, once we were a safe distance away and she relaxed her grip on the steering wheel a little.

"Better, honestly. Though I didn't like leaving them," I said, a little awkwardly and too loud.

"The Meat?"

"The other henches, yeah."

"Like you said, though: we didn't leave them, evac is going to get them."

"Yeah. It just *feels* like we're leaving them." Guilt bored into my chest, as I imagined the long minutes of terror those handful of henches were experiencing in lonely ambulances before our teams could intercept them.

Minutes I'd experienced myself.

"I promise, we aren't. We're just making Glasshole back there look worse."

"Mmm."

"Anna, we're the bad guys."

"That doesn't mean we're inconsiderate dicks."

"We'll take care of them, I promise. No hench left behind."

I was quiet a long moment.

"Hey," she said. "We're better than them. We're going to be better than all of them. I promise."

"I know what it's like to be hurt and left behind and I don't want to do that to anyone else." I leaned back. "But I need everyone to see what the damage these assholes do really looks like."

I saw a bit of movement out of my peripheral vision; I think she nodded. I felt a little more subdued, but then I looked down at my cane, remembered the feeling of tasing Glassblower, and a smile crept across my face again. Despite myself, I chuckled.

"It wasn't quite a cackle per se," I admitted a few days later, a glass of white wine in my hand. "But it was definitely an evil laugh."

Greg raised a glass of cider. "To Anna's first evil laugh!"

I grinned and bashed my daintier glass into his pint too hard. Darla, Nour, Jav, and Melinda all brought their glasses together with ours, clinking and shouting. Our celebration that night was twofold: the Glassblower mission had gone better than any of us could have possibly hoped for, and after a few weeks of prodding, I had managed to get Greg hired on in IT. He was positively beaming, over the moon to be able to set his impossible freelance schedule aside for something a little more reasonable. I hadn't seen him in months, and he looked exhausted under all his new-job excitement; he was thinner and his complexion was worse. I was looking forward to getting him some decent rest and catered lunches and clearer skin.

"Anna, you fucking crushed it," Jav said. My face went red, but I resisted the urge to demur and just thanked him. I knew I had crushed it, and I was proud; I tried to let that sink in.

"We took," he continued, "a hero's carefully guarded secret and made it a full-blown public catastrophe."

"He's never going to work again," Nour predicted.

"It's a disaster," I agreed, gleeful. Someone had got some video of Glassblower throwing liquid sidewalk directly into that Meat's eyes; the café owner, whose establishment was utterly trashed, decided to sue instead of appeal to Superheroic Insurance. Glassblower's team was doing everything they could to distance themselves from him, completely throwing the hero under the bus. Tardigrade released an official statement condemning him, and an even more vicious Instagram story. I was particularly moved by her saying that she'd "spit on him, but he'd enjoy it too much."

"So are we going to keep doing this?" Jav was eager.

I looked at him reassuringly. "We're just getting started," I said, and the table laughed.

Molly turned toward our laughter and grinned; they were dancing like a wet noodle on the dance floor nearby. I'd asked them, and the few techs who had worked on the new upgrades to my cane, to come out so I could buy them a drink in thanks; they were mostly keeping to themselves, but shyly accepted my effusiveness and a round of cocktails.

We had decided to meet at the on-campus canteen, a kind of trash-polka disaster of a bar that was apparently called Dr. Willicker's Holistic Wonder Bar but which everyone referred to affectionately as the Hole. My team deserved their well-earned drinks, and I figured our gathering was the best way for Greg to start to get a sense of the interoffice culture and feel like he belonged a little more.

I watched him carefully; he'd barely stopped smiling all night, perching in his chair like an excitable bird. I hoped I'd made the right decision, bringing him on—I hoped I hadn't fucked him over. He caught me looking and smiled at me.

I looked down at my phone in embarrassment, and saw a message from June.

> How's the fuckery

> Good

> Sure

> Let me have this

> Why should I?

I squinted at the screen. Something about this tone was off, too sour even for her.

> Are you pissed at me?

No.

> Dude

You were on the news again

> The fuck I was

I know it was you. That Glassblower thing.

> Oh. Of course it was me

I don't like seeing you on the fucking news

> Okay this is absurd. "See me on the news" can't mean "see anything I ever do reported somewhere"

It just freaks me out when something shows up in my feed and I know it's you

Well. I'm sorry. But if I do my job it's going to keep happening

You gonna keep doing this job?

Yeah it's great

She was quiet for a moment, and then sent me a selfie. Her hair was up in a wrap and her face was scrunched up, her brow drawn down into an exaggerated you're-out-of-your-goddamn-mind frown. I never realized how much I had missed June's face until I saw her and got all emotional about her pursed lips and merciless eyebrows. It made my heart ache.

If it was possible to blurt via text, I did.

You should come visit me

Fuck no. Getting in that place is a nightmare

> I guess the guest pass isn't the easiest thing

It's a fucking suppository

> We have ones you can swallow now

Oh yeah?

> I'll make sure they get you the older model

Asshole

> Exactly

This is why you have no other friends

A hand waved in front of my face, seeking my attention, and I looked up, startled.

"Hey, Anna." Darla, slurring a little, drew me back to the main conversation happening around me. I put my phone facedown on the table and let June swear at me unanswered. "Do you think Glassblower's team'll take him back?"

I grinned. "No, he's done. They're getting as far away from him as possible."

Jav nodded. "Way too much shit on his cape now."

"Yeah, they're throwing him to the wolves."

"Sad." Darla's performative regretful face was hilarious, a stretched parody of a commedia dell'arte mask.

"Tragic," Nour agreed faux-mournfully.

"I wonder what'll happen to him," I said, not idly. "Some heroes just can't survive on their own, and he hasn't worked solo in a decade and a half."

Greg's face lit up. "Anna, I got a question about teams."

"Fire away."

"How come we don't have any?"

Jav frowned a little and gestured around the room, leaping in before I could answer. "What do you mean? There are, like, people from five teams right here. There's I&I, R&D—"

"No, no, I mean, like, supervillains," Greg explained. "Heroes have teams and, like, group activities and whatever. Why don't, like, the villains do that?"

Nour furrowed her brow. "We have teams. There's the Dark Confederacy and the Untouchables—"

Greg shook his head. "No, those are shitty ones."

I took a long drink, and then finally answered. "You mean, why don't the real villains have teams?"

"Yeah, like, why doesn't Leviathan have a team? It would be so cool!" Greg was beginning to geek out, voice rising and hands gesturing. "Evil buddies to pull missions with and—"

"Absolutely not."

"But he could and—"

"Villains—real villains—aren't really big on group work."

"It just seems to me like—"

"Try and imagine it with me. Villains working with their peers. What are you picturing, dinner parties? Lunch and learns? Coworking spaces?"

He looked uncomfortable. "I mean, they need peers. Look at us right now. Maybe villains need that too."

"Do you know the last time Leviathan took any time off, or even left the compound?"

"Uh . . ." Greg floundered.

I knew I was being intense, but something had gripped me. I leaned forward. "Neither do I. He lives here. He lives *this*. He wears armor that's as much dark sorcery as chitin every moment he's awake. He doesn't go out. He doesn't unwind. His idea of relaxation is developing a new heat ray that melts human flesh more efficiently."

The table had grown suddenly quiet around me. Everyone's anxiety made me self-conscious, and made me pump the brakes on my full-on rant.

"I don't think you can win if you're not broken." I stared into my glass for a moment before looking back up. "That's why Leviathan's a real threat. He carries around all the 'evil' he needs." I paused. A thought congealed. "I think . . . I think that's how you have to be if you're going to stand a chance."

There was a beat of uneasy silence.

"Christ, Anna, sometimes you sound like one of them," Jav said.

I suddenly felt a bit awkward, and almost apologized. But I caught myself, and instead said, "Thank you," curtly, then flagged down a server to order some wings.

It was impossible to get used to the sound of Leviathan's office. "Sound" wasn't even accurate, it was more like a reverberation, a kind of noise that was felt more than heard. It came from the uncanny juddering of all of the equipment and devices, visible and otherwise, embedded in every conceivable surface of the space. It made me uncomfortably conscious of my body in an almost abject way. I could feel each tooth anchored in my jaw, wrapped in my gums; was keenly aware of the curve of my sternum and arch of my ribs.

More than that, being in that space made me more aware of the lingering ache in my leg, though over the months I had healed about as well as I was ever going to. The doctors who worked on Leviathan's compound were good, and had a lot of experience treating catastrophic injuries caused by vigilantes with superpowers; a simple compound fracture was an easy fix as far as they were concerned. I'd done a great deal of aggressive physiotherapy while I was healing, and kept my muscles from stiffening and atrophying too badly. In time, I could get around without my cane, quite comfortably most days. I limped only if I had to walk a significant distance, it was cold or rainy, or I was very tired. I hardly noticed my injury until those rare moments I was in Leviathan's office, when suddenly the frailty of my physical body was thrown into sharp relief by all the noise.

I leaned a little more heavily on my cane for comfort; I'd come to enjoy the feeling of security it imparted. After the encounter with Glassblower, I'd had it additionally weaponized, and there was even a tiny circuitry panel with some communication capabilities now. The cane made me feel both more balanced and more protected.

I had both of my hands resting on top of the handle as Leviathan moved his plated fingers across the touch screen display embedded in his desk, searching through some of my most recent memos and files.

"Not bad," he allowed, and I felt a curl of warmth catch in my chest. Praise wasn't something Leviathan doled out generously. "Not bad at all."

"Thank you, Sir."

He went quiet for another little stretch of time, and I let my gaze wander around his office. It landed, as it often did, on a mask. It rested in a special nook behind his desk that was custom built for it, lit gently from above and displayed on a matte black mannequin head. The mask itself was also black, though with the slightest bit of gloss, and one edge, near the left eyehole, showed some damage. He'd told me once that it had belonged to his mentor, Entropy; his tone indicated he would tolerate no further questions on the subject, and I respected his unspoken order.

Finally, he spoke again. "When I told you to make a space for yourself, I expected a great deal, but still you have surprised me." His eyes were down, darting between documents. "What has it been, nearly a year?"

"It very soon will be."

Leviathan nodded. "And in that time, you have become someone who helps dictate and guide our operations." He finally looked up. "You have ruined Glassblower. It's a success I would like to see repeated. Do you feel that you have the resources and cooperation you require to adequately accomplish your directives?"

"Yes, I do now," I said. "To be honest, Keller and Enforcement were initially resistant, but after the success of the Glassblower operation, they've grown considerably more amiable."

Leviathan nodded. "Keller is a military man—slow to change, but also able to recognize competence and strategic initiative."

I nodded. To his credit, Keller had come to show me a great deal more grudging respect in recent weeks, willing to give my suggestions and requirements consistently more time, attention, and manpower.

"You also proved yourself in the field, which he respects."

I acknowledged this with the slightest movement; I still vastly preferred to work behind the walls of the compound, but had found myself in the field more than once in the last few weeks, to help coordinate the more delicate operations. It still made me nervous, but each time the weight in my chest diminished and my hands were steadier.

Leviathan mercifully changed the subject. "How is your team working out?"

"Exceptionally well. I would like to give Javier Khan some assistance, though. With the additional missions we've been able to run, the flow of data has increased significantly. While he has been handling the workload satisfactorily, I don't want to create a situation where his accuracy declines or he burns out."

"Good foresight; it shall be taken care of. I'll call upon HR to provide you with additional candidates for you to select from."

"Perfect."

He cocked his head slightly to the side, the way a predatory bird might listen for the sound of prey. "Have you been screened for superabilities?"

The question threw me off, but I responded quickly. "Of course," I said. "Just the standard pre- and post-pubescent tests in school. My reading comprehension scores were above average and my dexterity slightly below; I had some markers, but nothing manifested."

There was a slight rumbling sound from the grill that shielded his mouth. "I want you more thoroughly examined—those amateurs miss a great deal in their rushing. I shall assign an abilities specialist to you."

"Whatever you think is for the best, Sir," I concurred. Filling out some forms and going in for some scans weren't terribly onerous requests, and Leviathan was known to be slightly compulsive when it came to fully gauging the capabilities of his employees. I knew they wouldn't find anything, but I was happy to satisfy his curiosity.

He cleared the screen on his desk with a dramatic swipe and eased himself into his chair, regarding me carefully. "I will soon call upon you for some additional missions, Anna. Not fieldwork, per se, but rather diplomacy."

I gave him a self-deprecating grimace. "Diplomacy isn't really my strong suit."

"I think you are mistaken." Leviathan's sense of humor was odd, nearly alien and often misplaced entirely. "I won't require you to act diplomatically. Rather, as our operations have grown, I have found the outward appearance of congeniality increasingly advantageous. All-out conflict with heroes is expensive and bothersome—too much of our budget is diverted to rebuilding."

I leaned forward a little, curious as to where he was going.

"The way in which you handled Glassblower inspired several ideas," he said. "You attacked when he was weakest, as Sun Tzu advises; you allowed other villains to take the direct and public credit—as well as the blame and repercussions—eschewing any form of larger ego gratification in favor of results; and you let him hang himself and bring shame down upon his name, do the bulk of our work for us."

"Flatterer," I said, and finally earned the slightest metallic scrape of laughter.

"I would like you to employ these strategies more, in lieu of direct confrontations," he said. "And on a larger scale. To do this, I think you need to spend more time in the odious company of heroes, in order to observe and gather information about them."

I wrinkled my nose. "You want me to start hunting bigger game."

"Precisely. And to do that, we must go on safari."

"I'll start packing." I began to turn, but then paused. "I'm not expected to be nice to them, right?"

A smile reached his strange eyes. "I expect you to be vicious."

It turned out I *did* need to start packing almost immediately. When I left my performance review and returned to my apartment, I found that flight details for the following morning had already been forwarded to my in-box. There was a small private airstrip at the northern edge of the compound, with a few augmented commercial-class planes and helicopters, even a couple of Hyperjets for emergencies. The vast majority of Leviathan's fleet were scattered, and stored, elsewhere.

We were going on what was ostensibly a diplomatic mission. It had been years since the greatest supervillain the world had ever known had regularly engaged in open conflict with heroes of any caliber, aside from the occasional bit of chest puffing and death-ray-warning-shot-firing with Supercollider. There was a point at which the constant aggression was getting in the way of his other plans: amassing power and influence, wealth-building, and R&D.

(I also suspected, though I never would have said so in his presence, that the ordinary violence of supervillainy had come to bore Leviathan. As much fun as the extraordinary weapons were to dream up, the consequences of being seen firing them were often more irritating than they were worth. He'd reached the point where it was far more convenient to hire some middling villain to take the credit, and the fall, and just place those munitions in the hands of another and set the wheels in motion. The pieces continued to fall into place, the blame landed elsewhere, and his empire continued to thrive. He took even greater pleasure in every small success, every tech acquisition or covert operation deployed successfully, because he counted each as a failure on the part of Supercollider to stop him.)

So, every once in a while, he did something that really distressed the heroic community: he set up a meeting and spoke reasonably to them. Few things made heroes more panicked than a civil conversation with *the* supervillain, which I suspected rather delighted him. The fact that he'd decided to give me a new opportunity to fuck with some heroes under the guise of friendly relations was just a bonus.

And, once I thought about it, was a pretty exceptional outcome to my first major performance review.

All of us on the mission were to gather on the airstrip early—the light was still dawn gray, and dew gathered on the scrubby grass that bordered the long, paved concrete runway. The air was so cool it felt bright and icy in my lungs when I inhaled deeply. I was nervous and so I was early, the first to arrive.

Our pilot was once a kick, then known as Gloom, who had natural low-light vision and a spatial awareness that rivaled that of a bat. The hero he'd been aligned with—the Gorgon—had treated him poorly, though, and after a fight with some villains that went particularly sour for him, he'd crossed the line. He was a composite now, having willingly undergone significant cybernetic upgrades under Leviathan's employ. His eyes, ears, and hands had all been replaced with complex machinery.

He was going over flight plans on his tablet, and as much as I was loath to interrupt him, I felt a kinship with someone who'd also found themselves on the wrong end of a hero's arrogance. I let myself hover and, soon enough, he glanced up, recognizing me.

"You're Anna, yeah?"

"That's me." I smiled and leaned on my cane a little self-consciously. "Forgive me if this is rude, but I don't know what to call you now."

"Not at all! I'm going by Vesper." He seemed pleased I would ask instead of bumblingly calling him by his old hero name.

"The bell or the bat?"

He grinned. "Bat; you're as smart as Leviathan has said."

I do not blush prettily, but go bright red and blotchy to the roots of my hair. I felt the heat rise in my face and became flustered.

"Is this reprobate bothering you?" That was Keller's growl. He and Molly strode across the airstrip together. Keller was built like an aging linebacker, one that could no doubt still play, making Molly's wiry frame and ridiculously long legs even more pronounced in contrast.

"I was being cordial to my newest passenger." Vesper sniffed.

"He was being a perfect gentleman," I said, glaring at Keller, letting my expression indicate I didn't think he could possibly understand what such a term meant.

I was still extremely irritated he'd maneuvered me onto the field, no matter how well it had gone or how accommodating he'd been since. Keller was completely impervious to my death glare.

I'd need to work on that.

A pair of representatives from R&D soon joined us: physics prodigy Rosalind Fife, who was terrifyingly young and profoundly neuro-atypical, and nanotech expert Ben Lao. Leviathan arrived last, of course, the soles of his boots giving off the oddest sound upon the asphalt—not hollow like rubber or a metallic clang, but an oddly smooth click. A single bodyguard, Ludmilla Illyushkin, accompanied him; she didn't speak a great deal of English yet, but then, he didn't require her to. She had lovely, old-fashioned manners that reminded me of a knight, but I was also uncomfortably aware that she looked at everyone and immediately calculated the quickest ways to kill or incapacitate them. Keller positively adored her.

"Morning, Sir. Systems nominal; we're ready to take off on your say-so."

Leviathan nodded and gestured for us to board.

As I walked by, Vesper whispered, "He's not a morning person," and I almost choked.

Once we were in the air, the small plane rattled contentedly through minor turbulence. Leviathan took a few sips of black coffee so dark it looked viscous. He sat with his eyes closed through this process, the filter that covered his mouth gently coming around the edge of his metal travel mug as delicately as the mandibles of a crab.

After several moments, he was able to keep his eyes open steadily, and became more receptive to anyone interacting with him, and a short meeting commenced. He referred to us all as "advisers"—which flattered me greatly—who would represent him at gatherings and provide support during key meetings. On this particular excursion, part of the team (Molly, Ros, and Lao) would be on their own, participating in "goodwill" technology exchanges. I'd be with Keller, Ludmilla, and Leviathan. We'd be meeting with the heroes first, as they preferred to operate during business hours, whereas villains still preferred to do business at night, as cheesy and cliché as the affectation was.

"We'll be meeting with the Ocean Four," Leviathan explained. "Riptide was injured badly last year and Abyssal is becoming increasingly nervous now that her brood of little barnacles are beginning to exhibit powers and might one day join the family team." He paused and drank. "They should be amiable to a ceasing of public hostilities with us and our allies."

"Abyssal is late in her first trimester of a new pregnancy," I said, and then paused for a second, unsure if my addition was appropriate. But Leviathan was looking at me steadily, interested, so I pressed forward. "I would think that might also be an impetus for their desire for peace."

"Dealing with her will be your priority," Leviathan said to me, and I nodded.

"And the black capes?" Keller inquired.

"Kronos and Hyperion." This was interesting; they were a big deal, former drug lords who had moved from narcotics to medical enhancement. They were quickly becoming one of the primary sources for cheap, under-the-table physical upgrades for thugs and aspiring villains without powers.

"Odd that they'd be willing to deal with us," Keller said. "By all reports, they have their market locked down."

"One of their doctors botched several procedures in a row—badly," Leviathan explained. "It seems he gained an unpleasant addiction that affected his ability to hold a scalpel. He was . . . dealt with and the errors covered up, but they are down a surgeon and demand is as high as ever."

"They want one of ours," Molly guessed.

Leviathan raised a finger. "And some of our tech. They are behind us, in terms of technical innovation, but as blunt and graceless as their methods are, there is always much to be learned from battlefield medicine. We may give them a few meager scraps, if it's advantageous."

The meeting wound down and I settled into my seat, peering out the window. The sun above the clouds was spectacularly bright, and the condensation on the outside of the window had long ago turned to ice. As I listened to the reassuring rattle and deep hum of the engine, I began to work the project, figuring in my head where I could get a prosthetic stomach once we landed. My expense reports were already notorious, and I expected Finance was going to lose their minds about this one. I also had no doubt it would be approved.

Thanks to some expert Googling and an exceptional courier, I was able to attend the meeting with the Ocean Four looking like I was about six or seven months along. When I walked into the meeting room—a circular chamber in the Ocean Four's base lit by a calm blue light, and dominated by an enormous tropical fish tank—I affected a slight waddle. I'd briefed everyone on my plan, but at the sight of me in maternity wear,

Molly had to surreptitiously kick Keller in the shin to help him regain control of his face.

The meeting was, for the most part, unexceptional. The heroes were fully decked out in their costumes and did a great deal of blustering and posturing, especially Riptide, Undertow, and the Current. Abyssal was much quieter, though, and I followed her lead, volunteering the occasional illuminating point but, for the most part, appearing content to hang back.

During a break, I immediately got up and went to the washroom, hedging a bet, and sure enough, while I was in the stall, Abyssal walked in. I timed my exit so that we were washing our hands at the same moment. She caught my eye in the mirror and smiled.

"How far along are you?" Her voice was quiet and kind.

"Oh, I still have a couple of months to go." I smiled back, putting a hand to my lower back and stretching.

"That's very exciting."

"It's my first; I'm pretty anxious."

"I remember that feeling." She paused for a moment, considering. "This'll be my third."

Pay dirt. "Really? Congrats! You can't tell yet."

Her hand crept to her stomach. "It's very early; we're just starting to tell people."

"Does it worry you?"

"Does what?"

I gestured toward the ceiling, letting the sweep of my hand take in the totality of their headquarters. "All of this, I suppose."

Her lips tightened strangely. "Of course it does." She was deciding whether to be annoyed at me or not; her suspicious WASP vibes were off the chart. I pretended to be oblivious to her discomfort and sidled closer.

"I don't know if I am staying on," I mock-confessed.

"You're quitting?"

"Thinking about it. Or at least, getting out of active duty, as it were. I feel so strangely fragile now."

Something in her face went watery. "It gets worse."

I tried to look crestfallen. "Well. At least my instincts are correct."

"Wait till the little one arrives. Boy or girl?"

I bet she was the sort to have a gender-reveal party. "This is embarrassing, but I don't know. Superstition?"

She smiled kindly. "Not at all. Having a baby is weirder than wearing a costume, somehow. You be as superstitious as you need."

I nodded. "I'm definitely taking a desk job after this." We walked out of the bathroom together. "Depending on how this goes, I expect a shower invitation," I said, and she laughed.

I realized, taking my seat back at the table, that this was an invaluable opportunity to run a critical experiment—a kind of A/B test. Here were four heroes with close-knit relationships and comparable power levels, all doing around the same amount of damage to the world with their every foolish endeavor. If we "intervened" (if we fucked with them), we'd have the unusual chance to closely monitor all of them and see precisely how each reacted to the stress, and how it impacted their careers. Maybe they'd end up doing less damage to the world, or maybe they'd become even worse. Either way, we'd be able to get an incredible amount of useful data with one action (and, potentially, reduce the harm caused by all four heroes at once).

To put this in motion, I had to arrange something to happen to Abyssal. Preferably her *and* at least one of her children. Nothing awful or permanently damaging, but something frightening enough that the rest of her team might follow her resulting cautiousness and let it declaw them.

I started plotting in my head, and settled on the relative advantages of a brief, nonviolent kidnapping. As soon as Abyssal was out of my sight, I typed up my recommendations to make sure her eldest child was held captive for at least a few hours sometime between now and her due date.

Working for Leviathan, every assignment and opportunity I was presented with was its own kind of test. I had to prove myself to gain extra tasks and responsibilities, and the way I handled them once they were given had an immediate effect on what would happen in the future. Leviathan liked my proposal and the oldest Ocean Four child was soon scheduled for a routine nonviolent abduction. (Most abductions were nonviolent; there was often far more to be gained from the psychodrama of when the target lost their beloved and got them back. In this case, the ransom mattered much less than the target's trauma from the experience, and their haunted relief at a near miss.) Leviathan viewed every bit of confidence he placed in someone as a risk, and I was proving a valuable investment.

The rest of the trip was a success on the black-cape front, with us getting a lucrative medical placement out of the deal (the tech team determined that inserting staff into Kronos and Hyperion's operation would effectively allow us to track a large chunk of the off-the-books cybernetic modifications under their purview). After that first trip, I found myself increasingly being called upon to accompany Leviathan when he traveled to various meetings.

In the next few weeks, I'd spent more time with my enigmatic employer than I had during the entire eleven months preceding them. I couldn't say I was getting to know him; it was impossible to know Leviathan, any more than one could know a volcanic eruption. You could study the phenomenon, have a solid working knowledge of how it functioned, but its sheer power and destructive capabilities were no less overwhelming or beyond comprehension every time you encountered them. I became familiar with his specificities, but I never lost my sense of awe.

I learned he found most heroes irritating. Rather than harboring any of the genuine enmity toward most of the do-gooders who plagued the villains of the world, he instead regarded them with bland distaste.

Leviathan's focus—one of the cornerstones of his psyche and the fuel for the inextinguishable rage driving him—was Supercollider. While details were hard to come by, even from his inner circle, the tension between them was monolithic. Their conflict had hardened into a cold war in recent years, but his determination to bring ruin down upon the hero never faltered for a moment. If ever a chance arose to cause Supercollider even the smallest harm or inconvenience, it was pursued doggedly.

Since inflicting pain and hardship on heroes was

fast becoming my specialty, Leviathan tasked me with dreaming up and doling out little miseries upon anything and anyone Supercollider came into contact with, extending the splash damage we inflicted to his associates. The prospect of a power failure at a ribbon-cutting ceremony the hero was attending, or Quantum Entanglement finding evidence of bedbugs in her hotel room, was enough to make him nearly giddy.

"I'd way rather be on our side," I announced to Molly, Vesper, and Keller in a hotel bar one night. On this particular occasion, we'd secured a new contract providing weapons for Infestation, a villain whose powers involved emitting a chemical that triggered an arachnid response.

"Oh?" Keller was now cheerfully blurry. He leaned toward me. Where I'd expected a career-long rivalry to take root, a weird, rough affection was growing between us. Every time I suggested something ridiculous, he grew warmer.

"Really. What's a hero going to do? Arrest you? Shrink you and keep you in an ant farm until someone busts you out?"

"Do permanent damage to your femur?" Molly offered, and I swatted them on the biceps.

"My point is: It's very boring. Straightforward. A hammer to a nail."

Vesper was nodding. "Tunnel vision."

"Exactly." I was using my almost empty glass to emphasize my gestures. "On the other hand, we seem rather pleasant compared to those arrogant pricks, but who knows what the hell we'll do to you?"

Keller let out a bark of laughter. "You're mistaking us for you, Tromedlov."

"Eh?"

"I'll just unleash the hounds on a problem; I'm pretty straightforward myself. It's you they have to worry about."

I laid a hand theatrically on my chest. "Keller, you say the sweetest things."

The aging dragon actually had the audacity to waggle his eyebrows at me, and I laughed.

One significant drawback to my increasingly ridiculous travel schedule and all of the accompanying responsibilities was that it pulled me away from my team more and more often. Instead of sitting with Jav and letting him lead me through the labyrinthine genius of his spreadsheets, he was sending me brief data reports. Instead of meticulously planning subterfuge and playing bad cop and worse cop with Nour, I was sending guidelines and instructions. Instead of getting lost down rabbit holes of data with Darla, I was leaving them to wander on their own. It wasn't at all that they couldn't handle it, quite the contrary, but I loved to be more hands-on in that work. It occurred to me that I missed it.

If the team's crankiness was anything to go on, they missed my presence too.

"I never see you anymore," Jav said petulantly.

I looked over my shoulder. I'd hopped into my office for a brief moment to try and find a document I needed on my neglected dumping ground of a desk. Jav was sitting facing me with his arms crossed, looking as though he were about to ask me if I knew how far past curfew it was.

I allowed myself to look guilty. "I know; I'm sorry. I'm being a terrible team head," I said. He pressed his lips together and I looked back down at my desk, hunting for a memo I was certain I had printed.

"You always come up with the best ideas," he said, a little pout left in his voice.

"You're all doing just fine without me."

"Nour and Jav resorted to prank-ordering, like, fifty pizzas to Stalactite's headquarters yesterday," Darla chimed in.

Nour, without missing a beat of her phone conversation, grabbed a Sharpie, scribbled furiously on a legal pad, keeping the phone pinched between her face and shoulder. She then held up a sign that said, "TAT-TLER!"

"After this meeting, I promise I'll be back in the office with nothing to do but ruin and torment with you all for at least a couple of weeks. Aha!" I found the sheets I'd been searching for. I'd apparently used a couple of them as coasters at some point in the recent past, but they were still readable.

"What's so important about this meeting?"

Jav was being unnecessarily difficult, but I decided to indulge him.

I heaved a sigh, using my cane as leverage to lower myself into my chair. Taking out a compact, I proceeded to powder my nose and retouch my eyeliner. "Flamethrower's an older hero, over fifty; his incendiary powers have kept him in the game longer than most, but he's retiring very soon and one of his idiot sidekicks is set to replace him. No one knows which yet." I carefully extended the wing tips of my eyeliner out a little farther, making the points sharper. "He's absolutely set against any kind of friendly arrangement with Leviathan, even if that means just mutually ignoring each other. Blowtorch and The Spark, however, are a hair more amiable, and we want to 'end hostilities, shepherd in a new age of mutual understanding' with them, blah, blah, blah."

"What's actually happening?" he asked.

"We have a DNA sample from Flamethrower on file; it's also common knowledge that Blowtorch and The Spark are twins. What we want to conclusively nail down is if they're also his children."

Jav's annoyance was suddenly obliterated by his curiosity. "Oh?"

"He was a lady-killer in his youth. When a couple of the kids he's got scattered about manifested powers, I think he took them on as kicks. Why hide their relationship otherwise?"

"But he still wants one of them to take over the family business even if he was shitty at paying child support."

"Exactly. Though, if and when we let the old man know that his kids agreed to work with us, even if it's just some sort of nonaggression pact . . ." Even in a hurry, this idea made me smile a little. I spread my hands. "I imagine it'll make the dinner table a little awkward. Might even start a small family coup."

"I miss you so much," Darla called, completely obscured behind an embankment of filing cabinets.

I swiped on fresh lipstick and rubbed my lips together, setting it in place with a pop. "Momma will be back soon, children," I promised. I snapped my documents into a briefcase, picked up my cane again, and headed to the meeting.

No one was in the room yet, but Blowtorch and The Spark were lurking outside the boardroom door, looking uncomfortable in their suits (costumes were considered hostile inside the compound; heroes generally expressed their commitment to a peaceful conversation by dressing in civvies). Jana from HR was walking away from them rapidly; from the blandly pleasant expression on her face, I knew she was furious.

She intercepted me on my way over and grabbed my arm. "I updated the brief, but just in case: since her transition, her name is The Spark."

"I made sure my tablet was synced with the update."

"Great." Her teeth were clenched. I raised an eyebrow in question. "Also, don't get too close to Blowtorch."

"Creep?"

She shot me some "good luck" eye contact and left, heels clicking with authority. I began to deconstruct how I could weaponize this new data.

"Friends," I said warmly, gesturing toward the open door with my cane. Blowtorch gave my body a long, full up-and-down look, which I chose to ignore. "Shall we take a seat and wait for my colleagues?"

The Spark nodded and walked through the entrance, but Blowtorch lingered, lounging in the doorway. He pointedly gestured for me to go ahead of him. I gamely walked forward, but kept a little extra distance between us.

As soon as I tried to pass him, he suddenly stepped in front, causing me to draw up short or else bump into his chest. "So," he said huskily, "what do you do?"

I smiled stiffly. "I handle information." I took a step back and raised the tip of my cane, shooing him into the room. He raised his hands in a gesture of mock defeat that implied he was anything but done and went in. It was going to take a mighty effort not to antagonize him before it was strategically sound.

I waited until he was lowering himself into a chair before entering the room. In the center of the meeting room's long table, there was a plate of muffins, a carafe of water, several glasses, and some bendy straws. The Spark was already pouring herself a glass. At the far corner of the room was a side table with coffee, and I fixed myself a cup before taking a seat at the opposite end of the table from the twins. I was acutely aware of Blowtorch watching me openly the entire time.

"Information," Blowtorch repeated when I finally sat down. He leaned back and rested the heels of his wing-tip shoes on the table. "Does that mean you interrogate people? Rip out fingernails with needle-nose pliers?"

I attempted to look scandalized. "Hardly. I'm a researcher; I generally only brutalize databases."

"Ah, nerd chick. Nice."

I let my smile become strained. The Spark cleared her throat. Her brother glared at her, annoyed.

"You look familiar," The Spark said uncomfortably.

"I doubt it; I'm generally stuck in the office." I tried to sound encouraging; I suspected talking to The Spark would be more pleasant than continuing to deal with her vaguely repulsive sibling.

"Mmm. Did you ever work for, what's his name, the Electric Eel?"

I fought to keep my shoulders from rising. "Briefly, back while I was still freelancing."

Her face lit up a bit and she nodded. "Yeah, yeah, I remember. You were in the room when he used the Mood Ring on the mayor's kid."

"I was," I said mechanically. "I was a temp at the time."

"Pretty badass," Blowtorch drawled.

"Not really. I wound up in the hospital. Supercollider shattered my femur."

They didn't know how to respond to this; The Spark looked suddenly stricken and Blowtorch made a blustering sound. I found I enjoyed the discomfort. I held up my cane. "This is a souvenir."

Blowtorch recovered first. "Pretty tough, then, for a nerd chick." Blowtorch let his eyelids become heavy and he smirked at me. "That's hot." He shot some sparks out of the tip of one finger for emphasis. It was extraordinarily embarrassing for everyone in the room.

I took that as the signal to humiliate him; putting up with him was no longer even remotely fun. I gave him the frostiest, most threatening smile I could muster. "Mr. Torch, what do you think my rank and role in this situation are?"

"Huh?"

"Let me rephrase for you: Why do you think I am at this meeting?"

He didn't understand the point of the question. "Taking notes, I guess?"

"No, I am not 'taking notes'; I just happen to be particularly punctual. I'm the head of my own department and one of Leviathan's representatives at this summit. Quite frankly, I find your behavior most unbecoming thus far."

His face turned ugly; he looked at his sister and jerked a thumb toward me. "Why would a supervillain keep this frigid auditor bitch around? No fun at all."

He angrily grabbed a blueberry muffin. I noticed the water in the glass nearby had started to boil.

"Sorry to keep you waiting," Keller said brusquely. I stood gratefully as he, Molly, and a couple extra suits I didn't recognize walked into the room.

"Good, some real conversation," Blowtorch muttered. He stuck out a hand and blandly shook each of theirs. He didn't bother to stand, but at least he sat up straight and put his feet on the ground. Keller gave me a questioning eyebrow and I shook my head slightly.

After the meeting, with overtures made, old grudges addressed, and a mutual plan to reduce tensions between Leviathan and the Flamethrower brand (once the torch had officially been passed to one of the siblings), Jana returned to escort the two heroes out. Blowtorch shot me a last, hostile look, while The Spark continued to look deeply ill at ease. As soon as they were safely out of sight, a forensics team descended like starving buzzards upon the boardroom, carefully collecting and bagging everything the heroes had touched, sipped, or left uneaten to harvest any DNA evidence. Surely there was enough spit for a good, old-fashioned paternity test.

The rest of the team had left for a dinner break, so I retreated into my empty office for a few minutes of peace and quiet. I rubbed my temples for a moment, breathing out the tension of the meeting. Feeling it start to seep away, I absently checked my email. Two immediately caught my attention.

There was a short message from Surveillance that read:

> Anna,
>
> Keller asked to see the video of your interaction with the heroes during today's meeting. Just a heads-up.

I swore quietly. I expected Keller would be trying to look for proof I'd been unnecessarily rude to the dirtbags, and braced myself for a small war.

A moment later, however, Keller wrote me himself.

> A,
>
> Way to handle those two asshats, Frigid Auditor Bitch (FAB).
>
> Cheers,
>
> Bob

I cracked a smile. I had won that bastard over after all.

That's *Head* Frigid Auditor Bitch to you.   —Anna (HFAB)

Two seconds later:

LOL

Sometime between when I finally went back to my suite rather late that night, and when I wandered back to my office in the morning, someone found the time to tape a sign to the door that read, WARNING: FRIGID AUDITOR BITCH. I opened the door slowly and was greeted by my entire team grinning at me.

"This is going to be a thing, isn't it?" I sighed. Nour giggled.

It was a good week before I realized that Greg had changed my email signature from "Anna Tromedlov" to "The Auditor." It stuck.

As luck would have it, I didn't have to go back on my promise to the rest of my team; I did, in fact, have a few relatively peaceful weeks in the office after whirlwind months of travel and meetings. While I'd enjoyed taking my talent for personalized misery on the road, it was a special kind of joy to be in my own element for a while. The team had done a fine job without me, ruining relationships and triggering superpowered migraines at a spectacular rate. But there could be no doubt that when I could be more present, our cruel little department thrived.

I also had to attend to the long-overdue task of hiring some much-needed relief to help take on some of Jav's workload, and after a great deal of screening and a hilarious series of interviews, we brought on a former temp named Tamara Ng. Several departments had used her to help solve data flow problems, and I saw no reason not to make the arrangement permanent. Her arrival brought its own kind of chaos, as our workflow and entire little department dynamic had to be retooled around her presence. It was a positive change, but good things are often extraordinarily stressful, especially in the short-term.

Since one of my standard problem-solving staples has always been to throw alcohol at a situation until it improves, to thank the team for holding down the fort while I was off sowing the seeds of discontent and also welcome Tamara into the fold, I called a "team-building" session at the Hole.

It took exactly a single round of drinks and twenty minutes of small talk before the team decided to drop the charade and worked up enough collective courage to start grilling me about Leviathan. I had started to take for granted exactly how unusual it was that I spent so much time in his presence, even for someone who worked for him.

"I haven't even met him," Tamara said. Her face was serious and solemn, as though she couldn't even imagine it.

"We've never spoken," Jav confessed. "I've been in the same room as him a couple of times, but that's it."

"He's terrifying," Nour said, almost whispering, as if he might overhear. "Have you seen him without his armor?"

I swallowed a bit too hard. "Um, no."

"Does it freak you out to be around him so much?" Nour stared at me.

"No, he doesn't scare me." This wasn't entirely true, but the feeling I had in his presence was extremely complicated and I had actively avoided dissecting it. I had to psych myself up before crossing the threshold into his office, but once I was in physical proximity to him, something in me uncoiled. I noticed my colleagues were visibly relieved when he left a room, whereas I felt the edge of something melancholy. "He's very clear in his instructions, which makes it easy to work with him," I said after far too long a pause.

Darla snorted. "We don't care about his management strategies, Anna."

Jav nodded. "Yeah, come on. Details. Weird, terrible details."

I thought a moment and then cracked a smile. "He likes *Coronation Street.*"

"He fucking does not!" Jav slapped the table.

"It's true; we had a lovely chat about how much he likes Hilda Ogden."

"My mind is blown."

"More," Nour demanded.

"I know for a fact that his Zune is loaded with Vengaboys."

"You are so full of shit."

"He has a Zune?"

"I think 'We're Going to Ibiza!' is his favorite."

"You'd better be lying," Jav said, crossing his arms.

"More!" Nour said.

I thought about, but did not tell them, the image he used as his lock screen and desktop across all of his personal devices: an engraving of Satan by Gustave Doré, with a quote from *Paradise Lost*:

> *. . . the Arch-fiend lay*
> *Chain'd on the burning Lake, nor ever thence*
> *Had ris'n or heav'd his head, but that the will*

And high permission of all-ruling Heaven
Left him at large to his own dark designs,
That with reiterated crimes he might
Heap on himself damnation . . .

It wasn't a secret, certainly, but something about it felt deeply personal, and speaking of it felt like breaking a different kind of confidence. Besides, my team didn't want intimacy; they wanted to be scared.

They crowded closer, faces eager. I cracked my knuckles one at a time.

"Do you guys know about the iguana?"

Nour frowned. "The villain?"

"No," Jav said, "that's the Iguanodon."

Darla looked like they were going to have an aneurysm. "No, but please tell me we are about to find out."

"He has a pet iguana."

"No!"

"Yep. Her name is Shannon."

"Shannon the Iguana."

"She's quite a lovely lady, almost five feet long. She has terrariums in both his office and quarters, though usually the office enclosure is hidden when he entertains. It took me quite a few visits before we were introduced."

"I just—wow."

"What did you do to earn the honor of an audience with Shannon?"

The truth was I'd just delivered a sit-rep when Leviathan, out of the blue, asked if I would be up for meeting "one of his inner circle." I said yes immediately, and expected to be briefed on an upcoming meeting or another round of travel. Instead, he touched a mechanism and a panel in one of the walls slid back, revealing a lush terrarium that was bigger than some studio apartments I'd lived in. I couldn't contain a moment of complete delight, and from behind his visor, I could feel him beaming at me.

I shrugged. "I'm extremely lucky."

I could see on their faces that my answer was entirely unsatisfying, so I launched into another story before anyone could call me on it.

"They're actually quite demanding to care for, and he's incredibly busy and often gone, so she has her own staff."

"Naturally."

I paused for a moment and took my time to theatrically refill my wineglass.

"And? Come on, Anna."

I swirled the wine in my glass, carefully considering its legs and bouquet.

"This is cruel and unusual," Darla protested.

I grinned, took a sip, and continued, "So, a few weeks ago, there was an incident with a staff member who hadn't worked with Shannon before. Although he'd been trained, he either hadn't paid attention or didn't think it would matter, because he left the heat lamps off for too long while cleaning her enclosure and she got a bit cold."

The team had grown completely quiet, like children around a campfire listening to a ghost story.

"Iguanas need UVA and UVB light, and are only happy between twenty-six and thirty-five degrees Celsius. This particular attendant let her stay too cold for a couple of hours before someone caught the error. Shannon recovered, but she was sluggish for a while."

"What happened?" Nour breathed. "Was he . . . was he disintegrated or set on fire or something?"

"No, no, nothing like that." I took a long drink. "Leviathan had the attendant's kid kidnapped."

"*What?*" Jav almost knocked over his pint glass and narrowly rescued it.

"He has a toddler, this attendant. The child vanished from day care the next afternoon right before he was scheduled to be picked up by his mother. He was found on his doorstep a couple of hours later, unharmed, except for a very mild case of hypothermia."

I let them stare at me in stunned silence while I casually finished my drink. "Anything else?"

The four of them shook their heads somberly, serious as children who believed in the boogeyman. A weirdly pleasant little surge of power crawled over me, as I realized that with my sheer proximity to Leviathan, they found me a little scarier. I wondered if I should reassure them that I found the incident deeply upsetting too, but in truth it bothered me far less than I expected. The combination of devotion and capacity for vengeance that he displayed at Shannon's discomfort warmed some neglected corner of my heart. So instead of reassuring my team, I let their uneasiness grow.

The next morning, as I was somewhat blearily walking to the office, my phone started buzzing frantically. I nearly muted it, but at the last moment saw the call I had almost dismissed was from June.

She was crying so hard that it took me a long time to understand what she was even saying, but between the sobs and blowing her nose I was finally able to make out that she and the Meat she had always refused to admit she was dating had broken up for good.

I tried to calm her down for nearly an hour before I accepted that this was a full-scale nuclear meltdown, and did my best-friendly duty: took two personal days (my first since I'd started), arranged for secure transportation back to the city, and headed over to her apartment.

It was late in the afternoon when I finally arrived. I stepped in through the door and faltered, not because the walk up the stairs had been difficult, but because her place was trashed. Pictures had been smashed, as well as some dishes, and there was broken glass sprayed across the carpet. One of her aromatherapy pillows was split open and dried lavender had spilled out. June was sitting on her couch, the one I had lived on for months, surrounded by tissues.

"Jesus Christ, are you all right?" I stumbled over to her, keeping my shoes on for safety, and glass crunched under my feet. I fell down next to her and grabbed her hands, trying to get a good look at her face, scanning for injury.

"I'm fine, I'm fine, fuck."

"You're *not* fine. What the hell happened?"

Her chin trembled. "We fought, like, all night. It was so bad. We threw things, at the end."

"I can see that."

"I shouldn't have looked at his phone."

"Ah shit."

"I know."

"Has /r/relationships taught you nothing."

"I know! But I did and he was a fucking liar and I told him so, and then—"

"Right."

"Fuck."

I shifted. "He left this morning?"

"Yeah. He broke a picture and I threw my mug at him and everything smashed and he left."

"Oh, babe."

"It was so fucking stupid. I knew what the fuck was up, but I had to look and then once I looked I had to do something about it because I couldn't tell myself I didn't know." She sniffed hard. "And now there's all this everywhere and I can't clean it up because then I'm cleaning up after a fight and there's glass—"

"Have you been sitting here the whole time?"

"I have to pee so bad."

I struggled up and went to find the vacuum in the closet. Behind me, I could hear her start to cry again.

I cleaned the glass and crockery chips out of the rug and off the hardwood floor, going over the same spots until I was certain there were no slivers left, and then she dragged herself up and into the bathroom. When I heard the shower running, I started the coffeemaker.

She spent the evening napping and crying, and eventually laughing while I enumerated everything that was wrong with her ex in excruciating detail.

"I couldn't tell if he had a picture of himself holding a fish, smoking a cigar, or posing with a car on Tinder, but then I realized: he has all three."

"It was a motorcycle." She was wheezing.

"Of course it was." I took a sip of the rosé I was drinking out of a teacup. "He looks like a handsome, scared turtle."

I paused after that to let her breathe.

I slept in June's bed with her like we were little girls having a slumber party, whispering to each other in the dark even though there was no one to catch us and tell us to go to sleep. I spent the day with her, helping her put her apartment fully back together and finding everything that her ex had left or reminded her too much of him and putting it in a box. I texted him later and arranged for him to come pick it up, and supervised as he collected it from the front hallway. He was smart enough not to say a word to me.

I was prepared to take another day, but June insisted that she was all right, that I had done enough. Once she was under an afghan in her now immaculate living room, I ordered us some takeout and told her that after we ate, I'd call for a ride back, and be at my desk the next morning. I settled on the couch after I'd placed the order; June lay back and put her feet in my lap.

"Should we look at Tinder?"

She made a face. "Like that's what I need right now."

"Not to talk to any of them."

"Oh. *Oh.*" She fumbled for her phone in the folds of the afghan and loaded the app, already giggling.

She swiped through a few profiles and then flipped her phone around, showing me a picture of a man's unpleasant face.

"He looks like a wet baguette."

She cackled and found me another one.

"He looks like Animatronic Abe Lincoln out for a night on the town."

"He looks like he has no sheets on his bare floor mattress bed."

"He looks like he has a collection of swords."

"He looks like a sentient boiled bagel."

"He looks like one of those stunted asparagus that never sees the sun."

"He looks like his shirt came from a bank's hot dog fundraiser."

"He looks like two different dudes glued together."

"He looks like a seagull that smelled a fart."

I had to stop for a while until she could breathe again; she was laughing so hard she was making little wheezing hiccups, and tears streamed down her face. Making her laugh was a particular kind of joy I had never found anywhere else; even now, as she was more despairing than I ever remembered seeing her, I still held that power. She wrapped her hand around my upper arm to steady herself, taking deep, calming breaths, only to erupt in peals of warm laughter again. I became aware of a deep ache in my chest. For months and months I'd only heard her voice on very occasional video calls; much more often, our only contact was text on a screen. Ever since that press conference, I'd put something else above her at every turn: the Injury Report over her comfort, my new job over our relationship. I hadn't treated her, and her laugh, like anything precious to me, and it suddenly hit me what a terrible mistake that had been. Tucked up with her on the couch, whispering and giggling and close again, I resolved not to let another pit open up between us.

I decided to stay another night.

4

The door shrieked open, and I jerked awake. The hinges had rusted and the door fit badly in the frame, making it both loud and difficult to open. I assumed it was a deliberate theatrical choice. It still startled me; I must have dozed off despite my best efforts to stay alert.

I slowly turned my face to the door, squinting against the too-bright fluorescent lights.

I could just make out the looming silhouettes of two men in the entranceway. I could feel the contempt even before I saw their faces. I noticed neither of them had their truncheons at the ready, though. They'd left the weapons clipped safely to their belts. Interesting.

I shifted so I was sitting slightly more upright, rolling my neck back and forth slowly to work out the terrible stiffness I'd earned from my doubtlessly very short nap. I was shackled to a metal chair in the center of a bare room, with a concrete floor pitted with several drains. It was almost disappointing that there was fluorescent drop lighting rather than a single bulb.

I stank, and the skin on my legs itched and stung. My wardens had left me restrained so long I'd pissed myself, which I was pretending didn't make me want to scream. They seemed to enjoy allowing me to wallow in my own filth for as long as possible. There was a bit of blood at the corner of my mouth, the taste of sharp copper when I moved my tongue over the inside of my cheeks, and a nasty headache was marshaling its forces against me.

All things considered, they could have done worse.

"Someone wants to speak to you," said one of my guards. He was a stout man with a close-cropped dark beard and wide-set eyes. He spoke with great reluctance, as though he deeply disagreed with whatever orders he'd been given. "Get cleaned up."

The second man strode forward. I thought I recognized his tightly curled red hair and round shoulders as those of one of my very first interrogators, one of the three who first bound me in this room when I arrived, but it was hard to keep track. He unlocked the shackles on my wrists; I'd been pulling against them to keep myself from falling asleep, and there were livid marks in my skin. It was hard to stand at first after so much time tied to a chair. My feet had gone numb, and when I put weight back on my legs a painful rush of pins and needles washed over them. All the blood in my body seemed to shift and my vision swam. I swayed and grabbed on to the chair for fear of falling.

The first guard unbuckled his truncheon. "Quit playing."

I straightened with as much sodden dignity as I could. "Just wanted to make you feel like you were doing a good job. Shall we? I don't want to be late to the ball."

His lip curled and he prodded me forward with the black, hardened piece of fiberglass in his hand. I was marched a short way down the hall to an empty group shower. They left the shackles on my feet, making undressing a struggle; I ended up tearing my stockings to get the disgusting material off my body. The guards stood uncomfortably close as I washed under a pitiful, shuddering spray of icy water, then threw a sandpapery towel in my face when I stepped out of it. They were trying to project an air of obvious disgust, as I awkwardly pulled on the hospital gown laid out for me.

"That hurt?" The second guard poked painfully at the one genuine wound that had been inflicted upon me so far: when I had been taken, my captors had immediately dug the subdermal implant out of my upper arm. Every one of Leviathan's employees had a tracking device and emergency beacon somewhere on their body. They'd located mine with a quick scan and dug it out with what seemed like a small, incredibly sharp melon baller. The hole punched in my flesh was no longer bleeding, but puckered and threatening some sort of infection.

"I wouldn't mind some antiseptic, actually," I said. I attempted to sound conversational, but my voice was ugly and dry.

My hair was dripping wet and cold around my ears, and I had to fight to keep my teeth from chattering. I was taken to a different interrogation room down a long, empty hallway. My bare feet were very quiet on the damp concrete, in contrast to the Vibram-soled combat boots stomping on either side of me. There was a metal chair riveted to the floor, but unlike in the previous room I'd been held in, this wasn't the only object in the space. Here, there was also a spartan steel table, affixed to the floor with bolts, and a very deep, comfortable-looking leather wingback.

"That's sweet of you," I said, making the barest of moves toward the fancy chair. "Thinking of my comfort—"

The guards took the opportunity to pounce on me, throwing me unceremoniously into the metal chair; I landed hip-first and couldn't stifle a hiss of pain at the jarring impact. "It might've hurt less if you'd shut the fuck up," the short one said. They shackled me again—hands and feet—and slammed out of the room.

The lights were a bit dimmer and it was slightly warmer; I was shivering less severely, anyway, which was something. I flexed my fingers and toes, trying to keep the circulation going as much as possible, and did the only thing I could do under the circumstances: I waited.

It was difficult to keep track of time. I knew that I had been held for more than one day and less than three, but that was about all I could calculate. My absence would have been noticed by now, I decided. Even stripped of my tracking beacon, they would know something had gone wrong when I didn't return. I had no idea what sort of a response it would raise, if any. Henching, even for a villain as powerful as Leviathan, was a job with significant risks, and I knew that I had taken those on freely. After my experience with the Electric Eel, however different my current situation seemed, I had to assume I was on my own.

I wasn't alone for very long before my mind returned to its favorite topic of the last twenty-four to seventy-two hours: my abduction. I kept turning those moments over and over, trying to find things I had done wrong. I knew that this was my traumatized brain trying to protect itself, to learn what mistakes I'd made so they wouldn't happen again. It didn't matter how often I told myself I couldn't have changed things.

The delivery driver called me, seeming confused about where to drop off the Thai I'd ordered. After a couple of attempts at instructions, I told June not to get up from her nest on the couch and made my way downstairs, cane in hand. Once I poked my head out of her low-rise, I saw a man standing outside, away from the streetlight, looking confused. I called out and took a few steps toward him.

As soon as I was next to it, the side door of the dirty white van parked by the curb slid open. The delivery driver charged forward and tackled me, and two men inside the van grabbed my arms. Their faces were covered with ski masks, but their eyes were visible. I yowled and squeezed a hidden trigger in my cane, managing to hit one full in the face with a blast of Inferno-grade, foam-based pepper spray. He squealed in agony and fell back into the van, but the other two managed to wrestle me in. My cane was ripped from my hands and thrown into the street. While one goon held me down, the one I pepper-sprayed fell to the floor next to me, drooling and heaving as we drove away.

I fought. I bit the remaining assailant hard enough that I tasted blood and raked my nails across whatever exposed flesh I could find. After cursing in pain, he stuck a knee in my back and stabbed a hypodermic needle into my thigh. My mind became unmoored after that, and the fight in me slowly bled away.

When I came to, I was shackled to a chair. I spent most of my time for the next couple of days alternately being interrogated and enduring hours of sensory deprivation in the dark, cold room. Their tactics weren't terribly inventive or even that brutal; they were clearly hoping to scare and unhinge me, rather than do any permanent damage. Leviathan provided resistance to interrogation training (part of his new employee orientation package), and I found I was shockingly well prepared for this. All the banging, screaming, and extremely theatrical violence employed was textbook, to the point of being predictable. I was exhausted and wanted to tear my skin off in disgust, but I was aware they could be doing a lot worse.

The door opened behind me. They hadn't left me alone very long this time, which was different. Also, the entrance was behind me now, so I could no longer see the guards as they entered, but I could hear the footsteps behind me, growing closer. My heartbeat hammered in my ears, and my throat threatened to close. It seemed like the moment they would do worse had arrived.

I made a point of sighing audibly. "This is very boring."

"I'm sorry to hear that." The voice was unexpected, but I recognized it immediately. I found it almost impossible to remain calm and collected for the first time since my capture. Supercollider's striking form materialized out of the gloom, his broad shoulders and narrow waist dramatically backlit by the lights in the hallway. He walked around the table and gently lowered himself into the luxurious chair across from me, the leather creaking in welcome.

I could do nothing but stare for a moment. He looked at me with a strange mixture of curiosity and gravity on his face, his dark eyes slightly hooded. He was freshly shaven and impeccably dressed; I even caught a whiff of Tom Ford cologne dabbed on his pulse points.

"You look dashing," I said. "I suppose I should be honored." I lifted one of my hands as high as I could until the shackle clanked, drawing me up short. "Forgive me for looking so terrible. The hospitality here is somewhat lacking."

"Again, you have my apologies," he offered. He placed his huge hands on the table between us, in a gesture that seemed almost supplicating.

There was a long, awkward silence. My heart still hammered in my chest; the aching rage I felt in his presence shocked me with its intensity, shot through with a healthy dose of fear and adrenaline.

"To what do I owe the pleasure of this meeting?" I asked finally.

He didn't reply, but continued to study me. I imagined my face, my swollen lips and the deep bags under my eyes. I wondered if it was pity I saw momentarily flash across his face. I wondered if he was even capable of the emotion.

"The authorities here," he said finally, "they want to arrest you. Have the police find some charges, extract whatever information they can from you about Leviathan, and lock you up for as long as they legally can."

I'd suspected I was being held under Dovecote, and these words all but confirmed it. I hadn't seen any obvious logos or other branding of the Draft, but the entire place practically reeked of Superheroic Affairs.

"That's an interesting proposition," I remarked coolly, "considering I am legitimately employed by a private corporation and have never had so much as a jaywalking ticket in my life."

"So. You would lie about what you do."

"No, I am very proud of what I do as an information specialist. I've had Legal examine my file and activities with a fine-tooth comb, and I'm clean. I know what you have on me, which is exactly jack."

He nodded. "We are aware of your record and the challenges in holding you long-term," he allowed.

I turned my hands palms up. The metal shackles slithered around my wrists.

"Well then. Don't you owe me a phone call?"

He got up and started to pace. The room was narrow and his strides were long, so he went back and forth quickly. It only made him seem more agitated. "You don't understand me. You're a problem," he said. "I didn't mean for you to be, but you are."

"I get that a lot."

"They think I'm paranoid." He struck a pose for a moment, placing his hands on his hips. Heroes never could keep from showing off for very long. "They think it's a waste of time and energy for me to follow up on every villain I encounter, every hench who gets away."

"I'm not sure it's accurate to say that I 'got away,' but go on."

His stride slowed and then he stopped pacing, his eyes growing vague. "The best piece of advice I was

ever given was from Doc Proton, when I was just starting out." He had a faraway look in his eyes, staring into
the middle distance. "I didn't take it at the time. I was
brash and young then. Reckless."

He looked back at me suddenly, as though remem-
bering I was there. "Doc Proton told me, 'You make
your own nemesis.' I didn't understand it then. I
thought it was one of those things a rambling old hero
said to sound wise. But it's been absolutely true. Every
evil, every great power that has ever risen to challenge
me, every archvillain who's ever been an actual threat,
was someone whose path I altered. I set our enmity in
motion, every time. A tiny action can cause an ava-
lanche."

"Poetic," I allowed. I'm not sure it registered. He
frowned, lost in thought. He was looking past me
again.

"I was foolish in the beginning and let my enemies
rise and become worthy foes. It took too long for me to
recognize them as threats, and eliminate them. Leviathan is my greatest failure." He paused, and something
very dark moved behind his eyes, while I imagined
how utterly furious Leviathan would be to overhear
that. He shook his head to clear his thoughts. "Over
time, and more near-defeats and close calls than I'd
care to admit, I have come to understand that there is

no benefit to letting your opposition thrive, to allow a sapling to mature into an oak."

I sucked in a breath. Supercollider had not only just validated my theory that superheroes were in fact terrible for the world, but proved I had not been thinking big enough. Not only were heroes responsible for all of the damage and injury they caused, they were even responsible for creating the villains they fought.

He looked at me then with a deep sadness. It chilled me more than the threat of any torture.

"When I saw you in the hospital, I knew what I'd done. I should have acted even earlier. But once again, my mercy allowed another evil to germinate."

"Don't be so hard on yourself." My bravado was failing, and my voice shook.

"I knew, but I let you recuperate. I let you turn further toward the darkness and begin to amass power against the forces of good. I hoped against hope that I was mistaken, but you have risen in the shadow of my weakness and hesitation."

Whenever I thought he'd finally reached the depths of his own jaw-dropping grandiosity, he managed to keep digging. A braver version of myself, one with fewer survival instincts, wanted to slowly clap (had my hands been free). I wanted to roll my eyes. But I knew his speech was leading somewhere terrible, so every insult died in my mouth.

"I'm not nearly that important," I managed.

His lip curled. "I've seen your work firsthand, in the field."

"I hate fieldwork. I vastly prefer my desk job."

"And from that humble seat you are destroying the lives of heroes and allowing evil to flourish."

"Oh, do go on."

He started to pace again. "Getting my hands back on the Electric Eel reminded me of you," he muttered, flexing his fingers. I hadn't heard he'd been taken in, and wished I had the capacity to enjoy the news. "After his capture, I happened to have a conversation with two promising young heroes. They spoke about you—one more warmly than the other—about your composure, your strength. They spoke of peace and alliance, but I saw what you were trying to do: sow the seeds of discord within that heroic family."

I stayed silent this time. For all his apparent empty-headed handsomeness he was occasionally brighter than most people might expect.

"You know what you did. What you're *doing*." His voice was blank.

I stared hard at the table between us.

"It matters not." He stopped pacing and towered over me. "I will no longer give in to my weakness in this regard. I have seen the signs and I know I need to trust my instincts. I have made an enemy and I must stop that adversary before she can rise against me."

"So, what's your plan," I said quietly. "Kill me? Old Yeller me out back and hope no one digs too deep when they landscape the yard?"

"No!" He looked at me, horrified. "No, of course not; we're heroes!"

I squinted up at him, disgusted.

"I know you might not understand," he said, sorrowfully, it seemed, "because you are still but a pawn. Do you play?" He didn't wait for an answer. "In chess, a pawn is the feeblest piece, and the most vulnerable—the most expendable. It's easy to ignore a pawn, to take it for granted while you concern yourself with the more powerful pieces. However, a pawn is also the one and only piece that, if left unchecked for too long, can become a queen."

I stared at him. *I am aware of what chess is.*

"I'm afraid that I'm going to have to remove you from the board."

He walked away from me and I began to shiver, more violently this time. He pressed the intercom button by the door and summoned my two jailers back into the room. They stomped in obediently.

"I want you to make her comfortable," he ordered, "and I mean that. She needs to be well rested and stable for the procedure tomorrow."

"Yes, sir," the two men said in unison, significantly cowed.

I felt like I was moving underwater as they unlocked my restraints and guided me to my feet. They were surprisingly gentle now. They led me to a cell and nudged me inside. There was a cot with an actual mattress on it, a toilet and sink, as well as a thin, stained but clean blanket. I wrapped it around me like a cloak. I curled up on the cot and tried in vain to be very still.

I must have fallen asleep at some point, the chalky weight of exhaustion winning out even over the fear, because I woke with a start to the sound of the door banging open. The two guards who stomped in didn't allow me the opportunity to fight. Still confused by sleep and aching everywhere, I'd barely managed to lift my head when they seized my arms and held me still. A third man had come in behind them, wearing scrubs, and while I squawked in protest he came up and injected something into the meat of my thigh.

In a few minutes I went limp, and they cautiously let me go.

"We can take it from here," the man in scrubs was saying, quite distantly.

"You sure? One of our guys still can't see."

"We have it handled. She'll be on a sedative drip soon."

They said a few more things but I couldn't focus on it anymore; it was like they were speaking in another room and I had cheap foam earplugs in. I tried very weakly to lift myself up on my elbows to hear better, but couldn't get the strength together. I heard boots moving away, and then the man in scrubs was pulling me into a sitting position, posing me like a limp, person-size doll.

The next few hours were a haze of movement and preparations I barely participated in. The drugs replaced my blood with molasses, the electric crackle of my synapses with guitar distortion. I was aware that I should panic. I thought calmly about fighting or tearing out my IVs, but the ideas were very far away, and the necessary effort to do so buried in fog. The only thing that seemed solid in my head was a deep, chemical calm.

Now and again, the smallest bubble of curiosity would pop to the surface, seemingly the only emotion

I still had access to. I was given new IV lines, which left me even weaker, pushed me even more deeply into myself. I was strapped to a hospital bed, but not flat on my back. Instead, I was secured on my side, my head tilted slightly upright.

Then I was in a room that seemed impossibly, hellishly bright. My eyelids were taped down, but white light shone right through them. There was a strange pain when someone injected local anesthetic into my scalp. It went in shockingly wet and sharp, like liquid glass, my nerves sending out one last distress signal before going quiet. I observed this with an academic kind of detachment.

The next thing I was aware of was a very loud buzzing beside my left ear. I couldn't feel anything other than a bit of pressure on my skin, but I could hear.

"Have you started?" I inquired. I was startled that I could muster the effort. My speech was slow, the words rounded off, and talking was laborious.

"Not quite," a male voice replied, calm and serene. "We had to shave your head first, just a bit, before we can make the incision."

The buzzing ceased. I smelled something that reminded me of a public swimming pool—the stench of chlorine—which I eventually recognized as iodine.

"Shouldn't I be unconscious?" I wondered aloud. No one replied.

I couldn't tell how many people were in the room with me, exactly. I tried to follow steps on the floor, voices, and the clattering of instruments on metal trays. There were some shuffling sounds and lowered voices; the surgical team held a brief conference. Everything was muffled, but I could just make out the words.

"This is not a complete slash 'n' burn and we're not dealing with powers; we're here to blunt and disarm. Minimal sensory damage and stay away from the speech centers."

I wanted to be scared, but my brain had misplaced the capacity for that emotion.

I was aware of them hovering over me. There was an odd feeling of pressure on my head again, and a tugging sensation. Then came another loud, mechanical noise, which made my face vibrate, my teeth rattle. There was the oddest, most unpleasant smell, which reminded me of being in a dentist's office and having a rotten tooth worked on.

"Ow," I said.

They stopped. "Does that hurt?"

"No," I admitted, "but it seemed appropriate."

"Keep going," someone else snarled, firing up the saw again.

After a few more moments of my entire consciousness being taken up by a noise that vibrated through my skeleton, everything stopped all at once. There was an instant of quiet, of soft voices and machines beeping and a bit of terrible scraping inside my head.

Then, one of the doctors hissed something and drew away from me. There were several loud noises outside the door, bangs and yelling, and the scraping noise stopped abruptly. There was a louder sound, almost an explosion, and a tray of metal instruments clattered noisily to the floor. The members of the medical team were soon screaming, first in indignation, then in terror.

Something cool and smooth touched my hand. It felt like fingers, but hard and with too many joints.

"Anna, can you hear me?" The voice was impossible, but unmistakable. Leviathan's hand closed over my wrist.

"What's happening?" I wasn't sure I actually produced the words, but I tried.

"Medical!" Leviathan's voice was a typhoon. "Get her out of here immediately."

There were hands all over me then, unhooking some

devices and attaching new ones, detaching me from one IV bag and hooking in another.

"No more drugs," I tried to say.

Someone squeezed my shoulder. "You don't want to be here for this."

There was a roar like the ocean crashing down on me, and then nothing.

"Anna."

"Mmmmm."

"Anna? *Anna?*"

"Fuck."

"Get him." I heard hurried footsteps, a door opening and closing. "Anna, can you understand me?" The voice speaking to me was closer now, low and insistent, but still gentle.

"Sure."

"Great. Keep talking."

"No." I felt like someone was sitting on my chest and my limbs were lead; it was almost impossible to open my eyes. My head felt stuffed with bandages.

"I know it's hard, but I need you to interact with me as much as possible, okay?"

I groaned.

"Can you move your hands?"

I flexed my fingers. I felt the tightness of surgical tape tugging the skin at the backs of my hands.

"Wonderful."

"Toes too," I said, wiggling them. "That hurt a little," I admitted.

"You're missing three toenails," she informed me.

"That's too bad. What's your name?"

"Oh, Susan. I'm Susan, from Medical."

"Hi, Susan." I feebly lifted my hand; she laughed softly and shook it.

"She's speaking?" Leviathan's voice was like a light being flipped on inside a murky room; I awoke a little more fully.

"Yes," Susan and I spoke at the same time, and she gave a nervous laugh. "She seems very aware and articulate," she reported.

"Auditor, do you know who I am?" I couldn't place the quality in his voice. It was one I'd never heard from him before. It was warmer, more liquid.

"Yes, Sir. Am I home?"

I couldn't explain how, but I *felt* his affirmative. "We extracted you successfully. You're where you should be."

A deep sense of safety settled over me. I let the first tendrils of sleep begin to coil around me.

"There was some . . . damage; we've had to repair you."

The comfort dissipated rapidly. "Repair?"

"Yes. It was complicated. Hearing you speak is a great reassurance."

Panic started to filter in. I tried to open my eyes and wake up more fully, but found only blankness. "Why can't I see?"

His hand was on my shoulder again, and I found it impossible to stay afraid while he maintained that contact. "It's temporary. I promise. Sleep now."

That command was a great relief. All of the questions I held, even the meaning of the ominous word "repair," were not nearly as important as doing exactly what he asked. I breathed in deeply and let my mind fall back into a deep, safe interior darkness.

At first, I couldn't do much but sleep. I often dreamed about being disassembled. Six spiderlike robot arms roamed over my body, eating away chunks, clipping or slicing or evaporating pieces away to carry off and repurpose. My flesh was not messy and did not leak as they worked, though, but stayed serenely, smoothly pink. My bones, when they started to show, looked like mother-of-pearl. While my brain manufactured these images, I was actually being put back together.

Piecing together what happened, how I had been rescued and returned to the compound, was slow, hard work. At first, staying awake for even a few moments was a struggle, and even after I was conscious for longer stretches of time, focusing on and retaining any information was a colossal effort. But I kept asking questions—of Susan and the rest of the medical team, of Greg and Vesper and Melinda and Keller, when they were allowed to see me, and even from Leviathan himself on the few occasions he appeared by my bedside. I asked them to tell me the stories, and wove the little pieces into a narrative in my head. It became a kind of talisman, an ever-growing bedtime story that I repeated to myself, over and over. I couldn't see those first few weeks in recovery, so I nurtured this story and watched it play out inside my head in ever-richer detail.

When I was snatched off the sidewalk and thrown into the van, I assumed that I was on my own. Everything in my previous henching experiences taught me that the second a hero had their hands on you, your contract was unofficially terminated. It turned out I was gravely mistaken.

The moment my subdermal implant had been ripped out of my arm, it sent out a distress signal; even though it was destroyed, that final beacon was enough to let Security know that something had gone wrong.

A team was dispatched to the last place a reliable signal could be traced, which was the street where I had been abducted. They spoke to June, who was panicked when I went to get the delivery and never returned. She was smart, and hadn't called the cops, so all of the evidence was still on the scene. My cane was in the gutter, broken but unmistakably mine. The team retrieved it, along with other forensic evidence: the residue from my pepper spray on the ground, one of my shoes that fell off in the struggle, impressions of the boot marks left by my captors, rubber from the van's tires on the road. It wasn't much to go on, but the tire treads and rubber composition matched Draft-issue trucks, and one of the moles we had on payroll at Dovecote's sister medical facility (affectionately called "the Vet," as in "veterinary hospital") reported several procedures rescheduled and one surgical theater suddenly prepped and on lockdown.

That was enough for Leviathan. While I was being interrogated, a strike was planned. Liberating me from the subbasement of Dovecote before surgery was almost impossible, but the idea was entertained. The story I heard, which I first assumed a lie, but a very sweet one, was that Leviathan had been prepared to raze the building to the ground and salt the earth when he heard what had happened. When I repeated the story to Leviathan, however, expecting him to refute it, he grew very still.

"They were kind," he said, "to describe my outburst so judiciously."

He was in such a towering rage that he'd become the storming, stalking, talking-about-himself-in-the-third-person supervillain not seen in years. The story was that it was Keller who eventually talked him down, promising greater success if they waited until I was moved to the Vet. He agreed to wait—just barely. Imagining that anger made me smile.

Leviathan and Keller saw their chance and green-lit the mission the moment they learned when I was to be transported to surgery, since the Vet was above-ground and far more vulnerable to attack. Supercollider had planned to watch the procedure from the surgical theater's viewing area, but a trio of villains—Tribulation, Ecstacy, and Rapture—were convinced (with money) that now was the time to test their "ascension engine" on a nearby courthouse. The strike team waited until Supercollider was occupied, cutting it as close as they dared. There was a critical balance between how long they could wait for Supercollider to depart, because as he was leaving I was being prepped for surgery, and the time the procedure was underway. They had a very narrow window to get me out of there, but they made it.

"They had opened you," Leviathan explained, during one of his visits in the very early stages of my recovery. "They intended to blunt your brain. Not to completely incapacitate you, but to effectively make you useless to me."

I struggled to find the words to describe the profound violation and disgust I felt about them invading my brain—especially since they had very nearly succeeded in "blunting" me. When the team stormed the operating room, my scalp had been peeled back and a small square of bone already removed from my skull. They'd intended to keep me conscious throughout the procedure, occasionally prodding me into talking while they worked, to make sure they didn't damage me too badly. A surgeon had only just made the first exploratory slice into my gray matter when the door was blown open and the strike team charged into the room.

When I asked what happened to the medical team performing my unwanted procedure, Leviathan simply assured me that they, as well as the guards posted outside the operating room, had been "neutralized." Keller provided quite a bit more detail, a play-by-play of the violence, and creatively described their state as "liquefied."

Back at the compound, I was immediately brought into surgery, where our own medical team was waiting. They were as prepared as they possibly could be; they'd even been able to get my previous medical records from the hospital I'd been admitted to after my leg injury, thanks to a surprisingly sympathetic emergency room doctor. There was some damage to my brain, especially where the surgeon, startled by the tactical team's assault, had slipped a bit with the leucotome.

Leviathan had worked with his neurosurgeons, supplying advanced technology it was suspected he'd used in his own augmentations and armor. He decided that I would not only be repaired, but upgraded. Rather than content himself with restoring partial sight in my left eye, the nerve was replaced with a composite of stem cells and some "donated" optic nerve fiber whose origins I elected not to ask about, and more bio-modded circuitry was embedded in my retina. The lesions on my brain were knitted with more custom cybernetics, which not only compensated for the damage, but enhanced me.

They did something else to me while I was open on the table, something I hadn't told anyone. There was a part of the procedure that Leviathan had only disclosed to key medical staff, and even then not completely.

He waited until we were alone to tell me, and I remember staring at him from my one unbandaged eye in utter confusion. My vision was still blurred and focusing was difficult. I didn't miss, though, that his armor rippled around his mouth, like an insect flexing its mandibles. I'd come to realize that it was a sort of nervous habit, like biting one's nails. It was one of a small list of things I planned to never tell him I noticed, so that he couldn't become aware of his tells and stop. Whatever he had to tell me was significant.

"The results from your scans were undeniable," he explained. "There was a well of untapped potential in you, which would occasionally seep into your conscious and subconscious minds. When you first came here, I deemed it too dangerous to activate your powers. But when the opportunity presented itself while repairing the damage those idiots had inflicted, it was the logical choice."

"I don't understand," I said. "I don't have any powers. I've never had any."

I was tested. We all were, as children. Superheroic Affairs mandated that everyone go through a screening process, so that the exceptionally talented could be raised to be heroes. For most of us, it was as terrifying as it was disappointing. It meant private training facilities and very few, heavily supervised visits with family. That prospect was more attractive to me than for most kids. But I went through the same standardized test that the Draft performed on everyone around puberty, and they came up with nothing extraordinary.

"They said there was nothing . . ." I tried to remember the words. "Nothing that needed further testing."

There was a rattle from the grate over his mouth, a small chuckle. "Anna, simply because you've built unknowingly on top of a graveyard doesn't mean those bodies aren't in the ground."

As I healed, I turned this over and over in my head. I felt no different, and had yet to accidentally levitate or set something on fire. As my mind became less clouded with painkillers and I could focus for longer periods of time, I could detect an ease and quickness to my thoughts, a bit of extra, sparkling clarity, but that was only to be expected from the upgrades I'd received. I wondered what he had found, and what would come. He'd flatly refused to tell me any details, and I realized it was possible that even he didn't know.

"Don't wear yourself down trying to figure it all out right away," he'd suggested with a strangely kind irritability. "Heal first. Come back to work."

"**This is** ridiculous."

Susan shone a light into my good eye, testing my pupillary response. "It's only for a few weeks, just until the implants fully heal." She nodded, satisfied with what she'd seen, and turned to make a few notes on my chart. I tilted my head up and down, still getting used to the feeling.

"I bet I look terrible." I'd lost weight while in recovery, which had hollowed my cheeks and made my features sharper. The hair on the left side of my head was beginning to grow back, a bit of comforting fuzz to mitigate the harshness of the staples holding my scalp together. It wasn't the general ugliness of my face that bothered me at the moment, however, but the new black patch snugly covering my left eye.

"It makes you look . . . distinguished?" Susan shrugged playfully. She was a Korean woman, a few years younger than I, with an annoying propensity toward optimism.

"It makes me look like a fucking pirate," I grumbled. I drew my robe a little closer around me in a sad attempt at shabby dignity. At least I was able to wear my pajamas while healing at the medical facility at Leviathan's compound, instead of a terrible hospital gown.

"Knock, knock." Greg poked his head in the room. "Whoa! Permission to come aboard, cap'n."

"You're fired," I spat.

"I'm not in your department," he replied cheerfully, strolling into the room with his hands behind his back. I flatly refused to smile at him when he grinned expectantly.

"I will find some way to have you fired."

"Y'ar, matey."

"I hate you."

"I come bearing chocolate?" He brought out the package he'd been concealing, a small confectionary box in the shape of a star.

"Bring that closer and I may let you live."

A moment later, Susan, Greg, and I each had a truffle in our mouths—mine was buttercream, Susan got a toffee, and Greg got the extremely cursed orange one, which I decided was an appropriate punishment.

"They still letting you out today?" Greg asked, searching for a new chocolate to get the taste out of his mouth.

"That's the plan."

"After one last quick glance from the docs to make sure everything's healing properly," Susan added.

Greg nodded to her, then turned back to me. "How's the noggin?"

"Weird," I admitted. "We won't know how the implants have taken until I'm fully healed and I can use this eye again. In the meantime, it feels . . . fuller, like there's more going on up there."

"Would you say you're officially a cyborg now? Are you a pirate cyborg? A piborg?"

I looked at Susan. "Remind me, is this thing weaponized?" I tapped the side of my head.

"I'm afraid not."

"Damn."

The medical lead soon arrived. After poking around my stapled-up skull and running a couple of quick cognitive tests, he pronounced me free to go. Susan promised to have the cards, flowers, and sweet gifts my colleagues had sent me moved to my apartment as soon as I was settled in. There was an excellent scotch from Molly, and a small army of cacti and succulents from my team. The pile of presents was dominated by a massive teddy bear from Keller and his goons. It was the size of a goddamn person, clutching a fabric heart that said, "Get Well Soon!" The thought of him, or one of his Meat, picking it out and bringing it over was delightful.

Susan offered to get a wheelchair to move me from the recovery room in Medical to the car waiting outside, but I declined. It felt important to walk under my own power, if I was able. Plus, Molly had gifted me with my newly repaired and upgraded cane, and I wanted to feel it in my hand again. I moved slowly, Greg hovering solicitously at my elbow in case I needed him, but I managed to walk the whole way through the building myself.

Outside the main doors, Melinda waited for me, smiling, the supercar purring behind her like a contented feline. It was a newer model, with a sharp, raptor-like body and odd, iridescent paint job, like an oil slick. "Your chariot, my liege." I giggled delightedly and she embraced me before helping me into the car, while Greg held the door. My crush on her had become a comfortable thing, a kind of warm aesthetic appreciation that meant I stammered less and complimented her more. Once I was settled, Greg hopped in next to me, and Melinda took her place behind the wheel.

"I'm riding in style today, I see," I said, running my hands over the plush, enveloping seats.

"I've only driven this baby a few times, usually when Leviathan really wants to make an impression. Seems he wanted to spoil you a little." I felt a pang at his thoughtfulness, and then wondered why the idea of him thinking of me would touch on such a tender spot.

Melinda dropped me off at my apartment with another hug, and Greg walked me up. There was a banner tacked above my door that read, WELCOME BACK, AUDITOR! It made my chest constrict, both painfully and pleasantly.

"Do you want me to come in? Need anything?" he asked when we were at the threshold, suddenly not sure what to do with his hands.

"No, I'm okay, thank you," I said, unlocking my door with the swipe of a key card I hadn't used in too long. "I appreciate you escorting me home, but I haven't been alone for more than a moment since I got back."

He swooped down and hugged me then, as tight as he dared. I briefly pressed my forehead into his shoulder and patted his back. It was like hugging a great bird, and I could feel his heart hammering.

"You'll be swashbuckling again before you know it, Captain Jack," he said, a catch in his voice.

"If you make any more pirate jokes I will get a cutlass from Keller and run you through."

"Y'ar," he said sadly, releasing me. I laughed at him and went into my rooms.

My suite was neat as a pin. It had clearly been cleaned, possibly repeatedly, while I was away. There was even a hint of eucalyptus in the air. I dove into my bed, burrowing into the clean sheets and bedding, feeling home. The simple physical comfort wrung a few tears from me.

I eventually sat up, pulling the blanket around my face like a hood. I decided to spend as much of my convalescence and medical leave in bed as possible. Looking around my room happily, robed in my comforter, I noticed something new on my nightstand.

The hand-thrown little pot was filled with rich black loam and a clutch of leaves so green and lush they seemed to glow. A single delicate stalk reached up, and blossoming from it were three black, velvety orchids.

There was no card, only a single thick piece of raw-edged paper. Burned into it was the alchemical symbol for sulphur—the Leviathan Cross.

I touched the branded surface with a fingertip.

One of the hardest parts of my recovery was screen time—or rather, the lack of it. Medical might have released me on my own recognizance, but I still had to check in multiple times a day with a team of specialists, and something all of them were adamant about was I could not overtax my injured brain or my eye. That meant as little time as possible staring at screens. It turned out, the few times I cheated (I was no better a patient the second time around), it was acutely painful.

This meant that communicating with June while I recovered was impossible, at least directly. While still in Medical I had to communicate with her via Greg, who would read her messages to me and take dictation back. When I was finally back at my apartment, I was told I could try and see if I could tolerate an hour a day. In case I couldn't, I set up some voice-recognition and voice-to-speech software so I could get my email narrated to me in a soothingly stilted robot voice. I wanted to save my precious hour or less of screen time for texting June.

Her responses, filtered through Greg, had seemed distant and generic; it must be weird talking through the filters of not only two devices but a human in between. I was sure she was saving her best material for the time we could digitally be together again.

I started by sending her a selfie of my stapled scalp with the caption:

peep my Frankenstein

And that's not all

And then I sent a second picture featuring my eye patch.

I got her read receipt, and then the three little dots that told me she was typing. I'd missed those three little dots, even if looking at them was already giving me a headache.

> Is this you? Like, you're talking by yourself?

> Yeah I broke out, I am allowed a few typing minutes a day and I'm wasting them on you

She was quiet a long time. The three composing dots told me she was writing something then erasing it, over and over.

Finally, right when I was about to put my phone down because of the discomfort, she sent,

> I can't talk right now but I'll message you later, k?

I smiled in relief.

> Sure thing, babe

It was working hours and she was probably in the middle of something. I put my phone to sleep and tried to catch a nap myself, as I had been told to do as often as I could.

The emails arrived a few hours later. Two of them, a few minutes apart. The first, coming from her official email, the one with the professional headshot for a profile picture that she sent all her résumés from, was cold and straightforward.

> . . . Do not contact me under any circumstances. This includes but is not limited to in-person contact, texts, email, social media messages, phone calls, and mailed postage. I no longer wish to be personally or professionally associated with you, and will be removing you as a contact on all platforms . . .

It was a breakup that read like a restraining order.

The second message was sent from the email address she'd had since sixth grade, the really embarrassing one that still had her flipping the bird while drunk off her ass as the profile picture. That email was only nine words long.

> I can't watch you disappear into another car again.

I stared at those words much longer than I was supposed to, until my good eye started to ache and blur.
I finally closed my laptop and walked in small circles
around my apartment for a while, numb.

When I missed a late-afternoon medical appoint-
ment, they first called to remind me, then sent someone
over to make sure I hadn't blacked out or my new circuitry hadn't gone haywire. I apologized, but I would
not go with them back to Medical. My throat was raw
from sobbing and my entire face hurt.

Distantly, I wondered what would happen next.
Would they send a different medical team, this one
with tranquilizers and higher security clearance, who
would just scoop me up and take me back?

Whatever the official protocol was never happened;
Keller came instead.

He knocked, but didn't wait for me to answer. I
yelped and leapt up awkwardly in surprise. He stood
there, looking at my swollen face gravely, taking in the
tissues scattered around the apartment. I was covered
in misery sweat and my face stung from salt. I made
some noise about him barging in, which he completely
ignored.

After a moment he gave a tiny nod and said, "Get
cleaned up and dressed, and meet me at the Hole in
an hour." He spoke with easy, complete authority, and

whatever barb I was about to lob at him dried up in my mouth. "Standing me up isn't an option." He nodded again, turned, and let himself out.

I seriously thought about standing him up, but I knew he'd just keep coming back until I relented. So after showering and holding an ice pack to my face for a while, I dragged myself down to the Hole to meet Keller, where he sat, smiling. Between my cane, the eye patch, and the still-fresh head wound, I felt monstrous. While we all worked for a supervillain, most of Leviathan's staff still weren't hardened enough that they wouldn't give me a longer look than usual. The scrutiny bothered me less than it would have a few months ago, but it still itched.

"You still look terrible." He smiled wider.

My lip curled. "I know."

Our server appeared, and Keller ordered a pitcher.

"I can't drink after—"

"Don't feel obligated." He waved his hand across the table. "Figured we wouldn't want to be disturbed by her checking up too often."

"That's . . . really smart."

He grinned and expertly poured himself a glass of something that smelled hoppy and fresh, just the ghost of a head collecting on top. "So."

"So how are you. How's the Meat."

He made a face. "Nice try. We're here to talk about how *you're* doing, smart-ass."

"Must we."

"Indulge me. How are you?"

"Wretched."

He grunted. I stared. "Well, you're here. Want to talk about it?"

I rubbed my forehead. "You remember June?"

"Yeah, I liked her. Terrible bitch—really funny."

"She . . . We can't talk anymore."

His face hardened a little. "Ah. I'm sorry."

Suddenly the cardboard coaster his beer was resting on became fascinating. I stared at it.

"You two involved?"

"She was my best friend."

"That's a rough one."

We were both quiet for a long moment, but not uncomfortably. He took another sip or two. There was a baseball game on the muted television screen on a wall behind me. Keller glanced up occasionally to check the score.

"This is when it starts happening, you know," he said.

"What?"

"People leaving you."

I was startled. "This is a thing?"

"Absolutely. You're a bit successful, getting a name. That's when they start abandoning ship."

"You have a funny definition of 'success.'" I sounded even more bitter than I'd meant to. "My name is a joke that stuck, and all I've earned from two encounters with Supercollider is a permanent limp and an eye patch."

"Names all start as jokes or insults, before we own them. And you survived Supercollider *twice*. He's a hell of an enemy to have."

"I will admit I am lucky."

"I refuse to let you dismiss my utter fucking *symphony* of an operation as luck."

"That's not what I—"

"Getting you out of there was a nightmare, but we did it. You do good work and we needed you here. That's why you survived."

"I—thank you."

"Self-deprecation has splash damage."

"Why are you being so goddamn wise."

"Because you're being impossible. As soon as you settle down, I can return to being a meathead again."

"I'm . . . getting accustomed to the idea that I'm valued here. I just didn't think I'd lose June when that happened."

"Oh?"

I felt my face become tight. I felt raw and ragged, the words ready to pour out, but it was Keller sitting across from me. I'd assumed he had all the tenderness and understanding of a water buffalo. But there he was, sitting across from me.

My throat was tight, but I pushed past it. "June and I started out together. We'd go to the Temp Agency, make ourselves feel better by making fun of everyone else when we were just as desperate, just as scared. We took the worst jobs, terrible assignments, whatever we could get our hands on. Because we could talk about it, mock it. We had each other, and that made it all bearable."

He was listening. His big hands were still on the table and he was looking at me, steadily.

"Even when I got hurt, when Supercollider . . . happened, she was there. She came to the hospital, to make it all a little less shitty. She set up a nest for me in her apartment when I had no one and nowhere to go. Painted my toenails . . ." I trailed off.

"But then you saw her a lot less."

I nodded.

"Was it when you got this job?"

"No, much earlier. Back when I started the Injury Report. We were living together, and she hated it. It made her anxious."

"Makes sense."

"Yeah. But I didn't listen to her; I kept working. Then when I got this job, it was worse. And it was my fault—I kept frightening her. She never came here. It freaked her out."

"And then you were taken."

"Yeah."

"They get scared that it's going to happen to them, you know. Like the violence is contagious."

We were both quiet for a bit. Keller drained his glass, refilled it, rubbed the back of his neck. Finally, he said, "You'd think people would be much more afraid to hang out with heroes and kicks."

"Why's that?"

"Well, they have a much higher mortality rate. You date a hero? You're their best friend? Their mom? The uncle who raised them? You're getting kidnapped three times a week, easy."

I chuckled. "True."

"'Course it is. When's the last time a villain's fiancée was spirited away from their engagement party and tied to the front of a speeding train for ransom?"

I actually barked out a small laugh at that. "They really should step up their game."

"You know why they can't get to our loved ones?" Keller asked.

"Because they'd never stoop to it?" I answered.

"Because we don't have any."

I made an awful choking noise, like he'd punched me in the throat. Now it was Keller's turn to stare at the table.

"My husband. He couldn't deal with the career change," he said. "He wanted to be respectable. He liked that. He liked waving me goodbye, waiting for me to come home." His big hands were cupped around his glass. There was a noticeable callus on the third finger of his left hand, where he must have worn a ring that was slightly too tight for his thick fingers.

"Why'd you put on a black cape?"

He bared his teeth. "The usual. Saw too many good men denied promotions or benefits. Too many honors given out to some powerful fuck's idiot kid."

I nodded and pressed my lips together. That wasn't all, but he was taking his time getting there.

"Plus, Leviathan was just smarter than anyone else. I wanted to be led by someone I wanted to follow."

"Did he come to you?"

Keller cracked a smile. "Back when he was more openly confrontational, I was part of a team that was called in when he was causing shit with this biomechanical submarine. Coast guard couldn't deal with it on their own, and all the supes powerful enough to confront him were conveniently tied up."

"Did you stop him? Was he impressed?"

Keller laughed, embarrassed. "Hell no; he massacred us. I speak figuratively in this case. He could have slaughtered us all, but didn't. He crippled our frigate and made a complete fucking mess of things. Turns out he was just doing some testing and the chain of command overreacted; we never should have been sent in there. He spun a damn cocoon around my little ship and boarded us like it was nothing."

I was rapt now. I knew the device that Keller was talking about, a defensive weapon that Leviathan called the hagfish. It shot something that was a bit like spider silk, but a lot more gel-like and awful. I enjoyed picturing it being used on something the scale of a ship; I'd only ever before seen it used on superheroes, which was funny enough.

"He had us captured, fair and square. I think he was about to toss us in the brig and just carry on. Then, like a joke occurred to him, he cocked his head to the side and asked if I wanted to come join him instead. Don't know what got into me, but I was mad as hell, so I said yes."

I was grinning. Keller looked at me and smirked proudly, but then his smile faded. He took a long drink.

"My husband decided not to come with me."

I swallowed. "I'm sorry."

He rolled his shoulders. "His prerogative."

"Do you regret it?"

He shook his head. "This is more honest."

"Henching never struck me as honest work."

He pointed a thick finger at me. "More honest than anything out there. I used to play at being a hero too, just not with a fucking cape. We were supposed to be noble, but we were just as cruel, corrupt, and selfish as anyone else. You just have to hide it, pretend everyone's doing good."

"With henching, you know where you stand," I allowed.

"Exactly. You own the cruelty, the scheming; it's all on the surface. No one wants to be a real hero; it's too hard. My husband didn't give a damn whether the work I was doing was noble as long as it *appeared* to be. When I killed someone then—something I did a *lot* more than I do now—it was for *the greater good.* It was such bullshit. So the second the pretense was gone, so was he. I didn't need that."

I admired the clearheadedness with which he'd made these choices, how he'd had some kind of internal direction and followed it, knowing the consequences. When I compared it to my own story, I saw just how much I had drifted and fallen, rudderless, in the beginning. "When I started out, I think I was playing at being a villain. I didn't think it was as dangerous as it was."

"You seem to have figured it out. Not everyone's cut out to risk limbs and eyes just because they're poor and pissed," Keller offered, winking at me.

"I didn't really choose this." I gestured to my whole body in a sweeping, dismissive motion.

"Yeah, you did," he said firmly. "You might not have known it at the time. But you went down the rabbit hole." He drank while I scowled at him. "Sure, you got your leg broke, but you could have bolted, gone back to school, and become a lawyer or some shit. You could have promised to be good so it never happened again. But here you are."

"Does that make me stupid?"

"Nah; it makes you a little bit evil, though."

"Flatterer."

"I'm serious."

"I'm petty and mean, maybe, but I don't know if picking on heroes the way I do fully counts as evil."

Keller suddenly raised his hands into claws. Deepening his voice, he spoke in a caricature of Leviathan's metallic rumble: "To seek vengeance and power instead of cowering when the world punishes you. That's what they think evil is, do they not?"

I burst out laughing. "I suppose so." My hand wandered absently to my scalp.

Keller watched my hand, and suddenly grew serious. "Look at you," he said quietly. "Look at how damn afraid they were. Look what they did to you just because you wouldn't be scared."

"Is this the alternative, then? Covered in scars and full of circuitry? Lonely as hell?"

"It's not all that bad," he said.

"How do you figure?"

"You know yourself. You know who you're working for. You're making choices with your eyes—well, eye—open."

I scowled at him again.

He gave an offhanded shrug. "And what have you got to lose? Not much more for you to be scared of, I imagine. That's what villains have that no one else does."

I picked up my soda water and looked into it. "Bleak, Keller."

"Not at all. It means we're tougher."

"You haven't addressed the crippling loneliness."

"Frankly, I'm hurt that you aren't counting my company."

"That's not what I—"

"I know."

I let a silence stretch between us, uncertain if it was uncomfortable or not.

"It's not that there's no one, Auditor. Sure, the pool's more limited, but everyone who's left are people who get it."

"So you're saying I'm not doomed to a solitary existence."

"Not for a lot of promotions yet. You're young, you'll be pretty again soon. And if I can rustle myself up a companion for a nice steak dinner now and again, you'll be just fine." He drank and waggled an eyebrow. He looked terribly pleased with himself and it wrung a smile out of me. "I won't lie—it's more difficult at the beginning, kiddo," he said. "But you'll get used to it. And hey: it's a hell of a lot harder for them to lay siege to you now."

I nodded. One of my hands wandered to my chest, and I pressed hard just below my collarbone. There was still a physical ache, a raw and bloody sense of loss. But it was healing.

I kept healing. It was a slow, extremely frustrating process. I hated the deep, loathsome itch of flesh repairing itself, and I hated how much time the process required. I tried to be better this time, to see my body as an ally instead of an adversary, but it was still immensely hard. As my skin grew back together and the grafts that re-placed the bone that had been sawed out of my head gradually solidified, I got stronger in tiny, agonizing increments.

My recovery kept me busy. This time, instead of being stranded on a couch for weeks on end with little contact, I had a steady schedule of appointments with specialists and therapists to make sure everything was knitting well, that my implants and upgrades weren't being rejected, that my brain was processing the new influx of data. I was always being evaluated, my treat-ment moving forward or scaling back, depending on how I reacted and progressed.

For important milestones, Leviathan would sit in on the assessments and occasionally order a test of his own. I saw him now more than I ever had before, and I found myself becoming increasingly attached to this new attention. The days I saw him were like rewards, something worth making progress for. His interventions weren't complicated and almost never very probing, just a few questions, a fingertip rest-ing against my temple or lymph nodes. I kept a small database in my head of every time he had touched me, and noticed that over time, he held the contact a little longer. A tiny upward trend.

After four months of recovery, however, I was called into his office for an unscheduled meeting. This piqued my interest. He'd flatly refused to entertain any questions about when I might be able to resume my duties, but I immediately expected that this was a first step toward getting me back to work. He brought a doctor into the meeting with him and said he wanted to supervise one last examination with his own eyes before he considered placing some weight back on my shoulders.

They were thorough, careful to the point of being anxious. He double- and triple-checked the doctor's work, going back and measuring again. For a long time, he worked on me in silence, concentrating on what was left of my wounds. I let my eyes close to pay attention to the other data: the light touches and pressures of his tinkering, the two of them talking to each other while he worked as though I weren't even there.

When the exam was over, the doctor left without giving me any results. Leviathan stared into my left eye, the patch that had been covering it discarded. His face was just a few inches from mine. Close up, his armor made a curious sound, the tiny scales sliding against each other like miniature tectonic plates.

After a long time, he spoke. "Good. This is very good."

"Thank you," I said, as though I had anything to do with what pleased him.

"Look up," he commanded, and pulled down my left eyelid. I expected his fingertip to feel smooth, but it was almost like extremely fine velcro.

"The implants are healing well," he said, releasing my face and stepping back. "How is your vision?"

"Odd," I admitted, sweeping my gaze over his office. His armor now had a slightly iridescent sheen to it, and a few of the objects in his office glowed. "I can see more than I could before. It's confusing."

He nodded. "That's to be expected. Your brain is learning to categorize the new data. The most difficult challenge now will be disguising your reactions; you may find you see some things that are unexpected. Do not be like the midwife who found herself gifted with fairy sight, starting every time she passed a sprite at the market."

Leviathan did like fairy tales. I smiled a little. "I'll work on it," I promised. I looked at the palm of my hand, wondering a moment at the details I could see now, the whorls of my fingertips, the fine folds of skin at each joint.

"I have decided that you will be working with Vesper while you adjust to the implants," he said, watching me closely. "He's had significant augmentations and has adjusted exceedingly well, especially to the sensory changes."

"Thank you, Sir."

He turned slightly away, satisfied. I was beginning to lose his attention. I could have dismissed myself, if I wanted. Instead, I lingered in my seat a moment.

"Do you have any other questions?" he asked automatically. He was already looking at the screen embedded in his desk.

"I have a request, if I may."

"Speak."

"I would like to be cleared to go back to work."

His body language remained quite relaxed, but his eyes snapped back to me, pale and probing. "Medical has recommended several more months before permitting you to resume even partial responsibilities, and I am inclined to agree with them. Not to mention learning to use your augmentations will take time."

"I am aware of my limitations, Sir," I said quietly. "I understand I have a long way to go, but . . . I have found being away from my work troubling."

He scanned my face, his gaze moving slowly, like a sensitive instrument. "I should refuse this. Having you fully healed is of great importance. Exerting too much effort too quickly could delay your recovery and cause you to perform at a level beneath your usual quality."

"I appreciate all of your concerns. You are right on all counts. This is a selfish request."

Something over his mouth shimmered. He was allowing me a small opening to speak my case, which I recognized as a significant indulgence. I let that give me courage and pressed forward.

"I feel that returning to work, in whatever limited capacity, would aid in my recovery."

His head tilted slightly. "How so?"

I made a fist. This was surprisingly difficult to articulate. I didn't know how to explain that, every moment, I knew the cost heroes wreaked on the world was adding up, with nothing to balance it out. I didn't know how to tell him that every day I wasn't working, I was being wounded by the constant, intrusive knowledge of those numbers ticking upward, unanswered. It was bad enough before I'd been enhanced; now it was so much worse.

I chose to say something I knew would resonate with him. "Every moment I am out of commission, I feel defeated. Like our enemies have won."

"Rest is a weapon."

"I am rested." I tried as hard as I could to sound patient. "Let me at least begin to sharpen myself again."

He was quiet for a long moment. In my head, I began processing his refusal.

"With regular evaluations from Medical, and extremely close supervision, I will allow it," he said quietly.

My head jerked up. I opened my mouth to start to thank him, but he cut me off, raising his hand before I could make more than an inarticulate sound.

"Your time at work, including engaging in any strenuous cognitive activity or looking at screens of any kind, will be limited. I will personally provide you with these guidelines and expect strict adherence. You are not to put yourself at risk in any way until I am fully satisfied with your resilience."

My smile felt like it might break my face. "Thank you, Sir."

He stared at me with heavy seriousness. "There are further conditions."

"Of course."

"There is a project that I had hoped to bring to you, pending your full recovery. If you insist on returning early, I require that it be on this specific endeavor, which will allow me to directly supervise both your work and recuperation. As I determine you are able, you may assume your previous duties, in time. Do you agree?"

I looked at him a long moment. I'd hoped to get back to my team, to resuming the work I loved. I had been actively daydreaming new ways to ruin heroes' lives. This was a disappointment, but also deeply intriguing.

"I defer to your good judgment," I said, curious enough to acquiesce.

"Goodness has absolutely nothing to do with it," he promised, "but there will be a great deal of judgment."

By the time I made it back to my apartment, giddy and stunned, there was a message waiting in my email, informing me that my first assignment was to meet with Vesper the following morning. We were to immediately begin work to help me adjust to and maximize the potential of my new augmentations.

We met in the courtyard absurdly early, when the light was still slanted and golden and the lovely little green spaces mostly empty. He brought coffee, like a human angel, and welcomed me to the "cyborg club."

Our first lesson together involved me looking at things around me and telling him what I saw. It was shockingly arduous.

"You have to keep in mind that you're already perceiving more," Vesper said patiently. "The data is already there."

"I'd say it hurts," I said, rubbing my temple, "but that's not quite right." I was struggling with taking everything in. There were days when I missed my eye patch fiercely, which was something I never thought I'd say.

"Your brain is blocking much of it out or ignoring it because it's new. That data is overloading your ability to process everything you're seeing."

"It's like I can see *less*," I protested. We were sitting on a bench in one of the larger green spaces, surrounded by grass. Everything was drenched in light. It was an overwhelming experience—all the new information being gathered by my implants and augmentations, my new eye—a frantic jumble in my head.

"The new data clutters up what you're used to," Vesper said, nodding.

"It gives me a headache," I admitted.

"I don't doubt it. Okay, let's try this: What's the hardest thing to look at out here?"

I squinted and swung my head around. "Flowers," I said. "Definitely the flowers. They seem to be throbbing."

"Ah, so you can see ultraviolet now?"

"And some infrared."

"You're seeing what the bees can. They can see ultraviolet light, so the flowers have special patterns just for them."

"It's like . . . extra visual noise."

"Yes. Like more voices in a crowded room. Now take it further: What do you think it's trying to say?"

I breathed in, attempting to beat back the frustration, and looked again. There was a brilliant shock of white and purple crocuses spraying out of a clump of dirt nearby. Laid overtop of the familiar colors were much deeper hues—glass-bottle green and bilious yellow—and in the center of each a rich core of indigo.

"Bull's-eye," I said suddenly.

He cocked his head toward me, the lens of one mechanical eye narrowing like a camera's zoom.

"The marks, like concentric rings—they must help the bees aim." I looked again, seeing every flower like a beacon, more semaphore than decoration.

"Very good. It's all like this. It's all data. Everything new means something, but in a language you're still learning."

I looked down at my hands and forearms. The familiar skin was now a complex, battered landscape of freckles and dimples, splattering errors of pigmentation, scars, and sun damage. An ocean of evidence.

"I'm not sure if this makes everything uglier or more beautiful," I said.

"Both." His face had a wise, robotic sadness in that moment.

"I like infrared better," I admitted. It was almost pleasant to study the way the body radiated heat. The slightly cool pits of the eyes, the warm cavern of the mouth, the pulse fluttering in the neck.

"That's how mosquitoes see us," Vesper said. "Always out for blood." He paused a moment and then suggested, "Try to focus on just that: just the heat. Push the other data away."

I couldn't isolate it entirely, but I did find that, with practice, I could focus on a single spectrum. Infrared was the easiest to sort out—seeping heat so different from the bounce of light. My infrared vision wasn't in color, like it would be represented if I were wearing goggles: the cooler blacks, blues, and greens, teasing yellows, surging reds and purples. In my new eyes, it was something else entirely—a depth and richness, an issue of saturation more than hue. I fancied I could almost smell it as much as see it.

I watched a young woman take off her jacket and stretch. I stared a bit, entranced by the hot vulnerability of her underarms, the veins and nerves so close to the surface. Something I didn't say to Vesper was that part of the unexpected deluge of sensory data was learning there were so many new things I was attracted to. Suddenly someone's heart rate was stunning, or their array of capillaries made me breathless. I had a whole new library of preferences to deconstruct and fret about.

"It makes me feel so naked," I said.

"How so?" Vesper was watching me carefully.

"I'm also giving off all of this information. Anyone could look at me and see where all my blood is, where my softest parts are, what the sun has done to my skin."

"Not everyone."

I looked at him sharply and smirked. "No, but you sure can."

"Well." He blushed. Or, rather, I watched a warmth surge to the surface of his skin. "Welcome."

"The strangest thing is that so much of what I can see now seems to be saying the same thing. Flowers, mammals—doesn't matter."

"What's it saying?"

"'I'm delicious. Eat me.'"

We fell into a pattern quickly. We'd meet in the court-yard, he'd bring me a coffee, and we would look at things together. I started learning to handle the visual data I was taking in broadly at first, getting a sense of the different spectrums I was seeing and what each new color or hue or intensity meant in a basic sense. It wasn't long before I started to get a much more sophisticated sense of what I was seeing, Vesper helping me decode it instead of my just coping with the processing. I started to see the difference between a nervous flush in the presence of a new lover and the way heat redistributed in someone's body when they were lying. I began to get a sense of what the color of fear was.

In the process, I learned that his innate gentleness and generosity were not the only reason he was willing to spend so much time with me. It took brain surgery and superpowers, but I was finally starting to learn how to decipher when someone found me attractive. His interest had scent and color, temperature and vibrational frequency. It was quantifiable and measurable, and there was something deeply comforting in that. I didn't feel capable of exploring the attraction, but I didn't discourage it either. I tried to treat his fondness with care, and found I hoped I would be able to give those feelings more space at some nebulous point in the future.

As overwhelming as it was for me, my enhanced data intake was still extremely limited. One of the most surprising discoveries I made during the early stages of our work was that Leviathan displayed almost none of the vulnerabilities I was learning to detect. His armor blocked any heat his body emitted, aside from the faintest ghosts of warmth around the joints and between the plates. And he was not a walking bull's-eye of ultra-violet light. Instead, he simply glowed, his armor lit up like the bioluminescence generated by the weird-est creatures dwelling in ocean trenches. His shoulder blades, I realized with a start, even had eyespots: a warning.

After just under a month of working with Vesper, I found myself sitting in the deep chair opposite Le-viathan's desk while he stood behind me, enduring the last screening before he decided whether he was going to permit me back on the job sooner rather than later. He'd called me in to unveil the new project he had in mind for me.

I was deeply interested in discovering what this was, but in the moments while he pulled up the files, I al-lowed myself to indulgently stare. I'd developed this bad habit whenever his attention drifted elsewhere, to an instrument or screen, filling those moments by just looking at him. Now, I realized after a few seconds that he was fully aware of me watching him steadily and was looking back with an expression I would have called amusement in someone I believed capable of the emotion.

I cracked an embarrassed smile. "I'm still getting used to the new equipment," I said, tapping the side of my head. "Forgive the vacant expression."

"Anything but vacant," he replied, turning away from me to change the wall-size display screen in his office from a lifelike view of the outdoors to a massive data feed. He began to pull up and organize files and folders on the desktop, layering things over each other.

"'Hyperfocused' is perhaps a better word," I ventured. "It's easy now to allow a single thing to command my attention."

"Your myopia will become less severe as your abilities develop," he said crisply, throwing images and documents onto the display as though he were dealing cards in a casino. "You will find yourself caught between the gravity of a specific detail and how that detail fits into a larger context. How you navigate that space will come to define you."

I wasn't sure if Leviathan was complimenting or threatening me (a common problem when interacting with him), so I didn't reply. Instead, I watched his hands for a few minutes, making quick, vicious little movements across the surface of the touch screen embedded in his desk. There was something barely controlled in the way he was handling the files, and it dawned on me that he was actually quite angry.

I turned my attention to the screen on the wall above us. He was now arranging the files, photos, media clippings, our own data files.

"If you wish to return to work," he said quietly, "then I require you to assist me with something quite specific."

"This is all about Supercollider," I said. The hero's name, image, or insignia was on every single bit of data scattering across the screen. "I'll do anything you need."

Leviathan's hands slowed. He pulled one photo of Supercollider out into a far corner of the screen: the hero in motion, one hand raised in a fist, framed by sky and sunlight as he flew. In another corner he placed negative publicity—culled from damage estimates, police reports, insurance claims—in an unsettlingly small pile. Other data, he tossed around seemingly at random, as though waiting for a pattern to emerge.

"What do you see?" Leviathan asked abruptly.

"Is this everything significant we have?"

"Nearly."

"It's . . . frustrating."

"Why's that?"

"Most of the data is useless."

"Explain that."

I sat back and considered the request. Then I leaned forward, rubbing two fingers across my left eyebrow, where there was still an ache from my implants healing.

"We have so little on him, and even less that could be weaponized."

"Go on."

"There's no way to get under his skin right now. He has no alter ego to reveal. He has no life outside of being a superhero—it permeates every aspect of his identity. He's a walking archetype more than he is a person."

"What else?"

"He's impervious, and I don't just mean physically—although knowing you can fire a nuke at the fucker and he won't stay down is annoying as hell." Leviathan made a rumbling sound I recognized as a laugh. "The entire world is invested in what he is, in maintaining and upholding it. Besides, there's no point in trying to tear down the facade because there's nothing beneath it."

He inclined his head slightly. I squinted at the screen. "May I?"

He gestured me over to the touch screen on his desk. It felt a little strange to be on the other side, with Leviathan so close, near my shoulder, watching, instead of across from me, demonstrating. Tentatively, I touched the surface, getting a feel for it. Once I got a sense of the friction of it, I started to rearrange things.

After working for a while, I asked Leviathan, "Now, what do *you* see?"

He was quiet a long moment, then said, barely audible, "He's hollow."

I nodded. "The reason we don't see anything to exploit is because there isn't anything. He—"

Something caught my attention and my brain refocused on it mid-thought. I'd come across a cached copy of a news story and now expanded it. It was coverage from my rescue from the medical facility at Dovecote.

I'd avoided reading too much about the aftermath of my time there, finding that any direct reminder of my near-lobotomy would suddenly make me feel as though my chest were closing in. As usual, the story was framed as an attack. But this time, the attack wasn't attributed to Leviathan, but another villain. Larvomancer had immediately, even gleefully, taken credit, claiming that his "exploding grubs" had caused the damage. Leviathan didn't need to tell me he'd invited the vivisectionist to take credit; Larvomancer was a diva always looking to bolster his reputation, so his cooperation probably hadn't been expensive.

What surprised me was that law enforcement was willing to go along with Larvomancer's story so readily. Despite the only tenuous evidence being that the damage to the medical building involved explosions, both the police and the Draft immediately adopted the narrative.

"Only Supercollider, Hero of the Burning Oceans Crisis and Right Hand of Superheroic Affairs, seemed disturbed by the Special Task Force's findings," the article read. "While the hero, who was in town on a diplomatic mission"—I snorted aloud at this—"would not elaborate, his face clouded throughout the press conference. In response to questions from the press, he merely hinted that he expected 'something even more sinister' was responsible for the attack."

I moved the story aside and pulled up a video search. It wasn't difficult to find a copy of the press conference in question, given at Dovecote immediately after I was broken out. The director of the Special Task Force was a dour man with terrible wire-framed glasses and salt-and-pepper hair. He said with a confident authority that they had their target identified and would be pursuing Larvomancer with all their significant resources. Sure enough, there stood Supercollider behind him, his face a grim mask.

Even looking at the hero's visage was difficult. It was suddenly impossible to breathe comfortably. I forced myself to study him, his controlled anger and disappointment. He was unmoving and implacable behind the podium. He was contained.

I paused the video and enlarged it so I could look at Supercollider's face more closely. It was pixelated, but there was something in the set of his eyebrows that bothered me.

"He knows," I said, mostly to myself. "He knows what happened and he's standing there like these normal people in suits can actually control him. He says almost nothing, even though he knows exactly what must have occurred. Even though he hates it, he's allowing them to pursue their incorrect line of inquiry. Why doesn't he just march the Draft up here?"

"The fool wouldn't dare," Leviathan spat. It occurred to me that staring at Supercollider's face might be difficult for him as well; I closed the video and turned to look at him. His posture was even straighter and stiffer than usual.

"Of course. Even he wouldn't be that reckless," I said soothingly. "It's just that he doesn't *insist*; he doesn't take control of the situation and begin any kind of response. He's waiting for the support structures around him to move into place first and then will follow."

Something else happened then: there was a shift in my brain. It felt weirdly mechanical, like a building settling on its foundations. I felt slightly dizzy and outside myself, for just a moment, before my mind righted itself. I found I was gripping the desk and my cane for support. Leviathan had moved closer. He wasn't touching me but was prepared to leap into action if I fell.

"His support structure . . ." I repeated.

I shook my head to clear it, and stood straighter. Letting go of my cane, I let my hands fall back to the touch screen. I started closing files on the display, clearing room. I could see something—a network, a web—so clearly in my head and needed to illustrate it.

I dragged the image of Supercollider into the center of the now empty screen and left him there. Around him, I began to arrange other images, web clippings, and files, like spokes in a wheel: Doc Proton, his mentor; the Collision Project, which had magnified his powers; the law enforcement agencies he collaborated with; Accelerator, the young hero who served as his kick; and Quantum Entanglement, his partner, who rivaled him in power, if not fame and reverence.

"This is what he is," I said. "This is what makes him a hero."

I added references to the scientists and government agents who had made him and supported him, as well as other old heroes who'd trained him.

"*This* is his identity," I continued. "It's not what's within him that's important. What's within him might be nothing. It's what's around and outside him that matters."

Both of us were silent for a long moment, staring. His photograph isolated in the center of the massive screen, Supercollider suddenly didn't look like a force of nature. He looked lonely and small.

He looked human.

As we both looked at the data in front of us, Leviathan came to stand behind me, very close. It was like being close to a server tower, filling me with a deep, subaudible hum. I found myself holding especially still, waiting for his hand to rest on my shoulder or support my arm, but he didn't touch me. "I thought I knew the depths of his treachery," he said very quietly. "I knew what a foul, duplicitous creature he was. But in the war of attrition that consumed us both, I allowed my anger to cool. I abandoned outright conflict for smaller, meaner victories. I allowed the ground between us to become unsullied by blood."

I turned my head slightly, looking over my shoulder at him. His hands were clenched so tight I swore I could hear the gauntlets creaking. I could feel the anger arcing off him, and I felt a ripple of an ecstatic kind of fear.

"I took peace for respect," Leviathan continued. "I believed that he thought, as did I, that we were too evenly matched as adversaries, that the glories had become too small and the costs too great for open aggression." He ground his mandibles. "I see now that he believes me weak." He looked at me. It was hard not to flinch. "He would dare to lay a hand upon one of mine, upon a trusted lieutenant?" He lifted a fist toward my face, and gradually uncoiled his fingers. He swept his hand close to my jaw and temple, over my eye. His gesture encompassed my circuitry. "That he would think he could do this is insult I can barely fathom.

"By the end, he will know how wrong he has been."

He looked back to the screen and the structure of information I had built, and I took the breath I didn't realize I was holding. I followed his line of sight.

"I shall have to remind them why they are so afraid of me."

"I know how," I said quietly.

His head jerked, and I felt him looking at me again.

I kept my eyes fixed upward. "I can see it."

"What would you do, Auditor?"

I thought a moment, got the phrasing right. This might be the best opportunity I'd ever have to prevent damage of this scale. All the lives the hero would blow apart, the people he'd hurt and the livelihoods he'd destroy; all the villains he'd create and all the evil he'd unleash; all of it might be avoidable. This could be my one shot to stop the natural disaster that was Supercollider. What would you say, if you could shut down an earthquake?

"I would cut every cable, knock down every beam, tear out every bit of foundation supporting him. I would rip the world down around him. It's everything surrounding him that makes him a hero, so I would take everything he touches and relies on away. With all that gone, if you met him alone on an empty plain, what would be left?"

I could feel sweat on my forehead and my hands were shaking. There was a long beat of silence, silvery and mercurial. I was certain for a moment that I had managed to say something very stupid. But then a remarkable thing happened: Leviathan threw back his head and laughed.

It sounded like a locust singing.

5

We went after Accelerator first.

The kick was an outlier. As I immersed myself completely in the data of Supercollider's career, I noticed almost all of the missions with the highest cost, the largest body count, involved Accelerator. When Supercollider worked alone or with other heroes, he wasn't exactly mindful of property damage, but with Accelerator in the mix he was a wrecking ball. Most remarkable, though, were the additional *civilian* casualties that resulted whenever Accelerator was on the scene with him. With the kick at his side, there was a surge in collateral damages.

I analyzed those missions and formed a hypothesis: Supercollider was more dangerous because he was *protecting* Accelerator. If a speeding car was headed for the kick, he'd toss it out of the way, regardless of the fact there was a family on the sidewalk and an old man driving. He'd knock a building down to save his charge, whereas if he'd been alone he might have only kicked in a few doors. He valued Accelerator's life above anyone else's he happened to encounter, and the cost of that value was spectacularly high.

Accelerator himself was relatively harmless. He was bad for the world, certainly, but nowhere near the scale of Supercollider. He could have been offset by becoming vegan and making regular donations to Greenpeace.

Personally I bore him no ill will. He'd been in the room when my leg was shattered, but he'd done nothing to cause the injury and, as best as our intelligence could determine, had no knowledge of or involvement in my abduction. By all reports, he was a perfectly decent, if slightly arrogant, young man.

But when he was around his mentor, he made the scourge of a hero so much worse. If Supercollider was a forest fire, Accelerator was the drought that turned the leaves to tinder. Neither the numbers nor the body count left any question as to our course of action.

I chose him first because he was vulnerable in other ways as well. He was relatively new to Supercollider's inner circle, so it would be harder to notice irregularities in Accelerator's behavior. His speed was physics-defying, to the point of being the subject of several Ph.D. theses. This made him nearly impossible to track and hit, and capable of mind-numbing feats of nimbleness. But his body was surprisingly fragile, uniquely adapted to deal with the friction, the wear and tear associated with speed, but he remained vulnerable to most kinds of damage.

When I proposed focusing our efforts on Accelerator, the challenge wasn't convincing Leviathan of the target. Instead, it was getting him to stick to the plan and exercise restraint. As soon as I mentioned Accelerator, he was ready to hire a double-jointed Russian cleaner to fire a blowgun dart into his neck and call it a day.

"I don't want to start with assassination," I explained patiently. "There are many ways that this can go. We ran a lot of simulations besides killing and the numbers look good in all of them."

"How would you set things in motion, then?" His arms were crossed and there were subtle patterns flashing across his armor, as if he were an agitated squid. He was clearly a little annoyed at being contradicted, but interested enough to at least allow the line of inquiry.

"Drive a wedge between Accelerator and the hero," I said, curling my hand around a cup of tea. We were sitting at the long table in his office. The display screen was off, and neither of us was paying attention to any data outputs other than each other. We'd both been in the mood for some good, old-fashioned plotting.

"And how would you sow these seeds of discord?"

"They're already planted, we just need to water them. Accelerator thinks his mentor is holding him back. It's out of affection, sure, but he feels too protected and believes he cannot prove himself while being overshadowed."

"Yet he does seem rather content in the shade cast by the colossus; he makes no move to spread his wings and seek the sky." Leviathan drummed his fingers on the surface of the table.

"Not yet, but let's give him a nudge and see what happens."

"A nudge."

"A romantic one, I think."

I assigned Nour to the job I had in mind. Nour, who inspired such trust and confidence in everyone she spoke to, who was so lovely and cordial, who could make you feel like her whole world revolved around you simply because of the way she listened. We scrubbed her record, got her an internship with the massive PR conglomerate that represented Supercollider's North American activities, and let her work her magic.

She and Accelerator were seeing each other within a month. She'd studied hard for the role. She took to wearing a perfume that smelled like vanilla, almond, and cinnamon to evoke his favorite cookies, and wore purple like his grandmother favored. And she listened—oh, how she listened. And we listened too, via the robin's-egg-size surveillance device she swallowed before every date. Though it was slightly muffled by the barrier of her body and distorted by the steady whoosh of her heart, we were still able to clearly hear that fast, fierce, proud boy pour his soul out to her with only the gentlest bit of prodding.

She made him feel like a young god. She made him forget how little experience he had and how often he felt afraid. She made him forget his mistakes and remember only his victories, see his potential as his present. He could be a great hero in his own right, she insisted, and could start right now to build his own legacy and gain the credit he rightfully deserved. She made him believe in that entitlement with every fiber of his being.

"He's smothering you," Nour cooed. "He doesn't mean to, but he is. Like a tree overshadowing a sapling, he's denying you light, keeping you small."

"What should I do?" he said fretfully, his lips at her neck.

"Reach for the sun."

After a few months of her making him feel invincible, Accelerator approached Supercollider and asked for things to change. He wanted a vastly expanded role in team operations. He didn't want to be a kick any longer, but a colleague. He wanted a full partnership.

The falling-out was legendary.

Supercollider felt Accelerator was asking for too much too soon, becoming ambitious before his powers fully blossomed and he was adequately prepared. He also knew that his kick was intensely vulnerable, more so than Accelerator would ever admit. He was that perfect combination of offended and terrified that made him explode like an overbearing parent.

Accelerator, of course, interpreted his hero's resistance as an attempt to put him in his place and belittle him, just as Nour suggested. Things got ugly. There were some very awkward media appearances where Accelerator went off script. He repeatedly no-showed for major crises where he was expected to assist, and even worked a few operations alone, without Supercollider's knowledge or permission.

Things got so tense I wondered if there would be a public confrontation, but it didn't come. Whatever happened between the two of them, those words were exchanged in private. Even Nour wasn't able to ascertain whether Accelerator was fired or quit. She had to write a report about the encounter—he burst into her apartment without warning, eyes feverish, still full of adrenaline from that final argument. She didn't have time to swallow a surveillance device, so she tried to reconstruct his manic ranting from memory. The phrase he repeated over and over was "I'm on my own now."

In the days that immediately followed, there was a scramble to assemble a hastily constructed narrative of personal growth and achievement, and suddenly Accelerator was setting himself up as an independent hero. A press conference was called. Accelerator alone spoke to the media, his words their usual blur. His elocution coaches were forever pressing him to slow down, take his time, but that day the words sped out of him.

He was grateful, so grateful, for everything Supercollider had taught him, but it was time to move on. "I'm ready to run at my own speed," he said, and the press gallery laughed obediently. Quantum Entanglement had a seat nearby, serene and achingly beautiful. She was there to congratulate the young hero on his new venture, while Supercollider was conveniently kept away by a top secret mission.

I was watching the press conference from my desk, running through possibilities for our next moves, when my head buzzed with the specific tone reserved exclusively for messages from Leviathan. I pulled out my phone.

> Shall we kill him now?

I smiled involuntarily.

> I'd rather maim at this stage.

> I am impatient.

> Trust me.

> I will. Do not let me down. It is time for blood, Auditor.

With that directive, I did something more direct than I had ever done before: quietly, with little fanfare, I placed a hit on Accelerator through a series of middlemen and false fronts. It was a common thing to do, and most heroes had a host of bounties out on them at any moment. For most henches, it was a "welcome to the neighborhood" type of hit, almost friendly, almost a courtesy. And it didn't necessarily mean that Accelerator was about to die.

I knew what I was doing; I knew I was placing him in danger. I wanted him to feel out of his league, and vulnerable. I wanted him to be hunted from the very moment he was on his own, to put him and Supercollider under more, ever-increasing stress. I wanted to give Leviathan everything he wanted.

Accelerator had spent too much time hiding behind the invulnerable muscles of his benefactor, and thanks to us had started to forget how much he needed that shelter. He believed everything Nour had told him, and believed himself so much stronger than he was. When the threats started coming, he didn't falter or retreat— why would he? He was a hero! He met them head-on. I didn't expect him to be quite as foolhardy as he was after those first attempts on his life. But instead of becoming more cautious, he took more risks. He refused to be afraid.

And then, in a crowded, dirty alley, he was jumped by a handful of mercs while foiling a botched mugging. According to the narrative that ended up on the news, Accelerator found himself penned in, trapped by brick and bodies, with not quite enough room to utilize his superspeed or agility. There was trash everywhere, and in the middle of the fight, one of the hired goons got their hands on a discarded wine bottle. He broke it against the wall and, with an awkward, awful lurch, shoved the glass into the young hero's gut.

The wound was jagged and deep, and right away it was hard to control the bleeding. Splinters of glass had broken off when Accelerator had been kicked, bottle still in him, as he defeated the last of the hit men. The police arrived quicker than usual and he was whisked off to a Draft medical facility at record speed. The doctors cut him open and sewed him up, then went back in a few hours later when he kept hemorrhaging. His intestines had been sliced up, and during one of the attempts to repair the damage, a surgeon unknowingly perforated his bowel. Whether it was that or the filth on the bottle from the alley, his wounds became hopelessly infected. It took four days for sepsis to take him.

Supercollider's face as he spoke at the public memorial was like sickness itself. He looked as though he wanted to run, and had turned pallid beneath his perpetual tan. He spoke of Accelerator's bravery and potential, his voice breaking. He said he wished he could have done more.

"I could have stepped between them—" he said, and then suddenly he could speak no more, and walked out of the room entirely.

Leviathan and I watched the memorial in his office. Leviathan was unabashedly thrilled, puffed out and proud as a bird, pacing up and down. I couldn't share that pride. I knew the data supported our success, but mostly I felt a weird combination of nausea and guilt. I left his office as soon as I felt it was reasonable to do so. I spent most of the night afterward fighting off strange waves of tears.

We collected Nour after the funeral. I expected to be able to debrief her and, after whatever leave or therapy she needed, welcome her back on to the team. Instead, she asked to be released from her contract. A little bit of the warmth had gone out of her eyes, and there was a hardness around her mouth and in her shoulders now. I realized I had sacrificed her too for this assignment, ruined a bit of the gentleness that had always defined her. It was something she would never get back. I hadn't accounted for that.

I tried to apologize in her exit interview, but she cut me off.

"I knew what I was getting into," she said. "You told me what to expect, and I said I could handle it. That responsibility is mine."

"There is no way you could have really known."

Her mouth tightened. "You tried to tell me, at least. I appreciate that."

There was nothing else I could say. I allowed her to

go and let her know the door was always open for her, even while certain she'd never walk through it again.

Leviathan gave me space. He let me return to my former work for a time, as I had to rebuild the team and our relationships as best I could. He also seemed to sense I needed to retreat into the numbers for a while, to run experiments that only impacted heroes' lives in much tinier, less consequential increments. A marriage gone sour here, terrible table service there. No one dying.

But while I worked, I kept an eye on Supercollider. There was a haunted, hollow look in his eyes that refused to fade. I knew we had struck home. I knew I had been right. And that meant we'd have to take another swing at him, whether I was prepared for it or not.

At the first signs he might be beginning to heal, to regain a little bit of the titanic strength that defined him—no more than a genuine smile after a successful operation—I found myself called back to Leviathan's office, looking at the map of data I had drawn months before.

"It's time to move again," he declared, and I knew that he was right.

I stared, not speaking, as the monolithic certainty of what I had to do next rose within me.

"What shall we destroy next?" he asked almost giddily.

Without a word, I expanded a photograph of Quantum Entanglement, and Leviathan crowed in sheer glee. Pleasing him ignited something in my chest, like I had a heart full of brimstone. As we plotted, leaning together over documents and data feeds, I felt a sliver of ice in my stomach whenever I looked at an image of Quantum's face.

"I'm going to be fired."

A thing I always liked about Keller was that he was nearly impossible to shock. He was a cinder-block slab of a man, physically and intellectually built to be left standing after a natural disaster. Between his military career and his work with Leviathan, there weren't a lot of crises that he hadn't sailed through with frankly irritating placidity.

So it was very rewarding whenever I could make his heavy eyebrows shoot up his forehead.

He got his face under control quickly. "Well, that," he said as he refilled the pint glass in front of him, "is the biggest load of horse pucky I have ever heard."

"You say that like it's ridiculous."

"What, you suddenly suck at your job or something?"

"Yes, Keller. Exactly that."

"Bullshit." He sucked a bit of condensation off the tip of a fat finger.

"I can't do this job."

"Your job?"

"This job."

"The fuck you talking about."

I took a deep breath. "I don't know if I can ruin Quantum."

He hummed. "You caught the feelings?"

"No. Maybe. I don't know." I rubbed my temple, letting my fingers trail into my hairline to the scar tissue there.

Keller's eyes followed my hand, caught the significance of the gesture. "After what he did to you, you don't want to tear him to the ground?"

I gritted my teeth. "It's not that. I want him to fucking burn." I looked down at my wrists, saw my pulse fluttering there. I concentrated on bringing my heart rate down, on cooling the heat flushes I could now see close to the surface of my skin in infrared.

Keller waited. "Good," he said finally. "So what's the goddamn problem."

"It's not her fault."

"So this isn't about him, it's about her."

"She didn't do this to me."

He looked at me impatiently. "It's not about her, it's about the numbers. Even I've sat through enough of your goddamn PowerPoints to know that."

I smiled sadly. "They're pretty good PowerPoints."

"And my *point* is"—I groaned at his pun—"the numbers work. You proved to us they worked. That kid died, but how many people get to survive because of it? I know you know. You're going to ruin this hero's life, but how many lives are better when it happens?"

I said nothing, but I did know. Every day I watched the cost of Supercollider rise.

"Also, fuck her. She's his partner. She warms his bed and cleans his cock and picks up his messes and makes his awful life more comfortable every day."

He was right. She gentled every edge in his life, lessened every blow he might have taken. She helped him immensely and her loss would reduce his capacity immensely. I'd run all that math and knew it worked out.

The numbers didn't lie.

"She's his right hand," Keller continued. He pounded on the table. "Chop it off."

I was quiet a long time. "I also think he makes her miserable."

He opened his mouth to say something, changed his mind, and waited. No one listened like Keller did when he really felt like it.

"I think she barely exists to him. She's as strong as he is, easily, but she's clipped and bound and confined in a thousand tiny ways to be a support to him instead of having the position she deserves. Accelerator needed to be in his shadow, but not her. She's stuck standing behind him, and I think she hates it."

He thought this over for a moment, then shrugged. "Love's fucked."

I shook my head. "I don't even think he likes her all that much; he ignores her as much as he can and treats her like a photo op the rest of the time. I don't think she likes him either." I didn't say it out loud, but in my head I played some of the hours and hours of video of their interactions I'd watched over the past few weeks. The way she carefully kept a bit of distance between them whenever she could and, when she couldn't, the way she micro-flinched when he touched her. You might only see it if you were looking for it, like I was.

Keller rolled his almost empty glass around in his hand. "Sounds to me," he said, leaning back in his chair and rubbing the stubble on his scalp, "that you'd be doing her a favor."

I felt something shuffle into place inside my head. I didn't feel any better about it. There was still an awful, sour pit in my stomach. But a few more tumblers had clicked in place.

Soon, Keller was yawning and we called it a night. Instead of going back to my apartment, I took a walk. I was irritatingly sober; one of the unexpected side effects of having a traumatic brain injury was that drinking was out of the question. Now my head was always clear, always crisp and humming cleanly; there was no way to look away from anything uncomfortable, or unsatisfying, or raw. I was always sheer and sharp.

So, I walked. Walking by myself was still frightening. Long after my stitches were out, hypervigilance left me constantly holding my breath, waiting for a van to pull up behind me, for hands to wrap around my mouth. I'd never been good at being kind to myself, so the only way through that I knew was exposure therapy. Safe in the fortress that was Leviathan's compound, I walked through my anxiety, through the lingering old fear, until it was familiar, worn smooth, almost friendly. Just an extra little jangle in the already crackling discomfiture in my head. The fear became comforting.

Under all the white noise and unhappiness, as I walked, I started to sift data. I thought about Quantum crossing oceans to take up her new position as one of the great heroes of our age, traveling from New Zealand and leaving everyone she knew behind. I thought about her early power assessments, her staggering ability to reshape the very fabric of reality around her. I thought about the interviews she gave where she talked about choosing to get her face tattoos, a deeply personal Maori rite of passage, when she learned she'd be working with Supercollider.

I thought about the private investigator whom Quantum Entanglement had hired nearly a decade ago, expecting to confirm her grim certainty that Supercollider was fucking his PA, or a cop, or a younger hero; I thought about how the PI had turned up nothing but the bland horror of his neglect. I thought about her dry-cleaning bills. I thought about the keyloggers installed on every device she touched, about all the reports that went back to Supercollider's team about her fucking a bodyguard, or a bartender, or a hero. I considered her partner's stark disinterest in these indiscretions. I thought about how her vast potential had been spurned and reduced to force fields and fireworks.

Looking for weak spots, I found myself holding the manuscript to an extraordinary tragedy. Probing for a way I could dismantle their relationship, I found that the bond between Supercollider and Quantum was hideously sterile, barren as a dead moon. Looking for things to undo, I found her already so awfully betrayed and undone.

I expected that whatever plan I came up with, whatever awful series of events I decided to set in motion, would be the great horror of her life. It hit me, though—walking through the sweet coolness of that night garden over and over again—that Supercollider was already the worst thing that had ever happened to her. I would just be forcing her to confront it. That realization gave me the last push I needed to finally set my plan in motion.

My leg ached by the time I finally let myself go back to my apartment. It was much warmer inside, and the sudden change in temperature made me feel at once clammy and oily. I showered irritably and, still wrapped in a towel, opened up my laptop and started to work.

"Take me through it. One step at a time." Leviathan sat behind his desk, fingers steepled. His voice was nothing but cool efficiency, and it worried me. I'd hoped for a hint of murderous glee at least.

"Were you displeased with my proposal?" I worked hard to keep my voice even, to tackle this like a logic problem. No amount of rationalizing could keep me from feeling devastated, verging on panicked, at the prospect of his disapproval.

He made a humming noise. "I wish to understand your thought process, how you arrived at this course of action." He was giving me space. I wasn't sure, however, if he was throwing me a line or giving me enough rope.

"Certainly." I stood—I had been sitting across from him—and hovered my hands over the touch screen on the surface of his desk, wordlessly asking *may I?* He inclined his head in assent and then turned his attention to the wall screen. I started to rearrange data, make it messier, more reflective of the place where I had begun.

"When I first tried to tackle this problem, I thought it would be fairly simple. My initial impulse was to find a way to destroy Quantum Entanglement's relationship with Supercollider."

"A logical first step." There was perhaps the tiniest bit of petulance in his voice now. I realized that he was hoping for something bloodier. I wanted to repeat one of his adages about patience back at him, but let him fume quietly on his own, changing course ever so slightly.

"It would be devastatingly simple; I would find all of the lies between them, all the little untruths, everything they kept from each other, all the pits and worms in their hearts."

He liked that; the sound he made was a slightly happier one.

"It would be a process that started slow, a gradual lifting of veils and ripping out stitches until one of them encountered something so abject and disgusting it ruptured them badly enough that I could really sink my hooks in." I moved some data files around for him to take note of: recorded phone conversations, PI reports, hotel reservations, audio clips from disgusted, gossiping security guards.

He scanned the data; I expected him to react to it differently, to recognize how damning some of it was. Nothing registered the way that I imagined. "And what is this unforgivable injury?" It occurred to me that since we were talking about relationships, I shouldn't expect him to have a recognizable frame of reference.

"To be honest, I was not sure which of these would be the final straw. I had guesses, but it would be up to them what represented the breaking point."

"Fair. Continue."

"Then, I figured things would happen quickly and terribly. They would tear each other and their relationship apart, and both of them live so publicly there would be no way it wouldn't spill over."

"What you have just described is the plan I expected from you." It took a mighty effort not to shrink away physically from his disappointment. "What I have before me is very different."

I nodded. "I know it is."

The grill over his mouth wavered in irritation.

I was not very good at speeches yet, but I summoned one. "Expecting to begin turning over rocks and find maggots wriggling underneath, I instead lifted the first stone and found only salt. With the lightest pressure, the facade of their lives fell away to reveal a stricken, barren landscape. Expecting excess and decadence and despair, I found only the stark, silent ugliness of something that had *already* been razed to the ground."

That startled him. He sat back suddenly; I fancied I could hear the liquid click of him blinking.

I pushed forward. "I realized I had to rethink this plan. I didn't need to reveal their awfulness to each other; that terrible task was long done. What I could do, however, was show the world just a bit of the horror I had uncovered. It wasn't Supercollider and Quantum I needed to rip apart; it was the world's infatuation with them."

"You are ruining a different kind of romance," he said, something clearly clicking into place for him. This was a kind of relationship he understood: he knew what it was to be loved, or hated, by the general population.

"Precisely. They aren't even bothering to lie to each other, so there's nothing there to ruin. They don't love each other, but the world still loves them."

"So how will you sully that love story."

"In almost the exact same way." I started to pull up different pieces of information now: images of public adulation for Supercollider, news stories that were obviously spun and wrong. "Imagine the world is Supercollider's lover. He's lying to them, and they blissfully believe him. Since these are the lies that have any meat—the ones with any love, any investment behind them—these are the stories we have to dismantle."

He stared up at the screen for a while, making his small thinking sounds. I imagined that he spoke quietly to himself while turning something over in his head, and it came through his armor's external audio feed muffled and strange.

"It's the first steps that trouble me," he said eventually.

"It's a deceptively benign beginning."

"Exactly. It strikes me as too conservative, in a way that you never are."

I realized that backhanded compliment might just give me the space to maneuver in this conversation that I needed. "When you're trying to ruin a relationship, you don't go for the big-ticket items first. It might seem logical to go straight for the deepest hurts: infidelity, abuse, drugs."

He didn't respond, but was listening, and carefully. If strategically exploiting weak spots in romantic relationships was not something he had much experience with, as I suspected, this would all be new data for him.

"When you aim for the core, relationships close ranks. Even if someone knows that what you're saying is true, they'll flagrantly deny it. They'll deny it harder exactly *because* it's true. Then the armor goes up and the daggers come out and you will find yourself facing a united front."

"You theorize that the public would leap to Supercollider's defense if you reveal the worst of his treachery at once."

"Yes. So we start inconsequential. Skirt the big issues and go for the irritants."

"The pain points they feel safe in admitting to."

I started to smile. He was following me, picking up the bread crumbs now. "If a partner has a gambling problem, start ruining the dry cleaning and the take-out orders. Add a few minor, unrelated expenses to a household secretly being bled dry. Those small bothers will burrow right down into the heart meat quicker than you can believe."

"I can believe it." There was a little buzz of excitement in his voice now.

"Even if the infection is slow to spread, it's better to let it fester long and deep."

He looked at the screen again, tapping his fingertips on the surface of his desk.

"Don't disappoint me," he said eventually, and my heart leapt.

Being dismissed from that meeting felt like a release, and by the time I got back to my desk my hands were shaking badly. Experiencing a sense of relief after leaving his presence was new, and I disliked it intensely. I collapsed into my office chair and cradled my head in my hands for a few minutes. I had pushed aside how stressful—no, how frightening—Leviathan could be when he was anywhere close to displeased. I was very lucky in that I saw it so seldom, that my competence dovetailed so well with his priorities. Being confronted with the fact that I was just as capable of irritating him or letting him down as anyone else was a rude reminder.

I thought of June with sudden, intense longing. I wished I could tell her how stupid all of my feelings were, so she could make fun of me. I pulled out my phone and stared at it for a moment.

I put it away.

Once I got my heart rate under control and started to consider next steps, I came to the deeply unpleasant realization that I was going to have to weaponize my own pain to pull off the plan I had in mind. This was something I had avoided. I'd watched myself become ever more dispassionately willing to sacrifice someone else's trauma to the gristmill (I felt a pang for Nour in that moment). It was now time to offer up my own badly knit flesh, the parts of me that were broken and unrecognizable. I knew it was the only way to get the best work out of myself.

There was a version of me that was still sympathetic. It wasn't what I was now, or more precisely, what I was becoming. Someone who was constantly performing elaborate equations to calculate the most accurate pain points and best places to sow misery was not someone it was easy to feel sorry for. I was now someone who saw in infrared and ran the math on death. But there were parts of me, the ragged parts I was rapidly discarding, that could inspire my pity.

My leg still throbbed. I'd never walk the same way again. I had been treated badly by both heroes and villains, and that wounded loneliness was something I could offer. I couldn't be the only one who'd escaped an encounter with Supercollider and was left in a similar state. There must be others he'd hurt. A reporter somewhere who'd been at the wrong place at the wrong time. Someone with an audience and a voice who'd been "Supercollided."

I didn't go to the gossip columnists with some of the uglier details I had found, offering a sordid and juicy tale of a sham marriage. I didn't go after the elaborate structures built to hide Supercollider's broken personality, or the less wholesome habits that Quantum had picked up to cope with her loneliness. Instead, I found an older, respected columnist with a complex spinal injury from his own now long-ago encounter with a hero. And then I put on what was unquestionably the most difficult voice I had ever assumed: my own. Shakily, as Anna, the scared and injured temp worker, I reached out to him to see if he could help me tell my story.

McKinnon was at first warm but brusquely professional, yet I knew I got my hooks in; the program I had installed to tell me when my emails were read showed my first message was returned to over and over, often late at night. The journalist recognized the bewilderment and betrayal in my writing, a feeling that could only strike home to someone who had been living with partial paralysis for twenty years.

The journalist wanted more details, and I seemed to spook. I had to be anonymous, I explained, because

I had been threatened in the hospital. I understood if this meant he couldn't help me, I said.

My tactic worked. McKinnon warmed, softened, lured me back. If there were other sources who could go on record, the journalist said, the piece would work. It would just take some time and digging.

McKinnon then threw deeply personal pain on the table, and instead of the flash of guilt I expected to feel, I felt an uneasy camaraderie. We'd been through the same thing, and the journalist wanted to help me, even if our goals were different.

There was a little part of me, the weakest part of me, that didn't want McKinnon to proceed. That part of me hoped the leads would go nowhere and the story would fizzle out. That I wouldn't have to retraumatize this probably decent person. That maybe I wouldn't have to hurt anybody. It was a frail, weak part of me I was listening to less and less. I knew McKinnon's leads would pay off, because I had already done the research myself. Once the journalist found what I had, the story would have to be written.

McKinnon got back to me in less than a week. The email was vibrating with carefully leashed excitement. Over a dozen people willing to talk, with very little prompting, and many more confirmed they had stories but were too exhausted or afraid to talk about it. Two of them were willing to go on record.

"Your story, however anonymous, needs to be at the heart of it," McKinnon wrote. "Your story, and mine."

A few days later, I met the journalist in a nearly abandoned diner for the interview.

McKinnon rolled the chair back from the table crisply when I entered, a gesture filled with bright excitement—McKinnon would have stood in old-fashioned courtesy if it were possible. The journalist's smile was thin-lipped but warm, and reached bright green eyes hidden behind dirty glasses. I'd worn my own old glasses to better assume the character of my former self, though I didn't need them anymore (laser surgery once I had unlimited benefits plus a reconstructed optic nerve took care of that). McKinnon's hand was pale but warm when I shook it, and I realized how cold my fingers were.

There was already a steaming mug on the table, a handful of sugar packets and leaking creamers thrown down next to it.

"I ordered you a coffee," the journalist said unnecessarily. "It's terrible."

"Oh?" The corner of my mouth turned up.

"That's why I like it here. Food's bad enough that it's usually dead. Lots of privacy."

I nodded. I gathered three sugar packets together, shook them and tore them in unison. I spent a lot of time prepping my coffee, pouring each creamer in one at a time to make sure it wasn't curdled, stirring. I was stalling. McKinnon let me stall, patient but watchful.

"This is probably a bad idea," I finally said, gripping my hands around the mug. I didn't have to pretend to be nervous.

A somber nod. "Probably."

"I mean . . ." I shifted. I was wearing what felt like a costume of myself: the last, now ill-fitting set of clothes I had from my old temp days. I was covered in less makeup and more anxiety. My hair was in its former, frazzled bun. And I let all the old insecurity, all the fear and despair that once drove me, settle over my shoulders like an heirloom shawl.

I took a deep breath. "He's supposed to only hurt bad people. He's a hero. If you get hurt, you're a bad guy, right?"

McKinnon nodded. Those green eyes never left me as the journalist reached into a jacket pocket to pull out a voice recorder. "Can I use this?"

"Oh. I guess. Sure. Of course."

McKinnon placed it on the table between us. "Can you say that again." It was a command. A little red recording light had come on, and I could see a digital readout of the rise and fall of our voices, of the sounds in the diner as they were captured.

"What did I say?" The waveform representing my voice looked thin and warbling.

"About Supercollider hurting people."

I took a deep breath. "We're all told that we're safe. That Supercollider only hurts the villains. That if you get hurt, you must have been doing something wrong."

"Were you doing anything wrong, Anna?"

I felt tears sting my eyes. Strategically, I let them come. Not fall, but well up. I looked at him. "They told me I would just have to stand there."

McKinnon was still, but those green eyes gripped me, in that strange way people have when they are trying to hold you up and hold you together because they need something. I didn't meet them.

The pain was all there, all real, but I wasn't afraid of it. I had enough callus built up that I didn't think it would draw blood even if the edges were still sharp. "I wasn't doing anything right, I can admit that. I was a hench. I did data entry and I didn't really accomplish anything. I was just kind of getting by. And to be honest . . ." I impulsively touched my temple—

the first unintentional move I made during the meeting—brushing that scar. It was becoming a nervous habit. "Sometimes I think that if something like this happened to me, then clearly I wasn't being 'good enough.' I wasn't good enough to be safe. On some level, I think for a long time I felt like I deserved it."

"What do you think now."

Until then, I'd kept my eyes lowered, giving only flickering eye contact. But now I looked right at McKinnon, steady. I could see more than a serious, focused face: elevated heart rate, excitement blooming at every pulse point. There was a crackle across the journalist's scalp, a lovely blue ozone light.

"I don't think anyone deserves this. Not even villains."

McKinnon sat back a little. "So it's not that you came to realize that what happened to you shouldn't have, because you were a decent, ordinary person."

I shook my head. "No. Even if I was everything I was afraid I was. Even if I was terrible. It still never should have happened."

"You don't seem terrible."

"You haven't spoken to any of my exes."

The journalist cracked a smile.

I grinned back. "I'm no less terrible than any of us. Say, oh, a receptionist for Black Hat. Or whoever sets up the AV equipment for Gangrene. Or the PA who brings Leviathan his coffee in the morning." (His name is Dennis.)

"Say you did deserve it, though."

"Did I deserve a spiral fracture, years of physio, losing my livelihood? Did I deserve the intimidation that followed?" I let real anguish creep into my voice. "Isn't it more monstrous if the answer is everyone thinks I deserved whatever came to me?"

"I don't think that." McKinnon was quietly angry now, angry about his own injury. Doc Proton, Super-collider's mentor, had left the journalist with spinal trauma when McKinnon was a photographer in his early twenties. Starstruck and hungry, McKinnon ran toward the screams to take photos of a great superhero triumph. Doc Proton used a lamppost like a javelin to stop Lady Sonorous (it was a different time) from taking off in her supercar. Doc left the scene with the villain in handcuffs.

He also left that young photographer with T1–T3 fractures.

"I know you don't," I said quietly. "But I think a lot of people do. And I think the people who don't bat an eye when things like this happen to citizens or henches are the same people who think it's perfectly fine for the Claxon to nail Harpy to the side of an apartment building."

"That's not—the same thing." McKinnon's brow furrowed.

"It's definitely not. *I* can't cause microfractures in your bones or neurological disruptions by screaming at you. I definitely haven't used it to shatter an actor's teeth." I took a long drink from my horrible coffee. "But even if I had, I don't think nonlethal crucifixion is exactly an appropriate response."

"Right."

"My point is just, if we're willing to tolerate that, who is going to care about a temp worker's spiral fracture?"

Or a photographer's spinal injury. I let that unspoken sentence hang. The journalist's experience had been similar to mine; Supercollider had learned so much of his manner and affect and approach from his old hero. Proton was vaguely apologetic, but once he was satisfied that the young photographer he'd catastrophically injured wasn't a threat (with no aspirations to villainy), the hero forgot about McKinnon entirely.

The journalist was quiet for a while, jotting down a few notes despite recording everything I was saying. "How are you getting on now?" McKinnon's voice was a little absent as the piece started to take shape.

I smiled a little. "Better. I found work. I finally feel like I am being appreciated."

He called the piece "Collision Course."

McKinnon told several stories. The journalist spoke to a former cop who was disillusioned with the endless, senseless hero worship displayed by his colleagues. He had to go on permanent medical leave when a superheated beam passed a little too close to him and melted his sidearm to his hip. There was the story of a young woman who had the misfortune of being taken on a single date by a lowest-tier hero; her endless kidnappings and eventual assault were treated as rote, expected, unremarkable. I haunted the piece like a ghost, too frightened to reveal my name, but giving just enough tragic detail of my encounter with the Greatest of Heroes and serving as the impetus for the story to be written. But it was the depth and poignancy in how McKinnon's own trauma was exposed, and the way that the world accepted that young photographer's devastating injury as necessary collateral damage, that warmed the cockles of my blackening heart. The journalist exorcised demons on the page, dragged out every wound. It was affecting. It was devastating. And even though he was barely mentioned at all, it roasted Supercollider alive.

By the time I got to my desk, Jav had printed out the article, placed it in a real-life physical frame, and set it up next to my keyboard. He was beaming at me, his teeth starkly white against his lips.

"You're so romantically analog," I said. I felt heat rising to my face.

"You're trending," Darla called over their shoulder, their attention darting between the various social media feeds across three monitors.

"I hope not. I was promised anonymity."

They gave a half grunt of a laugh. "*It's* trending."

I perched on the desk next to them. "What did you use?"

"#mycollision. Got people talking about the ways heroes have fucked up their lives. Used a couple of the influencer accounts and it took off." They scrolled. "Some of these are fucking heartbreaking."

Darla slowed down a little so I could see the stories that were filling up the hashtag. A budding restaurateur whose business was physically demolished by an errant eye laser. A makeup artist blinded by psionics. A parade of mortified flesh: burned, crushed, frozen, liquefied. Buildings people saved years or decades to afford reduced to rubble by a hero blundering through. The endless reams of psychological damage. A litany of heroes leaving trauma blossoming in their wake.

It was harrowing and grotesque. It was better than I expected. I could see the cost climbing higher.

"I should run all of these numbers," I said absently.

"Do it later. What's next?" Darla's voice was excited, hungry.

I focused back on them. "I want to see where this goes." I shifted to my feet. "I want to see what gets picked up where. What comes out in the next wave of think pieces. I want this to simmer for a couple of weeks."

They nodded. I felt their ripple of disappointment. "So we track it?"

"For now. Keep an eye out for the testimonials. I want to know who has the most gutting stories, who gets interviewed because of what they tweeted, who decides to write all the 'it happened to me too' follow-ups. I want to know who is out for blood."

Darla made a noise; I knew what I said registered, but their attention was already laser-focused on the feeds cascading down the screens; I left them alone.

I put Javier to work recording instances of the hashtag and its evolutions and permutations, all the types of damage and loss people mentioned (physical, economic, emotional) as well as mentions of Supercollider specifically. Many of the terrible run-ins people had with heroes involved other caped idiots, but his name was coming up a fair amount. I wanted to know what these stories had in common, what the themes were. I wanted to see if there was a pattern to how he hurt people. I wanted to know the cost.

With Jav and Darla running with their tasks, I turned my attention back to Quantum. Over the next hours and days, I searched tirelessly for any mention of her, any stories of heroic negligence and dismemberment and destruction that she figured in, peripherally or prominently.

For someone at the right hand of such a force of destruction, Quantum Entanglement showed up remarkably little. The most physical injury she could be considered responsible for was when someone suffered burns when one of her force field bubbles didn't extend quite far enough to shield them, but it was a stretch. Now and again, she was mentioned as being responsible for property damage, but those reports were rare and the damage not really extensive.

But there was a phrase that began to turn up repeatedly, something that chilled me every time I read it: "She just stood there." When she showed up in the accounts of trauma and terror, she was never the cause, never the one raining blows or pulling down buildings. She was simply standing aside, watching horror taking place around her. She was absent, an eerily silent bystander.

It haunted me. I wanted to know what happened to her. I needed to know how someone who could change matter around them had been reduced to someone who stood by. I knew whatever had happened would be her undoing; and I suspected that, if I could dig deep enough, I could break the shell she had become.

I kept the larger plot around Quantum close to my chest, but as I read the stories and analyzed the sentiment reports, I knew what I needed was some good, old-fashioned scheming. I decided to let Jav, Darla, and Tamara in on things, and invited Vesper for good measure (for all his generosity he could be delightfully cruel when he set his mind to it). The five of us took over a conference room, I brought a terrible amount of candy, and we set about methodically ruining our teeth and her life.

"Everybody loves adultery."

"Do you think that's the first thing we should go for?"

"It's a real crowd-pleaser."

"It's true. Seems cliché, though."

"It's cliché because it works."

"I am not disputing that, I just want to make sure we're leading strong."

"I think it's all in how we frame it. Make it interesting."

"Yeah, yeah. Like, how Supercollider can't satisfy her."

"Exactly. I like that."

"What could be wrong with him?"

"What could be wrong with her?"

"Is it her depravity or his dysfunction? I like leaving it open."

"Who should break it?"

"Is there any way we can arrange for someone she's seen to come forward?"

"Who is the most pissed off?"

"Thing is, she's pretty classy about it. Not a lot of bad feelings."

"Hmm. What about lingering sadness. What might have been. Can we coax out an ego who wants to weave a sultry, melancholy narrative or some bullshit?"

"Seems more likely. There's a former supe who's a cardiologist now—he's dropped some heavy hints and has an ego the size of the moon. It was a long time ago, though. She usually goes for lawyers, cops—anyone who doesn't like to talk."

"She's good at this."

"Strategic, for sure."

"Okay, here's the thing. Whoever talks has to think they're doing the right thing."

"Right. Right. Okay. What if—what if we do it in stages?"

"Explain."

"We start off just looking for people who know Quantum well. We want to do a piece on her because she appears so infrequently in the #mycollision and #collisiondamage tags. About how not all heroes are like that."

"Oh, that's good. We see who comes out of the woodwork."

"Yeah. I wager a few white knights who should keep their mouths shut about ever having known her swoop in to be all 'Quantum and I have a special connection and I can confirm she's blah, blah, blah not the worst.'"

"And then we zero in on those."

"The ones who already want to talk. Maybe we get one to do a more in-depth interview. But they're going to talk, they're going to talk too much, and soon enough someone is going to straight up admit they fucked her for a while, thinking they're being all gallant in exposing it or just to get some of that light shone on them a little longer."

"What are the odds he winds up dead, whoever he is."

"High."

"She doesn't seem like the murdering type."

"Her handlers, though."

"Mmm."

"Also, Supercollider has some real sharks on his team."

"Wanna bet on it?"

"Yeah, all right."

"Ten bucks. If he survives six months after he admits he fucked her, I win."

"Deal."

"Deal."

He didn't survive a week.

The support for Quantum was consistent and steady, unlike the hysterical and polarizing responses to stories about Supercollider. She was the kind of person everyone wanted to claim some small intimacy with. A security guard at Collision Tower. A caterer who had worked a police benefit and placed a glass of champagne into her perfect hand. Young heroes she had once almost smiled at. A firefighter she'd placed a force field around. A photographer who captured the diamond tear trickling down her cheek at Accelerator's funeral. A graduate student who had interviewed her twice.

She was shining and beautiful, and her walls were high and the moats around her deep. Everyone wanted to stake in her inner circle. They presented notes and signatures and tokens and things she had touched like holy relics. These were all poignant, but not damning. We needed to be patient.

He said he was her friend, at first. He was younger than her, but not by much, dark and thin with magnificent cheekbones and a generous laugh. He flew and had some moderate tactile temperature control powers; for most of his career he'd gone by Melting Point. They met when their respective teams had banded together to take on Electrocutioner, the time they pulled his flying fortress down.

They got to talking. They went out for a coffee. There was a connection, he said. A spark (pun intended). For a long time they would meet up here and there for dinner. She was funnier than anyone imagined, he said. No one would guess how warm and forgiving her sense of humor was.

I knew there had to be a greal deal more to their relationship than some laughter over appetizers. I quietly brokered a meeting between Melting Point and

McKinnon, and assumed he'd sabotage himself in the interview.

I was slightly wrong. It wasn't his ego that did him in, it was an ex. Immediately after a completely chaste and respectful profile about the "secret Quantum" came out, Melting Point's long-term, recently former partner went to the media. Fractured and devastated, the jilted lover had clung to something too, something he'd clearly been waiting for the perfect moment to deploy.

"Let me show you what kind of friends they were," he said at the ensuing press conference. "Let me show you what I found." He produced a pair of her gloves—her costume gloves—and a very torn pair of her tights. Both were ominously stained. There was still a bit of duct tape clinging to the balled-up gloves from where they had been used as a makeshift gag, shoved in someone's mouth and taped down.

He brought them out in a ziplock baggie in the middle of the press conference. He sobbed as he described finding them where they had fallen by the side of the bed, the side of *their* bed, careless and clumsy. Like Melting Point couldn't even be bothered to clean up properly. The ex had been gathering his lover's laundry, and instead of familiar pajamas and socks, there was the torn, debauched costume of the most powerful woman in the world.

"He didn't try and hide it." He closed his eyes when he spoke this line, grabbed the podium for support. "He didn't care enough." This was the clip they played, over and over, the force of his misery making him sway.

What made it so effective was that it was so pure. He bore Quantum no ill will, of course. She may have become a terrible symbol of his partner's infidelity, but when he said he didn't think it was her fault I found I believed him. His love for Melting Point had been so deep and so vast that it transmuted to hate with extraordinary completeness, the alchemical purity of gold into lead. Quantum was just splash damage.

I liked to imagine it was the press conference that sent someone on Supercollider's crisis comms team completely off the deep end. The endless loops of this man's pretty, ashen face, having his moment of vengeance, but taking no pleasure in it. After the constant bombardment of stories and testimonials, the continuous little slices into Supercollider's image, the rolling disaster of the past few weeks, it was inevitable that someone at the Draft would be pushed to the breaking point. Just the right combination of lack of sleep and overreaction . . . and the most surprising people will call in a hit man.

Four days after the press conference, the jilted lover announced that he had handed the tights and gloves over to a journalist and private investigator, in hopes that the spit and come and sweat could be tested for a match to Quantum, just to settle any questions of authenticity.

By that evening, he and Melting Point were dead.

They made it look good. The narrative all made sense: After thinking it over, Melting Point had gone to confront his ex directly. There was a struggle at the apartment the couple had once shared; when Melting Point microwaved his lover to death (the media even kindly called it a "misfire" of his powers, a terrible accident), the disgraced superhero killed himself. Froze his own torso, to be specific. It was a poetic touch, I thought, turning his heart into ice. The story was so clean that it almost made up for the fact Melting Point's powers did not work the way the coroner's report suggested. He worked by contact, and externally; the two bodies were cooked and frozen, respectively, from the inside out. The official statement, however, made no mention of this discrepancy. Someone chose not to play that card just yet.

When they announced Quantum Entanglement was going to make a public apology, I threw a party.

I booked the second-biggest conference space in the compound, hooked the livestream up to a digital projector, and sent out a company-wide invitation. I assumed almost no one would come, probably just my team and Greg and Vesper, maybe Melinda if she had the evening off or Keller if the knee-breaking business was quiet.

Instead, the room was packed. Once the chairs filled up, I watched my colleagues happily take seats on the carpeted steps and lean against walls. Vesper and Greg planted themselves next to me like an honor guard, deciding among themselves that they were my dates for the evening. This was a joke to Greg, who took on the role with goofy gallantry, but a little more serious for Vesper. It was remarkably comfortable watching the pair of them take turns getting drinks for the three of us and making a point to laugh at every remotely funny thing I said. I joked that they were going to make me start seeing the appeal of an entourage.

Melinda was not there but sent deep regrets; she was on call for Leviathan, but promised to watch on her phone.

Then the livestream started and the lights dimmed a little, and everyone settled in to watch the first lady of superheroism debase herself for the sake of her boy-friend's ego.

"I bet she cries," Greg said, angling a bowl of Chee-tos toward me.

"Absolutely not." Vesper's eyes narrowed so quickly I heard a mechanical whir. "She's going to read three sentences like a robot and run off."

Greg shook his head. "Scripted tears. The guilt has been tearing her apart. She's almost glad she got caught. All that shit."

I picked up a single Cheeto. "I don't think she's going to cry," I said, "but I think they'll leave her up there for a while."

"Yeah?"

I nodded, crunching. "This is her time in the pil-lory. They're going to make her field questions."

Vesper winced. "Cold."

"I'm just observing, not handing out the sentence." I sucked orange cheese powder off my fingers. "They're desperate. If they think public excoriation is the only way to make this go away, it ain't going to be pretty."

Greg opened his mouth to say something, but then a dour handler in an immaculate gray suit walked out, taking the podium like he was about to deliver a eu-logy. The dull roar in the room faded to the occasional snicker.

The representative (wearing a discreet Draft lapel pin, I noted) made a statement that was brief and damning. The "Family" was "shocked and reeling." Every time he said the word "disappointed," someone in the back yelled "Drink!" It happened four times in fewer minutes.

But it was not the Family making her do this, the PR flak was quick to specify. It was Quantum herself, who wanted to begin the "process of making amends to her partner and her public." At that, Keller exploded with an ugly bark of a laugh and the entire room cracked up.

Then the rep stepped back, and Supercollider walked out. The conference room filled with hisses and boos. Someone threw a Dorito toward the screen.

The hero took his place next to the podium, hands folded in front of him, eyes slightly downcast. His brow was furrowed and his lips set; his face was a better mask than any costume, the barest and blandest approximation of an emotion. I felt my lip curl in disgust.

Quantum walked out separately, wearing an extremely formal navy blue suit. I frowned and sat up straighter.

"They should have walked out together," I muttered. "Gripping each other's hands."

It seemed to take ages for her to get to the podium, despite her long, steady stride. When she reached it, she put both her hands flat on the wood and stared straight down. Her curly starlight hair fell over her shoulders. She looked unwell. She looked at once perfect and barely held together. She looked off script.

"How many times is she gonna say 'sorry,'" Greg asked.

"Twelve," said Vesper.

"Seventeen."

I put up my hand. "Something's up."

She stood a long time, just breathing, gathering strength from somewhere inside herself. Finally, she raised her head. There was something I had never seen in her strong, lovely face before: a strange, blind panic. The room got very quiet.

She opened her mouth. She gasped twice.

"No." It came out a croak. "No." It was clearer now. "I can't do this."

She drew a force bubble around herself, eerie and pearlescent. The microphone screeched with horrible feedback.

Then, she vanished.

The room exploded. Vesper grabbed my arm. Greg did a genuine spit take, rum and Coke soaking his shirt and the person sitting in front of him.

I stood as suddenly as I was able to, leaning on Vesper's shoulder. "I have to go."

I hadn't taken a full stride before my head was ringing with Leviathan's subaural tone. I felt it vibrate through me, making my flesh prickle and writhe, and I lifted my hand instinctively to my ear.

"Auditor." Leviathan's voice was ultraviolet.

"I'm on my way."

"There's a car outside." The call cut out.

Vesper was suddenly at my side again, grabbing my elbow to steady me so I could move faster. He helped me keep my balance and we dodged through the crowd. One of the R&D boys was calling after me, but Greg shushed him. He knew what was happening. More people began to call my name—offering praise, asking for an explanation—until it was almost overwhelming. Even if Leviathan hadn't called, I might have wanted to flee.

The supercar was humming anxiously and giving off heat. Vesper opened the door and I folded myself inside.

"My head's buzzing," Vesper said. "I need to get the jet ready."

I nodded. "Neither of us are sleeping."

In a moment of bravery, he leaned forward and pecked me on the cheek; the metal edge of one of his eye apertures clanked against my temple. "Be vicious."

I grinned. "Fly like the devil."

He shut the door with an efficient snap and the car roared to life. I looked in the rearview mirror and Melinda caught my eye; we grinned at each other. I gripped my cane, hard, and felt fear go to war with strange exultation in my chest. The ugly joy won.

When I walked into Leviathan's office, there was a gif of Quantum Entanglement up on the screen, of the moment she said, "I can't do this," and disappeared. It was playing over and over in a haunting loop. Leviathan stood in the dead middle of the room unmoving, watching it. He didn't react at all when I came to stand next to him. His armor was almost phosphorescent.

He didn't speak for a while; I stared at the gif playing in front of us, transfixed. It was hard, seeing the anguish on her face, the bewilderment in her dark eyes giving way to a terrible kind of resolve. I saw the tremble in her shoulders, the way her throat moved, the tiny shake of her head she gave before speaking.

Then, slowly, I realized that Leviathan wasn't watching her at all. His attention was fixed closer to the edge of the screen, where Supercollider stood. At the start of the gif the hero was looking at his disgraced partner; when she said "No," his practiced mask of shame and mourning slumped into confusion. I could see how tightly he was clenching his lantern jaw, how taut and strained the tendons in his neck were. And then, the moment she vanished, his face contorted into a pure, awful rage.

"It's time, Anna." Leviathan said it so quietly. "He can no longer hide what he is. His facade has cracked at last."

I suddenly felt cold. There was so much left to do. "A hairline crack—"

He shook his head. "More than that. Much more. It's fatal. No amount of *kintsugi* will restore him now."

A strange buzzing filled my head. I could practically smell Leviathan's neurons firing, feel the ecstatic tension coming off him in waves. His armor was so much brighter than usual, throbbing and iridescent.

"It's a solid blow," I said cautiously. "It's clear we've rocked him badly. The way he reacts now is going to be very telling."

Leviathan inclined his head sharply. "I have seen all I need to see. He is weak and wounded. It is time."

"Time." My head swam. I needed more time. "The plan is still very much in process, we have much more to—"

"No more hiding behind petty schemes."

I was shocked by how much that dismissal hurt. I swallowed hard.

Leviathan made a fist, the overlapping scales of his

gauntlets shivering and gliding together. "Blood is in the water. My prey is injured. It is time to strike."

"I worry that he is not injured badly enough. He is still very dangerous."

"Do you doubt me."

I felt like I was trying to breathe at the top of Everest. There was suddenly not enough oxygen and my chest felt full of liquid glass. It took all my strength to make steady, direct eye contact with him, but I did it, staring into the beetle-black apertures that he sucked light in through.

"There is nothing you cannot do if you wish," I said. I meant it.

The coiled violence in his body dissolved. Without changing expression, his face was flooded with uncanny warmth. He moved closer to me.

"Auditor." My name in his mouth felt so intimate. "Your faith moves me."

"I want you to be in the best position possible when you take him down." I felt like I was standing to the side of myself, watching myself speak. "I want him to be incapable of resistance. I want him to be wretched and kneeling, so all you have to do is tear his head from his miserable body."

For the first time in a long while, he touched me. He wrapped one hand affectionately around my throat, thumb pressed gently against my trachea, his four fingers reaching toward the back of my neck. His fingertips were slightly rough, and I was surprised again by how warm he was.

Let me do this, I begged inside my head. *Let me do this for you.*

"But it must still be a challenge," he said softly. "I am not collecting a prize; we are engineering his defeat. I want him weak, not incapacitated. I want him cornered, not neutralized."

I shivered. He must have thought that I was reacting to the contact between us and began to pull away, but I wrapped my hand around his wrist to stop him. It was the first time I had initiated direct contact between us, and I held on. I was not afraid of him—I was afraid for him.

"I don't doubt your ability to rise to this or any challenge," I said very carefully. "I am—"

"You worry."

"I do."

He smiled, I think. "You have not seen me fight yet, Auditor. Let me show you what I am capable of. By the time this is over, you will have nothing to worry about ever again."

He released his grip, and this time I allowed him to let me go. He looked at me just a moment, then turned away. Striding decisively toward the doors, I heard him call Vesper and demand his stealth jet, the Darkling, be ready; Vesper assured him that it was. He didn't pause or look back then as he left me alone in his office. The huge double doors closed behind him, clean and final.

I stood there staring at Supercollider's face, at the looping gif of his shock and rage. I saw him break and crumble, as Leviathan had, but I also saw something old and ugly crawl out. I saw it and, despite the disloyalty of it, I was so deeply afraid.

I wanted to believe with every ounce of my being that Leviathan could beat him, but powered by fury and rapidly losing the foundations of his support and control, I was acutely aware of how dangerous Supercollider was now. Leviathan was certain he was weakened. The hero I saw was desperate. If Supercollider had too much fight left in him (and the math I kept running in my head told me he was still far too strong for direct conflict to be safe), we could very well lose.

I could lose him.

I stayed in his office, alone, for a very long time.

6

At first, Leviathan just vanished.

Vesper had prepared the Darkling, but had not piloted it; Leviathan was more than capable of flying that bit of sleek machinery himself. The runway was cleared, the vehicle cloaked and the comms encrypted, and Leviathan rose into the sky alone. He did not share his flight plans nor check in whenever he arrived at his destination.

"I wonder if we'll ever hear from him again," Vesper said, like that was a reasonable sentence to speak aloud. He was sitting on my desk, drinking a coffee. I was staring blankly at my screen, pretending to work. I found it difficult to focus on anything, instead just replaying that gif of Supercollider in my head, captured by my newly eidetic memory. That, or suddenly being overcome by the ghost of the sensation of Leviathan's hand around my neck.

That got my attention, though. "We will." It came out a little harsher than I intended.

"You don't think he's been quietly disappeared into the belly of some supermax?" Vesper took a sip of his coffee and grimaced, realizing he could have ended the sentence with the phrase "like you were?"

I shook my head. "No." I spoke deliberately softly. "There is nothing about this that is going to be quiet."

"Why leave now?"

"He feels like he needs to do it himself."

Vesper swore and drank angrily. "He has every advantage and resource right here and instead he's run the fuck off like a goddamn hero."

"This room is definitely bugged," I reminded him.

"Whatever, he's definitely not listening and even if he was, good. I am sure your plan was good. Better than good. And it was working. It seems like folly to abandon it now." It was so rare to get a rise out of Vesper; I realized he was angry on my behalf.

I was suddenly terrified that I might cry; a sourness crept into my throat and I coughed. "I thought it was going well."

"It was going more than well." He stood up and was gesticulating now. He was going to make a fine villain himself one day soon, I thought. "You were going to bring him *down*." He paused. "Maybe that was it. Maybe he couldn't let it be your plan that worked, it had to be his."

I found I disliked that idea intensely, mostly because it was plausible. The tears that threatened began to transmute into my own anger. "There's a lot between them I don't understand," I said, which sounded vague even to me. I wondered what the strange tightness in my chest was. I wondered if I was jealous. I wished suddenly that I could see my own feelings with as much clarity as I now saw the ultraviolet spectrum.

Vesper was quiet a long moment, clenching and unclenching one of his hands. "We should be there," he said finally. "This is ours too." He suddenly looked over at me, the apertures of his eyes focusing sharply. "This is yours most of all." He gently tapped the side of my head, where the edges of my scars were visible.

I felt my jaw tighten. "I can't possibly pretend that I hate Supercollider as much as Leviathan does."

"It doesn't make your hate less valid. You deserve a piece of him too."

"I've carved out some pieces." I looked at my hands.

"But do you feel avenged? Do you think you've balanced the scales?"

I thought hard and ran the numbers. The imbalance added kindling to my rising anger.

"No."

Something in Vesper's face hummed. "You deserve to destroy him too."

I couldn't bear to agree with him aloud. The more I thought about it, the more miserable and cheated and furious I felt.

Vesper kept pressing forward. "What are you actually upset about—that Leviathan might be frozen in carbonite, or that we aren't at his right and left hands when that physics-defying jackass gets blasted out of the sky?"

"Stop." It was an ugly, furious word. I stared daggers at my monitor for a while. Vesper sat quietly, not pushing any harder than he already had. I wanted to apologize for no good reason, but fought down the impulse.

"What do you think is going to happen," he said finally. There was just enough deference in his voice that I felt like he earned my attention again.

I took a couple of calming breaths before answering. "What I am worried about"—I found the words slowly, turning each of them over in my mouth—"is that he's springing the trap too soon. I wanted more time—needed more time—to run Supercollider down. I don't know if he's badly wounded enough. I'm worried he's hurt just enough to be vicious."

"You think the Boss has a chance?"

I smiled a little. "He's got a lot more than a chance. But not enough of one for me to be entirely comfortable, you know?"

"I do."

"Stupidly, I wish he'd let me do a better job. I would have that bastard ground down to paste for him."

Vesper curled a mechanical hand around my shoulder. It didn't fill me with blissful terror, but there was a small flutter of something, like a night bird alighting on a branch. "You would have eviscerated him, and it would have been glorious."

I rested my hand on his. "Thanks."

The next day, there was a fire at a retirement home.

The Hadron was not your typical facility. Sure, there was shuffleboard and genial orderlies carrying tiny paper cups filled with arthritis medication, enduring the flirting of lecherous old ladies. The inhabitants were anything but ordinary, however, despite the expected incontinence issues. The Hadron was where aging heroes went, when they were finally too old or ill or unsound to get by in their neglected headquarters with doting assistants.

It was an incredibly dangerous place to work, despite the relative frailty of the residents. An old man capable of psychic manipulation was infinitely more dangerous to himself and anyone around him when touched by dementia; a venerable woman whose hands shook badly and could no longer control a powerful acid attack was a disaster waiting to happen.

Despite the advanced training and exceptional security, accidents here were commonplace, and sometimes a little thing could get out of hand. This was one such cascade of events, when an older fellow's pyrotechnic abilities started a small fire. It would have been rote, except a nearby oxygen tank got overheated and shot through a wall, which allowed the fire to spread farther than it should have, and suddenly what should have been contained by a small spray from an extinguisher required the evacuation of one full wing.

It wasn't until the flames were put out and the staff were doing head counts that anyone realized Doc Proton was missing. It took a lot longer—well, after almost everyone was settled back into their lead-lined, nonreactive suites and all of the security measures were triple-checked—before anyone started to worry.

I was staring at the press release announcing his disappearance and turning everything I knew about Doc over in my head when my phone buzzed in my hand.

Greg

We're placing bets

Melinda

$20

Vesper

How long til the ransom demand

Greg

I say 24 hours

Vesper

I say 12

Melinda

I say 48, when they can declare him missing

Greg

That only counts on tv

Melinda

People believe it though

Vesper

Keller has dibs on 72 hrs

An hour

Greg

What

Vesper

Ballsy

Melinda

oh shit

It's going to be fast. It has to be.

Vesper

You think Doc's gonna turn into a pumpkin?

He'll be sick in just a few hours now

Greg

I hate playing w u

I'll donate it to charity

My phone blew up with a string of texted expletives and I grinned. It was a brief but extremely welcome distraction. I'd done my homework, as usual, and
I knew the enhancements Doc had undergone in his
youth had caught up to him. I didn't know the specifics
of his condition but I had enough hard facts: He was
rarely away from the facility for more than six hours,
and typically needed about twenty minutes of treatment every four. He never left the compound without a
pair of doctors, one with a medical bag shackled to her.
He had a permanent picc line in his left arm, which
he sometimes concealed with a tensor bandage, making
jokes about his "tennis elbow."

I had precious few minutes to enjoy my small victory
before a different alert lit up the screen in my hand,
and I was suddenly issuing an all-hands-on-deck call to
my team. Leviathan had released a ransom video.

In a few minutes, we were all huddled together in
my office: Darla, Jav, and Tamara monitoring feeds
with me, tracking search terms, social media feeds, and
news reports. Greg brought a coffee for me and hov-

ered just behind my left shoulder, biting his lip. Melinda didn't need to be in the room, but her on-call was suspended in Leviathan's absence and she was deeply stressed out without a task, so I told her to be there in case I needed her. Vesper came and stood in the doorway, silently leaning against the frame. Everyone was as still as they could be while the video played.

Doc Proton was squinting. The room was dark and there was a bright light swinging about his face, making it hard to make out where he was.

"He's in the Observation Tower," I said.

Greg squawked and sputtered. "He's *here*?"

Vesper stood straight. "You sure?"

"Positive. That's the utility closet in the comm room." I'd hidden there once when the building had been raided, a minor heroic infestation. "Can you check to see if he landed?" I didn't take my eyes off the screen.

I heard Vesper nod; or, perhaps, a better way to explain it is I felt a burst of affirmative energy, and he left the room. Greg drew closer to me, hovering at the back of my chair. Jav twisted his hands together nervously. Tamara had her hands over her mouth, like a surprised little kid. Darla bit their nails. Melinda started pacing.

Doc lifted a hand to his face for a moment to shield his eyes from the brightness. "Is this really necessary?"

He was trying to sound bored, but mostly his voice was tense and wary. It had been a while since he'd been held anywhere.

"Forgive the disturbance," Leviathan said off-screen. "I will do my best not to take up too much of your time."

Doc Proton scowled at Leviathan, who was clearly behind the camera. "What is this about, son?"

There was a shocking amount of familiarity in that word.

"The second law of thermodynamics."

"What the ever-loving fuck does that mean?" Greg exploded.

"No idea," I said quietly. I hated not knowing.

Doc Proton looked confused for a moment, then his strong face fell, the smile lines sliding into misery, his eyes going wet. I might not have understood, but he did.

"Son, I know it doesn't matter, but I am so, so sorry—"

"This is not about an apology." Leviathan's voice was even more mechanical than usual, carefully robotic. "Certainly not from you, sir."

"Please—"

"I believe you have something to say."

Doc's head dropped down to his chest for a moment,

then he looked up square at the camera. For the first time, he appeared frail. "Supercollider." He paused a second. "My boy, don't come after me. There's a score to settle here, a scale that needs balancing. And I am happy to pay it."

"Noble. I wish she had such a choice."

"'She'?" Jav frowned.

I shook my head.

Doc swallowed hard, looked stricken.

"The universe will be set right today, all systems returned to equilibrium." Leviathan's voice was almost serene. "Do you acknowledge that all is as it should be?"

Doc nodded gravely. "I knew this day would come."

"I hope your protégé learns something from your shouldering of this responsibility, sir. I thank you for it."

Doc continued to stare directly into the camera for a long moment, and the live feed cut out.

My comm buzzed. Vesper texted:

> he's here

And then:

> Collision inbound

At that moment, I became aware of a weird hum that I felt more than I heard, something that set my bones vibrating and made the walls around me whine in protest. My leg ached; I thought I could feel every single once-broken edge of bone, every healed bit of calcium. Despite the pain, I stood.

A moment later, alarms went off, and the entire compound went on lockdown. I made a dash for the door, swearing, but the blast door at the front of our interlinked offices slammed down like a portcullis. I punched it in impotent anger, splitting my knuckles, and started to claw at the override panel.

The building was shaking more intensely now, throbbing like an arrhythmic heart. I should have been terrified, but the emotion was buried under the towering fury that I was going to be locked in my office while Supercollider blew the compound apart. That there would be nothing I could do.

I inhaled to scream, but let the breath out instead in an awkward, gulping squawk when the door slid open. Dressed in more body armor than a riot cop, one of the finer cuts of Meat stood there, plasma torch already unsheathed.

"Auditor. Keller ordered me to bring you to him."

I lunged through the door. I heard Greg make a

strangled noise behind me as the reinforced alloy panel resealed. The Meat handed me a bulletproof vest.

"This way," he said, already marching down the corridor. I strapped myself into the vest as I hurried after him. There was an earpiece in his ear that was clearly directing him, and twice he changed direction as we hustled through the halls. Once he stopped so suddenly I slammed into his back and bit nearly through my lower lip when my chin made hard contact with his armor.

When we reached a pair of exterior doors leading to the largest courtyard at the north end of the compound, there were two other Meat there waiting. They took up positions on either side of me and the three of them escorted me over to the vehicle functioning as the Enforcement Mobile Command Unit. It looked like an armored car mated with a surveillance van.

I barely got to glance around the courtyard before being respectfully shoved inside the Enforcement van, but I saw what looked like every piece of Meat in the entire compound wearing as much gear as they could find, more armored vehicles, and even some foam-based restraint artillery cannons. Keller had rolled out everything he could.

I also caught a glimpse of Supercollider. He stood at

the farthest end of the courtyard, just a sketch of a figure in a red suit, a blood moon, hands clenched at his sides. Although I was unable to see his face, his anger was still palpable, coming off him like a heat haze. The air around him blurred, seemed to shiver.

"Get her in," Keller barked from inside the van, reaching toward me. I hopped forward and the door slammed shut behind me, while the Meat ran off to join the rest of the enforcers.

"He's alone," I said, groping toward the empty seat next to Keller.

Keller muted his headset. "For now."

"What's he done?"

"Nothing. He's standing there and waiting. I'm not starting anything till he does."

I nodded. "Smart."

The inside of the van bristled with screens and surveillance feeds, every scanner and dish pointed toward Supercollider. Bent over keyboards and frantically processing the information, two other Enforcement commanders tried to make sense of what they were seeing and transformed that data into a steady stream of orders. So far, all those orders were some variation of: "Be prepared and keep steady. Wait."

I tried to keep my voice even. "Where is he?"

Keller didn't need to ask who. "No idea. But the

Observation Tower is empty." Keller had clearly been able to figure out where the ransom video was shot too.

"Does Supercollider know he was there?"

"It's still standing; I don't think so."

One of the panels started beeping anxiously, and outside I could hear a hum gathering momentum.

Keller slapped his comm to life. "Power down! Power down! No one fires so much as a rubber bullet before Supercollider makes a move."

The humming gradually wound down, and one of the commanders flicked the alarm off.

Keller sighed and sucked his teeth. "What do you make of this?"

I paused. "The Boss wanted a showdown. He sure is going to get one."

"He got a plan?"

"None he shared with me."

Keller looked over at me. "That doesn't mean anything, you know."

"I know." It was a little harsher than I meant it.

Keller nodded and handed me a headset. "Whatever is about to happen you deserve a good seat."

I smiled thinly at him, and we both turned our attention to the largest screen, the main video feed pointed at Supercollider. I tapped a button on my headphones and the external audio feed suddenly blared to chaotic life.

Over the engines and the voices and the weird tech being activated, I could hear Supercollider screaming Leviathan's name, over and over. It was thin and far away, but unmistakable, a study pulse in the background.

"Come and face me!" he said, his powerful voice worn to a rasp. *"Come and face me, you coward!"*

I clenched my jaw.

I became aware of a feeling that started at the base of my neck, sliding up the back of my skull like a shivering caress. I couldn't see or smell the cloaking device, couldn't hear the vehicle it shrouded (a near-silent slip car, if I had to guess), but I suddenly knew something else had arrived on the field. It didn't show up on any of Keller's devices, but I felt it, the spatial wrongness of it, with the dead certainty of a dog detecting an imminent volcanic eruption.

"He's here," I said.

Keller frantically scanned the devices around him, frowning.

"Trust me."

He looked at me for a long moment, then nodded. He tapped his comm back to life. "Pay attention. Boss is cloaked and on the field."

"Do we go for the hostile?" one of the field commanders asked, her voice raw. She was clearly starting to fray around the edges.

Keller's frown lines deepened. "No. Stay frosty."

I reached toward my temple, gritting my teeth. There was so much data. Between all the readouts in the van, everything happening outside, Supercollider's threatening violence, and the dreadful hum of Leviathan's presence, I was getting an ice pick of a headache. I tried to filter, to pay attention to the most important pieces in motion, as Vesper taught me. I looked at Supercollider on the screen, his red suit a wound. I let in the peculiar resonance of Leviathan's presence, let the sonar in my bones echo-locate him. There was a weird shiver on the screen, a convulsive bit of snow. I stabbed toward it with my finger. "There he is."

Keller hit the comm to speak, but before he could get a word out the emergency override crackled on and Leviathan spoke. He'd taken over all of the channels; he wanted to be sure that, before he saw him, Supercollider heard him.

"My old friend." The venom that he conveyed in those three words, digitized and distorted though it was, made me flinch. "You aren't needed here."

"Show yourself." Supercollider took several steps forward. He couldn't tell where the voice was coming from, and was looking in entirely the wrong direction. I kept my gaze locked on the screen, where the cloak around the slip car was subtly distorting visual reality.

"The debt will be paid. Not to worry. You can go home." Leviathan's voice was formal, almost courtly. He sounded rehearsed.

"Let him go."

"Who, the venerable Proton? I don't believe he wishes to be let go."

Supercollider's hands curled into fists. "Let me see him, you goddamn monster."

Leviathan laughed. Not his warm laugh, but the awful, high-pitched, eerie keening that sounded like a swarm of insects trying to replicate human mirth. It made me cringe. Keller squeezed my knee impulsively.

"You heard it from him yourself—he agreed to my terms. Someone has to set the universe to rights again, and he nobly stepped forward."

"He owes the world *nothing*," Supercollider screamed, swinging his fists. He was a little closer to the camera now, and I could make out his features a bit. His hair was stringy and sweat-damp, his face hollow. He looked like he'd lost a pint of blood. "He gave everything a thousand times over."

"Ah, but so did she. And they still murdered her, in the end. It's not fair that she should be gone, and he still remains, enjoying a comfortable dotage. And being an honorable man, Doc Proton agrees."

She.

"But don't take my word for it." Leviathan sounded downright cheerful. "Let Doc tell you himself."

The door to the slip car opened and Doc was shoved out; it looked for all the world like a portal had been ripped open. Doc fell badly. As soon as he was clear, Leviathan made the car do a sharp lateral leap, moving it fifteen meters away; Supercollider had lunged at the spot Doc had appeared from and missed the cloaked car by a handspan or two.

Doc moaned. Supercollider, gasping in agony, helped his mentor sit up. The older man hissed in pain, clawing at his hip.

"We're going to get you home safe, sir," Supercollider said in a hard whisper, crouching over his mentor protectively. It was the most concern I had ever seen him display. He curled his shoulders over the older man's much smaller frame, doing his best to block out any threats with the breadth of his own body. His hands seemed so big and useless as he tried to handle Doc gently.

Doc was shaking his head. "He said it had to be you or me, son." He smiled. "He'll leave you alone after this, and I believe him. It's only fair."

Supercollider's face contorted into an ugly snarl. "He's taking neither of us."

"Would you undo the grace of an old man's sacrifice for pride?" Leviathan's voice echoed around them. He sounded disgusted.

Supercollider gathered Doc Proton into his arms. He stood, unwittingly turning his back to Leviathan. He walked directly toward the command vehicle that sheltered Keller and me. I could see his face clearly now. His usual expression of bland heroic determination, a particular kind of practiced scowl, was gone. His face was awful, lips curled back from his teeth and his skin waxy. Despite being inside an armored car, I recoiled when he got close to us.

As gently as he could manage, Supercollider laid Doc Proton down. The old man could sit up, but barely, and with considerable discomfort.

"Don't do this," Doc said one more time.

Supercollider stood over him, and spoke as if he hadn't heard. "Don't worry, sir. This will all be over soon."

Doc swore and closed his eyes.

What had been a heat shimmer before became a nausea-inducing ripple as the slip car decloaked, and Leviathan stepped out. Supercollider turned, and the two faced each other.

I lunged for the door to the surveillance van.

"The fuck are you—" Keller grabbed for my upper arm.

"Help me get Doc inside," I ordered. No matter what was about to happen, Doc was useful. He was also a sick old man who desperately needed a cocktail of medication very soon to prevent his internal organs from shutting down, and if these were indeed his last moments, I had enough respect for him that I wanted him to be comfortable. Keller swore and half stood to help me.

By the time I threw the door open, Supercollider and Leviathan were locked in combat. Supercollider leapt up and aimed a punch downward, leaving a small crater where Leviathan had been an achingly close instant before. He'd moved with preternatural speed at an odd, skittering angle, taking a swipe at Supercollider with the blades attached to his gauntlets. Supercollider snarled and grabbed hold of the slip car; I screamed as he threw the odd, squat vehicle at Leviathan, who successfully dodged again. The car hit one of the foam artillery cannons, which exploded like a giant can of shaving cream left on a radiator. Several of the Meat standing too close were immediately engulfed; I could hear their muffled screams. The rest scattered.

You have not seen me fight yet, Leviathan had said the last time I saw him; now, watching him do battle with Supercollider, I understood his bravado. The hero had raw strength on his side, and was fueled by hideous anger, but Leviathan moved like nothing I had ever seen before. He bent in ways I did not expect, and his reflexes were uncanny. One moment he seemed to be a creature made of blades, then he was harder to hold than smoke. I was enraptured.

"We need to move!" Keller yelled.

I snapped out of it, and we made for Doc, both Keller and I doing an awkward, ducking run. Doc looked up at us, wary; he appeared much worse close up, his skin yellow and his lips dry.

"Sir, pardon the interruption, but we're going to get you inside," I said, bending down.

Doc's face crumpled into confusion. "That's—kind of you?" Keller and I each lifted him by an arm and we got under his armpits, and together we carried him toward the armored car.

He smelled strangely sour. Not unwashed, but ill. His breath up close was all ketones and copper. "Whose side are you on?" he asked us, slurring his words.

"Let's not worry about that just now." I looked over my shoulder; Supercollider was too focused on trying to rip Leviathan limb from limb to have noticed us.

"I see." Doc sounded wary but amused. "Well, at least you have good manners."

I slid the door open with difficulty, still trying to balance Doc's weight. He hissed in pain as we dragged him up and into the van. "Sorry, sir."

"It's all right," he lied. He was panting. I helped him sit on one of the bench seats, surrounded by bristling wires and video feeds. Keller slammed the door shut behind us. Proton looked very fragile to me, and I felt his unpleasantly damp forehead reflexively.

A sudden impact into the side of the van threw me forward, and I hit my face on one of the consoles. My already swollen lip started to bleed freely.

Keller bellowed and the two other techs in the van squawked in panic. Then, we heard footsteps on the roof of the van. I turned to look at the feed, but the screen had gone to static; the external camera had clearly been destroyed.

"Get me a visual," Keller said, and one of the techs managed to call up a feed from one of the backup cameras. There was Supercollider's boot, his chiseled calf, the sleek machine of his knee, as he walked on top of our vehicle.

"Keller, get us out of here!"

The big man was already diving for the driver's seat, shoving one of the techs out of the way. I found the seat next to Doc and tried to find a seat belt or harness; I had to content myself with hanging on with my fingernails when the van roared to life and was thrown violently into reverse.

The sudden movement was enough to dislodge the hero, and he was forced to leap down from the roof of the van. A moment later, he was hit in the back and knocked clear across the courtyard. I guessed it had been a blast from one of Leviathan's god particle cannons. It wouldn't have wounded him, but it was enough to send him flying away from us.

Doc was almost thrown out of his chair and I threw my arm in front of his chest to try and hold him in. He wheezed and gasped in pain, sinewy hands trying to find purchase on the seat cushions.

"You seem nice," he said, weirdly solemn. "You should get out of this line of work. Too dangerous."

"Well, you're retired and yet here you are." I scanned the inside of the van frantically, trying to find some information about the fight happening outside.

"Suppose that's fair."

The van screeched to a halt. "Can we get a visual on what the hell is happening out there?" I hated not being able to see clearly.

Keller left the driver's seat and clambered into the back with us, his face wet and ruddy. "I'll try. Hold on."

The largest screen hummed and then showed us the scene on the field: three foam restraint cannons were unloading on a spot on the ground where Supercollider had fallen. Under the impossible weight of the ever-expanding restraint cushion I could see him thrashing. Leviathan stalked toward him. It was beautiful.

I turned away from the screen then, grinning. I drew a breath to revel in how well Leviathan was doing, to call the fight early. I didn't see what happened on the screen behind me, but I did see Keller's face fall, his jaw go slack. I felt that joy grow cold in my chest. Before I could turn back, something again slammed into the outside of the van like a cannonball and the backup feed went to bleating static. I hit my head hard enough that things became hazy and distant for a few minutes. I couldn't understand anything happening around me; the wailing machinery and too much information reduced everything to an awful noise.

Then, everything else was erased by a terrible, metallic groan, then shearing metal, both impossibly loud. Like a can being opened, the roof of the heavily armored van was torn away; Supercollider had ripped it open with his bare hands.

He stared down into the van through the gaping hole in the metal he'd made, and locked eyes with me. The recognition and burning, awful hatred I saw there skewered me. There was a sensation like a vise grip in my chest and I knew he was going to kill me. He was ready. I had broken him. He had finally abandoned all semblance of propriety and was ready to pick up my fragile, ordinary little body and crush it.

"Oh god," Doc said. He was staring up as well. He had seen Supercollider's face too, had read the same murderous intent I had. "No."

Supercollider lifted me by my hair. I screeched and clawed at his hand, feeling like my scalp would tear free from my skull for those first few terrible inches, every line and knot of scar tissue in my head screaming. Keller made a move to grab my ankle instinctively but stopped, realizing he would make it worse. I managed to lock my hands around the hero's wrist and take most of my weight, holding myself up in a grotesque kind of chin-up, though it was still horrifically painful.

As soon as my head and shoulders were through the opening he'd torn in the roof of the van, he switched his grip, wrapping one of his hands around each of my upper arms. My shins scraped against the ragged metal as he lifted me out, tearing off strips of skin.

He held me out in front of him at arm's length, considering. I could feel his fingers shifting on my arms as he thought about tearing them off and dropping my body back into the van. I'd seen murder on enough faces by then to read it well. He decided against quartering and chose to wrap one of his huge hands around my neck. He pulled me closer, my windpipe in the cradle between his thumb and forefinger.

I could still breathe, a reedy whisper of air. But soon he was going to crush my throat.

"You deserve," he grated out, his breath all adrenaline and acid, "so much worse. But I want you gone."

I suddenly seemed to have all the time in the world. I thought about Leviathan. I wondered if he was dead too, if that was why I was in Supercollider's grasp once more. If this was the end, I didn't want Supercollider to be the last thing I saw; I looked over his shoulder, at the sky.

"Supercollider!" someone called. "We join you on the field."

Then I saw, for once in their wretched lives, a team of heroes was arriving in the nick of time. They were always showing up in the nick of someone's time, of course. But this was the nick of *my* time.

It was three of the Ocean Four (Abyssal was home with the baby, never to return to active duty). Riptide and the Current immediately leapt into the fray, engaging with all of the Meat who were, for the most part, attempting to beat a tactical retreat. Undertow, however, was headed right toward us.

I saw Supercollider's face take on a trapped, desperate quality. Whatever scrap of control that remained in him, whatever part of him that still cared about being considered a hero, kept him from tightening his hand. I saw it and somehow managed a rictus grin.

He turned, saw my smile, and he dropped me. I hit the edge of the sheared van roof, bounced down the windshield, and rolled onto the hood. I made an awkward, clawing grab but couldn't find purchase on the armored exterior of the car. I fell off the front, right between the headlights, knocking my head against the bumper as I landed. My vision started to narrow very fast.

The last thing I saw before I passed out was Leviathan, rising out of the crater into which Supercollider must have slammed him. I saw him blast Undertow in the back, sending the young hero pitching forward with an awful gurgling sound, his blue hair catching fire. I thought I saw ribs and vertebrae through the smoking hole in his back, but Leviathan never looked down. Without breaking stride he launched himself toward Supercollider.

I tried to stand but found that I couldn't. The world tilted and my consciousness winked out, like a screen going black.

"**It's not** him."

Greg wrung his hands. "Anna."

"Watch it with me."

"You need to stop."

I didn't reply. I was still wrapped in a recovery blanket, the crinkly silver material light and enveloping my shoulders. My first cape, I thought absently. I started the video I was watching over again.

Greg changed tactics. "Come on. Let's just take a break for a while."

I shook my head. Without taking my eyes off my screen, I took a sip of a coffee someone had pressed into my hands what seemed like ages ago. It had gone weird and watery, but I kept drinking it.

"Anna, please."

I wasn't sure what he was pleading with me for, exactly, but I shook my head anyway. "It's not him, Greg."

"Okay." He twisted his fingers together. I felt a pang of sympathy; I imagined the conversation had become very tiresome. "I don't want to argue."

"Thank you," I said absently.

He was quiet awhile; I watched the video sixteen more times.

It was a tiny clip, barely a minute and a half long. Four people in hazmat suits stood around a body. In the background, two Dovecote containment specialists aimed burrowing neutrino guns at the body on the ground between them. Carefully, the four personnel in protective gear maneuvered the body onto a stretcher. The body was covered in the twisted remains of a black suit of armor. One of the four slid a thick black bag over the stretcher, which immediately sealed around the body like vacuum packaging, then stiffened. The stretcher and its cargo were then wheeled, slowly, toward a containment van, and the video ended.

I rubbed my throat, which ached. I could feel the welts where Supercollider's fingers had dug into my skin. I imagined it was bruising pretty badly. I started the video again.

Greg saw my gesture and latched on to it. "You should have someone look at that. Let's get someone—"

"No, I'd prefer not to."

Greg's voice became shriller. "Fine, Bartleby. Then let's get you something to eat. And you need to lie down. You look—"

I didn't say anything. I started the video over again.

"Anna."

I shushed him. "I might have missed something."

There had to be a clue as to what had happened. Something I had missed on dozens and dozens of earlier viewings. So far, this was the only footage that anyone had been able to recover from the wreck of the command van. I had to find the answer in it; there might be nothing else to go on.

"Anna, please."

I was suddenly furious. I clenched both my fists around the edges of the emergency blanket, stretching the weird fabric tight across my shoulders. I wanted to spit. I fought it down, tried to breathe deeply, coughed from the rawness in my throat.

"I need to figure out what happened," I explained, summoning unnatural patience. "I need to know where he is."

It was Greg who exploded. "He's there." I'd never heard him snarl before. He swept his arms out and knocked over a stack of papers and sent my mostly empty coffee cup splashing to the ground, splattering sickly brown liquid as it went.

I turned my chair toward him a little for the first time. The intensity of his reaction caught my interest, briefly.

He leapt up and was pacing. "He's there. He's dead. He's fucking dead. He's on a slab, in a cryobag. It's right there. It's not going to change no matter how many times you watch it. He's either been incinerated already or is being dissected right now, Anna. That's where he is."

There was an eerie pause. Whatever energy had taken him departed suddenly, leaving him cold and empty. I saw it leave him as surely as though he had been possessed by a ghost. He sank to the floor and started sobbing. I watched him for a little while.

"I know it doesn't make sense yet." I knew I looked like I was in shock, and I might have been. There was dried blood on my face and huge handprints on my neck and arms. I was shivering with cold and sweating. "But listen to me. Greg, listen to me."

He was shaking his head, his eyes squeezed tightly shut. He was crying so hard he had stopped making any sounds that were anything like sobs, was just trying to suck air in horrible, choking gasps. A bubble of mucus came out of one nostril and I had to look away.

I turned my face back to the screen. "It's not him." I doubted Greg would have heard me if I had been yelling, and I was speaking very quietly.

Greg slowly composed himself and, after a long time, wiped his face hideously on his sleeve and stood. He said a few more things to me, but I was having trouble focusing and didn't reply. Eventually, he left. The door slammed behind him and I flinched when the force knocked something off the wall. There was the sound of glass shattering, and I turned to investigate.

It was my Villains' Union certificate that had fallen, the one Greg had given me long ago. "Congratulations, you have been Supercollided!" The metal frame had bent a little in the fall and the glass had shattered, a spiderweb of cracks radiating out from one corner.

I stumbled back from it, put too much weight too suddenly on my bad leg and fell hard. The pain in my tailbone shocked me back into my body. A sick, cold wave passed over me, and I dug the heels of my hands into my eyes.

In my head, I started to replay the scene once more. But what I was seeing wasn't the video I had been watching on an endless loop for hours this time. What I needed was there, waiting for me: the moment I'd first seen Leviathan's body myself.

When I'd woken up after Supercollider unceremoniously dropped me, it occurred to me that I'd hit my head hard enough that I might be concussed. I tried to get up repeatedly and failed, overcome by knee-buckling waves of nausea. When I finally stood and stayed upright, scanning the field, the compound was a mess of capes and containment specialists. There were a pair of moderately injured Meat zip-tied together a few meters away, being questioned before being loaded into a Dovecote prisoner transport van. I was vaguely aware I should flee the compound (evacuation procedures would certainly have been triggered by then) and retreat to a safe house. But dazed as I was, something caught my attention, and instead I walked forward.

A crowd was gathering, heroes and their handlers alike. They were all looking down at something. There was a body on the ground.

A strange cloud of numb unreality overtook me. I didn't want to know what they were looking at. My jolted brain was trying to protect me still, to lock out what I was about to see as long as possible. My heart was suddenly in my ears and an alarm started going off in my head, telling me to look away, to not get too close.

I kept walking forward. I felt like I was moving through liquid glass, at once sharp and surrounded by sucking sludge. A woman in a Draft suit escorted a journalist and cameraman closer. The crowd shifted then, giving me a better view, and I caught sight of a shattered shoulder plate, a black suit of armor.

I knew the elegant way those plates usually fit together. My throat moved but no sound came out. Leviathan was dead.

In my office now, sitting on the floor, I let out the choking sob I couldn't force out then. I dug my fingernails into my palms, and shook my aching head. Re-membering the wreck of his beautiful armor made me want to gag. My brain recoiled at the memory.

I took a few deep breaths and forced myself to think about what I had seen yet again, to think of the actual details. Because somewhere, my mind had made the leap from staring at his body to the certainty he was still alive. I needed to know where that insight came from. I needed to know if it was real, or a trauma response. I needed to know if I was rational. I bit the inside of my lip and called the memories back up again.

The arrangement of his limbs was wrong. One arm was twisted behind his back and arched up, and one of his legs was parallel to his torso, doubled back at an impossible angle. There was a smoldering wound in his chest plate. In a few places the chitin—usually a beautifully clean matte black, now filthy and ashen—was torn away completely, and I could see the skin beneath. Seeing his bare skin was somehow more awful than seeing exposed viscera. It felt like a violation to see him, the nakedness of it.

I had started to shake very badly then, and sank to my knees. Someone eventually tucked the silver recovery blanket around my shoulders and pressed that styrofoam cup of weak coffee into my hands.

In my office, hours later, my hands still shook as I relived those moments in my head. The video picked up where my brain left off, when the containment bag was wheeled over, when his body was sealed inside it, and what was left of him was taken away to be analyzed and processed, to endure every conceivable indignity in death.

Through the horror of that moment, a refrain started to gather momentum in my head: *It's not him. Leviathan isn't dead. He's not dead. He's not dead. He's not dead.*

My certainty felt different from irrational denial. There was something prickly about it, something bothering me. I was sure there had to be a fact not seen clearly, an image misunderstood, something my mercurial subconscious was able to process while keeping my surface mind in the dark. I was missing something, I was sure of it. There was more in my memory than grief, and more on that video than a record of the last moments anyone would see of Leviathan's mortal remains outside a clean room.

It had to be what I had seen *myself.* The hardest thing to think about, the images I had the hardest time focusing on most clearly, was the physical details of Leviathan's body. My brain was shying away from that trauma; the secret must be there.

I tried to recall the moment again, but my brain was becoming sluggish and confused. No matter how hard I willed myself to focus, my mind drifted. I touched my mouth and realized there was still dried blood crusted to my chin and neck, and my clothes were utterly filthy. For the moment, I conceded defeat.

I'm not sure how I dragged myself back to my apartment. The door was open and the place had been tossed, clearly searched by some overzealous Z-grade heroes and their kicks when they swarmed the place, all looking for a piece of Leviathan's downfall. There was nothing important there, nothing sensitive. Seeing my furniture tossed around and my clothes flung onto the floor would once have rattled me to my core, but now it left me weirdly emotionless. I absently picked up a few articles of clean clothing from the pile and all but crawled into the shower.

I sat on the smooth enamel floor while the hot water washed over me; standing seemed an impossible effort. My hair was still sopping when I crawled into bed— well, onto the mattress that had been tossed onto the floor—wrapping a quilt around myself like a cocoon. I don't think I even bothered to lock the door. I was so wrung out I wouldn't have cared if, during the night, I was cryovaced into a bag in a fridge somewhere in Dovecote myself, as long as they let me sleep.

I don't know how much time passed, but it was dark when I realized there was a hand on my shoulder, someone calling my name calmly and steadily. My mouth felt cottony and consciousness was a fight. For a moment I didn't know where I was.

"Anna. Come on, kiddo. Anna."

I sat up with great difficulty. It was Keller.

"I'd've thought you'd be arrested with the Meat." I felt like I was speaking through wet plaster.

"Doc wouldn't let them. It was the first time someone called me a 'nice young man' in a while."

Keller was on his haunches next to me, forearms resting on his knees. He looked downright concerned, his thick eyebrows turned upward and his frown lines especially deep.

"I'm all right," I said, rubbing my face. "Just tired."

"Greg said you'd lost it."

"Greg is an idiot."

"He adores you."

"He adores me and he is an idiot." Awkwardly and painfully I managed to get my feet under me and stagger to the bathroom. I avoided my reflection and loaded my toothbrush up with a really unnecessary volume of toothpaste.

Keller stood, his knees popping, and followed

me. "He said you were rocking back and forth muttering."

"Sounds like me," I mumbled, aggressively brushing my teeth.

"He said you kept repeating that Leviathan isn't dead."

"He isn't."

The worry in Keller's forehead creases deepened. I spat in the sink.

"Anna. I saw it too."

I splashed water on my face, dried it, and finally looked at myself. My face was hollow and the dark circles under my eyes were a deep purplish black. My lower lip was swollen and scabbed over where it had split. My throat was covered in terrible handprints. I looked battered and exhausted, but I was lucid.

I turned to Keller, walked a step or two toward him, and put one of each of my hands on his massive shoulders.

"I know this sounds fucking impossible." My mouth was as minty as it had been sour. "I do. But he isn't dead."

He looked like he was about to interrupt me, but then didn't.

I jumped on that little opening, the possibility of his

belief. "I can prove it. I swear. I just need some time. I haven't lost my shit. I know that it's a huge thing to ask, but I need you to trust me. I need to be able to count on you."

He looked at me a long moment, gaze flicking back and forth between my eyes. "It occurs to me," he said slowly, "that a good part of the latter half of my career has been believing someone who told me something impossible."

Relief hit me like a wave, and I let go of a tension I didn't know I was holding. Somehow, I found the capacity to smile. It hurt my face. I let it fall quickly.

"I *will* prove it."

"I know."

"I swear."

Keller wrapped his arms around me and squeezed. I let him hold me up for a minute, closed my eyes.

"Anna."

I stayed behind my eyelids one moment more. "Yes."

"I believe you. But we need to figure out what happens now. Can you do that with me?"

I drew in a long breath, held it, and let it out. Keller let me go. I opened my eyes and rolled my shoulders. I felt my brain humming, rattled but powerful. "Absolutely."

"It's going to be bad."

I nodded. "What is our situation."

He'd been speaking gently to me, his voice a soothing growl. He decided I had it together enough to slip back into his usual commanding brusqueness. "Most of the nonessential staff have evacuated. There's a skeleton crew here. The fail-safes fell into place as soon as they started searching so everything critical is buried under magma right now."

That was a relief. Leviathan's office, the labs, the vaults—everything truly valuable would be sealed and surrounded in molten rock. That also meant, however, that none of us had access to the best equipment and resources. That would be challenging.

"We need to take stock of who's here and what we have. I need to know what we had in circulation, what didn't get locked up, everything we have access to. Let's get on the emergency comms, figure out who is still available, and press them into service."

He nodded and started moving toward the door. I started digging through my smoke-and-blood-reeking clothes on the floor for my comm; I could use the equipment in my head to tap in to the emergency frequency if I had to, but it gave me a headache.

"Will you make the announcement, ma'am?"

"I'm on it." I found my comm and looped it around my ear.

"I'll get you a sit-rep and let you know what we have." Keller nodded crisply and ducked out.

My brain was still moving slower than usual, so it took me a moment to realize the terrible significance of that "ma'am": it meant that Keller had just decided, in Leviathan's absence, whatever it was, I was in charge.

I swallowed hard, straightened my shoulders to shed some fear, and tuned my comm to the emergency channel.

"All staff, this is the Auditor."

7

We couldn't stay at the compound. With Leviathan gone, the entire facility was on lockdown. Like most villains he was a control freak, and there were an awful lot of doors (and magma chambers) that once closed only he could open. Staff were already evacuated and scattering, and those who remained were edgy and exhausted. Some had even seen Leviathan's body and were badly shaken. Others expected heroes who had missed the action to show up any minute, looking for scraps to loot, or a fight; it was not an unfounded fear.

Keller and I decided that the best strategy was to let almost everyone go. Let the heroes think the henches were rats leaving a sinking ship. Much of the Meat and most of the henches were told to reenroll at the Temp

Agency (including Tamara), as though they were all back to the drawing board and looking for new nefarious work. We could keep them on the payroll quietly for a while, but they were to take jobs if they needed to maintain cover (though there weren't going to be all that many jobs with the market so newly flooded). Once they were settled, we got to work.

We moved the core of our limping, ramshackle operations to one of the shadier safe houses, a low-rise apartment building that usually served as the base of a small side business we maintained providing new, good identities when one of our team (or well-paying associates) needed one. If all else failed, we thought, at least we could get that last core team set up with new names.

Keller and what was left of Enforcement took over most of one floor, with Molly staking claim over a large corner unit with the few prototypes they'd managed to stash and retrieve. The other two floors became a chaotic mess of makeshift offices and living arrangements. I found an abandoned reclining chair and a battered desk, and planned to set up camp with the remaining Information team in a modest room. Keller made a bunch of noise that I should take more space, assert my dominance. I initially dismissed this as bullshit, stating that I felt more comfortable within easy reach of a keyboard.

"I'm not telling you to stop working," Keller said. "But do it from a place of power. Even if that place has black mold and leaks."

I saw his point, and claimed a space with a window for my own. I insisted, however, on keeping the chair.

Soon, I was also grateful for the privacy. I needed time to prove that Leviathan was still alive (the "and then what" part of the problem was something I actively wasn't thinking about yet). My team believed me, though some more adamantly than others. Keller had my back and Ludmilla would have followed the faintest bit of hope into hell. Most of the rest at least knew that my brain was weird enough to believe something I said that didn't seem possible.

In that ill-lit space with awful vinyl floors, I resumed torturing myself with the footage and my own memories the first moment I could. I knew he was alive; I just needed to explain *how* I knew—including to myself. I needed to make the math work. I needed to reward everyone who had given me their faith with facts. And I knew I had a very limited amount of time in which to work before the only responsible thing to do was disband everyone completely.

I just had no idea how to do it.

In terms of process, I monitored every social media feed and every major news source to see how Levia-

404 · NATALIE ZINA WALSCHOTS

than's apparent death was being discussed: what was being reported, what wasn't; what the tone was and what jokes were being made. The progress I made was agonizingly slow, however. It was all intensely painful to look at, and I found myself only able to work in short bursts before having to tear my eyes away or rest. Because of my injuries I could only look at screens so long and was worried about complications from my new brain trauma. It was also impossible to analyze what I was seeing with any critical distance. Every rehashed news story and clever quip was a fresh wound.

I felt the noose tightening when I learned to my dismay that Supercollider had vanished after the fight—probably personally escorting Leviathan into whatever containment pit had been devised for him. I tried not to think about that too closely, but the image came up over and over, unbidden. I wondered if Leviathan knew the world thought he was dead. I imagined Supercollider relished telling him that everyone was certain his lifeless body had been carted away, that no one was coming, that he'd be forgotten in a heartbeat.

The narrative around Quantum Entanglement was being carefully controlled as well, and not for the better. Someone finally decided, conveniently, to look at the details of the medical examiner's report, and noticed that there were some discrepancies between how Melting Point's powers worked and the circumstances of his and his ex-partner's deaths. There was now an official Superheroic Affairs investigation into her supposed role in the incident. Supercollider was clearly ready to string her up.

Through it all, I was flailing. I had data in front of me and could make no sense of it. I had resources (scattered and in shambles as they were), but no sense of how to deploy them. I couldn't relax, but had no capacity for work. I couldn't even text June; I ached for her now in a way I hadn't in months. I composed messages to her that I didn't send, describing the exact texture of my dread and the stakes of failure.

> I know you'd hate this, but I can tell you down to the month what I'll cost us all if I'm wrong

> I bet you'd love to see me be wrong

> You are a world-champion gloater. Prepare your finest artisanal told-you-so

I am glad you aren't here so this can't hurt you, but I miss you. So much

I was increasingly sure that I should just do my best to get everyone as safe as I could, set up in new locations with new identities, and walk away from all of it. I was on the verge of giving up, having just spent hours scouring the internet for any grainy, shaky phone video footage some overexcited kick might have uploaded after raiding Leviathan's compound, when Keller called.

"Hey, Ke—"

"Security feed, front door."

I clicked over to the video feed from the camera pointed at the building's main entrance. There was a tall woman, her hair tucked under a toque, ringing the doorbell. She had a small duffel bag in one hand, clutching the strap tight. She was wearing a hoodie and jeans, and I couldn't see her face, which was carefully angled away from the camera eye. But I would have recognized that queenly stance and the set of her shoulders anywhere.

"Well, shit."

The first thought I had was that she had come to kill me. She had somehow figured out that I was the person who had utterly ruined her life to get to Supercollider, and she was here for revenge.

But then my second thought was *Why is she knocking?*

"I can lock the foyer down and fill it with gas," Keller said.

"No, let me go down."

"I don't like it."

"Me neither, but she's doing us the courtesy of knocking when she could have fucking phase-shifted into the bathroom while you were taking your morning shit."

"First of all, I shit in the afternoons. Second, take Ludmilla with you."

I shook my head uselessly. "You can keep an eye on me, but I'm going down alone. Nothing threatening. She's waving a white flag, I'm not drawing a gun."

Keller made a noise.

"Trust me."

I could hear anger in his silence, and I knew he was sick and tired of hearing that line from me. I wasn't so sure I trusted myself. But this was the closest thing to a break we'd had, and we needed it badly.

There was no elevator in the building, and my hip was still in rough shape from my fall down the hood of the Enforcement van. I was slow. Walking down the three flights of stairs gave me plenty of time to get deeply nervous.

I caught sight of her as soon as I exited the stairwell, and my heart leapt into my throat. Seeing her in person, instead of through the distance of the camera, made the reality of this confrontation a lot more solid. Her eyes narrowed when she saw me.

I limped across the threadbare lobby and opened the heavy door with visible effort.

"Um. Hi."

We stared at each other for a long moment. Finally she said, "Can I come in?"

"Sure." I stood aside and she swept by me. She smelled like bergamot and citrus. I let the door close behind her a bit too loudly.

"Do you want a coffee?" I immediately felt stupid, but the offer made her relax ever so slightly.

"That would be great, actually."

"There's a kitchen down the hall." I led the way, and she walked authoritatively after me.

There were two Meat chatting in the kitchen when we walked in. One was shirtless, the other eating a bacon and tomato sandwich. Their eyes widened when they saw us.

"Can we have a moment, guys?"

"Um." The shirtless man openly stared at Quantum. Her powerful frame and the tattoos on her lips and chin were immediately recognizable without the context of her usual costume. This was the first time I had seen her tattoos up close, and they were beautiful, elliptical loops and interlocking shapes like a scientific illustration.

She raised a perfect, threaded eyebrow. The Meat eating the sandwich unconsciously let his arm waver, and a tomato slid out from between the bread and hit the floor. Shirtless grabbed a tea towel and tried to hide his naked chest behind it.

I cleared my throat. It seemed to snap them out of their shock enough to hustle out, Shirtless still demurely trying to hide behind the tiny square of cotton towel. I sighed audibly and Quantum made a sound that might have been a tiny snicker.

"The coffee's not as good here as it was in the old break room," I said, more wistfully than I intended. I focused on keeping my hands from shaking while I poured us both cups from the perpetually full old diner-style coffeepot. "I'm sorry we're so poorly appointed now."

"Hard times."

"For both of us, it seems."

"Mmm."

"How do you take it?"

"Milk and sugar, too much of both."

"Me too." I fixed us both mugs the way I liked it and carried them over.

She took a long swallow and made a sound of relief. I was beginning to realize she had no idea who I was and what I had done. "This is perfect."

I let myself smile. "I never managed to be a coffee snob. The Boss"—I found it unaccountably difficult to say his name in front of her—"had bean quality and roasting preferences and a whole nitrogen-infused cold-press thing he preferred."

"One of those."

"I'm proud trash."

The corners of her mouth trembled, and the banter I'd managed to keep up died. We both sat, not talking, both of us becoming more uncomfortable by the moment.

She looked around the shabby safe house kitchen, taking in every stain. I'd killed more than one roach in it already. "So this is the end of everything for you," she finally said.

"I'd like to think I have some fight left in me."

"I mean, you're still here, right?" Her face told me she thought this would be easier than it was.

"What can I do for you, Quantum," I prompted, not unkindly.

She didn't speak at first. I waited, letting more discomfort grow in the space between us. I took no pleasure in watching her tense up, but this was a conversation I was unwilling to lead. I wanted her to play every card she could before I had to show one of my own.

"I cared for him, you know."

I couldn't quite hide the disgust on my face. "No, I don't. Honestly, I don't understand how you could stand to be around him as much as you were."

Her face registered blank confusion, then she recoiled. "Not *him*. God, no. Melting Point."

"Oh. *Oh*. I'm sorry."

"Did you ever meet him?"

"No, but I saw how he stuck up for you. He seemed better than most." I wondered if she knew how much of a compliment that was.

Quantum stared at me for a long moment. A slow crawl of cold fear took hold in my stomach. I wondered if she had any inkling of our involvement in Melting Point's death and the pressure cooking of his lover. I wondered what she would consider fair payback, and hoped my exhausted face remained inscrutable.

"I think they had him killed. The Draft."

I felt a wave of relief. She wasn't here to kill me in particular, which I thought would be perfectly reasonable if she'd figured out what I'd done. That meant she wasn't here to wrench everyone in the building out of existence either. At least, not quite yet.

I drew a deep breath and let it out, hoping it registered as a sad sigh. "I am not surprised. I'm sorry."

"You are?"

She was testing something, and I wasn't sure what yet. So, to disarm her, I answered honestly. "Almost no one deserves what heroes dish out—even, sometimes, other heroes."

This confirmed something for her, and she gave a tiny nod. "You hate us, right? Them. You hate heroes."

Them. That was interesting. I took her lead. "I think they're an objectively quantifiable source of hardship and suffering for everyone in the world."

She blinked. This was not the monologue she was expecting.

"I can show you my charts if you'd like to see the proof," I continued.

"I—no, that's all right. I looked you up before I came here. I'd heard of you, and what you do."

"That's immensely flattering. So what can I, and my humble Excel spreadsheets of all your colleagues' sins, do for you." I braced myself. I expected that she was about to rattle off all of the reasons I must be at least partly responsible for what happened to Melting Point and, more crucially, to her. I was waiting for the other anvil to drop.

"I need to—I have—" She looked at the ceiling, clenched one of her fists resting on the table. Next to her hand was the coffee she was now letting grow cold. "I don't know why they turned on me now. Everything went to shit after Accelerator. After he . . .

"Supercollider wasn't the same; no one was the same. Maybe he didn't want the liability of someone close to him anymore, something that could hurt him. Maybe they just wanted him to be the lone hero again, 'wedded to the world' and all that maudlin crap. But they definitely wanted me gone, and now I'm here."

"It's not the nicest kitchen, but it is home for now."

"That's not what I—"

"I know. It's not where you ever expected to find yourself. But you are here."

"I need your help." Her voice was so sad, and so small.

This was what I had hoped for. She wasn't here to demand. She was here to bargain, and she was desperate.

I had nothing. I had no way to prove Leviathan was alive, and even if I could, I had no way to get him back even once I knew where he was. At most I could have arranged for a medium-profile kidnapping or a bank robbery with the resources that I had, but there was no way, with the skeleton crew that remained, we could ever hope to lay siege to Dovecote.

But now I had Quantum, and she was willing to talk. I needed to wring every drop from this opportunity.

All of this clicked together in my brain in a microsecond. I said, "What could we possibly do for you?" It was a mighty effort to keep my voice level.

She looked back at me, searching for words again. She was achingly beautiful. Her skin glowed like she'd had a facial the day before, and her eyeliner was sharp enough to cut yourself on. "Leviathan always seemed to *know* things. You all work for him; they call you the Auditor, right? If anyone knows, you do. Tell me who killed Melting Point."

I immediately started to calculate how to give her the safest answer. I was quiet a moment too long, and she took my reticence for disinterest rather than confusion.

"I don't expect charity; we can work something out."

I got my face under control and extended a hand across the table in a reassuring gesture. "Forgive me.

Unusual bedfellows and all. Just getting used to the idea."

That seemed to comfort her. "It's weird for me too."

"I bet it is."

She leaned forward. "You can do it. Find them. I am sure you can."

"Do you want the killer, or who ordered the hit?" The latter was a Draft crisis comms specialist named Harold who was addicted to Klonopin; he'd hired a couple of assassins (Keller once disparagingly referred to them as a "bonded pair") called Source and Sink. I considered exactly how valuable she felt that data was.

"Either. Both. Whatever it takes to clear my name." It sounded very expensive to me indeed.

"It's going to be a lot harder to get than it usually is."

"But you still can do it?"

I pretended to consider for a moment, then slowly nodded. "It might take a little while, but I can."

She studied me carefully. Her lower lip was slightly raw, as though she had been biting it out of nervous habit. Whatever she was looking for in my face, she found it, and nodded decisively.

I saw my opening. "What is this worth to you?"

"Leviathan is alive."

The room seemed to tilt. I gripped the table. Whatever unfathomable expression took hold of my face, Quantum looked deeply alarmed, as though she thought she might have made a mistake.

"Tell me," I rasped. "Tell me how."

"I—"

"I know he's alive. I am sure of it. Tell me how *you* know."

That seemed to completely shock her. She opened her mouth and then closed it again.

It took her a second to regain her composure, but she managed. "There's—there's a set of procedures in place, if we were ever able to capture him alive. The Leviathan Protocol."

"What are they doing to him?"

A combination of guilt and disgust twisted her face. "They fake his death to avoid a trial and media circus, show the press a dummy body, and then hold him up to twenty-one days. They've always wanted to study and interrogate him for as long as they could, and that's as long as the containment can reliably hold. Then they terminate him."

I stood up so suddenly that my chair fell over and hit the floor uncomfortably loud. "We have time," I said, not to her, as I paced. "We still have enough time." I looked back at Quantum. "I knew that body wasn't his."

My reaction was clearly not what she was expecting, and I saw her struggle to keep up. "How could you have known?"

"I don't know how, but I knew." Impossible hope rose in me like a radioactive dawn. "I knew he was alive." I wasn't sure if I was talking to her or myself at that point.

She seemed uncertain too. "Is this . . . Do we have a deal? You know how long you have, now you get me a name."

I had almost forgotten. It seemed like such an afterthought now. "Oh. Yes, of course."

"I'm not going anywhere until I get a name from you," she said. I supposed she might be threatening me, but I could not have cared less. My mind was already elsewhere, deploying our every meager resource to bring him home.

"Whatever you'd like." I touched the comm at my ear. "Keller? We got a room free still on the third floor, right?"

"You are out of your goddamn mind—" His voice was in stereo, weirdly doubled.

"I can hear you."

"Of course you can fucking—"

"I can hear you're right outside the room."

"Of course you fucking can! You think I'd let—"

"Come in here."

There was a long moment, and then Keller barged into the kitchen. He was breathing heavily through his nostrils and had his shoulders low and square, doing his damnedest to look as intimidating as he possibly could, which was adorable, considering how easily Quantum could remove us from this plane of existence without breaking a sweat.

I raised an eyebrow at him.

"I think you're out of your goddamn mind letting her waltz in here. Think of what could have happened to you."

"It didn't." I tried to call up some irritated imperiousness.

"We can't lose you too."

He sounded genuinely broken up and I gentled a little. "It was a good risk, Keller."

He didn't say anything, but the angle of his shoulders signified a subtle assent. He turned his attention to Quantum.

"You," he said, "better be ready to prove everything you just said."

She stood up slowly. "Are you calling me a liar."

"I am not risking anyone or anything on your word. You want a name, we need evidence."

She looked between the two of us. As much as I was already succumbing to hope, I knew in the cold cellar of my heart he was dead right.

"Can you corroborate this?" I asked. "Do you have a copy of a document, or know how to get one?"

"No. I can't even access my email." I recognized the look of near panic on her face as the same one she'd worn just before she blipped out of existence at the press conference. If we didn't give her something plausible, and fast, we'd never see her again.

Something shuffled into place inside my head. I gestured with my cane, using it like an exclamation point. "You can talk to Doc Proton."

"*What?*" This had completely blindsided her. "There is no way he's ever seen the Protocol, it's only—"

I held up a hand to interrupt her. "He's known our Boss—and Supercollider—longer than anyone else. Surely he knows something that can prove Leviathan's body wasn't real."

"I don't see—"

"That's the deal. Take it or leave it."

She glared at me. I was taking a gamble on the fact that she was not like most of her associates I had met and was therefore not about to do me a grave bodily injury. I saw a small, barely perceptible shift in her expression, like something was clicking into place. Maybe there was a reason she wanted to see Doc for herself, but whatever she thought, it made her suddenly acquiesce.

"Fine," she said. "It's stupid, but fine."

I closed my eyes. It wasn't very much, but it was everything.

"And you go in wired," Keller said.

I looked over at him and nodded in agreement. "I want to hear exactly what Doc says."

Quantum looked back and forth between us, trying to find a reason to refuse.

She nodded.

"We'll get you a surveillance egg," I said. I was starting to feel light-headed.

She frowned hilariously. "I hate them."

"How's your gag reflex?"

"Terrible."

I let out a dry little cough of a laugh. "Keller, can you take Quantum up to the empty room? I can't handle the stairs just yet."

He nodded gravely, gave Quantum his best "just try it" glower, and gestured roughly for her to follow him. Without checking to see if she was trailing him, he turned on his heel and strode out. Quantum didn't acknowledge me again. She took long, quick strides to catch up with Keller as he stalked loudly down the hallway.

I retrieved my chair from the floor and sat down before my legs gave out completely. I sat alone, just breathing, for a long moment. I couldn't make all the pieces fit just yet; the sides of the equation weren't yet balanced. But I knew, my brain knew, we had a way forward.

The coffeemaker was empty so I set about the business of refilling it, so there was a fresh pot for whoever wandered in next.

Once the dizzying moment of optimism wore off, I spent the next forty-eight hours convinced I had let my death in by the front door. What I had done was an absurd gamble at best and an utter disaster at worst. I had Keller and some Meat, but up against Quantum Entanglement I was defenseless—we all were. If she turned on us or simply decided she wanted out of our deal, we had nothing again. More, I barely knew myself why I had asked her to do what I did. Somewhere in the depths of my brain, in a panic, I had run some numbers, and this was the scenario it produced. I had no idea how Doc could prove her claim; I just knew that right now I had nothing, and if they talked we might get something real, something definitive, even if all it showed me was my hope was in vain. At least I would know and be able to move forward. I told no one else what she had told us; I didn't want anyone else to have to sit with the awful hope in case she was lying after all.

Quantum, for her part, was cordially hostile. She made it clear she was not interested in socializing or being exposed to any of us if she could absolutely avoid it; she trusted Leviathan's henches much less far than she could throw us. She spent most of her time in her tiny, spartan room, emerging only occasionally to make a sandwich or brew some tea while glaring at anyone she encountered like she was trying to set them on fire with her mind.

Watching her when I could, a horrible realization dawned on me: if Leviathan died, if it all fell apart, everything I had done would be for nothing. I would have killed Accelerator for nothing. I would have destroyed Quantum's life, and caused the death of her lover and his partner, and all of the other splash damage and ripple effects, for nothing. The math would fall apart, and I would be left with nothing but more lifeyears of debt than I could ever hope to pay off.

But there was no reason to torture myself with that impossible equation. He was alive. I could not ascribe any value to doubt.

The thing with the surveillance egg was that you could remove most of the bodily interference, the visceral noise, but you couldn't eliminate it completely. Lightened as much as it was, you could still always hear a heartbeat. I'd heard Molly complain about this, how it was distracting, but I'd come to find it an invaluable secondary source of information. You could tell if the person who'd swallowed the egg was nervous, if the tension in the room shifted suddenly, if they saw something they couldn't otherwise communicate, if there was going to be violence before it erupted.

Quantum's heart rate was elevated, its staccato urgency reaching my ears. She could teleport out if she needed; it wasn't physical threat that had her alarmed. It was that she'd been in hiding for weeks, and this was her first appearance in any sort of public venue since. Not to mention the headlines about her would be very different if she was detained at the gates to the Hadron, especially considering the fire and Proton's kidnapping: turning Supercollider into a supercuckold and maybe having something to do with her former lover's death was one thing, but if someone suspected she was up to something here, she'd be over the line for good. At that moment, I think, some part of her thought she could still go home.

We decided against giving Quantum an earpiece, which would almost assuredly have been spotted. Not everyone had the dubious luck of being in a situation to have a mic (of sorts) attached to their auditory nerve. It meant we couldn't talk to her, but she could speak to us.

"I know it's impossible, but I swear I can feel this thing in my gut. It's like I am pregnant. With an egg. Eggnant?"

"Oh my god." Keller had to put his head down.

"A hero with a sense of humor. She's too good for them," I said, adjusting the interference.

Security didn't give her a suspiciously hard time, but they were as cruel as they could be. They searched her thoroughly, got in subtle digs wherever they could, made her sign in twice.

"You must understand, we have to be extra careful after all the recent incidents," one of them drawled venomously. I could hear their hands on her through the walls of her body, feeling for anything they could harass her for. It made me unreasonably angry.

They couldn't stop her from coming in, though, because she'd messaged Doc ahead of time and he was over the moon to see her. Doc was guarded, not imprisoned, and could still do what he damn well pleased. He might have been weakened from his ordeal (he hadn't been seen outside the Hadron's walls since he was returned to their care), but he was still gripping his own agency tight. He wanted to see her, and without an excuse they had to let her in.

"Oh, honey," he said when he saw her, tears clouding his voice. "I am so glad you came."

"Hi, Doc," she said meekly. There was the thump and rustle of their hug; it sounded like he was sitting up in bed and he was bending over her awkwardly, his forehead making contact with her collarbone.

There was the scrape of her pulling a chair close to his bed, and she sat. "How are you feeling?"

He made a dismissive noise. "Bit tired, no worse for wear. Frankly, it'd been too long since I was in the middle of something. Made me miss it, got the blood pumping."

"They didn't hurt you, did they?"

"No, no. Downright civilized. I'm fine. But I'm worried about you, honey."

"I'm—"

"You look so tired."

"That means I look like crap."

"You are lovely as the dawn," he said, haughty and offended, and she laughed. "But anyone can see you're having a time."

"Do you know what happened?"

He sighed deeply. "Yeah, honey, I know."

"You must be so disappointed." She sounded so broken up I bit my lip at the pain of it.

"Not a chance." I could imagine him solemnly shaking his head. "I know this life is hard and complicated, and I am not going to pretend like I understand what you were going through. You don't owe me or anyone else an explanation."

"Not everyone agrees."

"I can't believe they tried to do that to you, make you go in front of all those cameras. I can't believe Supercollider allowed—"

"It was his idea."

There was a very long silence between them. Miles away in the safe house I could feel myself get uncomfortable, could feel sweat under my arms, on the back of my neck.

"Have you spoken to him since?" Doc's voice was hoarser now.

"No. I doubt I could speak to him now if I wanted to, which I don't."

"He didn't hurt you, did he?"

"He probably can't."

"'Probably'?" I said aloud. That was interesting.

"I know, I know . . . but did he try."

"No. Not in the way that you mean. He was just . . . It was terrible, Doc. It really was. I don't want to talk about it, I can't tell you. But it was so bad."

"It's okay, honey, you don't have to say anything."

Her heart was pounding now. "He's . . . He's just . . . He's not what everyone thinks he is."

Doc didn't answer her.

"I feel like I don't even know him."

"You might not, honey." He sounded so sad.

"Help me understand. Tell me about him, tell me what I don't know."

"I don't know what I—"

"You knew him. When he was practically a kid. You trained him. He looked up to you so much. Help me understand how he got like this, how he became whatever he is now."

"He's what he always was. He's a hero."

"Doc."

Proton sighed. "There was never any other path for him. Not from the time he was a tiny baby, I'd wager. This is always what he had to be."

"I don't understand."

"He didn't *become* like this, he always *was* like this. Nothing changed him, honey. He's always been this way."

"I remember him differently."

"Do you? Or do you wish you did?"

There was a long pause.

"We put all our hopes into him, Quantum. Everything we dream of. Everything we want him to be. It's the power of his that no one talks about."

"Holy shit," Keller said. I grabbed his shoulder.

But Quantum didn't understand. She made a sound in her throat, but Doc cut her off. "It's an incredible ability, when you think about it. More than all his strength. The real miracle is making people believe in him. I wanted the perfect protégé, I got it. You wanted a partner as strong as you, and he was that hero. Poor Leviathan wanted a nemesis, and there he was."

"It wasn't real?" She sounded hollow.

"It was as real as your force fields, Quantum. Real as he could tear a building to the ground. But he can't keep it up forever, see. You need to keep the hope, the dream, alive. And when it falters, and of course it does, he can't maintain it on his own. It fails. Without hope he goes back to what he is."

"What—what is that?" She sounded genuinely frightened. My hand tightened on Keller's shoulder. I was frightened too, and a childish part of me wanted to turn off the audio before I heard an answer. But I was also fascinated, and that infernal curiosity won.

"I don't know how to explain it, honey. What's left is . . . whatever it is, it's *hungry*."

"Christ." I let go of Keller. Doc was sobbing.

"Doc, you don't have to. Shh." The sounds he was making were suddenly closer and more muffled. I figured that she had sat on his bed and pulled him close, and he was crying onto her shoulder.

"No. No. I do. Supercollider should have left me. He should have let Leviathan do what he wanted. I deserved it, we all did, for what we did to him."

"I don't care what happened. I don't care what he looks like under that armor now—you didn't deserve that."

"No. Quantum. Listen to me. He's not *wearing* armor."

"Doc? That doesn't make any—"

"There *is* no armor. He's not wearing anything at all."

"I'll be fucked," Keller said.

I stood up so suddenly that I stumbled and would have fallen if Keller hadn't grabbed hold of both my arms to steady me. I felt a thousand things slam into place in my head at once; it was dizzying and difficult to process, but in my chest I also felt a surge of triumphant relief.

I brought up the memory of the last moment I had

seen Leviathan once more. I thought of the first glimpse of him I caught: his shoulder. The pauldron was pulled up and a little away from his shoulder, the rerebrace around his upper arm twisted away almost completely. I could see the skin beneath, some of it torn, some bits of the metal embedded into the flesh. My brain recoiled from the image and I forced myself to stay with it, to focus on his shoulder.

It was ugly, that broken pauldron. Not just because it was broken and begrimed from the fight; there was something innately repellent about it. Something wrong. Under the smears of dirt and blood and ash, it was dull, lifeless. There was no uncanny iridescence, no trace of the eyespots I had stared at in wonder whenever I could. The shape was right, but the texture was wrong. It wasn't *alive*.

I made a weird choking sound as my mind acclimatized to the idea that Leviathan's armor wasn't armor. It wasn't something that he put on and took off, a wonder of engineering; it was his body. That wasn't a grate over his mouth, but actual mandibles; the tiny flexible places I could see between each plate were tissue, not material; his gauntlets were his hands. It wasn't something he wore, it was what he was. The dead armor I'd seen in front of me couldn't be his because it could come off.

Leviathan was alive because that glimpse of naked flesh couldn't have been his body.

The second, simultaneous realization was that if the body was a fake (probably some poor unfortunate Meat or cop they threw a good costume on, and the kind of people the hero worked with could have made a fake that was very good indeed), they wanted everyone to *think* Leviathan was dead. Which meant not only was he alive, he was being held alive for a reason.

I found my balance slowly. Keller's face was a mass of worry lines, but I gently waved him off, promising I was all right. Putting these pieces together was exhausting, but I would push through and find new capacity. Because as much as I wanted to curl up in the moist-smelling reclining chair and never get up again, this was where the work truly began.

I called Ludmilla into the room. She needed to know next. Whatever else Doc and Quantum discussed, I could listen to the recording later.

It was not easy to get what we had heard to sink in.

"Watch it again."

Ludmilla looked stricken. It was obvious she could barely stomach it, though she at least had some idea what I was trying to show her.

"Trust me. Watch it again."

"I can't." Ludmilla was as gutted as I had ever seen her, pale and panicking.

"Watch it and tell me what's wrong."

"He's fucking—"

"No," I snapped, "he's not." I hated to be cold with her, but I would tolerate no more arguments. "Now watch it like this is proof of a hit. Watch it like this is a job. What's wrong with what you see?"

She took a shuddering breath and watched. After a few views, a different frown settled over her face. Something *was* wrong. Something was catching and tugging at her mind. Once the hook had caught I could point it out.

"The pauldron."

She frowned, and watched again. Her eyes narrowed and her brows drew in as she focused on it.

"The armor. It's . . . wrong."

"Leviathan has never *been* wearing armor. It's his *body.*" My heart was pounding. "That can't be him, because that poor fuck is *wearing* armor."

"Not him," she said. Her voice was steady, but seemed to tremble at the edges. "Not him."

I watched slow certainty break over her face. "We have a rescue mission to plan," I said.

At that, it was like Ludmilla sprang back to life,

gripping my hand with shocking intensity. "I am yours," she said, cheekbones like flint knives.

My hand creaked audibly as I stretched it out.

"Let's get him back fast," Keller said, already turning to leave the room and begin whatever preparations he felt were necessary. Ludmilla followed, vibrating with joy.

I was as elated as they were. But as I groped back to my chair and put my head in my hands, I found myself trying to hold the joy above water while exhaustion threatened to close in over my head.

There was a tiny courtyard behind the apartment building that had become our makeshift headquarters. Accessible through an alley that ran between our building and the next, it was little more than a staging area for garbage and old mattresses. A dry fountain, filled with dead leaves and cigarette butts and the odd frolicking pair of raccoons, stood in the center. There was also a busted couch that had once been upholstered in purple velvet that, despite being in a moderate stage of rot, was in remarkably good structural shape. It sat beneath the dubious shelter of a tarp-covered fire escape.

That's where Quantum found me when she eventually came back, sitting on the decaying velvet. It was slightly too cold to be entirely comfortable, but being inside was worse. The walls were making me feel claustrophobic. Besides, the wifi inside was terrible. I had been holding my laptop at awkward angles by my desk, trying to get a signal. A very important news conference had just started, and I needed to see it.

Outside, the video finally played, and the same Draft suit they'd had when they were going to put Quantum in the stocks was gravely addressing the press.

". . . a shame, a terrible shame, but the Draft, and Supercollider, believe we have no choice. In light of this new, conclusive evidence that Quantum Entanglement is responsible for the deaths of Melting Point and his long-term partner, with possible ties to Electrocutioner and the Rule of Nines, it is with heavy hearts that we must take this to mean that she has officially crossed the line. The Family asks that you respect our privacy during this incredibly difficult time."

There was an explosion of questions, and the suit held up a hand to wave them away.

What a joke, calling it "the Family" still. That was what the Draft had always called the unstable nucleus of Supercollider's inner circle. For the past twelve years it had meant he and Quantum Entanglement, and whatever other heroes or kicks who were deemed worthy enough, for a while, to be on the inside. With Accelerator dead and Quantum Entanglement excommunicated, who was even left to call "Family" now?

I lowered my laptop and saw Quantum walking toward me across the courtyard, her head down. It was like watching a thunderstorm approach over a lake. I closed the device out of courtesy and tucked it beside me, sliding over a little to make room. She sat down next to me and for a long time neither of us said anything.

She found her capacity to speak first. "I held up my part of the bargain. You'd better hold up yours."

I thought it was safer not to reply. The silence between us was deeply uncomfortable.

"Do you smoke?" Her voice was hoarse.

"No. I wish I did right now."

"That's a shame. It'd be fitting."

An alarm bell started to ring in my mind. I stuck my fingers into a hole in the fabric, felt it give and tear a little more. I touched the slightly damp stuffing, the sharp edge of a broken spring.

"You saw the press conference, I take it."

Her mouth tightened. "Was it you."

Everything suddenly came into hyperfocus. I seemed to be aware of every hair follicle and pore on my body.

It was a feeling I recognized now: brushing close to my death.

"I am afraid," I said automatically, "that you'll have to be more specific."

She leapt up then, so that she was towering over me. "Did you frame me. For murdering them. Was this you."

I was strangely relieved that I didn't have to lie to her. "I know this might look like my work, but I did not do this."

"I could make you tell me."

"The inefficacy of torture is well documented."

"I know what you are, what you do."

I swallowed hard, and hoped even that involuntary gesture didn't make me seem guilty. "I'm probably worse than what you know about me. But I didn't order the hit on Melting Point, and I had nothing to do with the Draft framing you."

Her face was terrifyingly unreadable. She was running some calculations of her own, but what they could be, I had no access to.

Sometimes, a small admission of guilt can cover up larger culpability. I decided to take that risk, a tactic that had sealed the deal on innumerable plea bargains. "I spoke to the journalist. McKinnon."

The potential for violence fled her body; I saw it

pass, like a spirit that had been possessing her suddenly loosening its grip. She slumped back down on the couch next to me.

"That was you," she said quietly. "When did it happen? That botched robbery with the Red King?"

"No. Nothing that bloody. The press conference the Eel held."

"When he kidnapped the kid?"

"I was one of the seat fillers, looking confused."

She stared at her hands. They had been clenched so tight, there were little crescent moon impressions on her skin from where her nails had cut into her palms. "I'm sorry. I shouldn't have threatened you. I should be apologizing."

I felt some of the tension leave me, sublimating through my skin. The likelihood of my imminent demise decreased, leaving me sweaty and tired. "You've had a day. I'll spot you this one."

We sat quietly together for a long time. I watched some leaves and garbage blow across the courtyard. There were a few crows on the building opposite, talking to each other and wondering if one of us was going to drop a french fry.

"When Doc told me about Leviathan . . ." she said suddenly. "Holy shit. I knew they'd use another body, but I didn't know *why*."

"I think part of me knew before the rest of me caught up. As soon as Doc said he wasn't wearing armor, though . . ." I thought about his hands. I hadn't been looking at gauntlets, but chitinous, segmented fingers.

"I guess . . . I guess neither of them were what we thought they were."

I shook my head. "It's not that. I just can't fucking believe what they did to him. It's so much worse than I imagined."

She nodded gravely. "If they put a dummy there, then he's almost certainly still alive," she said. "The Protocol is in action."

I nodded. While Supercollider and Tardigrade were generally considered the toughest known heroes, Leviathan outclassed them all in sheer stubborn invulnerability. There was some evidence of an advanced healing factor, but he was so impossibly difficult to injure there wasn't enough data to really tell. I didn't find that fact very comforting, though. There were a lot of unpleasant things you could do to someone without hurting them, and the words "study" and "interrogate" had been keeping me up at night.

"We need to get him out now," I said. "We need someone to take us to him."

"Who? No one's seen Collider since it happened."

"I see he's not super anymore."

She shot me some cut eye. It was one of her most attractive features and there were a lot to choose from. I let her intimidate me into changing the subject.

I started to pace. "He's going to stay underground playing with Leviathan and licking his wounds until there's a world-threatening situation that he can't ignore."

"Can't you make one of those? Isn't that your whole thing?"

I felt a ripple of unfathomable and useless irritation. "My 'whole thing' is data analysis. But even if I had every resource the Boss did and wanted to give it a shot, I'd be pretty clumsy at it, I think. We're running ops out of this shithole now with an eighteenth of the resources we had a week ago. I could commit arson or release a sex tape, but nothing on a scale that would necessarily lure him out."

Quantum's brow furrowed. "So how do we get his attention?"

Ruin him, I thought. *Make him furious enough to come after you again.* But she didn't volunteer, and I wasn't in a position to give orders.

What I was in the position to do, though, was be the bait.

There was a slow, terrible conclusion I had been coming to for a while: that my extracting Leviathan would probably mean dying by Supercollider's hand.

"I think I could do it, but I wouldn't survive it," I said. "Frankly I'm on borrowed time right now. As soon as Collider's bored of poking at Leviathan in whatever bunker he's keeping him in, I expect to wake up with a snapped neck. Or for this place to inexplicably become a crater if we're all unlucky. The next time he sees me he's going to kill me for sure."

Quantum was quiet a long moment, and I sat back down. Despite the fact that they had essentially signed her death warrant in that press release, she was still adjusting to the idea that Supercollider was capable of premeditated murder.

I decided to try something different, problem-solving by a more circuitous route. "How was Doc."

She snorted. "You care?"

"I do, actually. He was a perfect gentleman."

"You could have killed him."

"For what it's worth, his kidnapping had nothing to do with me at all. I almost had a fucking aneurysm when the ransom video showed up."

"That was—"

"The first I knew of it, yeah. I hate it when he doesn't tell me things."

She relaxed a tiny bit. "Collider was like that."

I disliked the comparison. "Usually he does. But he's not himself when Collider's involved."

"They definitely care more about each other than they do about us."

I swept whatever that feeling was immediately back into the pit from whence it came. "Hey, I'm just on the payroll," I said, and laughed raggedly.

"Right. You're on payroll, so come up with something." She turned herself toward me. "Such as: What the fuck do we do now?"

I dug my fingers into my scalp. "I don't have all of the pieces yet. But I am starting to put things together." I knew, though, that we needed to finish what we started. I told myself all the things I had been whispering to Leviathan: we must knock down his last two pillars of support—his public and his mentor. We needed to tear Supercollider all the way to the ground.

I said, "He doesn't have you. His relationship with Doc is strained but intact. As much public backlash as he's received so far, he could still recover from it. It needs to be something he can't recover from."

"Okay. What does that look like." She was holding me with her eyes, trusting I had a plan even if she couldn't follow. I really hoped I did.

"In the ransom video, the Boss said something I didn't understand. That the reason he was doing what he was doing had something to do with 'the second law of thermodynamics.' When you were talking to Doc, I think I figured it out."

Her eyes widened. "Entropy. The villain."

I snapped my fingers. "Got it in one. The Boss never spoke of her, but he kept her mask in his office. He grieves her, clearly. She's been dead a decade and a half and it still motivates him today, for some reason. And he blames Supercollider and Doc for it."

She was thinking hard. "The story is she died of a heart attack."

"The story always is. A heart attack. An accident. Collateral damage. Does anyone know what really happened to her, though?"

She made a sound. "Doc does. He never talks about it, but he knows for sure."

"We need to get Doc talking to someone."

"They won't let me in again, not after—"

"No, not you. It needs to be on record. Maybe the journalist who wrote 'Collision Course,' whom I trust. What Doc says needs to be devastating enough to make Supercollider want to rip my head off on live TV."

She looked at me. "You're willing to do that?"

"I am. So let's go."

"Where?"

"I just told you—we need to get the journalist to talk to Doc. You're coming with me."

"*What?* Why?"

"Because I want you two to talk." I stood up and gave her a savage grin. "Be prepared for some spectacularly shitty coffee."

McKinnon didn't think I was actually serious when I said Quantum wanted to speak with him. But there she was, flesh and blood and magic, surrounded by the smell of bacon grease and the ancient cigarette smoke that would never come out of the carpet, a real-life fairy tale ready to speak. When the Lady of the Lake points you in the direction of a sword, you don't demur or ask for time to speak to your editor or play hardball. You hit *record*, you listen, and you start composing in your head immediately.

Arranging for the journalist to speak to Doc was more complicated. Quantum couldn't go back now that she was an accused murderer, and security was still tight after his kidnapping, so McKinnon had to be expressly invited by Doc. And while Doc was willing to say all manner of things to Quantum privately, when he thought no other ears were present, convincing him to spill the secrets of his once-beloved protégé on record was something else entirely. There was the very real possibility that he would refuse, and we would fail.

I wrote him myself, in the end. I sent a message to his personal email, the one no one but close friends and Family were supposed to have. I reminded him who I was, about the little time we'd spent together in that demolished Enforcement van. I apologized for his treatment, and said, truthfully, I didn't know it was going to happen. I hoped that he was well, and that he was fully recovered from his adventure.

I then reminded him that Supercollider had lifted me out of the wreckage by the hair, how he had gripped my arms like someone thinking of tearing them off. I wrote about the handprints on my neck that I still had to hide from my more squeamish coworkers, how it hurt every time I swallowed. How if no one was looking, I'd be dead.

This is not all he's done, not even just to me. This is what you have seen yourself, and therefore I feel you are most inclined to believe it.

Holding this in mind, I am offering you a chance to balance the scales once more. Not with your life, as Leviathan offered, but with words. In many ways,

I know this is asking more of you, and it might be more difficult to give.

I would like you to think about the second law of thermodynamics. I would like you to think of his hands on my neck. And I would like you to consider speaking to a journalist.

What I was really asking him was *Do you believe in Supercollider, or do you believe in heroes?*

The old man chose ideas over the boy he'd loved, because that's what heroes always choose: their ideas and ideals. He *demanded* to be interviewed by McKinnon.

The journalist, in this moment of triumph, denied me the courtesy of letting me listen in, flatly refusing my gift of a surveillance egg.

I'm going to write the story
I want

I could hear the snarl in that text. McKinnon was a lot sharper than most, and could feel my manipulative tentacles wrapping around the work.

I tried to be reassuring.

> I'm not trying to control the narrative, I just want to listen

You'll see it when it's out

> I'm very impatient

You're probably not going to like it

I texted a string of threats and expletives, letting McKinnon feel like I was furious, while grinning the whole time. I sincerely doubted there was going to be any possible story I wouldn't be thrilled with, providing McKinnon had any journalistic integrity left. So long as spite for Supercollider still exceeded distaste for me, I could ask no more from our alliance.

McKinnon let me sweat for forty-eight hours after I knew that the interview was scheduled before a courier dropped a recording off at our ramshackle headquarters. I carried it up the stairs in my arms like a baby, awkwardly texting my thanks to the journalist on my way back to the office to devour it.

You're the goddamn Auditor

> Doc told you eh

> I should have made you wait

> You're going soft

> Fuck you

I grinned and locked myself in the office. I liked McKinnon quite a lot.

I fast-forwarded impatiently through the false starts and awkward small talk, until things began in earnest the moment McKinnon spoke the name of Leviathan's mentor for the first time.

"Tell me about Entropy," the journalist said, not ungently.

Doc Proton's mournful groan was audible. "She figured it out, didn't she. The Professor or whatever her name is."

"Hey, I took chemistry in high school. It's not the hardest riddle to solve."

"Fine. You're clever too. I still don't have to like talking about it."

"The story we have, the one we all know, is that the superhero, or *superheroine*, as she would have been called at the time, worked alongside you most of your careers. When you left active service, for the most part, you both chose to mentor particularly talented young heroes. Leviathan was in her charge. Despite being engaged in what we'd now call 'gray heroics'—and thus causing you two to ideologically butt heads—you had a profound respect for her. So much so that you spoke eloquently at her rather sudden retirement, and delivered a eulogy at her funeral six months later."

"That's right," Doc said in a husky whisper.

"What are we missing, Doc."

He made a noncommittal noise. Instinctively I knew it was too much, that void between his story and the official one. I could hear in that weird, groaning mumble his inability to get a mental handhold.

"Was she ill?" the journalist tried to prompt him. "Had she been experimented on? Did something go wrong?"

"Oh, a lot went wrong, son. But no, she wasn't sick. That old bird was supposed to outlive us all. I always figured she was made of titanium."

"What happened? Why did she retire?"

"*Retire* . . . ," he rolled the word around in his mouth, "is not exactly the word I would use. She and the Draft had started to disagree."

"About how the Draft treated those kids?"

"Oh hell, a lot more than that. She was furious about what had happened to her boy, and I certainly can't blame her for that. Leviathan was in some kind of chrysalis, in a coma after the experiments they—we—had done on him. We didn't know he'd live yet, then. The Draft had also started to catch wind of some . . . extracurricular tutoring she'd been doing with her charges, Leviathan in particular. She and the Draft decided that it was easier to part ways."

"So she *was* retired."

"That's right. But she didn't go away. That's the thing with Entropy, she was always so inexorable, so goddamn stubborn. She couldn't just leave Leviathan, and I understood that. She wanted to keep vigil until he woke up—*if* he woke up. Then, she wanted to be around while he recovered and rallied. I'd have done the same if it was my boy."

"It sounds like that wasn't all she did."

"No. No. When Leviathan was better—well, when he lived, and it was clear that the changes were what they were—she kept working with him, training him. Unofficially."

"Something I imagine the Draft objected to."

"Strenuously. They asked me to talk to her and I tried, I did, but she kicked me out and called me a coward. That . . . that would be the last time we spoke."

"Why did she think you were a coward?"

"For siding with the Draft, as she saw it. For continuing to work with them after we knew what they were willing to do to these kids. For 'choosing the greater good over doing good,' that's how she always said it. I said that was rich, coming from her, considering all the . . . unsavory things she'd done. She . . . she didn't take too kindly to that and that was the end of it."

"What did the Draft do next?"

"I didn't know they were going to ask him to intervene. I had no idea, I swear. I never would have allowed it."

"Asked who to intervene?"

"Supercollider."

"They sent him, what, to talk to Entropy?"

There was a very long, terrible silence. "He told me, later, that they wanted him to scare her. I don't think the woman would have been scared of the devil himself. But that's what the boy claimed they told him. 'Just scare her a little. Make her think about whether keeping in touch with Leviathan was such a good idea.'"

"Did they tell him what they wanted him to do to her?"

"I don't know. I don't know. I only found out what they had done after."

"After."

"He. Supercollider. He brought her to me."

"He kidnapped Entropy and took her to you?"

There was a pause where I could hear a strange, liquid noise: Doc swallowing repeatedly. I had no proof, but I imagined him shaking his head too.

"He brought me her body."

I heard McKinnon's shock in the silence.

Doc began again after a long time. "I believe that it was an accident, truly. He didn't want to hurt her, not badly. There was real panic in his face when he told me."

I wondered, absently, if that was the last time Supercollider had been afraid, really afraid. I hoped I got to see the next.

"How did she die."

"It's not—"

"I think it is. What did Supercollider do to Entropy."

"He picked her up."

Doc tried to stop there. His silence was a plea now.

"Go on." McKinnon was having none of it.

"He picked her up and leapt upward."

There was another pause. "He took her up . . . high enough. He was jumping over buildings, he said. She was cold. Her nose was bleeding."

"Then what happened?"

"He said his piece. She was to stop whatever training or communication she was carrying on with Leviathan, that she was to step out of the young man's life and stop undermining the Draft. That she needed to retire for real. And . . . And he . . ."

"What did he do, Doc."

"He dropped her."

"Oh my god."

"He didn't mean to, but he lost his grip. Just a little."

"Jesus, Doc."

"I dangled a lot of villains off of buildings in my time, and I wanted to believe it was the same kind of thing. But gone wrong."

"Very wrong."

"A few things happened at once, we figure. First of all, she had a heart attack. It might have been enough on its own, you know. It's a strange sort of comfort but I hope it was."

"What else."

"He *did* try to save her. But he caught her . . . badly. He just didn't know his own strength. He grabbed her too tight, much too tight, and—"

When Doc stopped here, the journalist didn't push him to continue. They both let the silence hang. The sound of that quiet, recorded, was awful. It was long enough for me to realize I had my hands clamped around my forearms, digging my nails into my skin painfully hard. I let go, flexed my hands, rolled my neck, tried to get some of the tension out of my body.

"What did you do," McKinnon said finally.

I could hear Doc shift, sitting straighter. "I did what I always did when things went sideways. I called my team. Neutrino, Siege Engine, and Cold Snap all came. I didn't want Atom Bomb to see. We talked through it with Supercollider, calmed him down. We figured out what we would tell people. It should always have a grain of truth in it, whatever you tell the public. Once he was presentable, we called the boys at the Draft and let them come and clean things up."

"So you taught Supercollider how to lie." The journalist wanted blood now.

"My boy, we all lie to the public all the damn time."

"Would you prefer to say you gave him a crash course in crisis communications?"

"You have no idea what it was like."

"No, I don't. But clearly you don't think what happened is something you can keep living with, or you wouldn't be talking to me. On that video it seemed like you were willing to die for it."

"I don't owe you anything. I don't owe anyone anything but Entropy, and Leviathan."

"What do you owe Leviathan."

There was another very long pause and some shuffling sounds; for a moment I was sure Doc was going to call the interview, considering the fury that had crept into his voice. He was willing to hang himself, but to be accountable to someone else was still an imposition he could barely tolerate. But, after a long moment, he sighed heavily, resigned.

"She told him that if something happened to her, it was no accident. She told him that they'd forced her to retire, and he should be vigilant. That if she died, or disappeared, or stopped talking to him, it wasn't her. That she'd never leave him. That it was the Draft that had come for her. So the next morning, when they announced she'd had a heart attack, he went to war. He was still a bit sick, but coming into his own. He needed help, though. He needed an ally. He went to his best friend."

"He went to Supercollider."

"Leviathan told him that something had happened to her, that they needed to stand up to this fascism even if it looked like heroism. You know. One of his speeches. He was already very good at speeches."

Imagining a young, heartbroken Leviathan summoning all of the still-developing powers of monologue he possessed to try and win over his friend and avenge his mentor made my chest contract painfully.

"And Supercollider lied to him." The journalist filled in what he saw as the next logical beat in the story, an unusual interview misstep.

"No. Supercollider told him everything."

McKinnon could have focused on many places. The article could have been an exposé on the broken system of drafting superheroes, beginning with the standardized screening that started around puberty. Maybe look at how the Draft found Supercollider before he was in middle school and conscripted him into a fight he couldn't possibly understand. Or eviscerate the system that took Leviathan, took a brilliant young person and completely annihilated him. Maybe even examine the problem of Leviathan's armor directly, which would have been the hardest to stomach, but which unquestionably would have exposed Supercollider and his vast system of handlers for the unconscionable liars that they were.

Instead of beginning with something new, however, McKinnon chose to focus on something the world had already seen: the ransom video. Homing in on the phrase "the second law of thermodynamics," and the way Doc's face had crumpled; examining the weight of guilt that crashed down on him in that moment, something everyone had seen played over and over again.

That festering mystery, something lodged just under the skin of discourse, held up to the light. What could make Doc Proton feel so awful that he'd be willing to accept his own death as retribution for it?

I thought, naively, that convincing McKinnon to work with me again and getting the article written was going to be the hardest bit of the process. After the interview with Doc, however, the story took over. McKinnon worked until exhaustion, until every word was a wound, and then filed it, triumphantly.

The editor, of course, rejected it outright.

For a moment, it looked like everything was going to fall apart in the most frustrating, mundane fashion imaginable. McKinnon said the editor was spineless and would publish whatever was filed. So it was, of course, this precise moment that the editor decided to invest in some vertebrae and refuse to run a piece that damaged his struggling online outlet's "already tenuous hero-civilian relationships."

McKinnon fought, of course, pulling rank and threatening to leave. The editor called his bluff and demanded a resignation. When McKinnon sent that update, probably from a BlackBerry while dry-heaving over a toilet, I bit the insides of my cheeks bloody, suppressing the urge to scream and break everything in my immediate vicinity.

"I don't understand," Quantum said to me, completely baffled. "They have to publish it. It's so important."

"We're the villains. No one wants to help us." I was lying in the broken recliner with a cold, wet cloth over my eyes. "I imagine that's going to take some getting used to for you."

"What about other villains?"

"We're not very good at group projects." I said it automatically, but I found I didn't believe it. Here we were, a skeleton crew working in a safe house in a last-ditch effort to save Leviathan. Quantum stood next to me, as long as I could convince her I could get her something she wanted, an extraordinary weapon I needed to figure out how to deploy. This rescue mission almost had a chance of actually succeeding if we could just keep our shit together long enough.

"Auditor?" I lifted the cloth off my eyes to find Vesper's strange silhouette hovering, concerned, in my doorway. The set of his shoulders was odd, tense, and I could see his elevated heartbeat fluttering close to the surface of his skin. "You available?"

"Always here, always at your service." I rubbed my temples.

"So, this might be stupid."

"It might be, but I definitely want to hear it, as

that is certainly the phrase that's launched a thousand schemes."

"We're going to ask for help, eh? Did I hear that right?"

"I appreciate you straight up admitting you were eavesdropping, and yes, we are considering all the options."

"What about Cassowary?" He looked at me expectantly.

I felt a few things move around inside my head, components suddenly fitting together.

"'What about Cassowary,'" I repeated, feeling the edges of each of the words. A former bored heiress who used her vast trust fund and family investments to seed her villainous career, she'd dabbled in a few other industries before finding her passion in being a professional antagonist. She'd funded some tech start-ups, done a bit of digital strategy—and publishing.

"How many outlets does she still own?" I dove for my laptop.

"No idea. She sold off a lot, but she kept a few."

"Her media holdings were all under a company she called Paracrax." I grinned. "Must have always had a thing for the flightless ones."

Sure enough, her company still owned a couple of transmedia conglomerates. A quick search turned up a stroke of infernal luck: one of those happened to be McKinnon's newly former employer.

I beamed at Vesper so brightly that he looked almost embarrassed.

"You know how to get in touch with her?" he asked the floor.

"Yes. I have Leviathan's contacts."

"What are you going to tell her?" I was suddenly aware of how uncomfortable, even afraid, Quantum looked.

"Everything, I think. The truth."

"That the Draft and Supercollider have faked Leviathan's death and we need to lure that broad-shouldered dickweed out so we might be able to sneak in and rescue him, so she needs to pull rank at a news outlet she doesn't remember she owns to make sure an article calling him out gets published," Vesper summarized while coming to stand behind my shoulder. I was sitting cross-legged on the shattered chair, already typing.

"Pretty much. Though you forgot the part about how the article contains Doc Proton's great confession."

"You are putting this into an email."

"Fuck it."

I'm not sure I honestly believed Cassowary would read the message I'd sent, and even if she did, I could hardly picture her doing anything but laughing openly at the absurdity. But when I woke up the next morning, my neck throbbing from the terrible angle I'd slept, still in my clothes from the day before, I had a string of frantic messages from McKinnon, who found himself suddenly and enthusiastically rehired. Apparently with a raise.

And his piece was running after all.

Beneath all of his manic updates was a two-word reply to my completely absurd request from Cassowary: "Good luck."

Greg happened to be loitering in my office, and read over my shoulder when he heard my yelp of joy. "She thinks we have a shot!" Sweet Greg. Optimistic Greg. Smart but about as perceptive as a lawn chair.

"Or she thinks we're signing our own death warrant and it's going to be interesting." My tone was surprisingly cheery even to me. "I'm grateful either way." I sent the most generous reply that I could think of: that I owed her a favor, and a big one, were I ever again in a position where I could repay anything. That I hoped I lived long enough for it to come to haunt me. I thought it might make her smile. Then I gathered the team, and we got to work.

8

With less than a day before McKinnon's article was due to go live, I started an orderly evacuation. Our ramshackle operations had blown under the Draft's radar so far, but as soon as that interview with Doc was out in the world, they would turn every resource they had toward tracking us down. While I actively wanted them to find me, there were many whose lives weren't on the table this time. Information specialists and researchers, my core team and a few other henches who hadn't been able to let go just yet—I wanted them safely dispersed, new IDs in hand in case everything went bad, and safely somewhere else when it was time to do the consequence math.

I had a plan, tenuous though it was. It had been brewing in my head for some time, and in those last

hours it all came together very fast. All of my edu-
cated guesses and napkin calculations wouldn't mean
a damn thing if the final pieces didn't fall in place,
and I had little control then over how it was going to
go. I'd tipped the dominoes and they were collapsing; what they spelled out now, though I'd carefully
engineered the design, was officially out of my hands.
And if I was wrong, very soon now Supercollider was
going to kill me.

It's hard to hold on to the fear of death when it's
an immediate possibility. It's too big an idea, even if
you've been near it over and over again. I'd be calm
for long stretches of time, giving orders and doing my
work in a reasonable manner, and then suddenly this
sick, cold terror would seize me and I'd have to hide in
the bathroom or a utility closet until the panic attack
passed. Maybe I saw a towel in the kitchen and the red
fabric reminded me of Supercollider's suit, or I caught
sight of one of my now faint and yellowing bruises, and
suddenly the memory of his hands on me, the effort-
lessness of his violence, the way I weighed nothing and
meant nothing to him, would splash over me all at once
like an acid bath of remembrance.

Every time I would breathe through it, drawing on
every self-soothing and CBT technique at my disposal.
I'd gradually extract myself from the vivid sense-

memory of his hands—his impossibly powerful hands ready to rip me apart—and back to a state of fear that was manageable. A terror I could work around. And when I could stand and breathe normally, I'd go back to whatever I was doing, the (very likely) possibility I was about to die placed just on the periphery of my mind for a few more hours.

I was recently recovered from one of these moments, almost absently cleaning out the tiny filth nest of my office, when Quantum came to find me. She had no roots here, so she had very little to do while everyone scurried around scrubbing their DNA off surfaces and packing up our scavenged equipment. I worked hard to appear my calm, ragged self, but my heart was in my throat.

"How much longer?" she asked.

I didn't look up. It seemed too dangerous. "Until we leave? Under ten hours; we're going to want to be long gone before that piece goes up tomorrow."

I waited for her to ask about Melting Point's killers, but she didn't. "And what happens then?"

I swallowed. "We go to Dovecote. Supercollider will never be weaker than he will be at that moment. Without you, without Doc, with belief in him critically damaged—we're never going to have a better chance than we will at that moment."

"What are your odds?"

I coughed out a small laugh. "Terrible."

She frowned at me and put a hand on her hip. "But isn't that what you do, check the odds and make the best decision?"

"It is," I allowed. "Sadly, our choices are all bad. We've chosen the best one, which isn't saying much. If everything goes perfectly, and we get in a few lucky blows with a brimstone laser, we might hit ten percent."

I let the silence hang between us. The fact was, there was a Quantum-shaped hole in the center of my plan, and if she didn't step into it, the whole thing would collapse. I needed to lead her close enough to that empty space that she'd be able to see it for herself and step into it, but not drag her over in a way that felt manipulative. I hoped I had done enough.

"I could protect you."

The wave of relief almost knocked me down. I put my hand on my desk to steady myself, and hoped the gesture looked more like surprise.

When I had my composure back, I looked at her, hard. Her hair was twisted up, and her short nails looked freshly bitten. Her eyes were tired and haunted, and she looked strong enough in that moment to have torn the city out by the roots.

"Can you?"

"I can. I'm stronger than he is. Not by much, but I am."

"This wasn't part of the deal."

Her lips tightened. "Let's make a new one."

"What do you want?"

"A piece of him."

"Do you hate him now?"

I thought that might make her angry, but she took the question seriously. Her brow knit, and she thought about it. "I hate everything that made him. I don't know if there's enough of *him* to hate."

I nodded. "He's empty. He's a collection of everything that made him."

She tilted her head to the side, considered. "You're right." She nodded once. "Yes. I hate him."

I had no way to let her know how grateful I was in that moment, so I said, "You know what's more criminal than anything I have ever done? That you've been overshadowed by that lantern-jawed cockwit when you're obviously better than him in every imaginable way."

Pain crossed her face. "Well. No one is willing to make some bitch the head of the greatest superhero team in the world."

She was repeating something that had been said to her; I could hear it in her voice. I dug my nails into my hands, where she couldn't see. I was so angry that I went quite still and quiet inside. I drew careful lines around that piece of anger and made a note to track down whoever it was who had first uttered those words in her presence and, if they were still living, solve that problem.

To her, I said brusquely, "Well, you're precisely the kind of bitch I'd like to see in charge more often."

She laughed. It was a little bitter, but a bit of sweet, syrupy catharsis crept in. "I'll take it."

She walked over and dropped herself down into my terrible reclining chair, like it was a bed at a sleepover. She leaned back, rolling her shoulders and stretching her muscular arms up onto the headrest. She was looking at the ceiling absently, and I let myself stare at her, at the strength in her biceps and the sharp line of her collarbone. For just a moment I allowed myself to imagine we were just two people alone in a bedroom, sharing space, with nothing terrible happening.

"I don't suppose it matters much if you clear your name now, does it," I said.

"You trying to weasel out of our deal?"

"Wouldn't dream of it."

"Then, what do you mean?"

"Since you're officially out of the hero business."

She looked disgusted. "There's a pretty big difference between a literal murderer and a superhero, you know."

I raised an eyebrow. "Is there? For people like us?"

Something lit up her face from the inside. "There should be."

I had touched a nerve, and so I pressed harder. "Is that what you want?"

She tossed her head, thinking. "I think the system is fucked."

"We're agreeing more and more all the time."

She threw up her arms, then let them fall to her sides. "If you're going to try and explain the math again, let me spare you the effort."

I shrugged. "It sounds like you're already on board with the idea that forcing anyone with powers to choose superheroism or be labeled a villain is deeply flawed."

She nodded, perhaps suspicious of our opinions aligning.

"So you want to try and be . . . something else?"

She looked away from me, weighing a thought. "You'll think it's stupid."

"Considering the schemes I am setting in motion this very moment, I find that extremely unlikely."

I saw her clench her jaw. "Someone needs to hold them all accountable. Someone needs to make sure that the 'heroes' act like goddamn heroes. There's got to be a way to keep them in check."

It was a wonderful fantasy to entertain: someone to haunt all of the heroes and keep them in line. I could imagine Quantum inhabiting the role perfectly, merciless and beautiful.

I calculated the risks, took a breath, and said, "I'll help you." I felt like I was watching myself speak the words.

Her eyes locked on mine, sudden and piercing. Her hair was up, but curls were escaping around her face. The black roots were growing out, contrasting the hyper-bleached white-gray of the ends.

"You would want to work with me?" Although it was subtle, I could swear I heard a slight emphasis on "you" and "want," and my palms got a little sweaty. I knew she was an invaluable ally. Someone who was unafraid of the Draft was someone I wanted on my side. And I liked her. She felt like a friend. She felt like she could maybe be more.

"Yes." I hoped it sounded real and solid.

"Really." She thought I was messing with her.

I put a hand to my chest. "I swear. This is an endeavor I can get behind."

She started to smile a little. "We're rather uniquely qualified for the role, aren't we."

"I think we'd crush it." I beamed at her, letting the fairy tale take root in my mind. If someone like her existed, people like me wouldn't have to.

"I'd need a different name," she said.

"Yeah?"

"This one doesn't fit anymore." I looked down. I could see all the little raw spots around her fingernails where she'd been picking nervously at the skin. Her shoulders were straight and strong, her body powerful and solid, but there was a remarkable vulnerability to her in that moment.

"Any thoughts about what you'd change to?"

"You don't think it's a bad idea?"

"No, not at all. Henches and kicks do it all the time when they cross the line."

She nodded thoughtfully. "I did always like 'Decoherence.'"

There was something in the name that seemed to take an almost physical shape as soon as she said it, like she'd breathed something into being. It settled around her.

I nodded. "That feels good. Spend some time with it, make sure it fits, before you take it on. But I like it a lot."

"You think your Boss would let you work with me?"

"I am sure Leviathan would see the wisdom of such

a collaboration," I said. I wasn't entirely sure if I was joking or not. She grinned at me, and I felt myself flush; it was the first time I'd spoken his name to her.

She was quiet for a minute, studying me, then said, "You're in love with him."

My chest was suddenly full of broken glass. I made an extremely unpleasant noise in place of answering. Delicate manipulation I had been prepared for, but this was a very different conversation.

She grimaced. "We don't have to talk about it."

I swallowed hard twice and tried to get my mouth under control. "Well, after that colossal failure to be casual, we might as well."

"So I'm right."

"It's more complicated than that."

"How so?"

"It's more like you're not wrong."

"Auditor, what the fuck does that mean."

"It means I don't know!"

"It's the only possible explanation."

"For what?"

"Oh, sure, people raid supermax complexes and overthrow superheroes for their bosses all the time."

"I'm a penal abolitionist, superheroes are a scourge, and he gives good benefits."

"I wonder what else he gives good."

"*Quantum.*"

"Don't be such a prude, you've thought about it."

". . . I've thought about it."

There was a very long pause. I kept wrapping cords together and securing them with velcro strips. I could feel Quantum getting more frustrated with each passing second. "And your thoughts are . . ." she said finally, exasperated.

"Well. It'd be weird."

"No shit. What else."

I changed tactics. "Have you ever *met* him, Quantum?"

She looked utterly startled. "Of course! We've fought—"

"No. Like when you were not trying to kill each other. Has he ever actually exchanged words with you." She opened her mouth to speak. "Delivering a monologue in the third person does not count, nor do general threats."

"Oh. No." She pressed her lips together and frowned, furrowing her brow and trying to think. "We've never—no, I don't think so. It's all been battlefield shit and posturing and ransoms and whatever."

I nodded. "That's what I thought. When this is over, you should meet him."

"Mmmm." The idea was clearly making her uncomfortable, so I directed things back to my own emotional hellscape.

"Anyway. I'm not sure either of us is capable of the kind of relationship you're talking about."

She relaxed, and grinned at me. "So you're not interested in how good he is with those pincers."

"It's not even about that! I'm academically curious, sure, but . . . Like . . . What does love with him look like? Are you asking me if I wanted to have romantic dinners alone with him, or fuck on his desk, or talk about our feelings?"

"If that's what you think a relationship is."

"Look. My point is, it's irrelevant."

"What is?"

"What my precise feelings are. I have a course of action and I am going through with it. The exact definition of my feelings doesn't matter; what they compel me to do, that matters."

She looked profoundly confused. "Okay. But even if the label on your own feelings doesn't matter, wouldn't you want to know how he felt about you?"

I tilted my head. "He pulled me off an operating table and rebuilt my brain. He killed people to get to me.

"What more could I possibly need to know?"

She couldn't come up with anything to say after that, and I continued packing up. The simple physical task was pleasantly numbing. I got so distracted wiping several hard drives that I didn't notice the precise moment she got up and left.

As we got into the last few Enforcement vehicles we had left, I asked everyone, individually, if they were certain that they wanted to come. A few of the Meat said they would rather stay behind with the noncombat henches, and serve as protection while they all fled to safety. All of the Meat who elected to come with us had to tell me, personally, that they were in. More than I expected decided to come. I tried to hold on to that as a thing to be proud of, to bolster my confidence, rather than making me guiltier for involving more people, more lives, in the gamble we were undertaking.

Keller was furious I even asked him, and I had to soothe him by reassuring him I was asking everyone. Ludmilla nodded, and curtly said, "Yes." Melinda told me she didn't trust anyone else to drive the slip car the way it needed to be driven. Vesper told me he would be my eyes.

Then Quantum was standing beside me. She didn't have a costume anymore; she was wearing high-performance athletic gear, all in black. It was more modest than her superhero attire, and a lot more intimidating. She was wrapping her hands like a prizefighter; it added a comforting press and weight between her fingers, she explained, a holdover from childhood martial arts classes. It also made her powers easier to control. Her hair was tied back, emphasizing her cheekbones and dark eyes. She looked harder, more powerful, surer.

"They're never going to forgive you for this," I said.

She finished wrapping her hands and flexed her fingers. She made a tiny force field blossom between her hands and then popped it, a move like cracking her knuckles. She looked at me.

"It's not so bad, really." She grinned at me and suddenly I could feel my face ache from the width of my smile. "I wasn't planning to forgive them either."

Molly had upgraded my cane for me one more time, despite limited resources. While the sensors were exciting, the fact that it had a concealed knife in the handle delighted me the most in a childish, James Bond kind of way. Ros, from R&D, hooked me up with a discreet little pendant I hung around my neck filled with nanotech that, if swallowed, would neatly liquefy me. It wasn't quite as dramatic as a cyanide capsule hidden in a molar, but it would have to do. If I failed at this, I was not going to give anyone the chance to dissect me again.

I didn't say goodbye to my team, or Greg. I watched discreetly on a security feed while Darla, Jav, and the rest climbed into an unremarkable passenger van, with a good driver behind the wheel and one of the Meat riding shotgun for a bit of extra protection. Greg glanced around briefly, frowning, before arranging his gangly limbs inside. Watching him made my stomach hurt. I didn't want that to be the last moment I saw his confused face.

Then Melinda was in the doorway and Keller was on the comm in my ear. It was time to go.

Once everyone who was leaving had a good head start, the rest of us prepared to meet Supercollider's wrath head-on. We all got into what was left of Leviathan's fleet of vehicles—a slip car, a surveillance and command vehicle, and a couple of lightly armored transports—and started the long, tense drive toward Dovecote. Quantum, Ludmilla, Vesper, and I loaded into the slip car, while Keller and the rest of the Meat loaded into the last command vehicle and some enhanced personnel-carrying cargo vans.

The plan was somewhere between direct and desperate. We were heading straight to the doors of Dovecote; Keller and the Meat would stay at a slight distance until Supercollider was defeated, and then together we'd storm the gates. We were counting on there being some collateral damage from the confrontation between Quantum and Supercollider to help us tear the place apart and make it easier for us to walk in.

"If you happened to knock him through a wall or two while protecting us," I said cheerfully, "that would be remarkably helpful."

"Blast a hole or four that we can widen," Keller added over the comm.

Quantum nodded. "I think I can do that. He's always been terrible at avoiding property damage."

"Show her the fucking PowerPoints, Auditor," Keller grumbled.

I ignored him, and started fiddling with the drink machine. "We'll use all his bad habits against him. The less we have to tear down because he's already done the work for us, the happier I will be." I got the hot water working and fished through the drawers for a tea bag.

"Are you making a motherfucking tea right now?" Vesper's face was so gray it was green, and his hands were locked on to his knees. Ludmilla was outwardly calm but whittling away at her cuticles with a butterfly knife.

I poured hot water into the small travel mug I'd unearthed from one of the storage areas under the seat.

When the steam rose I could smell the fragrance of bergamot and citrus, and something a little floral—there were cornflowers in this particular Earl Grey. "I am." I felt almost giddy. A sense of unreality had descended on me, as if I were watching myself from a small distance.

"Having a tea party in there?" I could hear Keller grinning. There was a crackle and a background bark of laughter. "Where are my goddamn crumpets?"

I actually giggled. It was probably mania, my brain finally gone sideways from the stress, but I hadn't felt as light as I did then since Leviathan went away. "Let me have a moment of peace."

"I feel like I am going to puke." Vesper sounded almost offended.

"Then I won't offer you a cookie." I'd found some gingersnaps. They were a little stale but also they were perfect.

Quantum took a handful when I offered. "Are you always like this?"

I thought for a minute, then dropped, "Fear accompanies the possibility of death. Calm shepherds its certainty."

Everyone stared at me.

"Did none of you watch *Farscape*? I'm disappointed." They stopped talking to me after that.

We still had an hour to drive. Outside the slip car, we were surrounded by brittle, late-autumn farmland just beyond the city, all limp barbwire and fallow fields in the early-morning light. My phone buzzed in my lap and I glanced down; McKinnon's article was live. I nodded toward the screen, as though it needed the acknowledgment, and turned the device off. I leaned back in my seat and closed my eyes. I trusted the team to document and manage the flow of data as best they could, to guide the conversation here and there, and generally do everything in their power to make the footprint of that piece as broad and terrible as possible.

An hour was not long enough for them to be able to come up with any kind of effective crisis comms response, but an hour was enough time that someone would have to tell him. An hour was just enough that his world would be narrowing to a terrible point. Enough that he would be on the verge of a meltdown, a towering monument to fury. He would have no time to think, to collect, to assess. I wanted him at his most uncontrolled and uncontrollable. Which also meant at his most uniquely dangerous.

The slip car was almost friction-free as it moved; I had very little sense of the road. The suspension was liquid smooth. Without the rattle and thrum of movement to distract me, I found myself becoming intimately aware of everything happening in and to my body. I could feel where the seams of all my clothes pressed in, the tag at the back of my collar scraping gently against my neck, the way the fabric folded and clung to the backs of my knees. I was aware of all the funny little aches and itches where my body had healed, or was forever healing. I could feel my heartbeat in all my pulse points, not a nervous flutter but a steady, defiant cadence. I felt a strange, overwhelming tenderness for my body all of a sudden. It had been through a lot.

I rubbed one of my thighs with the same long, reassuring stroke you might use to pet a big dog. *If we get through this, body,* I thought absently, *I'm going to be better to you. If this is it, I'm sorry. You did your best, all the time, and I appreciate you.*

"Auditor?"

I opened my eyes. Vesper was looking at me, the apertures of his eyes almost as wide as they went, making his face even more intense and owlish than usual.

"We're almost there," he said.

"We have some company," Keller's voice said at the same time, through the comm in my ear.

Just ahead of us there were several tactical vehicles waiting on the shoulder, cherries lit and motors running. As we drew nearer, I could see the logos emblazoned on the hoods and sides were the same concentric rings that Supercollider wore on his chest. When we were almost upon them, I could see there was a second logo, this one punched into the metal rather than painted on, much harder to see: a "D" for the Draft in a thick, brutalist font.

Two of the vehicles pulled out suddenly, quick enough to startle a less-skilled driver—Melinda sucked in a breath, but otherwise continued to handle the slip car with her usual, almost serene control. They didn't stop in front of us, though, or form a barricade; they matched pace and drove in front of us. A moment later, after we'd passed all the vehicles completely, the other two fell in behind.

All the calm I'd felt had vanished. All the fear and anxiety that had left me, briefly, slammed back into my body. My chest felt like it was closing in on itself. I tried, as surreptitiously as I could, to breathe.

"An honor guard," Keller said.

"Executioners," Vesper muttered.

"How kind." My voice sounded weirdly absent.

"They gonna fuck with us?" That was the most words I'd ever heard Ludmilla say all together.

I shook my head. "No. They're making sure we don't change our minds. They want us to be in the exact same place we want to be."

"I don't like it." Vesper's eyes were narrowed now, defensive pinpricks.

Then everyone was very quiet. I kept telling myself to breathe; after all, I might not be able to do that much longer.

"When we get there," I said, "everyone else stay in the cars. Supercollider, Quantum, and I are going to have to have a conversation." I tapped my ear. "That means you, Keller."

"Bullshit."

"That's the plan, deal with it. Everyone else stays put until Supercollider is sufficiently occupied. You're not dealing with him, you're dealing with Dovecote."

I locked eyes with Quantum.

She gave a sharp, definitive nod.

"Keep me alive."

She didn't say anything, but her mouth tightened. I chose to read that tightness as resolve. I chose to believe that she wasn't presently questioning that resolve. Then we were slowing, coming up on Dovecote's first set of security gates. I found myself wishing I could hear the ominous crunch of gravel under our car's wheels, could feel the tactile difference as a moment later we drove over the smoother, newer pavement. Instead there was only the slightest, eerie elision, the impossibly easy movement of the slip car winding down. The armored Draft vans circled around us and parked, waiting.

I pulled my comm out of my ear. The slight weight of it, custom-folded to my ear canal, was usually comforting. But for the next few minutes, I needed to be free of any distracting background noise, anyone vying for my attention, anyone else's worries or insecurities about the situation. I let the little earpiece dangle over my collar, still attached by a fine cable.

Vesper said something to me, but I didn't hear it. He reached out one of his hands, and for a moment I took it, returned the cold, jointed grip with a squeeze of my own. Ludmilla made a gesture to follow me out of the slip car, but when I definitively said no for the last time, she did not argue with me. Quantum and I shared a moment of eye contact. She was like a statue pulled out of the ashes of Pompeii.

Quantum and I got out of the car. The door and the cloaking devices seemed to close behind me together; the car didn't become invisible, but all the scanning disrupters were activated, making it impossible to get any kind of a read on who else was inside. It was strange to move through, like breaking the surface of a pool, then watching it grow still again.

It took me a moment to feel confident in my balance. Then slowly, cane in hand, I started to calmly walk toward the first security gate, which was just a small checkpoint shed surrounded by high chain-link and razor wire. Quantum followed, just behind my left shoulder, hands cupped and ready. I could hear something in the space between her fingers, a fuzzy sort of tearing sound.

"Drop your weapon!" The disembodied voice came over a loudspeaker whose exact location I couldn't pinpoint.

"What weapon?" I held up my free hand.

"Your cane, drop it."

"Really?"

"This is the last time I'm asking, drop—"

Then, as so many times before, everything happened both very slowly and very, very fast.

Supercollider came at us like an artillery shell, hitting the ground hard enough to tear a chunk out of the concrete as he launched into a run. He was a blur; Accelerator had been impossibly fast, and defied friction at the atomic level. Supercollider was nothing like that, but he did have his preternatural strength to move him forward, and while he was at least confined by physics, he could *move*.

The blow he landed, backed by momentum and

towering rage, did not fall on me. Instead, he pivoted back on his last step toward us and sucker punched Quantum Entanglement.

She didn't even have time to make a sound. I saw her body fly backward as though thrown from an explosion. She hit one of the Draft vehicles that had parked around us to block our escape. The heavy armor crumpled and the van flipped on its side, making a terrible shearing noise as the metal folded in around the site of impact. Around her body.

A spray of broken glass was falling around me, hitting the concrete like raindrops. It was too close to the first time I saw Supercollider, when he exploded in through the window. Then, as now, shards flew past me, narrowly missing my face. That time, the glass had been the long shards of windowpane. This time, it was the small, squarish bits of safety glass.

I stared at the van when it stopped scraping backward and rocked to a halt. There were muffled screams from inside the Draft's now destroyed vehicle. I saw one of the doors wrenched open and a man began to drag himself free, blood on his face.

There was no movement from the hideously folded metal that Quantum's body had disappeared into.

Then Supercollider was in front of me. He was breathing hard through his nose, a weird, stentorian whistle. I could smell him; his sweat was never dirty, just endless adrenaline and salt. It felt like I had all the time in the world before turning to face him.

He smiled then. It was the most chilling thing I had ever seen, that tiny smile. Not his practiced, cavalier grin from all the promo shots. It was small and broken, arranged by muscles that had mostly atrophied.

"You can't stop me," he said simply. His words were certain as gravity, as the Earth circling the sun. He put one hand on my shoulder, holding me steady. He was not trying to hurt me, but I was trapped by that grip as sure as an insect with a pin through its thorax.

"I understand," he continued quietly. "I do. You must love him very much."

I swallowed. There was a narrative in his head that he planned to execute perfectly, regardless of what I said or did. I let it happen. It gave me time to think, in those last moments I was ever going to have.

How completely stupid I had been, I realized, to think it was ever going to be possible to confront him directly. Even with his powers at his weakest, he was capable of pulverizing flesh beyond recognition. How utterly foolish to believe Quantum Entanglement, whom he'd kept under his thumb for the better part of twelve years, stood a chance in direct confrontation.

How could I think I was going to anything other than my death.

"People become selfish when they want to die," he was saying. "They jump off buildings and don't think of who'll see them smash onto the pavement. They step in front of transport trucks and force drivers to hit them. They pull guns on police officers and take aim. They don't care who they hurt.

"But you." He shook his head. "You *enjoy* it. I can't fathom how many people you took pleasure in destroying."

I knew the answer, down to the lifehour. I let the number slide through my mind one last time, made my peace with it. "Just you," I said.

He drew back his fist. I closed my eyes.

I felt him shift his weight to throw the punch, but then something was wrong. His momentum was thrown off, dissolved and dissipated. He made an awful, frustrated sound in his throat as he staggered.

I opened my eyes and took a gasping, gawky step back, sucking air into my lungs when it suddenly hit me I'd been holding my breath.

One hand was still cocked behind him, in the precise position he'd drawn it back. But it was pinned there; he couldn't release the blow he'd drawn. Instead he was standing weirdly in front of and below his own fist at the most awkward angle, tugging at his arm with his free hand.

I felt the hair rise on the back of my neck and an eerie pull in my stomach.

With a last grunt of frustration, Supercollider looked over my shoulder, past me. I felt the air shiver and rearrange itself behind me, and I followed his gaze.

The demolished Draft van seemed to be turning inside out. The torn metal pulsing and then undulating outward, like the time lapse of a flower blooming. Then Quantum Entanglement pulled herself out, lifting her body from the wreckage with a combination of magic and rage.

Her face was extraordinary. She was Grendel's mother; she was vengeance incarnate. If she'd had any doubt about what she was doing haunting the edges of her actions, all of that was burned up now. Supercollider had tried to kill her; a direct blow like that was a death sentence. If she hadn't used her powers out of sheer reflex she would have been smashed to pieces.

Supercollider snarled, then turned back to his trapped arm and gave it one more half-hearted yank. Then he dropped his shoulders as much as he could and hung his head. He chuckled.

"I should have known. How could I have known?

But I should have." He was talking mostly to himself. Then, he lowered his voice slightly. "You cunt."

I walked backward until I was just behind Quantum's right shoulder. She seemed to disturb the world around her, a strange, slipping sensation when I was near her, but I felt much safer there than being between the two of them. I stared at her a moment, trying to reorder my brain into believing she was still alive. That we were both still alive.

My mouth felt like it was full of ashes and my bloodstream a cocktail of every panic hormone, but I found my voice somehow.

"That's no way to address your better," I said.

"My *better.*" He retched the word. He yanked on his arm again and this time she released the tiny force field trapping his fist, let him succeed. He was not ready for it and the sudden change in momentum threw his balance; he fell. I laughed.

He scrambled to his feet and took a wide, aggressive stance, trying to reclaim some dignity. "How could you do this? How could you betray everything we stood for?"

"You didn't stand for much," she said. Her voice was absolute poison.

"My greatest folly was trusting you. I gave you so much and this is how you repay me—"

I hated how he was talking to her.

"Oh my god, shut up," I said. "You know perfectly well you held her back."

His face went ugly, and he stared at me. "Let me do this, Quantum. Let me take her out. It won't set anything right, but we can clear the slate. We can part ways as peers instead of enemies."

"You've never considered me a peer," she said. "I highly doubt you're going to start now."

"So this is your decision. This is all it took to send you over the edge to evil, a hair's breadth from the abyss this whole—"

"I can't handle this melodrama," I said. "Let us take Leviathan and go."

His face contorted, and he charged us, throwing his invulnerable body forward like a bullet train. He would have smashed us both in that moment. It was almost a relief to see him finally embrace the fact he was willing to kill us.

Quantum caught him with a force field. It wasn't like he hit a wall. No, it was more like he hit water from a great height. He broke its surface, but a strange kind of viscosity caught him. The world seemed to stretch around him for the smallest moment before his forward momentum was reversed, and she threw him backward.

Two of the other vehicles that had led us into the Dovecote compound were parked behind him, in front of the entrance to the security gate. His body hit both of them, unevenly, sending one spinning into the guard shack with an awful metal-on-metal squeal. His body smashed into the other and sent it flying backward with him through the security gate and into the inner courtyard. It was a rather pleasant parallel, I thought.

The heavy chain-link shredded and tore like wet wax paper, coils of razor wire wailing awfully as they were severed.

There's your hole, Keller, I thought.

The armored van scraped to a halt just in front of the second wall and gate, this one made of concrete. It had folded around Supercollider completely, both halves of the van bent toward each other and enveloping him. The metal had twisted together so that the site of the impact looked distressingly like a steel orifice.

It was eerily still. I felt frozen in place, trying to will the vehicle into staying still forever. I wanted him to be simply dead, like an ordinary person. Even though I knew it was impossible, for a moment, I wished.

Quantum, much more practically, strode toward the van before it had completely stopped rattling. I shook myself and followed, awkwardly arranging my comm back into my ear.

I was immediately greeted by Keller hollering, even before it was fully settled in place. "—now, we should move now, Auditor, we should—"

"No, stay put until this place is blasted open. It's going to get a lot uglier before I want any of the Meat deployed."

I listened to him curse as Quantum drew up short and I almost crashed into her back. The wreckage was starting to move again, a terrible rocking wriggle. The twisted armored panels rippled before being torn open, Supercollider furiously rending his way out. I wondered how much blood and bone of those Draft members inside was also being mangled in his effort to get out. I watched as his hands left awful claw marks on the van's body. He looked like something being born, or else summoned, slithering with wretched awkwardness out of the crash.

Quantum was on him before he could stand, trapping his feet to the ground, causing him to pitch forward violently. He would have fallen on his face if she hadn't shoved him backward, lobbing a force bubble contemptuously at his chest. He snarled and lunged at her. She almost absently avoided him, and responded by pinning him down more securely, phase-shifting his feet and calves down into the pavement and then leaving him there, submerged. He spat obscenities as he freed himself, ripping out a huge chunk of the concrete in the process.

I was riveted, watching Quantum fight for the first time. I'd seen her perform support: defending her teammates, rescuing hostages, gracefully dodging attacks, and redirecting the flow of a battle's energy. But that's clearly all it ever was: performance. I'd never seen her go to the wall. On paper her powers seemed ill-suited to offense, all force fields and shifting through matter. In practice, she was capable of using them viciously to frustrate, smother, and entirely overwhelm.

She was difficult to predict because she wasn't trying to wound, but exhaust. She repeatedly turned Supercollider's momentum against him, deflecting his blows so that instead of crashing into her he went careening into a reinforced concrete wall, or falling hard. She would block or surround other swings so that his limbs were temporarily trapped. She'd sink his nearly indestructible body into the walls or ground, forcing him to gouge out hunks of earth or asphalt to free himself.

He was still very dangerous. The concentration required to create and maintain the force fields, to sink matter into matter, was immense, and she was working so fast it was difficult to follow. More than once, he got his hands on her, and it was only by phasing out and through his grip that she narrowly escaped him crushing her.

Once, she sank her own leg into a wall along with Supercollider; he was trapped up to his torso, but there was a terrible moment when she went to move back smoothly and found herself tethered. She fell badly, crashing to her one free knee and scraping it bloody. For a moment she lost her control over the small circular force bubbles she had wrapped around his hands. He dug into the concrete wall itself, searching for purchase on her leg, for the flesh inside the masonry, and it seemed sheer luck she was able to sink farther into the wall and away from him before reemerging intact, shielding herself while Supercollider tore more chunks out of Dovecote's exterior walls.

Supercollider had a great deal in common with a diamond: aesthetically tacky; value artificially ascribed by corporate greed; cultural significance vastly overinflated; and incredibly hard to damage. I'd theorized that the only thing really capable of hurting him would be himself, the way that diamond was used to cut diamond.

Quantum was proving me right. She waited until he was struggling to keep his hands up, like a boxer deep in the late rounds of a title fight. Then she backed off, just a little bit, so I could have a go at him.

I opened my comm channel so that everyone on my team could hear, and tore into him.

Channeling my most disgusted and haughty voice, I told him how pathetic he was, how worthless. How false and feeble his artificial moral code was, and how now everyone knew. I told him he was empty and useless and impotent, until rage gave him a second wind. He turned, stopped trying to attack Quantum, and started going for me.

It was like taunting a vicious animal on the end of a long chain, standing just outside of its reach. I had to trust that chain would hold and snap tight an inch before his fists reached my face. It was impossible not to flinch and grit my teeth, but I managed to stay in place while he slammed into a force field instead of dashing my brains out with a headbutt.

My drawing his attention gave Quantum the tiny space she needed to really work. Now that she was not using every iota of concentration to keep herself alive, she could do worse to him. She threw up more shields to protect me as he flailed impotently, slamming his fists into the suddenly solid air over and over again. Then she focused a smaller force field around his lead leg as he surged forward. Instead of sinking his leg into the ground this time, she simply held him there. She threw more focus, more energy, into the fields around the thickness of his calf. After a moment it became harder to look at his leg directly. The air around it was thick and unctuous, glistening weirdly.

He slowed, then stopped attacking.

"What are you doing?" he panted. There were stress tremors in his arms and his swooping blond hair was plastered down with sweat.

Quantum was shaking as well, tensed and concentrating. She gritted her teeth and I became aware of a weird hum that seemed to be issuing both from the force fields around Supercollider's leg and also from within my own head.

"Quantum?" He dropped his hands completely, let his fists fall open. His voice was suddenly plaintive, placating.

She was talking to herself, mumbling quietly. I could make out every eighth word or so. Most of what I heard was vicious cursing.

"Quantum?"

I didn't know his voice could sound that small.

It happened all at once. Whatever Quantum was fighting against—the preternatural tensile strength of Supercollider's body, the limits of her own abilities, some internal checks holding her back, or a combination of all three—finally gave out. Supercollider's left leg spasmed in the grip of the layers of force fields, then bent, doubled over, and folded in on itself. Flesh sunk into flesh, sinew twisted and knotted, the porous calcium of bone braided through. She'd focused the fold in the middle of his calf, so his heel ended up bubbling out and through his kneecap, the toes pushed out through the back of his knee.

She let go with a gasp, putting a hand to her stomach. She drew in two huge lungfuls of air, gagging on the exhalations. I moved toward her instinctively to help and she waved me away, staggering. The agony of her exertion was too much to bear being touched, I realized.

Supercollider had fallen to his good knee, clutching at the thick, bulbous stump of his leg. His costume was torn away in places but I saw, to my horror, was also woven into and between the flesh where it had fused.

"What the fuck is happening out there, my god, Auditor—" Keller was losing his mind over the comm.

"Shut up."

"What?"

"She phased him. Into himself. Shut up."

"Oh. Jesus."

I stopped listening to Keller after that and just stared. That it was bloodless somehow made it worse. Supercollider was touching his own body in a kind of absent, horrified wonder, as though unable to believe that the limb, buckled and unrecognizable, was his anymore. He'd been able to pull himself free of metal and concrete because he was harder, stronger, more resilient than those materials, but couldn't free himself from the moors of his own flesh. He edged his fingers as far as he could into one of the folds, where his costume had been caught between and under his skin, and gave an exploratory tug.

It was then that he screamed for the first time. It was a weird, gulping shriek that seemed to surprise him as much as it horrified me. He tugged awfully at the places his flesh was most clumsily knitted, as though it were a mistake he could undo with force, like kicking a recalcitrant old television. There was a kind of creaking noise as he tried to pry the folded halves of his leg apart that made my stomach contract.

"Oh god, don't do that, please stop," I said, too quietly for him to possibly hear over the mewling he was making and the groans issuing from the strain he was placing on his supposedly invulnerable body.

As he moaned, Quantum recovered. She had been bent double for a few moments. Now, though, she pulled herself upright.

"Did you know you could do that?" I asked her.

She was quiet so long I wondered if she heard me.

Then she said, "This is the first time I did it on purpose."

"Ask him if he can wiggle his toes," Keller said over the comm.

I audibly gagged. "You're fucking disgusting."

Supercollider let out a wet moan at my words and I realized he thought I was talking about him. I decided not to correct the error.

He pulled at the halves of his leg a few more times, trying to ease and then jerk the folded flesh apart. When he failed again, he looked wildly up at Quantum.

"Put it back," he said. There was spit on his chin. "Fix it, fix it, put it back."

Quantum looked at me. Her face made it clear she had no interest in talking to him; if I wanted to negotiate, that was on me.

"Let him out," I said.

He stared back and forth between us, uncomprehending. It occurred to me he might be in shock.

"If you let Leviathan go," I said slowly, "Quantum will fix your leg."

The information filtered to him through the panic. He shook his head intensely. "No. No. I won. We won, I won. No."

He dragged himself up. He balanced awkwardly on one leg, hopping a little, a kid playing a schoolyard game. He stuck his arms out, groping, and found nothing nearby to hang on to.

"We match now," I said jovially. "Isn't that nice."

He lurched toward me and fell. It was a bad fall; he wasn't expecting it. He wasn't hurt, of course, but it laid him out. He got up very slowly. Instead of standing all the way back up again, he half crawled, half hobbled toward me, putting weight on the stump of his leg.

"Give him back and she won't do any worse." I sounded a lot steadier than I felt as he dragged himself toward me at a shambling crawl.

"Never," he spat. "Never."

He made a grab toward my ankle. He was still well out of range, but the sudden move made me leap back and my guts take a cold flip. I had to remember not to goad too much; he was still very dangerous.

He flung himself toward me again and this time hit a force field like a dog running into a sliding door it thinks has been left open. He snarled and flung himself away from the thin pane of superdense molecules. Quantum, recovered enough to be fully back in control of the situation, glared down at him.

"How dare you," he said to her. "How *dare* you do this to me."

"It's not like you even need the leg," I said conversationally. "Can't you fucking fly or something?"

A profound ugliness took over his face and I saw Quantum's shoulders tighten.

"No," she said. "He can leap, but he can't fly. He needs help . . . staying up." She glowered at him. "Don't you."

"Oh shit."

He was looking at Quantum as though he could bore a hole through her. I could feel his revolting sense of entitlement. She could use her powers for flight, and so she'd used them to support him. I'd read countless articles and reports that referenced flight as one of his superpowers, something that I had never seen questioned or challenged. But it had always been her, keeping him in the air.

He was glaring at her like he would rip the capacity for flight out of her body. Like he could pull it from her like a still-throbbing organ and swallow it down. She took a hard step back from that anger, from the terrible thought of what he might do to her if he could.

But I leaned in. Quietly, I said, "You don't ever have to hold him up again. You don't have to move him an inch if you don't want to."

The corner of her lip twitched and she bared her teeth. "Oh, I want to."

And with that, she distorted the air around him and picked him up.

"You want to fly." She lifted him higher. "Let me help."

He struggled in her grip, but the force field around him held as she took him higher. Soon he was a dot, and she pushed him, right over the top of the main building of Dovecote. I thought I could hear him yelling something, but it was far too faint to make out any words.

She was sweating, and talking to herself again. "A little, just a little," she murmured, over and over. Then, when she was content with his positioning above the prison, she dropped him. He made a sound like an incoming mortar, and when he hit the building I could feel the impact in my body as much as I heard it.

Keller was screaming gleefully into the comm in my ear. "That's right, girls, tear that motherfucker apart." He sounded so proud.

I expected Quantum to lift him straight up out of the crater his body had made in the building, but instead she dragged him *forward*. The walls gave before his body did, collapsing as he was pulled through plaster and drywall and rebar and concrete. She used his nearly indestructible flesh as a battering ram, blasting a wide hole in the front of the building. Once he cleared the walls, she threw him into the yard where we were standing once more, an explosion of dust and debris following him like the tail of a comet.

"That a big enough hole for you?" I asked Keller over the comm.

"Downright lovely, thanks," he said.

"Go, then. Now. Find him."

As soon as I gave that assent, the doors of the vans and armored command vehicle finally slid open. As the Meat piled out, they were met by the Draft security forces, who suddenly disgorged from the remaining vehicles that had followed us in.

Supercollider dragged himself up, chunks of half-frozen earth and construction debris falling from his body. At the same time, Dovecote began to evacuate. An awful siren took up, a deep squalling pulse, and the supermax prison's staff fled out of emergency doors, a few climbing out of the hole in the main atrium itself. There were few people; one of the features of Dovecote was how automated it was. I noticed no one in leg irons or surrounded by containment fields being taken out under guard; they'd clearly left all of the prisoners behind.

"Keller, let most of these fools go," I said. "But grab every security pass and key card that you can."

Over the steady pulse of an energy weapon, he barked, "Bit busy, but I'll see what I can do."

My reply was cut off when Quantum grabbed my arm and pulled me behind her. Supercollider was stalking us down again, moving at a hobbled but inexorable crawl. The dust on his face and in his hair made him look almost demonic, just the wet pits of his eyes fixed on us.

"If I have to use you like a fucking wrecking ball to get to him, I will," I snarled.

"Never." He spat out a gout of mucus and plaster dust. "I'm the only one who can get there. Rip it all down. He'll rot down there."

"This can be hard or easy."

"You can't make me. You can't make me let you in."

As soon as the words were out of his mouth, the energy between us shifted. Quantum changed her stance. I crossed my arms. He slowed; fear and confusion blotted out the anger in his eyes. With the building wailing behind him and Quantum and me staring him down, I think it finally occurred to him that maybe, in fact, we could.

"We choose to take that as a dare," I said. A humorless smile pulled at my face.

Supercollider dragged himself up onto one knee and the gnarled stump of his leg, misplaced toes grotesquely convulsing. He raised his hands to Quantum, for the first time not threateningly, but pleading. His hands were up and open, showing his palms.

"Quantum," he said. "Please."

I groaned, suddenly overcome by nausea. The air

around him started to get thick again, to hum even over the steady siren. My teeth hurt.

She started with his shoulders. She stretched one arm out, and for a moment it almost seemed to elongate before she bent his own arm back, dislocating it at the shoulder socket and folding it across his back. She pressed the arm into the flesh on top of his shoulder blades, the hand wrapped around the opposite shoulder, until it was completely under the surface, even the fingers submerged. His left arm was now buried inside him, a hump across his upper back. Then she went to work on the other arm, folding this one down and around, into his torso.

It was hard to watch. I wasn't squeamish, but when she started to change his face I had to look away, gagging. It was the way his jaw stretched and popped, his grotesque babbling losing any resemblance to recognizable language. I could still hear the awful sound of the rearrangement, something like high-tension wires under impossible stress, and all the fleshy, oozing bodily sounds that came with it.

I could hear him crying. I couldn't find it in myself to enjoy it.

It wouldn't have been nearly so bad if he were more fragile; someone without powers, or even just without his kind of invulnerability, would tear like a wet paper bag, be thrown into deep-shock trauma, then completely come apart. Supercollider was living through it, which made the process much worse.

She stopped when she got a nosebleed. She held the sleeve of her hoodie up to her nose, pinching the nostrils shut and breathing loudly and laboriously through her mouth. Her lungs had the reedy sound of someone who had just run a long distance.

On the ground in front of her was a pile of flesh that had once been shaped like a person. I kept my eyes away from him; glancing at him long enough to make sense of what I was looking at made me queasy.

"Don't you dare barf," she threatened. "I'm a sympathy puker and there is so much blood in my mouth already."

I nodded and averted my eyes more sharply, fighting back the nausea.

With Supercollider undone, I started to pay attention to what was happening around us at Dovecote fully for the first time. Security forces from the escort cars and Dovecote itself were giving the Meat a problem, and while we were meaner and prepared for a fight, they definitely had us outnumbered. I was taking stock of the situation, scowling, while Quantum managed to get her bleeding under control.

"What this situation needs," I said, "is an old-fashioned head on a pike."

"How about a floating flesh bag?" She gestured toward Supercollider, who had begun to make very upsetting noises.

"I think that will do nicely."

Quantum obligingly floated the skin potato over to the center of the confrontation and dropped the sodden mess rather dramatically in front of the Dovecote security forces. One poor bastard puked into his riot mask. After Keller got on the loudspeaker and asked if anyone else was interested in being folded up into a "human asshole" (he always did have a way with words), everyone was suddenly much more reasonable.

With Dovecote's security actively retreating, I was able to pull some resources for the rescue mission itself. I grabbed Vesper to help with the security measures and Ludmilla for sheer creative brutality, and a small team of Meat both to offer additional protection and to carry what was left of Supercollider. Whatever we were about to encounter, he was coming with us; I knew we weren't going to be able to reach Leviathan without him.

Melinda had to stay behind to be our getaway. I ordered Keller to stay with the rest of the Meat and take care of things outside. He half-heartedly protested even though he knew I was right.

"We can handle it," I said, and then, more quietly, "she can handle it."

"I know," he said, too gruffly, and I realized that he felt left out.

"Besides, I need you to make sure we've fully secured the upper floors. It's critical. The last thing I need is some fucking lingering Draft security assholes who stuck around trying to rappel down a goddamn airshaft or some nonsense at the eleventh hour, giving us headaches we don't need."

He was visibly mollified. "We can do that."

"Besides, if—when—we walk out of here with Leviathan instead of this dickless lump, I want a clean, smooth extraction with no fuckery. I need you to make that happen."

He nodded once. "Careful down there. Bring him back."

"We got this," Ludmilla said crisply, and I barked a laugh.

He grinned at that, turned sharply, and started ordering Meat around, once again back in his element. Quantum sidled over to me as we walked to the building, looking gray and close to spent but still smirking.

"If these tough-ass motherfuckers had any idea how much we take care of their dumb feelings, eh?" she said quietly.

I made a strangled noise and doubled over.

"He getting to you, ma'am?" one of the Meat asked, so concerned.

"I'll live," I said, hoping I sounded grave instead of choking on laughter. The Meat hefted Supercollider onto their shoulders, adjusting their grip, and we entered the shattered walls of Dovecote.

The steady wail of the evacuation alarm was muffled when we made our way through the main, working portion of Dovecote and descended to the lower floors. No one much cared if anyone down here could be evacuated in a timely manner or not. No one was going to risk as much as a singed eyebrow rescuing the supervillains locked in its bowels. The staff could get out quickly, the place would go on lockdown, and anyone trapped down there would be left to starve or smother. It made me furious, because it was so obviously part of the design.

We reached the floor that I had been held on during my several days of interrogation. When those doors closed behind us, any trace of the alarm disappeared. It was exceptionally soundproofed on that level; couldn't have anyone overhear what might be going on in any of the interrogation rooms.

A strange, disembodied sensation came over me at the particular smell of that place, concrete and aggression and fear. It wasn't really the look—if anything, it was much more drably corporate than I remembered, almost dingy. The lighting was sickly and the gray walls made the place feel like a neglected hospital. But the smell was exactly the same, and it shook me.

"This was the last place we spent time together," I said to Supercollider, trusting that he was being dragged along close enough to be within earshot. "It's almost romantic, isn't it."

There was no response. I didn't turn my head to check if he'd heard me; I didn't much like to look at him by then.

I turned to the Meat who were not presently carrying Supercollider. "Check each of the rooms down here. If anyone else is being held, let them out." I looked over at Vesper. "Help them."

A pair of enforcers and Vesper peeled away from the rest of us and started systematically dismantling the doors that led off the main corridor. I was disassociating at that point and feeling increasingly unreal and dreamlike. It didn't feel like I was moved by compassion, but rather disgust, and a deep need to take apart absolutely everything that the Draft had built.

The sounds of the doors opening and the shouts or moans of relief elicited a kind of mournful slurping sound from Supercollider, which was satisfying.

We left that floor and made our way through one more security checkpoint before coming to a stark, imposing pair of elevator doors. Their featurelessness was particularly off-putting. The elevator wasn't marked, had no LCD screen to display which floor the car was on. There was also no button to press to call it, just a flat panel of black sapphire glass set directly into the wall.

"Five bucks says it's biometric," I said.

Vesper came to stand next to me and tapped the side of one of his eye sockets. "Handprint and DNA signature, by the look of it."

"What are the odds it's geared to the flesh bag over there."

"High enough to risk whatever terrible booby trap security measures are in place."

"Is that elevator loaded with mustard gas?"

"No, because it isn't the First World War. The system just goes on lockdown, and then we're not getting any deeper in this building without mining equipment."

"While that's not impossible to arrange it's an inconvenience I would rather avoid." I turned behind me to look toward Quantum, trying to keep my eyes fixed on her and not the gibbering mess two of the Meat were dragging behind her. "Do you think you can get one of his hands free?"

She frowned like she was doing long division in her head. "I think so."

"We need intact fingerprints."

"I'll try."

She turned to Supercollider, who made a panicked sound and wriggled at her approach. I was not so ashamed of losing face that I turned my back completely so I didn't have to watch whatever process happened behind me. There was a weird keening sound from the felled hero and one of the Meat coughed and gagged through it.

"You don't need anything above the elbow?" Quantum asked me, her voice shaking a little with effort.

"No, just the flat of the hand, I think."

"Okay, good, one was mostly free. I got it, I think."

I heard a horrible, wet popping sound. I looked to see what she'd done and immediately regretted it; it was like a hand stuck to a plate of undercooked ham. I ordered the two Meat who had been on Supercollider duty to take a break and two fresh pairs of arms and gag reflexes came forward. They picked up the mass of flesh and carried Supercollider over to the elevator doors to position his hand against the glass panel. I took the opportunity to close my eyes and rub the bridge of my nose; Vesper put a hand on my shoulder and squeezed. I rested one hand on top of his metal fingers; the cold was comforting.

"He won't touch it!" one of the Meat complained. I reluctantly opened my eyes to see them struggling with Supercollider, who was shaking convulsively.

"What do you mean? *Make* him."

"He's made a fist. He won't put his hand down. I can't—eeeeeiiiiiiiiiii!" The Meat shrieked and let go of Supercollider, causing his compatriot to also lose a grip on the undulating flesh sack they held between them. He was screaming because two of his fingers had been crushed by Supercollider's one freed hand.

"Goddamn it, get him out of here," I said, my voice raw and more frustrated than I expected. "Get him help," I added, trying to gentle my annoyance. The Meat's buddy took that to mean he should take his injured friend back upstairs and in the vicinity of some gauze and a tourniquet. The bleeding Meat kicked Supercollider as the two of them left. I appreciated it for the sentiment even if it was entirely ineffectual.

Supercollider's one free hand was clenching at the

air rapidly, at once absurd and grotesque, but even so profoundly limited as he was, he was still dangerous. I ordered everyone to step away from him. On the bare concrete he looked a bit like an action figure melted into a pool of plastic in a microwave. I pushed down the wave of hysterical laughter that threatened to bubble up at the image, smothering it with irritation.

"I can put a force field in the palm of his hand to keep the fingers open," Quantum suggested, "but that will only do so much good."

"Sink his arm back in," I said.

"But that'll—"

"Leave his palm and the underside of his fingers on the surface, but submerge the rest."

She frowned for a moment, trying to picture it, then slowly nodded. She flattened his flailing hand, bending it back at the wrist and splaying his fingers out, then sunk his arm all the way down into the lumpen wreck of his body, like burying a knife up to the hilt. When she let go, the back of his hand was fused into his flesh, but the palm and fingers were still at the surface on a flat plane of flesh. It might have once been his shoulder.

The Meat left with us lifted his body and held his hand, as it was, against the glass. He was shaped so awkwardly and had so few handholds now. One of the

Meat complained aloud, as they shifted and struggled and tried for a long time to get his hand positioned correctly, that he was wet all over. I wished I didn't have to think about that.

After several laborious minutes, they finally got his hand pressed against the glass; the elevator rewarded us with a deep, uncomfortable hum as the handprint was registered and the car began to move toward us. The Meat sighed with relief, eager to drop Supercollider if they could or at least adjust his weight in a way that was easier to carry. I heard one of them mumble about needing multiple showers, which made me notice how sticky and abject I felt.

The doors opened to a starkly lit, smooth metal interior, without mirrors to counteract the sense of claustrophobia. It was an elevator designed to contain and intimidate. The Meat dragged Supercollider in and the rest of us followed, standing as far from him as we could.

The elevator started to move, but very slowly. A laser scan passed over us and I felt a fresh rush of panic.

"Unable to register facial recognition. Please face the doors," said a calm, cheery robot voice.

"Ah shit," Vesper said. Ludmilla stepped closer to me, protectively, as though she were going to be able to fight the elevator robot with her fists.

"Get him up," I said. "Hold him up so his face is where it should be."

The Meat grunted and lifted Supercollider higher off the ground. The lasers swept again. The robot again pleasantly informed us we'd failed the scan. "Two more attempts. Please face the doors."

"Higher," Quantum said, "he's taller than that." Her voice was even and authoritative but the set of her shoulders had become tense.

The Meat groaned and hauled Supercollider's torso—he was really all torso now, his face lodged somewhere in the center of his chest and grotesquely blended and elongated, like the Blemmyes in the *Nuremberg Chronicle.*

"It's not going to work, look at his fucking face." There was raw panic in Vesper's voice.

"I am trying not to. Shit. Shit."

The lasers screened the elevator a third time, cool and efficient. "Unable to register facial recognition. One more attempt. Would you prefer a retinal scan?"

"Yes, we would prefer that, for fuck's sake." Vesper was rattled. He didn't like enclosed spaces.

"Unable to process your answer, Supercollider."

Quantum had her phone in her hand, her brow furrowed. "Shut up," she said, frantically hunting. "One second, one second." She put the phone to her ear.

"Are you taking a fucking call right now or—" I kicked Vesper to shut him up while Quantum glared daggers at him. I motioned for everyone else to be silent.

"Would you prefer a retinal scan?" the robot sang.

Quantum's face lit up. She switched her phone to speaker and played a clip. It was tinny and weird, but Supercollider's voice. "Yes, I'd like that. Can we—" She cut it off.

"It sounds like you would prefer a retinal scan. Is that correct?"

Quantum played the clip again. "—message. Yes, I'd like that. C—"

"Retinal scan indicated. Scanner active." A panel slid open and a rectangular box descended from the ceiling. It came down to face height for someone around six-four. There was a thin slit of glass in the device. "Please look into the mirror, Supercollider."

Ludmilla and Quantum moved to help the Meat position the ruin of Supercollider's face exactly right in front of the aperture. He couldn't do much to resist, but he was trying. He wriggled like a pupa about to split open before the cicada emerged from the husk.

"Please look directly into the mirror, Supercollider," the robot chided. "Unable to register retinal scan. Please try not to blink."

"Keep his eyes open," I said. "He's not looking."

"I'm not sure I can hold his eyelids open without damaging them," Quantum fretted. She was visibly sweating from both physical strain and focus.

"I don't care, none of us are dying in this box."

She gritted her teeth. Of everything she had done to him, this was obviously the most horrific for her, the most difficult. Supercollider squalled pathetically, and one of the Meat turned his face away suddenly.

After a tense second, the robot chirped happily.

"Retinal scan confirmed. Thank you, Supercollider. Proceeding to special containment."

The collective sigh of relief was immense. Everyone dropped Supercollider to the ground, unable to keep supporting his bulk, and he lay in a grotesque puddle as we continued our descent. Quantum turned to one of the walls and rested her forehead against the cool metal surface, looking defeated. I approached her and she raised a hand, telling me to let her be.

"It's almost over," I said. "That should be the last thing you have to do."

"I don't think I can—"

"You won't have to. It's done. You're done now, okay?"

"Okay."

I resisted the impulse to touch her comfortingly,

knowing it was the last thing she wanted, and moved as close to the doors as I could. I wanted out of this metal box as quick as possible.

After a distance that seemed impossible, the elevator finally ground to a merciful halt. The air had become so thin and close and sour I felt like I was suffocating. The doors slid serenely open and I slipped a little in my haste to get out; I didn't want to think too hard about what might have made the floor slick.

Everyone stumbled and staggered out of the elevator with the almost sobbing relief of people who had been trapped underground for weeks and were just experiencing fresh air again. The landing we reached wasn't much to celebrate. There was just barely enough room for all of us; the space wasn't much bigger than the elevator itself. It was gray and sterile, sealed concrete. There had been no attempt at all to make the space hospitable or comfortable. It was clear this was not somewhere anyone came very often.

The ceilings were low and the short corridor in front of us was narrow enough that two people could barely stand abreast, tight enough that the Meat lifting Supercollider had to switch their grip so they were carrying him like a piece of furniture, with one in front and the other behind.

The corridor led to a pair of doors with a short foyer

between, which was at least better lit than the hall-way in front or behind it. The foyer housed a pair of negative-pressure doors, the kind that might be found in an isolation unit on a hospital's critical-care floor. A sign told us brusquely the second set of doors would not open before the first was sealed, to prevent con-taminants from either entering the rooms beyond or escaping out into the rest of the facility.

"We can't all fit between the doors at once," Vesper said, rubbing the back of his neck.

"I'll stay here," Quantum said, too quickly.

I turned, surprised. "You sure?"

She nodded once. She looked as unwell as I had seen her, gray and clammy, her lips almost bloodless.

"You deserve to be there. We can go through in shifts. This is your moment too."

"I'm fine." She flinched at how loud her voice was in that lonely space.

I realized that she was terrified, and backed off. It was easy to forget that to her Leviathan was still the boogeyman; to most people he was still the scariest thing in the world. Even underground, even impris-oned, even in whatever condition he was going to be in, she'd spent all of her career as his adversary, think-ing he was the incarnation of everything to be fought against in this world.

"No problem. Guard the exit." She was visibly re-lieved, and seemed especially so to have a job to do, an excuse not to enter Leviathan's cell.

I gritted my teeth before speaking again, realizing that the best way forward was going to put me in a ter-rible situation. "I think we can only fit three at a time. In case we need to disarm another fucking bomb with Super Meat Sack's farts or something, one of you"—I pointed to the Meat—"and I should take him through first."

The Meat looked at each other, stuck their fists out, and threw a round of rock-paper-scissors (they'd propped Supercollider against the wall as we problem-solved, like a piece of luggage). The loser (rock) swore and turned toward me. "Can you help me carry him through? He's heavy."

"I'm not sure how useful I can be, but I'll help you drag him." I was wearing a harness that had a special loop for my cane; I was able to sling it across my back to get both my hands free. I had avoided much con-tact with the sheer abjection of Supercollider's present physical form, but there was no way I could avoid it now. The two Meat got him through the first set of doors, but then one of them left and I had to take his place. The doors closed behind the three of us and then—but for one bullet-headed enforcer with a blond high-and-tight—I was alone with the ruined bloat that the hero had become.

Most of his costume had torn, having been used over and over to lift and reposition and drag him. There were still shreds and chunks of it, grotesquely woven between the places where his flesh was folded over, effectively creating handles to pick him up with. He was awfully heavy, almost impossibly so; I suddenly had a deep pang of sympathy for the Meat who'd been taking turns dragging and carrying and hoisting him throughout the facility.

Despite his indestructibility, his flesh was still warm and elastic, still had the deceptive give that made me think it would be fragile. It made me wince to drag him across the floor, imagining that flesh catching on the sealed concrete, but I couldn't scrape or abrade him if I tried. It would have taken Leviathan's most advanced technology to so much as make him bleed a little.

I hated touching him. He was damp all over and actively wet in some places, sweat and drool and possibly piss; I couldn't tell which orifices were folded up where or how, and frankly I didn't want to look closely enough to have that clarified. His eyelids were mercifully not destroyed, but they were swollen now and his eyes were oozing with thick, clear lymph. He wasn't making sounds anymore, and his eyes were closed as much as they could be. I decided he must have lost consciousness.

Sweating, negotiating with the exhausted Meat about who needed to lift what and who needed to shove when, I didn't feel triumphant. I felt tired and full of revulsion. I was anxious to get to Leviathan at last and also secretly terrified about what I would find, how he would be. I was just raw and scared and wanted it to be over.

After too many struggle-filled minutes we got him to the other side of the doors, set our burden down, and got them sealed. I leaned heavily against the wall, my face pressed against its comforting immovability and coolness with my eyes closed, for the much quicker span of time it took for everyone else to get through the negative-pressure lock. I didn't move until Vesper came and put his hands on my shoulders; I felt the internal whir of his finger joints tightening to give me a small squeeze. When I didn't move immediately he took my cane out of the harness across my back, and handed it to me when I wearily turned around.

There was only a single door now. It was more like the entrance to a vault, with a heavy rotating lock mechanism. The handle looked like something that would open an ancient submarine. There was also a keypad, and a flat panel that looked unhappily like it might be another biometric authenticator.

"Want me to try and talk to the lock?" Vesper offered kindly, digging in the pocket of his tactical vest for a cable he could plug into his temple.

I made a noncommittal sound and walked a little closer, trying to figure out a plan of attack least likely to get us gassed or nuked. A proximity sensor went off when I got a bit nearer, and the panel hummed to life.

"Welcome, Supercollider, we've been expecting you," the robot said solicitously. I hissed a curse. "Streamlined access still active. Please stand on the pressure plate for final scan."

I suddenly realized there was a round spot on the floor, right in front of the door, that was inset in the concrete the smallest margin; it must be weight sensitive.

"Set him down there, slowly," I ordered the Meat. "Put half his weight down and then the rest of it, like he's taking a step onto the plate."

"We'll try," the thick-necked blond said, and laboriously began to maneuver Supercollider onto the pressure sensor.

"Streamlined access!" Vesper was disgusted. "I bet the asshole doesn't even have two-factor authentication enabled."

I chose not to remind Vesper that streamlined access was probably the only reason we were able to do this. Ludmilla drew close to me, expecting things to go badly as always. Her pessimism was one of the most comforting things in the world, steady and unchanging as the tides.

"Thank you, Supercollider," the robot hummed. "Please deposit a DNA sample to be granted access."

A tiny slot opened in the blank panel by the door, containing a buccal swab.

"Of course."

I gingerly took the swab in my hand and made my way to Supercollider, careful not to step on the edges of the plate. Mercifully, he was "face"-up, his features emerging from the swollen and irregular landscape of his chest like a volcanic island rising out of the ocean.

He hadn't been able to speak since Quantum had sunk his head into his body; his muscles were so out of place, and his jaw anchored by the flesh around it. His lips were parted and bunched over to one side, out of which he'd been drooling steadily. I got the scraper end of the swab in the dribbling aperture, ran it roughly over the inside of his cheek, and stepped back.

"Pick him up," I ordered. "The robot needs to think he's dropped the swab in himself, and it won't work if he's still on the plate."

The Meat was not excited about having to lift Supercollider so soon. "You sure?"

"Better safe than sorry."

He hefted Supercollider off the plate, arms shaking, and I waited a beat before dropping the swab into the little slot. It disappeared into the mechanism next to the door and the computer hummed happily.

"You can drop him now," I said, almost as an afterthought, and there was a sound like a side of beef hitting the floor of an abattoir that made me wince.

The door thought for a moment and then obligingly slid open.

"Thank you, Supercollider," it said serenely.

The room beyond was painfully bright. I flinched and squinted, waiting for my eyes to adjust, at once wanting to rush in and wanting this last delay to stretch out into infinity.

Anxiety had my stomach in a vise grip. Being in Leviathan's presence was always a nerve-racking experience, no matter how much weird affection grew between us. There was no real way to gauge if a force of nature returned or was even aware of one's attachment. The few weeks we had been apart made me awkward and forgetful; I was suddenly gripped by the stupid panic that I wouldn't know what to say to him.

I also didn't know what state I would find him in. His near-invulnerability was a great comfort, but Supercollider was supposed to be indestructible too, and we'd been able to do unspeakable things to him. The Draft had far more resources at their disposal, and Supercollider was not as intelligent or creative, but certainly matched us for malice. I was worried I would find Leviathan in pieces. I was worried he would be an empty shell.

He didn't smell like a human who was suffering confinement—the stale body odor and accumulated filth, the sourness of starvation. The smell in the room was dry and warm, kind of brittle, a bit like fallen leaves late into the autumn, after frost had touched them and they had just begun to decay.

The room was bare to the point of featurelessness. The light further washed it out and made the space seem unreal, at risk of melting away. A toilet and a sink were set firmly into the wall and floor. There was a weird hum I could feel more than hear, which I suspected was interference from a Faraday cage.

The light made it difficult at first for me to locate him on the infrared scale, so the first thing I saw when my eyes were still adjusting was a smear of ultraviolet defiance. He was seated with his back to the wall, legs bent and arms resting against his knees, a pose that was strategically defensive but appeared almost rakishly casual. His head was down but carefully angled, cocked and listening.

Ludmilla strode past me into the too-bright room and went to stand by her regular place at his right side. She left a careful distance, ready to help him up, but not moving to touch him until he gave assent. I allowed her momentum to propel me forward, coming to stand in front of him.

"You look better than I thought you would," I managed, hearing my voice crack and letting it happen.

He didn't move or respond for a long moment, and I felt an ugly rush of panic in my gut. Maybe what I had first seen as hypervigilance was in fact crushed defeat; maybe what looked initially like careful wariness was emptiness.

Then, he lifted his head an infinitesimal amount. "Now, this is new. This is interesting."

Of course he thought this was a tactic, another piece of whatever psychological warfare he'd been subjected to. I didn't try and reassert my own reality, didn't beg him to recognize me. The best way to convince him was to be steadily, stalwartly real.

"Can you stand?" I asked.

A ripple passed across him, a kind of grim amusement. "How kind of you to ask."

"Leviathan. Are you hurt, Sir?" I felt a sour welling in my throat. I rolled my eyes up, trying to will myself not to cry, but the lights were too bright and my eyes started watering immediately, the exact opposite of what I wanted to happen.

He lifted his head a little more at the smell of salt water on my face. "This is good, this is very good. Your best so far, in fact."

I felt a little bewildered, unsure what the most helpful thing to do or say would be. I looked behind me for support; the Meat were waiting respectfully in the hallway, unnecessarily guarding Supercollider, while Vesper stood warily at the threshold. The openings of his eyes were tightened as much as they could and the brightness was obviously horrifically uncomfortable for him, so he was keeping a bit of distance between himself and the full intensity of the light.

I turned back. "You can leave whenever you like," I said, clearly and steadily. "Let us take you home."

He sighed. "The voice is very convincing, I'll give you that."

"Leviathan, it's me."

"You would have me hope. It's crueller than you usually are. You would have me stand and try to walk out the door, perhaps even let me get a step through, before whatever you have devised next as punishment befalls me. Clever indeed, but not clever enough by far."

"No one will try to stop you."

"Oh? Is Supercollider not behind you?"

"He is, actually."

Leviathan looked at me then. Whatever script he was following in his head, this was not in it. His dark eyes, which I used to think were screens or lenses, but I now knew were as biological as my own corneas, were inky and unreadable, but there was a tiny bit of doubtfulness hovering around his shoulders.

"I brought you a present, Leviathan. Would you like to see?"

I ordered the Meat to bring Supercollider into the room. They hefted him between them and carried him in, with a scuttling kind of crabwise gait. They were close to exhausted and moving him was becoming more of a challenge every time. They couldn't put him down gently anymore, and instead flung him more dramatically than was strictly necessary at Leviathan's feet. He landed facedown with a sodden thump. There was a wet, slurping noise against the floor.

Leviathan stood. He was visibly thinner than when I had seen him last, his waist waspish, and the planes and angles of his body made harsher, more insectoid, by what I suspected was dehydration. His movement was not predatory but defensive. He was something cornered, moving a bit too slow and ready to sink his fangs in at a wrong move. The Meat sensed the threat in him and backed off, chests heaving with the effort. They smelled like fresh sweat; the thing on the floor was bile and fear and ruin.

Leviathan prodded Supercollider with his boot—not a boot, but a jointed appendage, like a mantis's hydraulic foot—and the hero made a miserable gurgling sound. It might have been a plea, or just unhappy jabbering. Leviathan met my eyes again, his gaze wild now, panicking, and kicked Supercollider over onto his back.

Twisted almost beyond recognition, sunken into the center of his chest, mouth reduced to a grotesque orifice, there was just enough of the ghost of Supercollider's face left that someone who knew him, really knew him, would know whom they saw. Leviathan knew exactly whose defeat he was witness to.

Leviathan screamed.

I had prepared myself for a lot, for maniacal laughter or complete disbelief or even rage. I wasn't sure if Leviathan would be grateful or furious, gleeful or too distraught and confused by his confinement to understand what was happening. I made myself imagine the possibility he wouldn't be conscious. But as he lowered his forehead to touch the floor, and my stomach turned to ice and ash, I realized I was completely unprepared to deal with his raw, unfathomable grief.

Vesper would always let me be quiet. It was a great gift of his. Greg would yammer on to fill the silence, shoving his glasses up his nose, hands awkward and always a little flailing. Keller would try and be rational, talk me through things, problem-solve. But Vesper would let me sit for a long time, thinking, and simply take up space with me. He'd sip his coffee contemplatively, and let me take my time. Then, with unerring accuracy, as soon as something finally shifted in my head and I was ready, he'd ask a question.

This time, he'd been standing in my new office—my new office in the compound—admiring the art I'd chosen for the walls, his head cocked contemplatively while I worked. Three beautiful, brand-new monitors glowed happily on my desk, each displaying a different set of social media feeds and data arrays, windows overlapping each other. There was the faintest smell of fresh paint still palpable in the room, and muffled by the walls I could just make out the very distant bang and mechanical whir of construction happening somewhere else on the floor of our building. Finally, he turned to me like he was about to remark on the weather.

"So, is he talking to you yet?"

I'd been waiting for this. I stared straight ahead, pretending I still cared about what was on the screen in front of me. "He's making sure that I am kept apprised of his wishes."

His eyeholes whirred and contracted. "This isn't a status report. Is he speaking to you, using his mouth, while looking at your face, while you are physically in the same room."

I winced. "No."

"Any change at all?"

"He did forward me an email directly."

"Any words attached?"

"No."

"That barely counts."

"It feels like not much but something."

"Sounds like not much."

A long but comfortable silence stretched between us again. I wasn't expecting Leviathan would use something as crude as internal messaging if he wished to speak to me. The subaural tone hardwired directly in my head would thrum the second he had any interest in my presence or opinions. It had, since we'd brought him home, remained completely silent.

I stood up to refill my mug from the coffeemaker, which was also new, and which sang a little tune when you selected how many shots of espresso you were in the mood for.

"I choose to believe this"—I swept my arm around

me to encompass my beautiful workspace, one of the very first restored in the rebuild—"is a gesture of affection."

He made a small, disgusted noise. "It is literally not even the least he could do."

Vesper wasn't wrong, but I wasn't sure how to even begin arguing with him.

"Is this what you thought would happen?"

I shoved my hands deeper into my pockets, aware that the gesture was such a cliché. I wished I had a can to kick. "I don't know."

Vesper found a lovely new chair to perch on, which creaked when he settled onto it. "I think you do."

"I thought—I hoped—that he would be okay . . . or okay enough. That we would get him back and—"

"Things would be the same again?"

"I didn't think he would be so . . ." I trailed off. "I didn't think it would be this hard."

"When we got him back?"

"If we got him back. I thought there was a good chance he'd be whole, that they wouldn't have been able to—"

"How did you think he would be with you?" Vesper was trying so hard to be kind.

I considered lying, but didn't have the energy to try and hide my feelings from someone who'd taught me how to read people. "I just . . ." I let it hang. This was deeply embarrassing when I looked at it. "I thought he'd be happy."

"And grateful."

"Yeah."

"You did more, and better, than he could have imagined. You expected, somewhere, that he would notice."

I swallowed hard, and didn't answer. We were both quiet a moment, in an awkward but not unpleasant stalemate.

"Is the clean-out done?" He decided to let me off the hook for a moment.

"Long done." The safe house had been dealt with as soon as we had Leviathan.

"I'm going to miss your awful recliner."

"RIP in peace."

"Did they send in the nanobots?"

"Nah, just a little arranged arson, maybe a small EMP. Our roots there weren't very deep."

"Why be elegant when you can be effective."

"And explained away."

"So. Now what happens?"

"That depends on if Leviathan will ever talk to me again."

"He will."

"Probably."

Vesper looked at his hands, and fiddled with the tip of one of his long, mechanical fingers. "Have you heard anything about her?"

My stomach dropped. "No," I said. "Nothing since she blipped out."

I thought back to the last moment I'd seen Quantum Entanglement. I didn't know I'd be laying eyes on her for the last time, so I'd committed precious few details to memory. Almost all of my attention had been on Leviathan. For long moments, he would not move nor allow anyone to touch him. He stayed curled on the floor, racked by awful, rattling sobs. When I drew near him he flinched in open revulsion, and I couldn't bear to try again. I wept silently. It was Ludmilla who finally coaxed him up and carefully led him out of the confinement room. Everyone followed them out, not speaking. We left Supercollider leaking on the floor.

When we got through the doors, making a grim procession toward the elevator, I was lost in my own terrible thoughts. If I had not glanced up I might have missed her completely: the moment she saw Leviathan, her face registered raw shock and panic, and she phase-shifted out of sight.

At first, I thought that she was overwhelmed simply seeing him. A weakened Leviathan was still terrifying, and she had been through a great deal. As we withdrew from Dovecote, taking a few liberated villains with us but leaving most to find their own way back to their lairs, I expected her to reappear once she processed what she'd done. But she never returned. My focus was entirely on getting Leviathan to safety, and though her disappearance worried me, it was buried under far more pressing logistical and emotional problems.

It was only much later, when Leviathan was recovering under medical supervision and the lights were back on at the compound, that Darla said I needed to see something. They'd been processing some of the data we'd taken from Dovecote, ripping things from whatever hard drives we'd liberated, when they found something on a laptop one of the Meat had grabbed on her way out.

Anything related to Leviathan was flagged for a manual review, and once Darla broke the encryption, they called me over immediately.

It was the Leviathan Protocol. Much of it was extremely technical, detailing the exact specifications of his confinement room, from the pH balance of any liquids he might come into contact with to the thickness of the concrete that made up the walls. I discovered I was right about the Faraday cage. The Protocol even theorized how many lumens might be necessary to cause him pain.

There was only a single specification that didn't match, but it meant everything:

> Under no circumstances is Leviathan to be kept alive for more than 48 hours after capture. All study and interrogation must take place within this window, after which he must be terminated. No extensions will be granted under any circumstances. Within the 48-hour allowable confinement period any attempts to break confinement or escape must be met with deadly force. Once death has been confirmed (see Appedixes 6 and 7 for instructions on how to pronounce subject officially deceased), study may continue.

Forty-eight hours. Not twenty-one days.

When Quantum came to us, she was lying; she thought he was already dead. She expected us to find a corpse in that room, or nothing at all. It was only because they *couldn't* kill him after all (which I uncovered in an increasingly panicked series of memos among Dovecote staff) that our mission was still a rescue, and not retrieving a body.

Her deception hurt me, but her departure wrecked me. I was furious at first, storming around the office and ranting at anyone unlucky enough to be in my field of vision. Slowly, however, an aching kind of betrayal set in. Whatever I had felt, whatever connection I thought we had made, was once again misplaced. When things went wrong, when what she was using me for didn't work out the way she expected, she vanished. It made me think of June, which made me feel even angrier and more pathetic.

"I hope she got what she wanted," I said, much more viciously than I intended.

"You got what you wanted," Vesper reminded me. I turned my face away from him, disliking the number of questions hovering around the edges of that statement. It also drew my attention to my own hypocrisy: I'd lied through my teeth to Quantum, often and at length. I manipulated her into putting herself in very real danger to achieve my ends. She did the same to me to enact vengeance (on Melting Point's hapless murderers, maybe; certainly on Supercollider himself, in the end), and it was unfair to blame her for it.

That didn't stop me, however. I couldn't let go of the fact that she would have let me find Leviathan dead, or simply vanished. I hated that look of total fear I'd seen on her face, however briefly. She only helped me because she believed he'd never see the light of day again, because she thought he was already in pieces.

"*Did* you get what you wanted?" Vesper was still staring at me; I'd left him unanswered far too long.

I ran my tongue over my teeth and swallowed. I couldn't banish the thought any longer: What if Leviathan never got over the knowledge that he hadn't been able to free himself, and needed to be rescued? What if he never recovered from the fact that his archenemy's ex-girlfriend defeated his greatest foe instead of him? What if he couldn't process the idea that Supercollider might never recover, would never pose a threat again? What if his feelings of vulnerability and inadequacy turned into a new kind of hate—for me?

"What I wanted," I said softly, "foolishly included Leviathan speaking to me." And a great deal more than that, I thought but didn't say. I stared out the window—my new office had a window—across the demolished courtyard. There were several large craters from the fight still blasted into the ground. A few mangy pigeons strutted about the yard, pecking the asphalt between tattered dead leaves and cigarette butts. Soon, it would be freshly landscaped again. I couldn't bear the thought that I might not be wanted here anymore.

I thought of Jav and Darla and Tamara (whom we'd immediately rehired) working quietly in the semi-open space they shared next to mine. I felt a sudden sharp tug of affection for them all, working so hard to sort out the math, to keep an eye on the damage and help balance it. Even if I was never forgiven, and couldn't stay, I hoped that, just maybe, they'd be able to hum along without me, to keep our little disaster engine careening forward.

"If he doesn't talk to you soon—and grant you your every whim for the rest of your days, quite frankly—he's not nearly as smart as we all thought he was," Vesper said. He was fierce and intense, and I felt a twinge of affection for him too.

"Worse comes to worst," I said, "I'm counting on you for a reference."

I don't know if Leviathan listened in on that conversation, providing an impetus for him to speak with me again. It could have been a coincidental matter of timing. But the day after I spoke to Vesper, my head rang with his summons at last.

I did what anyone did when Leviathan called them: I went to him. It was the longest elevator ride I'd ever taken in my life. I'd always been anxious stepping into his presence, as would anyone with a shred of self-preservation, but this was paralyzing. My heart hammered in my throat and my chest squeezed so tight I wasn't sure I would make it to him. Despite the urgent humming in my head, I stood outside his doors longer than I should have, willing my courage to come together.

Finally, I stepped across the threshold, the massive doors smoothly opening for me. The smell of that room, and the noise of it, the buzz I could feel in my entire body, sent such a rush of aching familiarity through me that I thought I would lose my composure. I had missed this. Missed this weird, vast, terrible office so badly. I could finally put that longing down—if only for a moment.

I saw his eyespots first. They were shining like bioluminescent creatures deep in the ocean, bright on his shoulder blades. He was sitting with his back to me. Something had his attention, and it let me gather myself and step forward.

When I felt I could do so, I spoke.

"You look well, Sir."

He unfolded himself from his chair, stretching long, angular limbs. He was still thinner than he had been, but was recovering from his confinement. As he moved, he gleamed. I studied every joint and segment and took in the truth and beauty of him; there was no longer an unspoken underneath to wonder about.

"That is kind," he said quietly, "from someone who knows what they are looking at."

It occurred to me, for the first time, he might be ashamed to have someone know.

"I've always known exactly who I'm looking at."

That took him aback; it passed across his face like headlights through a window. He covered his surprise by turning quickly to activate one of the huge screens behind his desk. Then, he came to stand beside me. I heard his joints click into place, and felt the eerie warmth he emitted. I could have leaned toward him, the familiar sense impressions of him were so comforting. Every moment he was alive and whole released tension I forgot I was holding.

"I had a great deal of time to think, Auditor." He tapped his tablet and a single image appeared on the screen in front of us. "All it seemed I had was time. I returned, over and over, to that which you accomplished, and all you would have deployed if given the chance." He paused, and I swallowed hard. "Time to sit with the consequences."

With a hand on my shoulder he turned me to face him. The abject misery I had seen before was no longer there. Instead a deep, mindful grief had settled over his face.

"No matter my personal feelings"—there were oceans in those words—"I had to lay them down. When

I could do so, when I could allow my thinking to ascend, I saw your plans as though for the first time."

"Thank y—"

"No longer bound to consider each cog and coil, I saw the vast machinery all at once." Whatever genius he thought I possessed, he was not interested in hearing me talk. "You proved that it works. You have given the world, given *me*, decisive evidence that once the pieces are assembled, a hero can fall. A king can fall. No matter how absolute the stranglehold of power might seem, I can take them down. The data is there."

"I knew it would work," I said quietly. I still ached for the glory that could have been, for the parts of my plan I was never able to execute.

He knew what I thought, as he always had. "I am through getting in your way, Auditor."

Agreeing with him seemed dangerous, but I nodded and closed my eyes. This was his apology. It was far too little bandage over too large a wound, but I could also see what a mighty effort it was for him to offer it at all. I'd find a way to keep that wound from festering.

"The strategy is clear," he said, gesturing toward the screen, where the massive, stylized logo of the Draft loomed above us. "We must see if it scales."

The vastness of his proposal was a blow. Instead

of taking on hero after hero, destroying them one by one, he wanted to take on the Draft. He swept his hand across the screen and another logo popped up: Superheroic Affairs. As his fingers moved, more images assembled: the governmental agencies involved with selecting, transforming, controlling, monitoring, and deploying heroes. Every part of the process, every bit of the Draft. He wanted to take it all down.

Everything.

"It will scale," he said to himself, so low I almost missed it. "I am sure of it."

My lips parted in shock. I wanted to scream at him, to throw my cane across the room. I hadn't predicted this. I thought once we took out Supercollider, it meant we could theoretically take out anyone. To Leviathan, it meant we could take out *everyone.*

We are still rebuilding, I shrieked in my head. This could do so much harm; even if the math worked out, we were already covered in so much blood. *Look at the cost,* I wanted to scream. *Look at what it cost us.*

But that's not what I said.

I looked at the screen, feeling the engine of my brain warming up and humming. My hand reached for his but I didn't quite touch him.

"I'll run the numbers."

Acknowledgments

I'm incredibly lucky. I know that's a thing people say fairly often when giving speeches or talking about their lovely wife and kids or whatever, but I mean it differently. I'm lucky like a cockroach is lucky: irritatingly resilient, and if you see one there's an army of them in the walls somewhere. I realize I've just called my friends, colleagues, and loved ones cockroaches, which gives you an idea of how good I am at feelings, but what I am trying to get at is that I am surrounded by an entire community of hilarious geniuses without whom I would not have been able to accomplish a damn thing.

Thanks to Ron Eckel, my agent, who put an incredible amount of faith in me when I was a freelancer gleefully making enemies on the internet. He and his team at CookeMcDermid took such good care of me, I am still in awe of it. He has been my champion from the first and having someone on my team and in my corner the way he has been is invaluable.

Thanks to my editor, David Pomerico, who grokked what I was hoping to do immediately and became a crucial ally. Because of his input, and because he believed in it, this book is dramatically better, and I am profoundly grateful for the trust he placed in me.

Thanks to my team at HarperCollins. Taking a manuscript and making a book out of it still feels like an act of genuine magic to me. I was fortunate enough to work with a team of actual wizards, and am deeply grateful for all their expertise, enthusiasm, and kindness.

Thanks to Professor Ilan Noy, whose work on measuring the impact of natural disasters was incredibly influential for me (and the Auditor), and who graciously allowed me to quote him in this book.

Thanks to everyone who read early drafts of *Hench* and offered invaluable input, criticism, and encouragement, especially Jonathan Ball, Nicolas Carrier, Izzie Colpitts-Campbell, J. Dymphna Coy, Heather Cromarty, Chris Dart, Trista Devries, Stacey May Fowles, Haritha Gnanaratna, Christopher Gramlich (who taught me about blood transfusions), Ryan Hughes, Rachel Kahn (who drew Anna for the first time), Max Lander, Jennifer Ouellette, Erin Rodgers, William Neil Scott, Mariko Tamaki, Audra Williams, and Jennie Worden. They were my cheering section for literal years and their support, love, and friendship mean the world.

Thanks to the Cecil Street Irregulars: Madeline Ashby, Jill Lum, David Nickle, Michael Skeet, Hugh Spencer, and Alan Weiss, and the late Sara Simmons and Helen Rykens. Their input and guidance from the very first drafts were crucial, and being able to tap into their collective talent and wisdom has been transformative.

Thanks to all of my friends, who have kept me in one piece and have brought joy to existing on this blasted hellscape of an earth. Every time I have made one of you laugh, a little devil earned its wings. If you think you recognize a flattering depiction of yourself in this book, you're probably right. If you recognize an unflattering one, you're *definitely* right.

Thanks to my parents, Harry and Margaret (who are endlessly proud of everything I do), and my brother, Michael, and sister-in-law, Kacy (who are more brilliant and kind than humans have any right to be).

Above all, thanks to my partner, Jairus Khan, without whom this book would never have been finished. He built me custom word counters and disaster math spreadsheets, helped me through every plot hole and problem, and unfailingly, unwaveringly believed in me. There is no part of this book, as there is no part of my life, that isn't better for him having touched it. I used to feel lucky because I lived; now I feel lucky because he loves me.

About the Author

NATALIE ZINA WALSCHOTS is a writer and game designer whose work includes LARP scripts, heavy metal music journalism, video game lore, and weirder things classified as "interactive experiences." Her writing for the interactive adventure The Aluminum Cat won an IndieCade award, and her poetic exploration of the notes engine in Bloodborne was featured in Kotaku and First Person Scholar. She is (unfortunately) the author of two books of poetry: *Thumbscrews*, which won the Robert Kroetsch Award for Innovative Poetry, and *DOOM: Love Poems for Supervillains*. Natalie sits on the board of Dames Making Games, a space for queer and gender-marginalized people to create games freely, where she hosts interactive narrative workshops. She plays a lot of D&D, participates in a lot of Nordic LARPs, watches a lot of horror movies, and reads a lot of speculative fiction. She lives in Toronto with her partner and five cats. This is, arguably, too many cats.

HARPER LARGE PRINT

We hope you enjoyed reading
our new, comfortable print size and found it
an experience you would like to repeat.

Well – you're in luck!

Harper Large Print offers the finest in
fiction and nonfiction books in this same larger
print size and paperback format. Light and easy to read,
Harper Large Print paperbacks are for the book lovers
who want to see what they are reading without strain.

For a full listing of titles and
new releases to come, please visit our website:
www.hc.com

HARPER LARGE PRINT

SEEING IS BELIEVING!